IF ONLY YOU KNEW

IF ONLY YOU KNEW

Alex Hairston

BET Publications, LLC
http://www.bet.com

SEPIA BOOKS are published by

BET Publications, LLC
c/o BET BOOKS
One BET Plaza
1900 W Place NE
Washington, DC 20018-1211

Copyright © 2004 by Alex Hairston

All Kensington Titles, Imprints, and Distributed Lines are available at special quantity discounts for bulk purchases for sales promotions, premiums, fund-raising, and educational or institutional use. Special book excerpts or customized printings can also be created to fit specific needs. For details, write or phone the office of the Kensington special sales manager: Kensington Publishing Corp., 850 Third Avenue, New York, NY 10022, attn: Special Sales Department, Phone: 1-800-221-2647.

BET Books is a trademark of Black Entertainment Television, Inc. SEPIA and the SEPIA logo are trademarks of BET Books and the BET BOOKS logo is a registered trademark.

ISBN: 1-58314-395-5

First Printing: March 2004
10 9 8 7 6 5 4 3 2 1

Printed in the United States of America

For my grandmothers with love
Betty K. Perkins
and
Chrissie Hairston

For our young people everywhere
and the decisions they make

Acknowledgments

I'm incredibly blessed and I know it. That's why I thank God each and every day. He's part of everything I do and that will never change. I am forever humble.

I'd like to thank my #1 sample reader, my wife, Kim. Thanks for having my back and being so supportive. I love you.

I used to joke with my wife, saying that I was going to keep her and the kids a secret because I'd sell more books if women thought I was single. That still makes me laugh, but that's not my style. I'd never do anything like that because I'm so proud of my family. I always keep my family first because none of this would be possible without them.

To my loving parents, Alex Sr. and Marie, I can't thank the two of you enough for being so supportive.

A very special thanks to my #2 sample reader, my sister, Erica. Love you.

I have so many people to thank for the success of my first novel and I can't possibly mention you all by name, but know that I love you and appreciate everything you've done. Here's a special thank you to all of my friends, relatives, bookstores, book clubs, and fellow authors. Hopefully, this way no one feels left out.

I'd like to thank BET Books for introducing my books to the world. Very special thanks to Linda Gill, V. P. of BET Books, and Glenda Howard, my editor, for believing in me. Guy and Kicheko, thanks for all of your hard work.

Thanks to two special ladies, my publicist, Felicia Polk, and her partner in crime, Robin Green, for spreading the word and putting together my first book tour.

To my readers: I can't thank you enough for supporting my dream. Thanks to all of you who took the time to e-mail me with your wonderful comments. That really keeps me going. And I still want to hear from you. I love you and I need you!

A quick note: I decided to write *If Only You Knew* to show that I could write about other characters besides Eric Brown Jr. I still might do a sequel to *Love Don't Come Easy* one day. Too many people thought I was writing about my life. Just a reminder, I write fiction. This book is very different from the first. Enjoy! Thanks again for supporting my dream.

Lots of Love,
Alex

www.alexhairston.com
alexhairston@yahoo.com

Part I

Deception

Chapter 1

Jamal

Winter is my least favorite season of all. In general my world is already cold enough without any additional frigid days and nights. Winters in Baltimore are usually bitter cold and I hate being outside for extended periods of time. The finest aspect of winter is the pure white, untouched snow cover, which adds beauty to almost any landscape regardless of whether it's urban or rural. Spring is an exciting season; the environmental changes are so dramatically different from winter. Spring gives life to a multitude of brilliant colors. Summer is just a more intense version of spring. Summer's heat and humidity somewhat diminishes its appeal, but cool water from an ocean, river, lake, stream, pond, or even a city fire hydrant adds an entirely different perspective and appreciation. Autumn is definitely my favorite season of all. As a visual artist, I can really appreciate the vibrant blend of colors found in October and November. Almost nothing compares to the stunning scenery of a drive through western Maryland during autumn. Armies of trees with pale green, amber, auburn, and crimson leaves line the hillsides. The mountains are breathtaking and seem to reach heaven. I love to paint vast landscapes, but sometimes a simple visit to a park can inspire a work of genius.

My girlfriend, Jessica, and I were out for a drive and I decided to stop by the Robert E. Lee Memorial Park to take in its beautiful and tranquil atmosphere. This park is probably one of the best-kept secrets in the Baltimore area. It's a perfect rendezvous spot for lovers and an amazing retreat for nature enthusiasts as well. I can't get enough of the sights and sounds. There's a huge lake that runs down into a frothy white waterfall, and then the water flows into a small peaceful stream. Trees surround the lake and their fallen autumn leaves seem to dance with the wind to a bird's song. Sunlight glistens off the ripples of the motion-filled lake. These are just a few things that get my creative juices flowing.

As I sit on a huge rock enjoying the scenery, I stare into the disappointed face of my angel. I ask myself, how could anyone not enjoy this place? I can sense that at any second hell is about to break loose from the mouth of my angel. Jessica can't resist spoiling my peace.

"This is so boring. How long do we have to be here?" Jessica says as if I'm wasting her precious time.

"Please, not right now. You're spoiling my mood. At one time you used to love this place." I pause for a second, taking in a breath of fresh air and at the same time taking in more of the scenery. My eyes move from left to right, then focus back on Jessica. "I can't believe we're getting all this priceless beauty for free."

"If you weren't so broke, we could be taking in the beauty of the mall, but instead I'm sitting here with a starving artist. I need to stop by Hecht's, Macy's, or Nine West for some shoes."

"I'm not trying to hear you right now. I might be broke, but I definitely have potential wealth."

"Huh? What the hell is potential wealth? Whatever it is, you sound stupid talking about it," Jessica says with sarcasm and laughs in my face as if I'm a big joke.

"You know what, I am stupid, but for an entirely different reason."

"What's that supposed to mean?"

I don't say a word. I just give her this wouldn't-you-like-to-know look.

I'm twenty-five years old and I thought that after eighteen months of being a dedicated friend and lover to Jessica we'd be a lot closer to making the ultimate commitment. But after all this time I feel like marriage is a distant concept that just keeps evading my grasp. I really want to get married one day, but Jessica is what I often refer to as my *Ms. Right-now.* Someday soon *Ms. Right* will suddenly appear and steal my heart and mind. To be honest I live for that day. I live for the day when I can have an intelligent conversation with a woman.

Physically, Jessica has it all. She's everything I could ask for in a woman. She's a pretty little brown thing who reminds me a lot of Chilli from the group TLC. I'm in love with Jessica, but I wish that we had a healthier relationship. If she could just say something nice or just say that she loves me once, she'd be making a major step in the right direction. When and if she says she loves me, I hope she means it. All I want is a fifty-fifty relationship, someone who's willing to meet me halfway. Shit, I'm even willing to go the extra mile for real love.

Recently I've had the feeling that Jessica's been doing me wrong. Sometimes her emotions don't match the situation at hand and that's a sure sign that someone else is on her mind. It's obvious to me that another man is influencing her. For months I tried to persuade her into becoming a sports fan, but I failed. All of a sudden she knows all about different sports and athletes. She has developed an undying passion for sports. Jessica talks about the Baltimore Ravens like she knows them personally. Michael Jordan's return to the NBA and his retirement are two of her favorite topics. The whole sports thing is cool, but I was pissed when I found an empty Lifestyles condom wrapper that didn't belong to me in the backseat of my car this morning. I figured it must have belonged to Jessica's new man and the asshole accidentally left it in my car.

Jessica stares at me, still waiting for an answer. I say, "I was going to leave this alone, but look what I found in the backseat of my car this morning."

I pull the condom wrapper from my pocket and flash it in front of Jessica's pretty little face.

With a surprised look Jessica says, "What's that?"

I think, *Stop tripping, you little freak. It's your boyfriend's.* Instead I say, "You should know. You had my car last night and this wasn't there yesterday."

With a straight face she says, "It's not mine."

"Well, it doesn't belong to me either. I only use Trojan condoms."

"It's probably mine from a while back. It might have popped up from under the seat or something. Remember that night we had sex in your car? I pulled out a Lifestyles condom for you."

Jessica is trying to be slick. She's playing a Jedi mind trick on me. Like a dummy I say, "I guess, but I can't remember."

Jessica does have her own little trusty supply of condoms and it's possible that I used one of hers. I can't remember, so I just drop the whole thing.

In less than a minute she flips the script on me. She says, "So, do you think I used the rubber with somebody else?"

Without hesitation I say, "I don't know."

My response sparks anger in Jessica's eyes. "You don't know?"

I guess I'm asking for it, because I say, "No, I don't."

Jessica yells, "I can't believe you! Take me home!"

"I'm sorry. I'm just confused about us right now."

That was an attempt to calm the flames, but my comments only add fuel to the fire. Jessica hops off the rock with a major attitude.

Out of frustration she yells like a fool, disturbing the park's tranquillity, "Take me home! Take me home right now!"

She walks away leaving me sitting on the rock with a confused look on my face as she blazes her way to my car.

Jessica is silent during the entire ride to her apartment. Her silence sends me deep into thought. She has a unique way of stealing my energy and happiness, putting a halt to my creative flow. As an artist the last thing I need is someone interfering with my momentum. I try to stay inspired at all times.

I can't wait to get Jessica home. She lives in what she likes to call an urban contemporary duplex apartment in the heart of downtown Baltimore. This is her way of staying in touch with the *streets* and *keeping it real.* She lives a few blocks from the Baltimore City Jail and a couple of blocks from the cultural center of the city, which has a symphony hall, an opera house, art galleries, and museums. It's hard for me to believe how uncultured this girl is, but still I love her.

Jessica remains silent. In her presence I'm alone and it bothers me. She won't talk to me, but she has the nerve to change my radio station without asking. No matter what, I refuse to give her the argument she's looking for. With my hands on the steering wheel I give her quick little stares and loving smiles, but she's too focused on being mad to even notice. Jessica knows that I'm deep in thought and that she's the centerpiece of my thoughts. Even with that in mind she continues to ignore the hell out of me.

Jessica's helplessly stuck in the middle of two worlds, the battle between good and evil. She has issues with her father and I think she's looking for a man who can compensate for the love and material possessions he used to give her. I can only give her so much, but she wants the world on a silver platter right now. At this point all I can give her is love.

Maybe I'm wrong for accusing her of being with another guy, but something's up with her. A man usually knows when his woman is messing around.

I can remember back when things were better between us. We were both huge music fans. As a matter of fact, we met at Best Buy while browsing the same crowded CD aisle. Jessica and I grew up in the same neighborhood, knew a lot of the same people, but we had never met until that moment. When our eyes met for the first time something happened inside me. It seemed as if Jessica felt something special too. Her eyes spoke to me and my heart listened. I thought it was love at first sight.

We had so much in common back then. In the beginning everything seemed so divine. Jessica gave me the impression that she was the ideal woman for me. Instantly I knew that this had to be my soul mate. So what if I'm a poor judge of character? I've always been a sucker for a pretty face.

During the good times Jessica and I used to go to concerts. I'll never forget seeing Erykah Badu in D.C. at Constitution Hall. I took Jessica to see Jill Scott and Musiq Soulchild. We sat front-row center at the Meyerhoff Symphony Hall twice and both times Jill put on heart-pounding and breathtaking performances. Music and poetry, it was a spiritual thing. Musiq Soulchild reminded me of a young Marvin Gaye.

At first Jessica and I were both big fans of Jills, but now Jessica is more into DMX, Ja-Rule, and Jay-Z. Sometimes she reminds me of a fake-ass around-the-way girl. It's funny how a new man can drastically change a woman. I don't have any concrete proof that a new man actually exists, but my suspicions and fears have almost been confirmed. I know it's just a matter of time before the truth is revealed. All I can say is, whoever Jessica's new man is, he'd better have plenty of patience and a decent cash flow because Jessica can be a real gold digger. I'm not exactly the poorest brotha around, but again I do have potential wealth.

I'm a gifted artist with the talent, ambition, and determination to make anything happen. I have the power to change negative to positive. I'm a triple threat: young, gifted, and black. I like to think of myself as a financial success waiting to happen . . . potential wealth.

I pull up to Jessica's apartment and she still doesn't say a word. She doesn't even look my way. She simply opens the car door and gets out.

I say, "Look, I'm sorry. Call me later and maybe we can hook up and do dinner and a movie."

Jessica slams the hell out of my car door and says, "Yeah, right. Go straight to hell, Jay."

"Okay, I'll meet you there, with your little smart-ass self," I say as I pull off and make my way home. I think, *Later for her.* It's getting dark and I need personal time to plan out my life and my next course of action.

I'm a simple man. The less complicated my life is, the better it is. It doesn't take a lot to make me happy. I work full-time as an assistant manager at an arts and crafts store. I am a starving artist, but I'm happy. When the time comes I'm going to be rich and somewhat famous. I say somewhat famous because most artists hardly ever achieve fame. Until opportunity presents itself, I'm just fine working every day at Peaches' Arts and Crafts and teaching an art class there every Thursday night at 7:30.

My family is originally from Baltimore. Well, the part that I know of, because I never had the *pleasure* of meeting my father. My mother always told me this lame story about how she met my father when she was eighteen. She was fresh out of high school and he was in the army at the time. My father was a few years older than my mother. She never told me his exact age and to be honest she probably never knew. My mother told me that they met on base at the NCO Club in Fort Meade, Maryland. She got pregnant with me and my twin sister, Kali, around the time my father got orders to go to Germany. Somehow they lost contact with each other and my mother had already lost the nerve to tell him that she was pregnant with twins. My mother's story is so shaky that I've always had the suspicion that she was the victim of a one-night stand and just too ashamed to admit it.

My father's name is Thomas Butler and that's a name that constantly sticks with me. I like the fact that my mother gave me her last name, which happens to be King. My family's last name has a royal and powerful appeal, but I often describe my family as a group of misfits, except for my grandmother and my little sister, Kali. I shouldn't refer to Kali as my little sister because she's a big-time coanchor with Kyle Williams on the local ABC affiliate's noon and six o'clock news broadcasts. I'm extremely proud of Kali and I love her to death. Little Shadow represents the family real well on TV every day. My relatives nicknamed Kali Shadow, because she used to follow right behind me as if we were attached or something. Somewhere along the way Shadow branched out and led herself into a successful broadcasting career.

Kali and Kyle's faces are plastered all over town, from billboards to buses. Everyone knows and loves Kali and Kyle, the hottest and cutest couple in local news. The thing that most people forget is that Kali is happily married to John. My brother-in-law is a successful financial advisor. He now runs his own firm. John lost his position at American Financial Incorporated after a merger with the Harrington Financial Group that should have been called a takeover. The whole thing left too many chiefs and some of them had to go. John happened to be one of them. It was a blessing in disguise.

I never liked any of my sister's boyfriends, but John's my boy. Kali and John live in a very exclusive area of Owings Mills, Maryland. They live all alone in a huge $350,000 brick colonial. It's hard to believe that Kali and John are only twenty-five years old, because they live like an old rich couple. Everything about them is stylish, from their house to their cars and clothing. Kali is always dressed in her business attire and it's rare to see John wearing anything but a nice Armani suit. They're the pride and joy of our family. Kali and John are the perfect couple living perfect lives. The only thing missing from their tiny kingdom is a little rug rat. They keep saying that I'm going to be an uncle soon, but because of their careers they're probably not trying hard enough.

My grandmother, Connie, is the queen of everything. I owe her the world for everything she's done for me. She raised me and Shadow because our mother, Karen, was and still is a world traveler and one of those crazy full-time, lifelong students. My mother is an extremely intelligent woman, but she has some serious underlying emotional issues. She has been in school so long that I lost track of her degrees somewhere between her psychology and law degrees. I'm not exactly sure how she's able to go to school like she does, because she's never really had a job. My mother knows a lot of wealthy old men and I'm sure they help her maintain her eccentric lifestyle. At this point I'm not sure of her actual address. She uses my grandmother's address for business purposes only. Occasionally we get to see or hear from her when she's expecting some important mail or when somebody dies.

Home, *sweet* home. I'm not ashamed to admit that I still live with my grandmother. We leave in a row house in an area of west Baltimore called Edmondson Village. This area has a notorious reputation for crime, but I don't really understand why. As long as we've lived here, we've never been victims or witnessed any violent crimes. I have noticed some drastic changes in this area over the years.

When I was a kid this street was lined with shady trees and well-maintained homes. There was a certain pride and attention given to lawns and hedges and an unmistakable feeling of unity. Today there are abandoned houses that have been boarded up for years. Most of the home owners have sold their homes, died, or turned their homes over to their kids and moved into senior-housing complexes. The majority of the residents on my street are renters who take little pride in the exterior appearances of their homes. There used to be a row of garages that stood in the alley behind my grandmother's house until a crazy juvenile-delinquent arsonist burned them down. Now there's a long narrow lot where the garages once stood.

We used to have an annual summertime block party where neighbors would eat, drink, and party for hours. Back then everybody knew everybody and now we're just strangers coexisting in a common area. I'm not sure what to call it, urban blues or urban decay. It's not so bad around here. This could be a rat-infested dumping ground like some other neighborhoods around the city.

I decide to pull my car around to the back of the house and park on the lot, hoping to avoid my grandmother at the same time. I'm just not in the mood for conversation right now because my grandmother has the tendency to lecture me for hours.

Grandma is so incredible, an ageless beauty. She's the type of woman that cooks, cleans, fights your battles, curses like a sailor, and prays like a saint all in the same breath.

As soon as I open the basement door, my grandmother hears me enter the house. She yells down the basement steps, "Jamal, that you?"

"Yes, ma'am, it's me."

"You better stop sneaking in here scaring me like that. Dinner's ready. Wash your hands and come up."

"Okay, I'll be right up."

The aroma of my grandmother's cooking fills the air. It's Wednesday night and that means fried chicken, homemade biscuits, mashed potatoes, collard greens, and macaroni and cheese. What could be better? I love living here. I've transformed this basement into an exquisite art studio and gallery. I rarely refer to it as a basement. It's more like a cozy lower-level apartment, my bat cave, or my fortress of solitude. I actually can afford a better apartment somewhere else, but it's home and I'd rather pay rent to my grandmother instead of some faceless landlord. In addition to that, I don't think my grandmother could afford to keep her house or keep up the maintenance without my help. It's hard for her managing things on a fixed income and all. It's really important to me to keep this house in the family. We've got a lot of history in this house and ghosts that no other residents would understand. My grandfather and aunt died years ago and we're convinced that they still hang around the house.

There's a knock at the back door.

A male voice says, "Yo, Jamal, let me in."

It's my best friend, Kenny Thomas, banging on the door like a fool. Kenny is better known around here as Church. I gave him the nickname Church Boy when we were kids. Although he hasn't been to church in years the name stuck to him like glue. Over the years his name was shortened to Church. He's a preacher's kid. Reverend Thomas is the pastor of my grandmother's church. Since I can remember, Church has always been in some type of trouble whether minor or major. I guess that's typical for a preacher's kid. Church was a shy quiet kid similar to myself. We used to collect baseball cards, play basketball and arcade games. I think Church got tired of playing childish games, because he started stealing cars, shoplifting, and hustling on street corners. I never got involved in that madness because I feared going to a place like the Hickey School for Boys, and more than that I feared my grandmother. Church ended up doing time at Hickey. When he was released his parents kept the boy in church every Sunday and at least two to three weeknights. I'm not sure if it was the time at Hickey or the time in church that made the difference, but Church has been legit for years.

I open the door and say, "What's up, Church?"

Church is a big boy, so naturally the aroma of my grandmother's chicken automatically steals his attention.

"What's up, Jamal?" Church pauses and takes in a deep whiff. He says, "Damn, it smells good up in here. What's Grandma cookin'?"

"Our usual Wednesday night meal."

"Chicken? I'd kill for some home cookin' right about now."

"You can forget that. My grandmother can't afford to feed your greedy ass. So, what's up?"

"A bunch of bull. I just lost my damn job."

I'm still not in the mood for conversation, but being the fool I am I ask, "How?"

"Over forty cents."

"What?"

"Yeah, forty goddamn cents. This morning a dude I work with asked me if he could borrow forty cents for the vending machine and I gave it to him. This evening I saw him at the vending machine with a handful of change, so I asked for my money back. The dude goes, 'I can't believe you sweatin' me over forty cents.' I told him it was a loan. He refused to give me my money back and called me a sucker. I snapped. One thing led to another and the next thing I know, we were exchanging punches. It took my supervisor, his secretary, the janitor, and two other guys to break us up. The next thing I know, I'm in my supervisor's office with a pen in my hand about to sign a termination slip."

"Damn, they don't play."

Church scratches his head and says, "Well, I was already on probation for that truck accident two weeks ago and for getting caught stealing trash bags, soap, and paper towels off the job."

I burst out laughing. "You idiot. All I can say is, you better start job-hunting 'cause the holidays will be here before you know it. Your girl, Keisha, won't like you being unemployed."

"You ain't lying, dawg. Four years on that job all wasted over forty cents. I worked my way up from the loading docks to being a full-time driver."

"Yeah, and I can't believe you blew it all over forty cents. Damn, I would've given you forty cents."

"Yeah, right, you're just saying that now. This other guy owes me twenty dollars, you gonna give that?"

"I guess you better track him down and whip his ass too, 'cause I'm broke."

"See what I'm saying? I might have to hit the streets and start hustling again."

"Yep, and your ass will end up right in jail with the rest of 'em."

Church laughs like I'm joking. "Speaking of jail, remember that guy, Tank?"

"Yeah, what about him?"

"I heard he'll be home soon."

"Who'd he kill?"

"I can't remember. All I know is, he's been in jail forever."

My grandmother yells down the steps, "Jamal, I told you to wash your hands and get your narrow ass up here before your dinner gets cold."

Church and I laugh. My grandmother considers it an insult when dinner is ready and I don't come running. I say, "Yes, ma'am. I'll be up in a minute."

Church yells, "Hi, Ms. Connie. Sorry for holding Jamal up, I'm on my way out."

"Who the hell is that?" my grandmother says with much attitude.

"It's Church. Sorry I can't stay for dinner."

"I'm not! I can't be feeding the whole world. I'd love to feed you, but you eat like every meal is your last," my grandmother says with brutal honestly.

Church and I laugh.

I say, "I told you, you are greedy."

Church says, "That's okay, I just had a super-sized extra-value meal from McDonald's. It's not home cooking, but it'll do." Church drops his tone to a whisper and says, "Damn, your grandmother is mean. Let me go before she kicks my ass out."

"Alright, remember what I said, stay off the streets."

"I will, for now anyway. Peace."

I go to the bathroom to wash my hands and head upstairs. Grandma's brother, Uncle Richard, is the first thing I see when I enter the kitchen. He's sitting at the kitchen table eating mashed potatoes and sipping a can of Ensure. My eyes focus on the mashed-potatoes and Ensure foam on his lips and in the corners of his mouth. There goes my appetite.

My uncle lives two houses down from us and he's probably the strangest character in my family. He's my grandmother's youngest brother. He's only about nine years older than my mother and just a few years older than my mother's sister. Basically, Grandma has been like a mother to my uncle too. Nobody in our neighborhood knows my uncle's real name because for years they've always called him Coach. Even my family refers to him as Coach. He picked up his nick-name because he's been coaching Little League teams since anyone can remember. Over the years he's coached football, basketball, base-ball, tennis, and he recently added lacrosse to his résumé. My uncle has always been an avid sports fan and probably the best damn Little League coach in the country. He's been a role model and father figure to thousands of kids. Coach used to remind me of one of those intimidating loudmouthed inmates from *Scared Straight*. Parents and kids respect him because he's a tough natural-born leader. At the same time, Coach is a very private type of individual . . . a real mystery man.

The only person who really knew Coach was my Aunt Alfreda. Everybody called her Freda. She smoked and drank herself to death. She always loved to give me hugs and kisses. I can still hear her vicious smoker's cough and see her tobacco-stained teeth. As long as I live I'll never forget how she reeked of alcohol and those pink-and-black-pickled alcoholic lips courtesy of Miller's beer and Seagram's gin. Aunt Freda and Coach never married, they just lived together for countless years. After my aunt's death, Coach turned into an even more difficult puzzle to solve. He has always been weird, but he's my buddy.

Coach is a disabled Vietnam veteran. And by no surprise, only a small percentage of his disability is actually physical. A major percentage of his disability is mental. Actually the Veterans Administration has been good to him. Unfortunately, Coach was diagnosed with liver cancer about a month ago and his doctor said if he lasts beyond the next couple of months it would be a miracle. Coach has been sick for a long time, but he just kept putting other things and other people before his health. Although he's always been a proud and independent man I'm going to do whatever it takes to help my uncle. He has been the closest thing to a father that Shadow and I have ever known.

Grandma has her back toward me as she wipes down the stove. She doesn't say a word to me. I think she's still mad that it took me so long to come upstairs. She gets insulted too easily when dinner is ready and I don't come running. All I can do is focus on Coach. I hate seeing my uncle look so pitiful. No matter what, I try my best to act natural.

I ask, "What's up, Coach?"

He says, "My time, my time is almost up. What's up with you?"

I feel a lump develop in my throat, because hearing Coach talk like this hurts. We all know that he's dying, but it's weird to see and hear him act so cool about it. Maybe it's a good thing or just a bad case of denial.

I say, "Stop talking like that."

Grandma says, "I keep tellin' him to stop talkin' like that."

"Why? Y'all know I'm dying."

Grandma says, "We don't know nothing. I told you to stop listening to that damn doctor, he ain't God. My Lord can do anything but fail. You just keep praying like I told you and He'll keep you."

I say, "That's right."

Coach says, "Y'all talking a bunch of shit."

I say, "Can we just change the subject?"

Grandma says, "Yeah. Your aunt Hunk called here today."

Aunt Hunk is Mother's mean, badass lesbian sister from east Baltimore. Aunt Hunk picked up her nickname in prison because the women there used to tell her that she would make a handsome man. I'm still not sure if that's a compliment or what. But my aunt walks around the city like she's one hunk of a man ready and willing to fight the toughest men and date the finest women.

I ask, "What did she want?"

Grandma says, "Her stupid ass is in jail again for beating her girlfriend's husband in the head with a hammer. Now she wants me to put my house up to get her out."

"I guess she'll be there for a while. 'Cause I know you're not puttin' this house up."

"You know I ain't that crazy. She'll be okay. She must like jail 'cause her ass is always there. I'm not gonna worry myself to death, 'cause God takes care of babies and fools and she ain't no baby."

I laugh and ask, "Have you heard from my mother lately?"

Grandma says, "No, I'm worried about her. I'll just put her in God's hands too."

Coach goes, "Don't worry, you'll be seeing her soon. She'll be here in a few weeks for my funeral."

Grandma says, "Please stop that, Coach!"

Coach says, "I'm just tellin' the truth. I've got some good insurance and I want March Funeral Home to have my body. My insurance policies are on the left-hand side of my underwear drawer. I wanna be buried at the Veterans Cemetery. I've got my gray suit hanging in the closet all ready to go 'cause that's what I wanna be buried in, y'all hear me?"

I nod and say, "We hear you. I'm going back downstairs. I need time to think. All this talk of death has made me lose my appetite."

I lie in my bed staring into space. Seeing my uncle deteriorate like that makes me think about my own mortality and certain choices I've made in life. In high school I was a pretty good athlete thanks to my uncle spending so much time with me. The one thing that I kind of regret most in life is not going to college or to an art school. I guess I'd like to get a bachelor's in fine arts. The downside to getting a degree in fine arts is that it will only help me earn a little more than I make right now. A degree in graphic design would probably be a better choice. Since the age of three I've had a natural talent for art. The first portrait I ever painted was of a black Jesus. J.J. from *Good Times* kind of inspired that piece and it still hangs on my grandmother's bedroom wall.

I'd like to take some type of art history or art appreciation class, so I can instantly recognize works of art and be able to discuss all the great artists of the past and present. I'm very confident in my abilities as far as sketching, painting, and sculpting go. I may not understand some technical skills and terminology, but in the end my portfolio speaks for itself. Right now I make very little money off my artwork. I'm okay with that because through networking I plan to become a featured artist in a well-known exhibit one day. Most of the time I sell my artwork on my job, at African-American art shows, festivals, flea markets, and even over the Internet. I can't forget about the beauty salons. The women of Perfections, Edie's Creations, Pamper Me With Jazz, and Hair Explosions have shown me some major love. I met a woman about a year ago who has a Web site that features young, up-and-coming African-American artists. She sells artwork on consignment. Most African-Americans I know don't seem too interested in my paintings of landscapes; instead they love my paintings that depict ghetto life, sports themes, images of slavery, famous blacks, and Egyptian themes. The most money I've ever received for my artwork was three thousand dollars for a portrait of Malcolm X, which was sold at a local auction. I wasn't able to attend the auction and to this day I have no idea who purchased the painting. Right about now, I'd be happy to get a couple hundred for any of my paintings, framed or unframed. I usually won't sell any of my sculptures for less than a hundred dollars regardless of size.

I thank God for my job every day. Mrs. Harvey owns Peaches', which is the only African-American-owned arts-and-crafts store in Baltimore and probably in the entire state of Maryland. Mrs. Harvey's son, Dennis, is the manager of the store and he has never liked me too much. He resents the fact that I have a little authority in his family's business. The thing that bothers him the most is that I'm ten years younger than him and his mother has a schoolgirl crush on me. I can get his mother to do almost anything for me. I'm strictly talking business. Dennis accused me of stealing art supplies from the store before. His mother shot down his accusation almost as fast as he got it out of his mouth. Mrs. Harvey and I have an agreement that I can take as many supplies as I need within reason, as long as I make her aware and keep some type of record of what I take. I run the Thursday night art classes practically free of charge and the classes have turned into a real moneymaker for the store.

I have a pretty good life and the only thing that's missing is a good woman. I want someone who appreciates me for the person I am, no matter how broke, how different, or how boring I might appear to be. I wish Jessica could just have stayed the way she used to be. I can still remember way back when she was my sweet little Jessie. Now she's just Jessica a.k.a. *Ms. Right-now*. No matter what, I love and miss her.

Chapter 2

Jessie

I don't like when Jamal refers to me as Jessica. Most of the time I call him Jay, so he should relax a little and call me Jessie like he used to. There are so many things I dislike about him and how he addresses me is just one minor detail. Jay thinks I'm a gold digger, but I'm not. I just like nice things. I wanna look good and be treated special. Sometimes a girl has to pamper herself and get the hair and nails done.

I love money. I'm a bank teller for Bank of America. I handle stacks of money and it hurts like hell to handle thousands and thousands of dollars each day only to go home absolutely broke. My savings account was recently closed due to a major lack of funds. As of today my checking account balance is $27.50 and that's just ridiculous. My goal isn't to become filthy rich, but more like financially stable. I want to be like some of my customers with over ten thousand dollars in their money market accounts and investments up the ass. I'm so broke right now I could die. I used to have a Honda Accord until it got re-possessed. I was mad at Jay for a while because he couldn't help me keep my car. A man should be able to assist his woman in her time of need. He's a good lover, but that doesn't pay my bills. On the real, our relationship is in serious trouble. Most of the time it's me with the problems and he really deserves a break. I think I love him, but I can't see myself telling him. Check me out, sounding like a good girl. That used to be my style, but I'm different now and Jay can sense that something's up. He shocked the hell out of me when he found that condom wrapper in his car. When he confronted me about it I almost pissed in my panties. At first my mind went blank and I couldn't even come up with a good lie about how it got in his car.

Jay and I have a mutual friend named Trey. Trey's a lot closer to me, I mean, *a lot* closer to me. Trey and I made love for the first time two nights ago, but it wasn't the first time we had sex. Usually he does it rough, but oh my God, he made *passionate love* to me. Trey is three years older than me and Jay. Jay has a pretty smile and a tall, slim frame with boyish characteristics. At one time all that turned me on a lot, but now I need a change. Trey's a little more masculine, a real physical type who looks like he knows how to hurt something. To most guys he has a threatening appearance, but to most women it's a turn-on. He's a straight-up thug type with a serious cash flow. He reminds me of DMX, only about seventy-five pounds heavier and a few inches taller. Trey's from a rich family and he owns two barbershops and a car-detailing business. He has a house in the city and one in Prince George's County. He drives a white Infiniti Q45 with twenty-inch rims and I like that a lot. Jay drives a weak-ass Chevy Cavalier that he got from a public auction in Pennsylvania last year. I don't like driving Jay's car, but right now it's my only real source of transportation. I hate driving a damn hoopty.

Trey and I made love in the backseat of Jay's car and Trey's stupid ass left the damn condom wrapper in the car. I hate lying to Jay. Sometimes I want to leave him, but something's keeping me with him. Having two men in my life beats the hell out of only having one any day. Anyway, men do that shit to us all the time. I had a dream that Jay's potential wealth prophecy came true. He does have a special gift with his art. Jay can create almost anything. If he makes it big I want to reap all the benefits. Damn, I really sound like a gold digger. Maybe it's just in my blood.

The women in my family have such bad luck with men. My mother, grandmother, and two of my aunts are all currently single and have never been married. Only my Aunt Brenda is married and just about all of the women in my family are jealous of her. It's probably because Aunt Brenda has a good man in her life. My uncle Will and Aunt Brenda are probably the most perfectly matched couple I've ever seen. They've been together so long that they even look alike. After twenty-five years of marriage they're still going strong and it appears that their relationship is getting better and better. My uncle got a job promotion and they just purchased a new home in Atlanta, Georgia. It's funny how often good things happen to them. I guess that old saying is true, *Good things happen to good people.*

Women are forever hating on other women in successful relationships. I guess jealousy is a way of life for some women. I can still hear my mother say, "How did she get him? She doesn't deserve him. I go to church every Sunday, why won't God bless me with a husband like that?" Jealous women set traps and give bad advice to spoil the happy relationships of naive women. It's true that misery loves company.

My mother, Tierra, is truly a miserable person. She's downright wicked and that's why I had to distance myself from her. All my life I tried to gain her respect and acceptance, but nothing worked so I finally gave up. I graduated from Western High School, which is an all-girls school with one of the most challenging academic programs in the state of Maryland. My mother wasn't impressed at all. She told me she would have been impressed if I had graduated in the top 5 percent of my class. I was completely crushed. I think that was my main reason for not going to college right away. I planned to only take a year off and that year soon turned into seven. Although I hate my job at the bank I'm too comfortable to go anywhere else.

A major part of my mother's resentment against me has to do with the fact that I look so much like my father. His name is George Weaver and to say the least he's a real trip. My parents were never married, but we all lived together as a happy family for years and I thought that was the way it would always be.

My father was an ordinary type of guy who worked for a roofing contractor, but to me he was my everything. My mother said he was an ordinary type of guy when it came to everything else except dealing with women. He really put me and my mother through something. At first I had no idea that he was such a womanizer. When I was seven years old we were on our way to pick my mother up from work. It was a Friday evening, payday for both of them. I remember it as if it were yesterday. My father's car was clean. He was dressed to kill and he smelled like he had bathed in Polo cologne. He and I were on Edmondson Avenue at a red light when this woman pulled up next to us. I watched from the backseat as this woman caught my father's attention. It was as if he forgot I was in the car or he thought I wasn't paying attention.

Maybe he just didn't give a damn because he turned toward the passenger-side window and blew the lady a kiss and mouthed the words, "I love you."

She mouthed, "I love you too, baby."

I was blown away. I thought, *Ooh, I'm gonna tell my momma.* But I didn't tell because I wanted to protect my daddy. The last thing I wanted was for my parents to split up. I knew my momma would have killed him. I later found out that my father was already involved in a relationship with that woman. At that time I was too young and innocent to understand exactly what was going on with my parents. The next thing I knew my father ended up leaving me and my mother for that woman and her two kids. The part that hurt the most was that my father was my best friend and he turned his back on me. I love him so much.

Every night I could count on him to give me a piggyback ride to bed. We used to play board games like Sorry, Life, and Monopoly for hours. I couldn't have asked for a better father, but when he left us, my mother was too bitter to even sit down and play a quick game of Uno with me. Instead of giving me a piggyback ride and tucking me into bed, she would beat me for asking when my father was coming back home.

The sad thing was that my mother didn't give up on trying to get my father back for years. She would run behind him, begging him to come back. My mother even fought his girlfriend a few times. She was a wreck, but all the while she was hard on me. She gave me advice that she wasn't even trying to follow herself. My father eventually married his girlfriend and became too busy with his ready-made family to look our way again. And people have the nerve to wonder why I'm the way I am. When my father was with us I had it all, jewelry, designer clothes, leather, and fur coats. After he left, my mother and I had to give up just about everything we had to make it. Now I have someone in my life like Trey who spoils me with nice things the same way my father used to. That's what I really wanted from Jay and he knows it, but he never did anything.

I called Trey late last night on his cell phone to see what he was up to and he caught a nasty-ass attitude with me. It wasn't like I was trying to keep track of his whereabouts, I just wanted to see him again.

When I called I said, "What's up, Trey?"

He said, "Chillin'. What's up?"

In a sexy tone I said, "I want you. Ooh, I need you so bad."

"Oh, damn, what's up, shorty? I ain't know it was you."

I said, "Wanna come over and make love to me?"

"I can't 'cause I'm chillin' with my baby mother tonight. I can't talk right now. Here she come."

I got pissed. I said, "Well, fuck you then!"

"Bitch, don't never talk to me like that, you hear me!"

"Whatever, nigga."

I hung up on that ignorant bastard. I deserved that for messing with his trifling ass. Like a fool I keep asking myself, what do I see in him? Like a lot of people I suffer from instant-gratification syndrome. I wanna be rich now, like yesterday. For real, Trey has the riches right now. He's sexy and all, but realistically he lacks a certain degree of class. He's really bringing me down. I'm not the same cultured pearl I used to be. Sometimes Jay can be a real intellectual and he stimulates my mind. He's the first artsy type of guy I've ever dated and most of the time it's hard for me to appreciate his perspective on the world. If he had more money I'd pretend to be interested in whatever he wanted me to focus on. At first I thought it was weird that Jay still lived with his grandmother. I never dreamed of messing with a guy that lives in his grandmother's basement, but after he explained why he still lives there, I thought he was really sweet.

I was completely out of line at the park today. The scenery was beautiful and I spoiled a perfect romantic setting. Jay deserves better. I know it and he knows it too. Trey had me so messed up that I couldn't think straight. Our argument over the phone kept playing in my head. I love Jay, but sometimes I yearn to be with Trey. My attraction to Trey is obvious and that numbskull stays on my mind too much, but later for him and his *baby mother*. I can't believe that gold-toothed, iced-out, platinum-wearing, ballin', shot-callin', ebonics-speakin', punk ass hasn't called me yet.

My phone rings. I check my caller ID: Trey Bryant.

I scream, "Yes, it's my baby." I grab the phone and say, "Hello."

"Hey, Boo."

"Oh, now I'm your Boo again. Yesterday I was a bitch," I say with a serious attitude. I changed up real quick.

"I'm sorry, shorty. You know I can't stand when people yell or curse at me."

"Same here and I'm sorry for cursing at you. I miss you."

"I'm glad 'cause I ain't think you wanted to talk to me again."

"I wanna hook up tonight."

"I can't, but tomorrow's better. I need a big favor, shorty."

"So do I. My bills are due again."

"Didn't I just give you some money?"

"Yeah, and it's all gone. It's not easy being me. You know I gotta look ghetto fabulous." I laugh. "You owe me big time anyway."

"How you figure? 'Cause you sexed me last night?"

"No, dummy, because you left your condom wrapper in Jay's car and he found it."

Trey bursts out laughing. "Oh, shit. What did he say?"

"Not a whole lot. I convinced him that it was his. Next time we should do it in your car."

"Hell no! How we gonna have sex in a Q45? Not on my leather seats, I can't see that happening."

"I'm tired of quickies. We need to get a hotel suite again."

"I bet Jamal don't wine and dine or take you to nice hotels like I do, right?"

"No. He can't afford it."

"Well, stop sweatin' me, you know what I'm saying? Sometimes all I have time for is a quickie. You know I'm a businessman. The sex is good, right?"

"Yeah." I wanna say, *Yeah, right, you minuteman.* We only really had good sex once.

"Alright, that means I'm doing my job. Look, Boo, you gonna have Jamal's car tomorrow night? 'Cause I need you to pick me up."

"I can't because it's Thursday night and I have to pick Jay up from work after his art class. Why do you need to be picked up? What's up with your ride?"

"I have to drop my car off at the dealer for some work and it won't be ready until Friday morning. I'm going to New York Friday and I want you to go with me. If you come get me tomorrow, I'll hook you up for real. I'm saying, whatever you want, whatever you need. Some good sex and some serious shopping."

"I do need to go shopping and I need some good sex too. I don't want a quickie either."

"Don't worry, I'm gonna give it to you real good."

"Okay, you better. I'll see you tomorrow."

"Oh yeah, tell your soft-ass boyfriend I said hi. You can bring him to my party Saturday night."

"Now why you calling him soft?"

"He is soft. Okay, check this out. Look at his driver's license and see if he's smiling. If he is, that's a sure sign of a soft nigga."

"Leave him alone. I bet he's not smiling. You just made that up because your mug shot and your driver's license look exactly alike."

"Yep, hard-core till I die."

"Stop being stupid. What's your party for and where's it gonna be?"

"My house in P. G. County. It's kinda like a housewarming and a welcome-home party for my man Tank."

"Big crazy Tank?"

"Yep, that's my man and stop calling him crazy."

"Okay, but you know that boy ain't right. I gotta go. Bye, Trey. See you tomorrow."

What kind of nonsense have I gotten myself into? Big crazy Tank is a straight-up murderer who I haven't seen in about ten years or more. Tank and Trey used to terrorize our neighborhood when they were younger. They were two people that nobody wanted to mess with. I can't remember who Tank killed. I just remember him shooting three or four kids at his high school. Tank has been crazy all his life and I really don't want to see him, but I can't miss Trey's party. Jay probably won't wanna go, but I'll talk him into it.

I never ask Trey what other type of business he's into, but I know he's not detailing cars or overseeing his barbershops all night long. I really don't want to know. But if he hangs around people like Tank he's probably involved in something illegal. All I know is that he keeps my bills paid and he's about to get me another Honda Accord or my dream car, a Mercedes Benz coupe.

My doorbell rings, but I'm not going to answer it. Usually, if I'm not expecting company, then my so-called company shouldn't expect me to answer my door. I always tell people to call first because their asses won't get in.

Anyway, I make my way downstairs to the front door and peep through the peephole. Jay is on the other side of the door looking lost and kind of pitiful. He looks like he just got off a short yellow school bus and the only thing missing is his safety helmet. He has a blank expression on his face and a dozen long-stemmed red roses in his hand. I open the door slightly and look him right in his face.

I smile and say, "Thank you."

I take the roses and try closing the door in his face, but Jay jams his foot in the doorway to keep the door from closing.

He says, "Girl, stop playing and let me in. I've got something else for you."

"Slide it through the crack."

"That's exactly what I wanna do."

The next thing I see is a big, black, long, erect penis slide through the crack in the doorway. I almost do a Lorena Bobbit and chop that bad boy right off with the door, but I like that thing a little too much to chop it off. Sisters just don't go to that extreme. Plus, I'm not sure if I want Jay to be the father of my kids one day.

After about a minute of taunting him, I finally let Jay inside. The last thing we need is for my landlady, Mrs. Jenkins, to see a big black penis peeping through the doorway. Only God knows what would happen then.

Jay looks even better than earlier. I guess he calls himself trying to impress me and I can't lie, it's working. He shaved his face and neatened up his little mustache and goatee. His skin looks smooth and his boyish charm is in full effect. I want to run my hands across his face, but I'm playing that stuck-up, hard-to-get role. To top everything off, Jay's Nautica cologne is starting to have an effect on me.

"Who you trying to impress coming over here dressed up with a fresh shave, Nautica cologne all flowing, and pulling out your thing? It must be for Mrs. Jenkins, 'cause I ain't impressed," I say in a joking way.

"Yeah, where's ole girl anyway? She's probably due for a good work-out. I know somebody else who's past due for a good workout, but I won't mention any names. Let's see, how long has it been?" Jay jokes as I pulled him by the hand leading him up to my apartment.

When we get up to my apartment I reach for the switch to turn on my lamp because the place was completely dark except for the bright glow from the streetlights below, a little moonlight, and a dim candle-light coming from my bedroom. As I reach for the lamp Jay grabs my hand and puts it around his waist.

He says, "I like it just like this. There's just enough light for me to see your beautiful face and the darkness helps to set the mood."

"What mood?" I say in a playful way. The mood is right and the last thing I want to do is spoil another romantic setting like I did earlier.

"Just flow with me, girl. Let me take you there," Jay says as he caresses my face and lays a soft kiss on my lips. In a sexy sort of way he says, "That was nice . . . real nice. I'm sorry for the way I treated you earlier."

He apologizes and instantly I feel guilty. "I'm sorry too. I spoiled everything with my attitude, but I'm better now."

"Good, 'cause I need my sweet little Jessie back."

"I like that. She never left, I'm right here for you."

"Please don't change anymore; if anything, we need to get things back to the way they used to be. Can we spend the night together?" Jay asks as he kisses my hand.

I say, "Slow down a bit."

"I can't, I'm in love with you."

Jay is so expressive. His eyes even speak to me. I know he's in love with me, but I have to tone this down a bit.

I ask, "Are you sure it's not a bad case of lust?"

"Well, to be honest it's a little bit of both and there's nothing wrong with that, is there?"

I think, *He's good.* I smile and say, "No, I guess it's okay."

"I'm glad we're on the topic of love. I need to know if you love me."

"Yes, I do." I think, *Why now? If I tell Jay that I love him, it's like telling him this is serious and this is permanent. No love . . . no commitment . . . no broken heart, that's my motto.*

He says, "Okay, but can I hear you say that you love me?"

I look at Jay like he's crazy. I think, *Damn, gimme a break. This brotha's trying to get the world in one night.* "I said it already. You asked if I loved you and I said I did."

"It's not even the same. I said I loved you and you just agreed."

"What's the difference?"

Jay loosens his tight embrace and says, "I think I should leave now."

"Answer my question," I say in a forceful tone.

"It means so much more when the words *I love you* actually flow from your lips. It's not that hard. Watch and learn. *I love you, Jessie.* See how easy that was for me? And after eighteen months it should be just as easy for you to say."

I pause for a few seconds. With a shy little smirk on my face I say, "I'd love for you to spend the night. Was that close enough?"

My remark makes Jay's eyes widen. He shakes his head, saying no, but at the same time he pulls me closer. I think, *Sending mixed signals, huh? Typical horny male, thinking with the wrong head.*

He says, "Not exactly what I was looking to hear, but it'll do for now. I've got a lot on my mind right now and I need to have your body close to mine. I swear, I'm gonna make you love me. If it's the last thing I do, I'm gonna make you love me."

"That sounds good to me."

Jay looks at his watch and says, "First, let me call my grandmother to let her know I'm not coming home tonight."

"Huh? You need permission from your grandmother? What kind of man are you?"

"I'm gonna show you in a minute. Stop trippin'. It's not a matter of getting permission. It's more of a respect thing. I like to let my grand-mother know when I'm not coming home. She's old and the last thing I need is to make her worry herself to death."

"I understand. Just hurry up."

It's morning. Sunlight wakes me and the aroma of my citrus mist candle drowns out the scent of my sin. But my guilt quickly reminds me of what I've done. I'm guilty of keeping a lie going. Oh, what the hell, I'm only human.

I look around my bedroom and there are clothes everywhere. My panties are all the way across the room near my closet. My comforter is on the floor with Jay's black Calvin Klein boxer briefs on top. All I'm wearing is a sheet and a smile. I usually won't admit it, but I got worked. Jay has some type of unexplainable affect on me. As he sleeps I stare at his face in amazement. I think, *If only he could make money like he makes love, he'd be a rich brotha.*

I wake Jay with a kiss on his lips. With his eyes still shut he pulls me in tightly against his bare chest.

I whisper, "I love you, Jay. I love you so much."

He opens his eyes with a surprised look on his face and says, "I love you too, baby. Thank you."

"No, thank you for everything. Thanks for the roses and for mak-ing me feel so special. You're too good to me. I don't deserve you," I say with a feeling of guilt possessing my mind and body. Telling Jay that I love him feels good, but I still have Trey on my mind.

After I gaze into Jay's eyes for a few minutes something hits me. I ask, "Can I see your wallet for a minute?"

"Why? I don't have any money in it."

"I just wanna see your license real quick."

"All right," Jay says with a clueless look on his face. He reaches on the floor to pick up his pants, then hands me his wallet.

I pull out his license and to my surprise he does have a big-ass cheesy smile on his face. I think of Trey's exact words, *a true sign of a soft-ass nigga.* Without saying a word I gently tuck Jay's license back into his wallet.

Jay looks at me and says, "What is it?"

"Nothing, baby, I was just checking. You look real handsome on your license," I say as I kiss his lips for the second time.

Jay has taken care of some of my needs, but there are still some other needs that only Trey has the power to take care of. Having two men can be fun, but sometimes it can weigh real heavy on the conscience. I feel like I want to make Jay my one and only. It's just hard as hell to figure out when to let Trey go. When would be the right time? After Trey pays my bills, after the New York shopping trip, or after I get him to buy me a car? I would look so good rolling in a Benz. Damn, decisions, decisions, it's hard being me. It's even harder keeping a lie going. I have a strange feeling that soon the light will be shed on my dark secret. Within a few seconds I decide to hold on to Trey a little longer, because a vision of me riding to the mall in my Mercedes Benz coupe pops into my head.

Jay asks, "Baby, why you looking so serious? Everything's good 'cause we're in love and with love we can conquer anything," he says confidently as he lays a deep passionate kiss on me. After we kiss Jay doesn't say a word, he just stares at me and smiles like he's the happiest man on earth.

I think, *Poor little crazy boy . . . so handsome . . . so sweet . . . so broke. If only you knew.* I'm glad there's no way for him to decipher what's on my mind.

Usually, I never like to tongue-kiss first thing in the morning because of morning breath. I'm not going to complain, because I'm in love and love conquers all, even morning breath.

Chapter 3

Jamal

I'm on my way home from Jessie's place and I can't stop thinking about how incredible last night was. My life is so perfect. I'm complete again. My little Jessie is finally back. We're back on track, together in love. I'm an artist perfecting his masterpiece. I'm painting a perfect picture, a picture-perfect life. My girl said she loves me. She actually said those words. Now I see her in a completely different light. That girl might have a ring coming her way real soon if she keeps this up. Call me crazy or call it a love high. Whatever it is, I'm happy.

I march through my grandmother's front door like I shot the sheriff and the motherfuckin' deputy. A night of good sex can do that. I give Grandma a kiss on the cheek and she gives me this I-don't-know-where-your-lips-have-been kind of look.

I say, "Goooood mornin'. Don't look at me like that, Grandma."

"You need to stop."

I laugh and ask, "What? Stop what?"

I make my way to the living room past a traditional framed picture of Jesus. Next to that is a picture of Martin Luther King, John F. Kennedy, and Robert Kennedy, with notations under their images describing their contributions to the civil rights movement. I give them a quick salute. I'm in a silly mood.

Grandma is right on my heels. We sit down together on her fine-looking plastic-covered beige sofa, which matches her plastic-covered love seat and chair. This furniture has been covered so long that I hardly ever notice the plastic anymore. I'm not exactly sure what it's being protected from, but I can see this plastic has done one hell of a good job. This stuff still looks brand-new under all this thick, hot-ass plastic.

My attention goes back to Grandma as she continues her lecture. "You and that girl are living in sin. I raised you better than this. You need to make her an honest woman."

"She's already honest. Jessie doesn't lie to me."

Grandma laughs and says, "Stop making an ass of yourself. You know what I mean. I'm gonna pray for y'all."

"Thank you for being so concerned, but I just might be gettin' married soon."

Grandma's whole demeanor quickly changes. "That would be nice. Oh Lord, please tell me you're gonna have a church wedding."

"Of course."

"I'm gonna tell Pastor Thomas you wanna get married at our church. And when I tell Shadow, her and John will probably pay for the wedding."

I give her a funny look and say, "No, I'll save them for a rainy day. Me and Jessie can handle this. It's our wedding, so the least we can do is pay for it."

I'm talking pretty big for a man with no money. I've always pictured me and my lovely bride having a big church wedding followed by a fancy catered reception. Damn, that would be sweet, but it's starting to look like a courthouse wedding and a cheap backyard reception for us.

Grandma says, "You're right about paying for your own wedding, but to be honest, you ain't got a pot to piss in. It won't hurt to ask them. Rich people are supposed to help out their less fortunate family members. Shadow loves you and I know she'd love to help y'all."

"I said it's okay. I hate asking John and Shadow for help. They have their own bills already. We'll talk about this later, I gotta get ready for work."

"Slow down. You're late every day anyway, so sit here and talk to me for a few more minutes, Mr. Assistant Manager."

"Okay, what's up?"

"My foot if you say *what's up* to me again. Have you taken a good look at Coach lately? He looks so bad. He's really suffering. That damn chemotherapy is killing him. The hospital van will be out in a few minutes to take him for his appointment. I sure wish you could take off to go with him."

"I can't today, but I promise to go with him for his next visit."

"The way he looks, there might not be a next visit. You should see how skinny he is under those clothes. He can't keep nothing on his stomach. I'm gonna have him move in here with us to see what we can do for him. We can't turn our backs on him."

"I don't plan to. Coach is like a father to me and you know I'm gonna look out for him."

"I know, I'm just scared, that's all," Grandma says with tears in her eyes.

"I got this, don't worry."

"Thanks, Jamal. This is a tough time and we all need to stick together."

"Everything will be fine."

Grandma smiles and says, "I love you."

"I love you too. Now stop being so dramatic, I gotta go to work. I can't go to work all teary-eyed, looking like a punk."

That makes Grandma laugh.

It's 7:15 P.M. and I see some of my students start to stroll in and head to the arts-and-crafts room in the back of the store. I've been here since 9:00 this morning and I feel better than I expected, even after a fairly busy day around here. Jessie caught the bus here early to pick up my car. She should be in front of the store at 9:30 sharp, no excuses. She has this ritual that she does every time she's late. She fills my gas tank in hopes of making me forget how late she is.

The store owner, Mrs. Harvey, spots me in the store's main aisle. "Hey, Jamal, got a minute?"

I look down at my watch as if I don't already know what time it is. She grabs me by the arm and gently pulls me aside just out of the flow of customers. I really don't look forward to talking to Mrs. Harvey, because she has a way of giving me this hungry, sex-starved look. Don't get me wrong, she's a very attractive older woman, but I really don't want to be involved with my boss like that. I like the way things are right now. I get extra-special treatment for being who I am and for the good work I do around here. Mrs. Harvey is an influential woman in the community with lots of connections. I'm sure she could help advance my art career somehow. My only fear is what she'll expect in return. I always keep in mind that Mrs. Harvey is a married woman with a husband that looks like a strange mixture of Nick Ashford and Ron Isley. I ain't trying to get none of his sloppy seconds.

I play it cool and say, "Sure, I got a minute, my class doesn't start for another fifteen minutes. So what's on your mind?"

She smiles and says, "Expansion."

"What you gonna do, knock down some walls around here or what?"

"No, nothing like that. I'm looking at some properties in Baltimore and Anne Arundel County. And that's where you come in."

"Okay."

I have no idea where this is going. Usually, I just smile and nod to give the impression that I'm flowing with every detail. Something tells me that this is different. I'm just happy Mrs. Harvey and I are having a normal conversation without her usual hungry, sex-starved look.

"You've been an assistant manager here for about a year, right?"

"Yeah. It doesn't seem like it, but that's about right."

"You're a valued member of this team and I think you'd make an even better manager. I'd like you to manage one of the new stores. It's time for a change, wouldn't you agree?"

"Yeah, but you know this is only temporary. I'm an artist and I'm looking forward to pursuing my dream of having a successful career in fine art, not management."

Two of my students, Mr. Allen and Ms. Verdene, walk past and greet me and Mrs. Harvey. They're a cute little elderly couple that look a lot like Uncle Ben and Aunt Jemima together. I tell them to head back to the arts-and-crafts room and I'll join them in a few minutes.

Mrs. Harvey asks, "And what are you doing to pursue this career in fine art? It's not an easy living being an artist. You need to eat. I know you like to have fun and entertain your little girlfriend. Look, this is right here right now. I'm offering you a solid future with this company and you can still pursue your dream. I'm willing to help you in any way I can. I'll even introduce you to some of my friends—rich friends. Anyway, I'm always talking about you." All of a sudden that hungry, sex-starved look appears. She smiles and says, "Can't you see everything I'm doing for you? What you gonna do for me? You scratch my back and I'll scratch yours."

"What?" I look at her as if she were crazy and we both burst out laughing. "Mrs. Harvey, I appreciate what you're doing and all that you've done for me in the past, but I need more time to think about this."

"I told you to stop calling me Mrs. Harvey. I'm Peaches to you." She grabs my hand, scratches my palm with one of her long colorful nails, and a chill runs through my entire body. I pull my hand away just as two of my other students, Tamar and Lyndia, arrive. They're two sexy young girls both about nineteen years old. They say hi as they walk by, then laugh at what they just saw. I'm a little embarrassed, but they probably have no idea what they actually witnessed.

"Look at you acting all funny. Now I see what you like. These young girls don't have nothing on me. I know you need to get back there for your class, but please give my offer some serious consideration. If you want we can showcase as much of your artwork as you like during the store's grand opening. Shit, I'll even fix it so you can have your own exhibition at a gallery. How's that sound to you?"

All women have to do is mention sex or my artwork and I'm putty in their hands. In this case mentioning the exhibition does the trick. I'd love that kind of exposure.

With a big smile I say, "That sounds good. I'll definitely give it some serious consideration."

Mrs. Harvey says, "You are so gorgeous and you're good for business. I think a lot of these women come here just to see you."

"Yeah, like Tamar and Lyndia, right?"

"Right. You don't realize how sexy you are. I'm leaving now, but Dennis will be here to close." There goes that hungry look again. "Good night, Jamal. I love you."

"I love you too." I'm lying. She always says that to me. I started saying I loved her and I ended up with my own office and a raise. Sometimes I feel that I bring this harassment on myself because I continue to play along with Mrs. Harvey, digging a deeper ditch. Sometimes it's a use-what-I-got-to-get-what-I-want kind of thing. Just last week, Mrs. Harvey entered the danger zone and felt me up. I should say, she felt me up and down. She actually grabbed a handful of me. It felt good for a second and then I quickly recovered from my temporary lapse from sanity. I suddenly regained my senses and realized that her touching me was totally inappropriate. Besides, I don't cheat on my girl. In the future I just have to remember my limits.

My worst fear is that one day I'll look up and *Peaches* will have me trapped. I'm an artist and the last thing I want is to be stuck in a career as an arts-and-crafts store manager. But there are worse things. I could be Peaches's sex slave. *Oh, hell no!*

I head back to the arts-and-crafts room, which resembles an elementary school art classroom. The room still looks a little junky and cluttered from Mrs. Harvey's Tuesday night crafts class. It looks like everyone is present except for one person, Richard, and I'm sure he just wants to be *fashionably late,* so he can make his grand entrance and steal the attention of everyone in the room. Here he comes now, twisting like an ugly little girl in heat, with his mascara, a purse, and a tight-ass Versace outfit.

He puts his hand up to his mouth and says, "Oh my goodness, am I late? I'm always the last one here."

I say, "It's okay, I'm a little late myself. I got caught up talking out front."

Tamar and Lyndia look at me and burst out laughing. I think, *Oh, shit, they know that I was being sexually harassed by Mrs. Harvey.* I look the other way and try to remain composed and not laugh at myself.

I say, "Okay, let's get started. Tonight I want to concentrate on landscapes. You can pick any setting, any season, whatever you feel comfortable painting. Tonight is about artistic freedom."

Usually I have everyone paint the same picture and I get ten different interpretations, which is fine. Versatility is good and tonight my class has the green light to freestyle.

"I was inspired by Bob Ross to do this activity."

One of my least favorite students, Betty, yells out, "Who's Bob Ross?"

Her stupid eighteen-year-old son, Anthony, yells out, "Yeah, who's Bob Ross?"

These two irritate the hell out of me. They irritate me about a hundred times more than Peaches's long, colorful fingernail scratching my palm. I'd rather listen to the screeching sound of a thousand fingernails slowly sliding down a chalkboard than listen to their voices. It's almost as if they share the same dilapidated brain. Most of the time Betty is Anthony's mouthpiece. Even if he initiates a conversation Betty cuts him off midsentence and finishes his thought. I love for my students to ask questions, but Betty likes to waste everyone's time by asking questions that she already knows the answers to. She has a bad habit of cutting off the person trying to answer her question and elaborating more than the other person ever could on her own question.

Betty says, "Oh yeah, the artist. Bob Ross is that white guy from public television with the Afro. He was an incredible artist. He loved to do paintings that depicted nature. I mean, the man could create a masterpiece within minutes. He died in July of 1995. God bless his soul."

Anthony adds his two cents, "Oh yeah, the artist, the white guy with the Afro from public TV, I remember him. He died."

I think, *Oh my God. If murder was legal.* Instead I say, "Thanks a lot for those interesting biographical descriptions."

I pass out some sample paintings and carry on with class as planned.

After a long hectic day of working like a slave and instructing my art class, I can't believe that Jessica's late picking me up. She knows the routine, but she never ceases to amaze. I start my class at 7:30 and I'm out the door at 9:30 sharp. Why would Jessie have me waiting like this? Damn, I was just starting to build up confidence in her again, major confidence. The kind of confidence you have in a fiancée. She doesn't know it, but I purchased an engagement ring for her about three months ago. I often carry it with me, waiting for the perfect moment to propose to her. I never gave her the ring, for two good reasons, the first reason being, she started acting crazy and changing up on me all of a sudden. The second reason is, being the gold digger she is, there's no way she would appreciate this gold quarter-carat diamond engagement ring. Whenever I mention an engagement ring, all she knows is a platinum two-carat diamond ring. Now how could I possibly flash a gold quarter-carat diamond ring to someone who expects a two-carat diamond ring? And to top it off, she expects platinum.

I watch car after car pass by and not one belongs to me. Hold up, I see the headlights of a car like mine. If this is Jessie I won't be so mad. Damn, it's not her. It's just some dude driving a Cavalier like mine. Okay, if she can get here within the next thirty seconds, I won't be mad. It's ten minutes to ten and still no sign of her.

Dennis is still inside the store. Instead of wasting money on a disgusting diseased pay phone I decide to go inside to call Jessie. Mental note: *Get a cell phone.*

All of the store's lights are off, except for a dim light coming from under Dennis's office door. I think something must be wrong, because usually he would be out the door this time of night. As I pass his office I hear one of my favorite Sade songs, "No Ordinary Love," playing softly in the background. I can hear a quiet whimpering sound like a small wounded animal. Now the pace of the whimpering speeds up and it sounds like a person getting the thrill of a lifetime. Oh, shit, Dennis is gettin' busy with some woman. I've heard enough. I go to my office to call Jessie. It's dark, but I don't need any lights. The combination of streetlights and neon green exit signs in the store provides just enough light for me to see. From my desk I can see outside and still there's no trace of Jessie and no answer at her apartment. It's now 10:05 P.M.

I hear Dennis's office door open and I can't move quick enough to close my door without looking like a fool or scaring the hell out of him and his girl. Anyway, I'm curious to see what type of woman Dennis attracts. He's always talking about this mystery woman, but I've never seen her.

I hear Dennis's voice, "That little asshole, Jamal, left his office door open."

I can't believe he just called me a little asshole. I hear his date laugh and more of Dennis's loud, obnoxious voice.

As he steps in front of my office door he says, "If it wasn't for my mother, that—"

He stops midway through his sentence and stares me right in the face. He's completely thrown off guard. He just stands there speechless and motionless like a kid caught with his hand in the cookie jar. I hear his date's footsteps suddenly stop behind him. Without saying a word, I hop out of my seat and head toward the door so I can see his girlfriend. But who I see, who I see completely catches me off guard. I'm shocked and nervous as hell at the same time. It feels like my heartbeat is in my throat. I thought by jumping up from my desk to see Dennis's girl like that I was getting payback for him calling me a little asshole, but the embarrassment is more than any of us can handle. I should have known that Dennis was a homosexual. Richard, the flamboyant gay guy from my art class, is standing there, mascara, purse, tight-ass Versace outfit, and all. "No Ordinary Love" starts playing in my head and for now and forever that song will have an entirely different meaning.

I say, "Oh, shit, I mean, I'm sorry. I'm waiting for my girlfriend and I came back inside to call her. Hope I'm not interrupting anything."

Richard twists up his lips, sucks his teeth, and rolls his eyes.

Dennis turns into a stuttering idiot. He says, "I . . . I . . . I . . . We . . . We were just—"

I ask, "What, leaving?"

Dennis quickly answers, "Yeah. Leaving. C'mon, Rich, let's go."

Richard struts right past me still twisting like an ugly little girl in heat, mascara, purse, tight-ass Versace outfit, and all. The funny thing isn't that they were together, but that asshole Dennis was about to explain to me why he and Rich, as he called him, were locked in the store after closing hour, in his office sounding like a small whimpering animal with Sade playing softly in the background.

It's 10:30 P.M. and I'm standing outside the store in the crisp, cool night air watching cars drive past again. Jessie is an hour late and I'm pissed. Okay, finally this is my car coming. I can see Jessie's little peanut head. I wish I had a rock, because my aim is good enough to take her out from here. I'm mad because she treats me like shit.

Jessie pulls up to the store as if everything's fine, just like she is on time. I'm too pissed to drive, so I get in on the passenger side.

Jessie goes, "Hey, sorry."

I say, "Hey, sorry nothing. Where the hell have you been?" My car smells funky and it's all stuffy inside. I ask, "Why does my car smell like hot lake trout and butt sweat?" I can't wait to hear Jessica's answer.

"Stop trippin', Jay. That's my dinner you're smelling."

"Where is it? I want some fish."

"It's all gone."

"That's okay 'cause I didn't want none of your stinking fish anyway," I say in a joking way.

Jessica has this weird expression on her face. She looks as if my little joke actually hurt her feelings.

"I'm just joking, girl. Stop looking like that."

"You're not funny."

"Alright, I'm sorry. Damn, you did it again."

"What did I do now?"

"That Jedi mind trick thing that you do. You have a way of switching things around."

"Like?"

"Like you being late picking me up and me apologizing for a stupid little joke."

"I got caught up talking with Kim, Toya, and Rachael. You know how we do."

"Yeah, I do. I know how *you* do. Trust me, I understand."

"What's that supposed to mean?"

"Exactly what I said, I understand."

We're cruising down Martin Luther King Boulevard. We stop at the light on Franklin Street and I feel something roll out from under the seat and hit the heel of my left feet. I reach down to see what hit my foot and it's a beer bottle.

I say, "I just want to know one thing."

"What?"

I ask, "How long you been drinking Heineken beer?"

Jessie has this *What-you-talkin'-'bout, Willis!* look on her face.

I say, "You have either a split personality, early Alzheimer's disease, or a secret boyfriend that's trying to set your ass up by leaving all kinds of shit in my car."

"You're so paranoid. That probably belongs to one of my girls."

I'm silent. I don't have anything to say to Jessie's lying ass. I look down at my gas gauge and it's full. Yep, another sure sign that she's up to no good. Every time she's late or has done something wrong she calls herself making up for it by filling up my gas tank. This time it's not enough.

Jessie says, "I filled up your gas tank."

"It was the least you could do." I pause for a few minutes because I'm being so mean. This whole situation is messed up. Last night was so sweet, but maybe I'm crazy for expecting something that simply isn't here. All that good sex may have left me with a false sense of reality. Every man wants a good woman and I want to trust and believe in mine. I hate to argue more than anything in the world.

Jessie is my weakness. She's so beautiful that it's hard for me to stay mad. I have something special planned for her tonight and I can't let anything spoil it. Call me stupid or softhearted, I don't care.

Out of nowhere I say, "I believe you."

"You do?"

"Yep."

"Just like that?"

"Yeah, and I'll never mention it again. You have no reason to lie to me. If you say the beer bottle belongs to one of your girls, then it does."

"Thank you. I thought you were going to be angry all night. Again, I'm so sorry for being late. How was your day?"

I smile at Jessie and give her a kiss. "Thanks for asking. I had a crazy-ass day and I don't know where to start."

"Start anywhere, except for the ending, 'cause I kinda ruined that part."

"No, you didn't, 'cause tonight has just begun. I need to be inside you just like last night."

"That sounds so good, but I'm not in the mood."

"You're not on your period, so what you got, a headache or something?"

"No, I'm just not in the mood."

"Give me a minute and I can fix that."

"There's nothing you can do to fix it. Guys always want to fix things. You don't understand the female psyche. For women sex is much more than a physical thing."

"So, you're saying you aren't attracted to me anymore."

"No, it's not that at all. It's just that mentally I'm not there right now. Can we just sit here and talk for a minute?"

"I understand where you're coming from. I'm fine with some good conversation tonight, but can we do it inside your apartment?"

"I'm tired, but okay. Remember, we're just talking."

"That's cool. I'll just make love to your mind."

We get upstairs to Jessie's apartment and everything's real mellow. She turns on some music. I'm getting aroused just being here. There's something about being in the place where my love dwells that turns me on. Jessie doesn't like incenses, but she loves the aroma of scented candles. A light aroma of peach blossom fills the air in the living room. Her sex appeal and the aroma of her apartment are intoxicating enough to make a brotha go crazy.

Jessie says, "I wanna shower real quick. If you're hungry, there are some leftover grilled tuna steaks in the frig and some coleslaw."

"Sounds good, but I wanted some lake trout."

"You should've said something and we could've stopped somewhere and got you some."

"Nah, the tuna's good, but where did you get the lake trout, anyway?"

"Up on Reisterstown Road. I had potato salad and string beans too."

"Shit, all I smelled was fish in the car."

"Boy, you need to stop. I'm gonna get my shower. See you in a minute."

"Can I join you?"

"No, a sista needs a little private time."

"Alright, see you in a minute."

Jessie closes the bathroom door leaving me lonely, abandoned like an unwanted pet. Here I am in a deserted living room with nothing to do. I know I'm wrong, but everything in this room is open for search and seizure. I usually respect a person's privacy, but Jessie was stupid enough to leave me out here alone. Trust is out the window for a minute, 'cause a brotha has to protect his interests. I'm not snooping too much, just some light snooping. I quickly sift through a pile of mail on the coffee table, bills . . . bills . . . bills. Damn, more bills. There's a stack of books, *The Coldest Winter Ever*, *Satin Doll*, and *True to the Game*. These are all good books, but not typical reading material for Jessie. She used to be into contemporary romance novels like *Love Ain't Goin' Nowhere* by Eric Brown.

Ooh, the caller ID box. I review the numbers. Jessie's mother's number, mine, mine again, Kim's, Toya's, Trey's, Jessie's mother again, and mine again. Everything looks okay, but why is Trey calling here? I guess it's cool, a male friend here and there is okay, but I don't trust him. Trey is a mutual friend of ours. I've known him forever because my grandmother used to baby-sit him along with his younger brother and sister. We used to lie and say we were cousins. Trey is a few years older than me, but we were still close. Over time we just kind of grew apart. To be honest he chose one road and I chose another. He chose the thug life and I chose the everyday hardworking-class lifestyle. Not to say that his life isn't hard, because it is. The most difficult part of a hustler's life is watching his back for cops and crooked people trying to take what he's got. He constantly has to anticipate certain moves, know who to trust, and most of all know how to survive on the streets. After really thinking about it, being a hustler sounds a lot harder than I thought. I guess that's why I chose the path I did. I have little respect for hustlers, especially those who stay in the game too long. A smart man knows when to quit, because around here a hustler's life span is brief.

Trey was the weed man when we were kids, and only God knows what kinds of drugs he's dealing now.

The shower stops. I reposition myself on the sofa. The bathroom door opens and Jessie steps out looking beautifully refreshed from her shower. She looks brand-new. I described her as looking like Chilli from TLC, but right now she looks just a little bit better.

She says, "You okay over there? It was awfully quiet out here. What were you doing, masturbating or something?"

We laugh.

I say, "How'd you guess? I'm fine now. I can't believe you left me alone like that instead of letting me join you for a hot sexy shower. But it's okay. We're here, we're right here connecting mentally, and I love it."

She smiles and says, "You're so stupid."

Jessie stands in her bedroom doorway. She grabs her underwear and dresses with the towel still covering her body. I hate when she does this.

"Alright, see, you're wrong for getting dressed like that. Girl, you better drop that towel and let me sneak a peek, cop a feel, or something."

"Nah, see, we're right here." She moves her index and middle finger back and forth in front of her eyes like Martin Lawrence. "We're connecting mentally, remember?"

I jump up from the sofa and rush Jessie, tackling her to the floor. We begin to play-fight like little kids in love. She is so beautiful, feminine, and strong at the same time. I ease up a bit and gently stroke her wet, long black curly hair. She gives me a deep passionate kiss.

I say, "I love you so much."

"I love you too. You better stop 'cause I know where this is headed. Now, tell me about your day."

"Damn, I don't wanna stop. I like where we were headed."

"Tonight is about connecting mentally, remember?"

I smile and say, "Okay, I was offered a promotion. Mrs. Harvey is expanding the business and she wants me to manage her new store."

"Oh my God, baby, a promotion. That means more money, right?"

"Yeah, but I didn't accept it yet."

"Why? Oh, I know why." She laughs. "You still being sexually harassed?"

"Yeah."

"So what? You better go 'head and give that sexy old chick some of that good loving. If you do it good enough she might put you in her will; then if you sex her to death we'll be rich."

"Yeah, right. Stop playing."

"You know I'm just joking. She better stay away from my man. Did she put her hand on you?"

I think, *Not this week.* I say, "Hell, no! You know it's not like that."

"Not yet. Give her a little time and she'll cop a feel. Don't be surprised."

"Oh, guess who's gay?" Jessie shrugs. I say, "Dennis."

"Who?"

"Dennis, Mrs. Harvey's son."

"Oh yeah. Don't tell me the son's coming on to you too."

We laugh.

"Nah, fuck you, okay? He was having sex in the store with this real flamboyant gay guy from my art class."

"I'm not surprised."

"Well, I am. He always talked like he was such a ladies' man."

"Those are the main ones, working too hard to hide something."

"I never thought of that before."

"I knew it. See, the female psyche. Welcome to my world."

"You're crazy. What about your day? You talk to anyone interesting today, last night?" I think, *Go 'head and lie, I dare you.*

Jessie says, "Not really. Oh yeah, I did talk to Trey."

I can't believe she told the truth. I love this girl. I say, "Really, about what?"

"He's giving a party Saturday night at his house in Prince George's County. He said it's a housewarming and a welcome-home party for Tank."

I laugh. "Tank? I forgot all about his crazy ass, until Church mentioned him the other night."

"Well, the party is for him."

"You sure it's for Tank?"

"That's what Trey said."

"That nigga's crazy. Who the hell did he kill, anyway? I just remember him shootin' like ten kids in high school and terrifying the entire neighborhood."

"I can't remember who he killed, but I know he only shot like three or four kids in high school. The other stuff was just made up."

"Crazy-ass Tank, the original urban legend. I can't lie, I was scared of his ass for real when we were kids. I bet I'd whip his punk ass after all these years. I bet he's a punk for real now after all those years in jail, long, hard years in the penitentiary with grown men. I bet they wore that ass out. You know he was tried as an adult, right?"

"Yeah, but I don't care about all that. I still wanna go to the party."

"Shit, you must be crazy. I ain't trying to go. It'll just be like one big thug reunion."

"Yeah, you might be right, but I heard Trey's parties are better than P-Diddy's. Anyway, you said Tank was a punk and you could whip his punk ass."

"True, but I still don't wanna go. I don't care how good Trey's parties are supposed to be or who's supposed to be there. It's not my type of crowd."

"I'm gonna be there. And don't say stuff like, 'It's not my type of crowd.' You sound like an old stuck-up white man saying shit like that."

I laugh and say, "Ooh, that hurts a lot. I guess you're right. I do need to loosen up a little and hang out with my boy Trey. You know he's my pretend cousin, right?"

"I know, baby. Oh yeah, before I forget, I'm off tomorrow."

"Me too, and I wanna do something special with you."

"Aw, baby, I'm sorry, I already have plans to go shopping in New York with my girls tomorrow. We're going on an overnight shopping trip."

"Damn, I guess I gotta do this tonight."

"What are you talking about?"

"Shhh. I gotta take my time with this." I pause. "Has anyone told you that you were beautiful today?"

Jessie smiles and says, "No."

"Well, you are. You're the most beautiful thing in my life and I need you. Everything's starting to come together. It's almost picture-perfect. My job is going well. Our relationship is going well and I haven't been this happy in a long time."

I drop down to one knee and Jessie looks at me as if I were absolutely crazy because she has no idea what's happening. I reach into my pocket and pull out a black velvet ring box. Now Jessie is looking at me as if I were really crazy, but there is also a look of excitement in her eyes. Within seconds her eyes flood with tears.

"Engagement rings symbolize love, but no ring can possibly express the love I feel for you." My voice cracks and now my eyes are teary. "You're my everything and I want you to be my wife. Will you marry me?"

I nervously open the velvet box, revealing Jessie's ring. A ring that in no way, shape, or form measures up to the one she probably has pictured in her mind. But this is her ring, my gift to her. This is a ring that can't possibly be appraised by anyone, because my love is behind it and that makes it priceless.

Jessie is speechless. She bites her bottom lip for a few seconds, then says, "Oh my Lord, I'm in shock right now."

"So am I." I look at the ring, then stare at her and ask, "What's your answer?"

"Yes, I'd love to be your wife."

I'm not sure what surprises me more, Jessie's pleasant reaction to seeing the ring or her accepting my proposal. I'm too excited to do or say much. I quickly stand up and embrace her. We kiss and our destiny is almost sealed.

Chapter 4

Jamal

Trey's party is off the hook. I'm smoking, drinking, and dancing my ass off. I've danced with Jessie and most of the girls here. Most of these girls are freaks. They've been grinding and feeling all over me. Jessie watches as I dance with this freak. She seems to get sexually aroused watching this girl seduce me as we dance. Jessie even coaches her along.

She yells, "That's it, girl, play with his thing. Make him hard."

Jessie is drunk and so am I. Everything is going pretty good, but they just keep playing "Atomic Dog" by George Clinton, over and over. As a matter of fact, it's the only song they've played all night.

I yell out, "Work that ass, Jessie!"

When I look again Trey and Tank have my baby in a sandwich, treating her like a cheap little trick. Jessie looks like they're hurting her.

I yell, "Jessica, c'mere! Get the fuck off my girl. I'll kick your punk asses."

Trey and Tank let go of Jessie and instantly they're right in my face yelling at me.

Jessie breaks us up. "Y'all ain't his type of crowd and he will kick both your asses. Especially yours, Tank. 'Cause he said those men raped you in jail and made you a punk."

Everybody at the party starts laughing. They laugh so loud that I start laughing too. Tank doesn't laugh at all. He is so mad that his eyes become bloodshot red. I'm so drunk that it looks like Tank is crying blood. He pulls out a handgun and starts pistol-whipping me in my head and the whole time I'm laughing and so is everybody else, especially Jessie and Trey. I feel so weak that I drop to the ground. Tank stands over me and aims the gun at my head. I can't talk. All I can do is smile and that makes Tank even madder. He is about to pull the trigger when Coach comes running through Trey's backyard screaming, "Stop!"

Tank pulls the trigger and the bullet penetrates my skull near my left temple. Instantly my body is completely numb, except for the most excruciating headache I've ever felt in my entire life. The pain seems to radiate through my head in waves. It's completely dark and "Atomic Dog" finally stops playing.

I open my eyes and realize I was dreaming. My alarm clock reads 3:20 A.M. It's still dark and my radio alarm clock went off playing "Atomic Dog" for some strange reason. That whole scenario was a stupid dream. But the pain on the left side of my head is too real. I have a killer-ass headache. I decide to get out of bed and go upstairs to the kitchen for a drink, because my little refrigerator is empty.

When I open the basement door leading to the kitchen, I instantly notice that the kitchen is dimly lit. The refrigerator door was left open. It looks as if somebody made a late-night refrigerator raid and got a little careless. All of a sudden I hear some mumbling coming from the living room.

The voice says, "I know I'm going to hell for what I've done."

My eyes widen, trying to focus in the darkness. As I get closer I say, "Coach."

He replies, "Yeah."

I reach for the lamp and place it on its dimmest setting. The light reveals a disturbing sight. Coach is sitting in my grandmother's recliner wearing plaid flannel pajamas, an old yellow hospital bracelet around his left wrist, one brown corduroy slipper, and his old reading glasses. If he was a candy bar he'd be called Good N' Crazy because that's exactly how he looks. His eyes appear weak and his dark, skinny, winkled face is scantily covered with the last of his little straggly gray hairs. The chemo has caused Coach to lose almost all of his hair. I would give him a shave later, but soon he won't have a trace of body hair. Coach sips from a can of Ensure. When he puts it down I feel the can to see if it came out of the fridge. The can is still cold and that's a good sign that the fridge hadn't been left open too long.

I ask, "Why are you sitting here like this? Where's your robe and who were you talking to?"

"I can't sleep and it's too warm in here for my robe. Your aunt Alfreda was just here. She looked like a beautiful angel. I guess she doesn't want me to die alone. She was here to help me cross over."

An eerie feeling overtakes me. Hearing Coach mention my deceased aunt's name is unnerving. The thought of Aunt Freda being here gives me chills all over my body. Poor Coach is delirious. I want to ask him if he could see the proverbial light that dying people always talk about, but I don't.

I say, "You're a little confused. The doctor said to expect some confusion."

Coach frowns and asks, "Who you callin' confused? Freda sat right there smoking her Newports and drinkin' a fifth of gin."

I smile and think, *That doesn't sound like a beautiful angel to me.* I ask, "You could see her in the dark?"

"As clear as I see you right now. I couldn't believe it was Freda. Thought my eyes were playing tricks on me. That's why I put on my glasses. She's mad at me, told me I was going to hell."

Now I want to ask him if he could feel the flames, but I don't. I often wish I could save the world. Since that's impossible, I just wish I could save my uncle from his pain and suffering. What exactly do you say to a dying man?

Time seems to be Coach's greatest enemy. As time passes his cancer grows, stealing every ounce of life from his fragile body. I can't imagine my body betraying me like that. He's nothing more than a scared, withering shell of the man he used to be. He fears death, but the longer he lives the worse he feels. This is torture in its simplest form. He's pitiful. I want to cry, but I'm too strong to shed a tear.

I say, "You need to go to sleep."

Coach says, "I told you I can't sleep. I'm sittin' here reminiscing, talking to your aunt's ghost." He pauses for a few seconds. "I know what this is all about. I see everything so clearly now. I've seen both good things and bad things in my life and now I'm being forced to relive the bad. Some things from my past are coming back to haunt me. I've done wrong and now I gotta pay. I'm going to hell and I know it."

Coach starts to cry. He struggles to continue. "I remember when my parents died. I knew my day was coming, but not like this . . . not like this. Cancer is my death sentence and a living hell all wrapped up in one. Jamal, there's so much I wanna tell you, but I just don't know how to tell you."

I say, "It's okay. I don't know what you've done and I don't wanna know. All I can say is pray. Are you saved?"

"Yeah, I accepted Christ in my heart in the hospital. That's what dying people usually do when they're lonely and afraid."

"It's okay. You accepted Christ and that's what counts. He won't let you down."

"He won't? Then why is He allowing me to suffer like this?"

"You're asking me a question that I can't answer. You should try to focus on the good things in your life. You've had a good life. You helped raise so many kids. You were a sergeant in the marines. You've been around the world twice. You have a nice house and a new Cadillac. How many men can say that they've owned three Cadillacs in one lifetime? Remember your first Cadillac?"

Mentioning the Cadillac does the trick. Coach instantly brightens up. "Yes, Lord, how could I forget? It was a white 1976 Fleetwood Brougham. My Eldorado was my favorite though. The Fleetwood was used, but the Eldorado was brand-new."

"I remember. You taught me how to drive with that car. I owe you so much for being like a father to me. Remember how you used to play Teddy Pendergrass and the O'Jays all the time?"

Coach smiles. "Yeah."

"All the kids in my class were trying to rap and I was singing love songs."

We laugh.

"It was good for you, turned you into a real lover, right?"

"I don't know about all that. I remember that one Halloween when you sent me to school dressed as a pimp. Boy, did I look stupid. I had no idea who or what I was supposed to be dressed up in a suit with that big hat cocked to the side and all that jewelry."

"I remember. I drew facial hair on you and put your grandmother's fur coat on you too."

"Aw, man, I was trying to forget about all that. Thanks a lot for reminding me."

"Back then I used to complain about you and Shadow running

around the house, yelling and acting crazy. I'd love to go back to those days again. Have you talked to Shadow lately?"

"No, it's been a few days. She's so busy, I try not to bother her too much."

"Call her. I want y'all to stay close. I'm proud of the two of you. You're an artist and she's a news anchor. I'm damn proud of y'all. Connie and I did a good job raising y'all. I just wish your mother would come see me before it's too late. I miss that girl."

"I wish she'd come too, but after all this time, I wouldn't count on it."

I hear Grandma coming downstairs. She enters the living room looking as if she is half asleep. She asks, "What's going on down here?"

I say, "Coach can't sleep, he's busy worrying."

"I've got a good reason to worry. Look at me." He holds his arms up in the air. "This ain't me. This cancer is eating me alive and the chemo is killing me even faster. I'm weak, nauseated, and my hair is gone." Coach pauses for a second. "Freda was here and she said I was going to hell."

Grandma yells, "Lord have mercy! Stop talking like that! You're scaring me, Coach."

"I'm scared, sis, I'm scared."

Grandma says, "No disrespect to Freda, but that ain't nothing but the devil trying to scare you and I can't have that in this house. The devil's wrong if he thinks this battle is his. This battle belongs to the Lord and the victory will be yours. If you don't understand what I'm saying now, you will. God knows you will. Let's pray."

We all hold hands as Grandma begins to pray. She's such a spiritual person. She prays a mighty prayer. Her words and presence are comforting to me, and most of all to Coach. My grandmother and God are the only things keeping this family together.

Coach keeps telling us that he loves us, and asking if we love him. After a little reassurance we're able to help Coach relax. Now he is sleeping like a five-foot, nine-inch, 135-pound baby.

Finally I can return to my bed. I can't understand it, but my headache is gone. All I can think about now is Jessie. I wish I could call her right now.

Chapter 5

Jessie

I can't believe Jay. He is so sweet. And look at my ring. It's not a platinum two-carat diamond engagement ring, but it's mine and it's beautiful. For the second time this week I woke up with a smile on my face. I owe it all to Jay. He's filled my world with vivid colors. Everything's so clear, bright, and beautiful. The sun has never shined like this before. I'm somebody's fiancée. This isn't exactly what I expected, but I like it. It was a pretty unavoidable thing after I confessed my love for Jay. He's more of a man than I gave him credit for being. He's my Jamal.

I didn't want to send him home last night like I did after his wonderful proposal. He deserved some good sex for real, but my coochie was way too sore from messing with Trey to do anything else. I'm good, but not that good. All I really want to do is lie around the house all day and relax because I have more drama in my life right now than a damn soap opera. My life reminds me of some shit you'd read about in a novel.

Jamal is a real trip. He thinks he is so slick. I know he doesn't trust me and he has every right not to trust me. Especially since stupid Trey is always leaving evidence at the scene of the crime. He acts like he wants to get caught or something. Trey has nothing to lose. On the other hand, I will definitely lose Jamal and that would crush me and our future plans.

I pretty much gave Jamal the freedom to snoop around my apartment last night while I was in the shower and I know he did. At first I didn't realize that he probably scanned through my caller ID until he kept throwing hints, asking who I'd been talking to lately. I finally caught on that he probably knew that Trey called. I planned to be honest anyway. I ain't even mad at Jamal. I call that watching his plate so another man can't eat his food.

My phone rings. Speaking of the devil. My caller ID reads *Trey Bryant*.

"Hello."

"What's up, shorty?"

"Hey, Trey." I sound a little surprised, as if I don't know it is him.

"There's been a change in plans. The trip to New York is off."

"That's fine as long as the shopping is still on."

"We can do that and I still wanna spend the night with you. How does the Embassy Suites sound?"

I smile and say, "Hot, real hot. Can we go to Prime Outlets in Hagerstown?"

"Whatever makes you happy, 'cause I know you were lookin' forward to going to New York."

"Not really, I was just looking forward to going shopping."

"How 'bout I come by around noon?"

"We have to move quick 'cause Jamal is off today and he might be staking out my apartment."

"Why?"

"Maybe 'cause you fucked up last night and left your beer bottle in his car."

"Don't worry about that. I bet he was mad for five minutes and then everything was normal again. He could have found me butt-naked humping you in his backseat for all I care. He's sprung and no matter what he ain't never gonna let you go. He's in love." Trey laughs.

"That's not funny. Just hurry up and get here. When you pull up I'll be ready to hop right in your car."

My phone beeps. "Somebody's on my other line. Let me go and I'll see you in a few minutes."

"Alright, it's probably your lover man, Jamal."

"Gotta go, bye."

I click over to my other line. "Hello."

"Hey, girl, what you doing?"

"Hi, Jamal, I was just talking to Rachael and Toya, we're about to leave for New York."

"I miss you. Can I come over for a little good-bye kiss from my fiancée?"

"No! I mean, that sounds nice, but my girls will be here in like two seconds, I think I hear them now. I gotta go. I love you and thanks again for last night." I hate being so abrupt with him like this, but it's very necessary. Finally I hang up.

Trey pulls up to my apartment at 11:45. I hop in his car like a bank robber getting into a getaway car. I'm not trying to get caught.

Everything is taken care of. My girls are really out of town, so Jamal shouldn't run into them. Anyway, they know the deal. Trey and I speed off on our way to I-695, then to I-70 West.

Trey's outfit steals my attention for a minute. He has on a Sean John denim suit and butter Timberlands, typical gear for him. But he's wearing an African Holocaust T-shirt. It's nice, but not his usual style. I just look at his shirt without commenting.

The weather is perfect for shopping. It's a clear, sunny autumn day, about sixty-eight degrees. The sky looks incredible. It almost looks airbrushed, a shade of powder blue with a few puffy white clouds.

Trey asks, "Why you so quiet?"

"Just looking around and thinking about stuff."

"That's cool. Probably thinking 'bout shopping."

"Yeah."

We laugh.

I think of Jamal and how the scenery out here always excites him. Guess I've been around him too long, because for the first time it really excites me too. It's so pretty out here this time of year. I miss Jamal, wonder what he's doing right now. Wonder if he is thinking about me, about us.

Trey and I drive past Turf Valley Country Club and see some golfers. Not a black face in the scattered pack of golfers. Where's Tiger when we need him most? I'd love to see him and his big teeth out there representing the black race or whatever race he represents.

Trey says, "That's what I need to get into, golf."

"Who are you, Tiger Woods?"

"Nah, I ain't trying to be like that or nothing. I'm a businessman.

The golf course is a good place to meet people. You know, networking and shit."

I laugh. "Yeah, networking and shit. You better not go to an exclusive country club talking like that."

"Hey, I'm just being me. People respect that in a man. That's how I got where I am today, being me. I've got friends in and outside the ghetto. So what you saying, huh?"

"Nothing at all. You know better than me. You're speaking from experience and I'm speaking from my sheltered little world and generalizations."

"I'm glad you recognize it. In some way, everybody can relate to the ghetto and the hip-hop lifestyle. I guess we owe that to MTV. Being black and being around black people is hot right now, without a doubt."

"Okay, you got me, Mr. Businessman."

"Driving out this way brings back some bad memories."

"Like what?"

"Like that cold winter morning a few years ago when they were shipping my black ass out to the Maryland State Correctional Facility in Hagerstown."

"Ooh, that sounds rough. What did you go to jail for anyway?"

"Nothing. I didn't do shit."

"I heard that everybody in prison is innocent. They're all there for the same thing, nothing."

We laugh.

"Just half, the rest are probably there for possession of narcotics with the intent to distribute."

"Damn, I got you." I want to ask a question, but I'm kind of hesitant. If I can't ask my man, who can I ask? "Do men really get raped in jail or is that just something that happens in movies and made-for-TV stuff, like *Oz*?"

Trey takes his eyes off the road and looks at me like I'm crazy. "That shit only happens to people that want it to happen to them. Men have sex in prison, but those are the homos. Why would you ask me something like that?" Trey asks defensively.

Yuck, a vision of Trey with another man pops into my head and it makes me laugh. He'd better not hide something like that from me. He doesn't look like the type that would be washing somebody's drawers or getting traded off for a pack of cigarettes.

I say, "No real reason. Jamal and I talked about prison last night."

"What does he know about prison? He wouldn't make it an hour in Central Booking. I hate when people like that talk about shit they've never experienced."

"You're right again. Do you still mess around with drugs and stuff like that?"

"What? Shorty, don't ask me stuff like that."

"Sorry." I feel so stupid. All of a sudden I feel as if I were twelve years old, because all this is new to me.

Trey smiles and whispers, "Just a little. Can't talk in the car, alright."

I whisper, "Sorry."

I feel like such a little geek. I should've known better. After all this time we've never discussed Trey's involvement in any illegal activity. I've never seen Trey act so paranoid, especially in his own car.

"I don't know about any drugs, but I know my detailing business is doing real good and so are my barbershops." Trey is talking like he's reading a script or something and he sounds like he's on a third- or fourth-grade reading level. He continues, "My investments are doing good too. I'm doing alright. John is my financial advisor."

"Who?"

"John, your boyfriend's brother-in-law."

"Oh, that John. Can you stop talking like that?"

"Like what? Alright, let me stop. But for real, that nigga is a genius. The stock market is nothing but a guessing game and sometimes I think John's a damn psychic. He made me a lot of money back when those tech stocks were hot. He sold them at the right time too. Now he's being a little more conservative with my money 'cause the market's kinda cold. I turned a bunch of my homeboys on to John."

"I can't relate, 'cause I'm broke. A lot of my bank customers made money off those tech stocks too, and I'm happy for all y'all."

"Don't hate. We can work on getting you some investments too. I'll talk to my man John, a'ight?"

"Yep, right after we spend all this loot shopping."

We laugh. That's how I know that Trey is paid, he laughs instead of getting mad when I talk about spending his money. Broke men get mad with a quickness when you mention spending money. Jamal is a prime example. That brotha even gets mad when I spend my own money. I guess he can feel it just before I'm about to hit him in his pockets.

We've just entered Carroll County.

I ask, "What do you think of all these white kids in Carroll County using heroin like crazy?"

Trey says, "No real opinion."

I forgot I'm talking to a drug dealer. He's probably thinking too bad for them and good for him.

Trey says, "Well, they gotta do something. It's boring as shit out here in farm country. Look at those barns and cornfields over there. That shit is boring to a teenager. Now, the heroin is like a great escape to never-never land. To be honest, nobody gives a shit about the thousands and thousands of black heroin addicts in Baltimore, now, do they?"

"I guess not."

"Nothing's ever an issue until it affects white America."

"True."

"I'm tired of all this drug shit, anyway." He yells like he's insane. "You hear that, I'm tired of this shit!"

"I hear you. Calm down."

"I'm not talking to you. I'm talking to them."

My eyes widen. "Okay." He's completely lost it. "Who's them?"

"Them. The ones who put this shit in our community from the start. I don't care if my car is bugged or not, nobody's gonna control what I say."

"Stop being so paranoid. I don't think anybody has this car bugged."

"Those damn feds got me going crazy. I don't feel safe talking in my own car, because I can't keep my eyes on it twenty-four hours a day. They could easily bug this shit. I feel like they're leaving me alone for a minute so they can set me up for the kill. They raided my detailing shop about three months ago, but they didn't find shit. They just wanna shut me down anyway. 'Cause a black man ain't supposed to have a successful business. I've sold drugs, but now I'm ready to be legit, ready to finally leave all this madness behind."

"You should. You're wearing that African Holocaust T-shirt and contributing to a new African Holocaust."

"Check you out, being all righteous and shit. You don't say stuff like that when you're spending my money. I know that we never talked about stuff like this before, but you had an idea what I was into. Am I right?"

"Yeah, you're right again."

"I deal drugs, but I have a conscience too. Some nights I wake up feeling like shit knowing that I sold drugs to some kid's mother and that kid probably won't eat 'cause his mother used all of her money to get high. I hate to admit it, but they're gonna get it from somebody, so why not me? Why not me? That's my excuse, what I keep telling myself, how I keep myself in this. Growing up, I used to think of my mother as evil. Not the woman you know as my mother, she's my stepmother. My biological mother was weird, always tired or emotional. I later found out that she was a heroin addict. I actually watched her kill herself. At first I just thought of her as an alcoholic, until I caught her shooting up in the kitchen in front of my little brother and sister. I must have been like ten years old. When I close my eyes at night, I still see her and it's got me messed up. I was the one who found her dead on the bathroom floor with a needle sticking out of her arm. It hurts so much, nothing but the same nightmare almost every night. I can't believe I'm opening up to you like this. I was trippin' earlier. I don't really think my car is bugged, I just don't like talking about my business. What I do isn't everybody's business. You know what I'm saying?"

"Yeah. It's okay talking about your problems to me. It's a good thing. I'm your friend and if you ever need to talk I'm here for you."

We kiss.

"Thanks, shorty. Now you know about my demons and my weaknesses, but I better not hear about this from nobody else, you know what I'm saying?"

"Yeah. You don't have to worry. I'm good at keeping secrets."

Trey never opened up to me like this and it's almost scary. Must be the fact that we're so far from the city and his drug-dealing friends. This country air and scenery are having some type of unexplainable effect on his criminal mind.

Trey says, "I wanna change, but it's going to take a miracle. Nothing's gonna change any time soon 'cause I just can't. To be honest, once you're in, there's no way out. It's like there's a no-way-out clause in my contract. When we get back home I'm gonna be right back in the same shit. Because of who I am, who I know, and how good I am at what I do, I'll never change."

Trey is really in a no-win situation. He knows that he'll never change, and deep down I know he won't either. Only one thing changes a brotha like this. There's only one sure way to get Trey out for good. I don't even want to think about it because I'll make myself cry. This day is too pretty to ruin with ugly thoughts. Here I go doing what I do best. Giving men a false sense of hope.

"You're already off to a good start with changing. At least you have a conscience. You're halfway there and you don't even realize it. I respect you and I think you're a good person."

"Alright, that's enough about me. I've told you about my demons, now let me hear about yours."

"There's nothing to tell."

"You're lying. Everybody has demons."

"You really wanna know?"

"Yeah, tell me and don't hold back. This is for my ears only."

"It involves you. You and Jamal."

"C'mon with it."

"I love Jay and all, but you offer me something he doesn't."

"Like what?"

"Let me finish. You have an interesting and exciting lifestyle. You're paid. You look like DMX and you know how much I love him."

We laugh.

I continue. "Jamal gave me this ring last night and proposed to me."

"Damn, I didn't even notice. It's kinda small."

"So what? It's mine and it's beautiful. You didn't put no ring on my finger."

"No, but I can. That's cool. I got a lot of respect for Jamal doing something like that. He's crazy, but I guess it's good."

"He's crazy for falling in love with me, because look where I am, with you."

"If that's really a problem I can take you back home." He laughs.

"Stop playing, I'm serious. I love him, but I need you in my life too. I feel so bad for deceiving him like this. I'm living a lie and one day I'll have to pay for this."

"Did you accept his proposal?"

"Yeah."

"Stupid question. I guess you did, you're wearing his ring. Why the hell would you accept his proposal when you know that you can't commit to him?"

"He was so sweet and sincere last night. It was the things he said and how he looked. This man is planning a future with me. I'm part of somebody's future plans. He's constantly thinking about us."

"You're my girl and all, but if this ever becomes too much for you, let me know and I'm out, you know what I'm saying?"

"I appreciate that, but no. I said I need you. I'm just like you and I'll have to learn to deal with the pain and guilt."

Too bad I can't have all of my needs met by one man. It's hard to find that special someone to satisfy my every little need.

We're just a few minutes outside of Hagerstown. I can see mountain ranges in the distance. My ears stop up as we ascend this steep incline. Mentioning Jamal's name really makes me miss him. I wish I could share this experience with him. He'd get a kick out of this, trees and mountains as far as the eye can see.

We're on a narrow two-lane highway. The speed limit is sixty-five miles an hour and everybody wants to be aggressive, including Trey. I should say, especially Trey. He is blowing his horn and flashing his high beams off and on.

I yell, "Slow down, Speed Racer!"

"Nah, this bitch just cut me off and that other bitch better get off my bumper. I swear to God if he hits my car I'm gonna kill his ass."

"It's okay, he just backed off and the other guy is signaling to exit. Look, they're gone now. You okay?"

"Yeah!"

"Oh, stop being so mean. I think it's funny how everybody's a bitch to you, male or female."

"I don't discriminate. A bitch is a bitch regardless."

"What exactly is a bitch?"

Trey looks so stupid right now. He looks so puzzled that he laughs at himself. "Hold up . . . hold up. I'm thinking. Stop making me laugh."

"I like to hear you laugh and I love to see your smile. I'm starting to see a softer side of you and I like it, I like it a whole lot."

Trey stops laughing and the smile disappears. "Ain't nothing about me soft. I don't have a soft side. Hard-core till I die and don't forget it." He pauses for a second. "That's what a bitch is in a male sense, a soft man. Like Jamal."

"My man is not soft."

"And you're a bitch in the female sense. I mean that in a good way of course. You're strong, intelligent, you don't take a lot of shit, and you know how to get what you want. And no matter how shit goes down, you demand respect. I didn't mean any disrespect when I called you a bitch the other day. In this generation, we kinda flipped the script to make derogatory terms mean something positive. Like when I say my nigga I mean, my brotha, my partner, my homey."

I look right at him and say, "That's the stupidest shit I ever heard in my life, except for the part about me being strong, intelligent, and demanding respect. That was sweet and everything else was just plain stupid."

We laugh.

We take exit 29 and head over to the outlets. I've been here so many times that the salespeople at Nine West, DKNY, Coach, Tommy Hilfiger, Liz Claiborne, and Ralph Lauren all know me on a first-name basis. Shopping here is fine, but I'd much rather be in New York shopping for Burberry, Prada, Gucci, Fendi, or Dolce & Gabana. On the other hand shopping is shopping, especially when I'm spending somebody else's money.

Trey says, "I wanna do something different today."

I have no idea what he means by that. We park the Q45 and walk down the strip to the Kay-Bee Toys outlet. I look at Trey like he's crazy. My whole expression changes when we get to the Barbie aisle. There are dolls and accessories as far as I can see. I instantly turn into a little girl again and Trey loves it.

With excitement I say, "Ooh, look, a Barbie styling head. I used to have one of those when I was little. My father used to surprise me just like this. Can I get one?"

"Get it." He picks up four Barbies, clothes, a Corvette, and a camper. "Get these too. Want a dream house?"

"Oh my God, you better stop. You're spoiling me."

Trey moves in close, putting his arms around me. He says, "I'm supposed to. You make me happy and I wanna do the same for you."

"Okay, I'm happy, but put the dream house back."

"Alright, but we gotta get this Britney Spears karaoke machine."

"I know you're trippin' now."

"Forget you, I like Britney Spears."

I know it's silly, but I plan to get these toys and decorate my bedroom with them.

When we get to the register the clerk says, "Some little girl is gonna be real happy."

"Yes, she is," I say with a smile big and pretty enough to land me on the cover of *Essence*.

We head back to the car to unload my toys, so we won't have to walk around looking like Santa's little helpers. On the way back we notice that the jewelry store is having a big sale. This time I lead the way. Right away I see this beautiful one-and-a half-carat diamond pendant.

Trey says, "Want it?"

"Yeah, but how much?"

"Don't worry about that. Excuse me, miss."

This lady steps over to help Trey. I laugh because she looks too much like Mrs. Garrett from *The Facts of Life*.

"Yes, sir, how can I help you?"

"I'd like to see this diamond pendant, please."

"It's beautiful, isn't it?"

I cut in and say, "Yes, it is."

The saleslady smiles, puts on her glasses, and says, "It also comes in white gold and platinum."

"Yellow is fine because it matches my ring." I proudly flash my ring, but she doesn't look impressed at all.

She dips her head, looks at me from over her glasses, and simply says, "Yes, I see."

The saleslady hands Trey the necklace. He comes from behind, pressing himself against me, putting the necklace around my neck at the same time. It looks so pretty that I almost melt. It's such an elegant piece of jewelry. Today I'm a queen.

I say, "Can I have it?"

Trey says, "Yeah, but how are you going to explain it to Jamal?"

"I'll tell him that it's costume jewelry. He can't tell a real diamond from a fake."

Trey looks right at my ring and says, "Yeah, I can tell."

"Low blow, but I set myself up for that one. That's gonna cost you an extra outfit."

The saleslady laughs and says, "You go, girl!"

I look her up and down and think, *No, you better go, girl. Before you catch a serious beat-down, all up in my business.* Instead I say, "Please, miss, I was talking to him."

By this time I've had enough of Trey and Mrs. Garrett. I hate that old-ass expression, *You go, girl.* White people just picked it up last week and are running it in the hole. They steal old stuff from our culture all the time. They're still impressed as hell with moonwalking, Lionel Richie, and braids, the eighth, ninth, and tenth wonders of their world.

Now Mrs. Garrett is eyeballing Trey's platinum-and-diamond jewelry. "I love your jewelry. Where'd you find that?"

Trey smiles. "New York, Jacob's, custom made. You ain't down with this."

"I know that it's beautiful and expensive too. It's tight."

I say, "It's tight. Oh my God, I can't take it, she said 'it's tight.'" I have to laugh. "Stop sweatin' my man like that. Trey, can you pay for my necklace, so we can go? This woman is killing me."

When we get outside I say, "Thank you, sweetheart. Now I'm ready to shop."

"What have we been doing?"

I give him a funny look and say, "Oh, baby, that was just a warm-up. You know how I do. I wanna get some boots, a leather jacket, another Coach bag with the complete leather-care kit, a few dresses, a pantsuit, a couple blouses, perfume, and whatever else catches my eye."

"Damn, shorty, I don't feel like all that walking. Here's my debit card. It's okay, I made you an authorized user."

"You did?" I have the biggest smile on my face. "My name is on your account? You're too good to be true. I feel like crying. Sure you don't wanna come?"

"I'm sure. I'll just sit here for a minute and make some phone calls, and then I'll go down to the Timberland outlet. Meet me at the food court in an hour."

"Hour and a half, okay? See you, sweetie."

An hour and a half later I have so many bags that I'm not sure how I made it to the food court.

I see Trey and yell, "Trey, baby, I'm right here! Help!"

He just stands there and laughs at me struggling with my bags. Finally he stops laughing long enough to help me to a table in the food court.

He says, "You don't make any sense. Did you leave me any money?"

I hand Trey his debit card. "All I can tell you is that it worked when I left the last store."

"I'm just playing, you couldn't have done that much damage."

"I did, and I got the receipts to prove it."

Trey laughs and kisses me on the lips. "What are you in the mood for, pizza, Chinese, cheese steaks and fries, or do you just wanna skip the food court and go to a restaurant?"

"Chinese is fine. I'll have General Tso's chicken with lo mein. Thanks, sweetheart."

I sit at the table watching the people around me. A young black guy smiles at me. I think, *Oh no, shorty, if you want to keep your pretty face stay away from this table, 'cause I'm with a fool that will beat your little young ass senseless.* He must have read my mind because he has just done an about-face. Good. I feel a tap on my shoulder. I turn around to see a tall handsome white guy. He must have scared that first guy away. Now it's his turn to get scared off.

He says, "Excuse me, miss, is this seat taken?"

"Yes, it is. My husband will be right back. We just got married, so you better step off, 'cause he's a little touched in the head and very, very possessive."

"Sorry, ma'am."

This goofy bastard damn near trips over a chair trying to get away from me. I laugh until I notice this couple at the table across from me. Oh, they're sweet. They're so expressive speaking in sign language. They look so happy, silently laughing. Anyone can see that this couple is in love, deeply in love. I think it's great. I don't really want to stare, but they're so cute together. Makes me grateful for what I have. Five fully functioning senses and pretty good sense. No impairments. All of my loved ones are healthy. I'm so blessed. My eyes tear, but I'm happy. I'm happy for the couple and with myself for the time being.

I'm too busy being nosey to notice Trey standing next to me with our food and drinks on a tray.

He asks, "Why you looking like that? Where's that pretty smile of yours?"

"You scared me. I didn't notice you. I'm smiling on the inside."

He smiles. "I couldn't tell. Did I do something to make you smile on the inside?"

"Always. This time it's you and that cute little deaf couple over there communicating in sign language."

"Look how happy they are. I couldn't be that happy if I couldn't hear. Wonder if they can talk at all."

"You could be that happy if you were deaf, especially if you were born like that. You can't miss what you never had. His girlfriend is so beautiful and I'm sure that's why he's smiling like that. They're so in tune to each other, who cares if they can or can't talk?"

"Stop staring at them. You better eat before your food gets cold."

"You're right. This smells so good."

We get in the car and the last thing I want to hear is hip-hop beats. During the entire ride up here we listened to nothing but rap music. I like rap, but a little bit of R&B or jazz would be cool. Trey starts the car and hits a button on the CD changer. I brace myself for the first big beat. The first thing I hear is a mellow trumpet, Miles Davis. Thank God. I look at Trey.

He asks, "What's up? You ain't down with Miles Davis?"

"No, I didn't know you were down with Miles." I don't mention it, but Jamal was the one who put me down with Miles Davis.

"It's a nice break from all that rap from earlier, right?"

I smile. "Sure is."

Trey's car is so classy. He makes me feel like a queen and I look like one in his Infiniti. The car's interior smells like new leather. I recline my seat and it seems to caress me. It's comfortable and Miles Davis sounds so good. We speed down the highway. We pass tree after tree, hill after hill. The sky is so pretty. This warm beautiful day is slowly turning into a cold dark night. My eyelids are heavy. My head feels light and so does the rest of my body. I yawn. I'm so tired that all I can do is relax.

I wake up feeling refreshed. Feels like I've slept for hours. In reality, only thirty minutes has passed. Trey was just on his cell phone, but I was so out of it all I heard was mumbling.

I ask, "Where are we?"

"We're about forty-five minutes from the hotel. Did you realize that this ride takes us through about five counties in the same state within an hour?"

"No, that's some real useless information. You must be tired."

"I'm okay. What makes you think I'm tired?"

"You start to say crazy stuff when you're tired."

"You think you know me, don't you?"

"Yep, especially after this trip. You never opened up like that before and now I feel like I know you, the real you."

"Well, I'm back, this is the real me now. Forget about all that other stuff I mentioned earlier."

"Stop acting like that. Let's talk some more. What's on your mind right now?"

"Okay, all of a sudden you're like a damn psychiatrist or something."

"Psychologist, consider me your psychologist."

"What's the damn difference? You're more like a nosey friend."

"A psychologist doesn't prescribe medications, and you're angry. Talk to me."

"You're scaring me."

"Good, you have fears."

"Stop!"

We laugh.

I say, "Now be serious and talk."

"I was thinking about my brother and sister. Carlos wants to get into the family business, but we won't put him down. He's not cut out for this. He's too hungry, and greedy people don't last long in this business. He has no loyalty and he'd probably make deals with too many people, all the wrong people. A madman like that can't be trusted. I worked my way up slowly, at a snail's pace. Nothing was too trivial or difficult for me to handle. I came up under the tutelage of my father and my uncles. This shit's in our blood, but Carlos is only twenty and he wants to run shit now. He's trying to be the king, but my father is the king and I'm the prince and we ain't going nowhere. So that's why I figure my brother needs to stay in school at Morgan and become an engineer or something. He's in college trying to be a gangster living off the family rep, when he should be trying to learn something and stop wasting his time and my father's money."

"That's deep. Talk him into staying in school, because no matter what he'll always have that degree to fall back on. When he earns that degree nobody can take it away, not a thief, cop, judge, your father, or you. Make him stay in school. What about Danielle?"

"She too materialistic. It's seems like she expects too much. She acts like I have an endless supply of money. She doesn't know how to plan for a rainy day. It's always spend, spend, spend, I need, I want, and gimme. People don't value my money like they do their own. Does the way I make my money make it less valuable or more expendable? That bothers me. Money is money regardless of how it's made or where it comes from. She needs to appreciate it more. Am I right?"

I'm not sure what to say. "This isn't a topic for me to comment on because I'm guilty of the same thing and I'm sorry."

"No, I'm sorry because that wasn't directed at you at all."

"Regardless, you just described me perfectly whether you want to admit it or not. I do think it's important to plan for a rainy day."

"True. You're my lady and that makes you an exception whether you want to admit it or not. You work for all this and you do a damn good job. You keep me happy, real happy. You make me twice as happy as that deaf guy in the food court. I've never said this before, but I love you."

Tears flow from my eyes and I'm speechless for a minute. What did I do to deserve all this love from Trey and Jamal? I'm so confused right now.

Trey says, "I said I love you."

"I love you too, and I like the way you explained what I mean to you. You're like a different person and I'm loving this."

"I know that you're someone's fiancée, but to be honest, that doesn't faze me at all. You wear his ring, but my pendant is right by your heart. Fuck his ring and him too."

We kiss. Poor me. Here I go. Love? This is beginning to feel like a competition.

I say, "I don't know this side of you at all, but I like it. Please don't change. At first you seemed so shallow, so angry, and excuse me for saying this, but dumb. You've used words today that I've never heard you use. I never knew you were so articulate."

Trey smiles. "You thought I was dumb, that's funny. I'm far from dumb. Thanks for being so honest, brutally honest. That's why I love you. Jamal isn't the only one making future plans with you in mind. I added your name to one of my bank accounts. I have a substantial insurance policy with you and my baby mother listed as the beneficiaries. Back to the dumb thing, I can be very articulate if I want. I went to Howard and Morgan."

"Really? I didn't know that. I had no idea you thought enough of me to put my name on an insurance policy, especially a substantial one. Thanks for loving me that much. What's your baby's mother's name? After all this time I've never heard you say her name."

"It's Alicia. I can't believe I never mentioned her name around you."

"Nope, you've never mentioned her name. You always refer to her as *my baby mother.*"

"Is that how I say it?"

"Yeah, you don't say baby's mother, you say *baby mother.*"

"I never picked up on that. *Baby mother.* I say that all the time and people probably laugh at me too. *Baby's mother.* No wonder you thought I was dumb. I really did go to Howard and Morgan as a student, not just for step shows and homecomings."

We laugh.

He continues, "I never graduated from college. It took going to two colleges for me to figure out that I wasn't college material."

"Don't feel bad. I never got up the courage to go to college."

"Regardless, you're still special to me. Nobody else had the balls to tell me that I was pronouncing that shit wrong. You're a bad bitch, you know that?"

"Yeah, and you're my nigga, you know that?"

"I'm gonna take you on a run. You down for it?"

"I'm down for whatever."

"I canceled the New York trip 'cause my partners, Kev and Mike, decided to come down here for my party and they're in east Baltimore right now handling some business. I was gonna go by myself, but I want you to meet them."

"Good. Now I get to experience your world."

Chapter 6

Jessie

Trey and I pull up to a brick row house in northeast Baltimore near Northern Parkway and the Alameda. This is a nice middle-class area and it isn't where I expected Trey to bring me. There I go again making generalizations. Trey never mentioned exactly what's going on. I'm not sure if we're here to pick up or drop something off. I'm kind of nervous, but Trey looks very relaxed. This type of thing is routine for him. He gets out of the car and goes to the trunk. He comes back and grabs my purse.

I ask, "What are you doing?"

"Here, put this in your bag."

"What is it?"

"A nickel-plated twenty-two, my first gun, and now it's yours."

"I don't like guns. If I need a gun I shouldn't go in."

"You really don't need it, but just in case."

I look at him as if he were crazy.

Trey says, "Don't look at me like that. I said just in case. If something goes wrong stay low and aim high. Aim for the enemy's head." He laughs.

"Stop playing. I'll take it, but if the police find it on me, my story is that you planted it in my bag. If I have this, what do you have?"

"My Glock."

"You got a Glock and I got a damn cowboy-lookin' gun."

We laugh.

I let him put the gun in my bag. Sirens blare in the background. I'm not sure if it's an ambulance or the police. It seems as if the police are coming for us because they know that there's a gun in my bag and we're up to no good. I'm nervous and my heart is beating at a rapid pace. We get out of the car and Trey leads the way to the front door carrying a medium-sized black nylon duffel bag. I'm not sure if it's filled with money or drugs, but all I know is that it's a damn good thing we didn't get pulled over on the highway. As we get closer to the front door I hear music playing. Somebody's partying to some classic Tupac. Trey rings the doorbell and almost instantly a middle-aged, dirty-blond-haired, jelly-bellied, white woman with thick-ass, free-clinic-lookin' glasses answers the door. Not at all who I expected to see on the other side of the door. I feel at ease. She's the most nonthreatening-looking character I've ever seen. Trey acts all familiar, even gives this woman a kiss on the cheek. He introduces me to Kelly and we all head upstairs to her apartment.

The music is coming from the first-level apartment. Now they're playing something by Jay-Z. This place is a duplex that looks and smells a whole lot better from the outside. The hallway is hot and musty with a faint aroma of marijuana smoke in the air. The old carpeting seems to trap every single odor. The walls are in serious need of a paint job. Looks like somebody scuffed up the walls, probably moving furniture. I'm sure it wasn't Kelly's furniture that scuffed up the walls, because when we enter her apartment it's empty as hell. Without saying a word, I quickly scan her apartment. She has the nerve to have two black 1970s-lookin' beanbags in two corners of the apartment. The only other pieces of furniture are a folding table, two folding chairs, a lava lamp, a giant yellow flashing traffic light, a dusty boom box, and a bright-ass lamp with no shade sitting in the middle of the living room floor. This is obviously a spot where people come to get high and hang out. I bet they get high on ecstasy or something. This entire setup reminds me of something I saw once on HBO's *America Undercover.*

Kelly asks, "Y'all want something to drink?"

I look around and see an old McDonald's cup in the windowsill and an empty milk carton on the floor next to an ashtray filled with cigarette butts, ashes, and an old piece of gum. I'm real funny about where and what I eat and drink.

I quickly say, "No, thank you. I'm fine."

Trey says, "I'll take a beer."

In a low tone I say, "Yuck."

Trey nudges me on the arm. "Stop!"

He recovers just as Kelly reenters the living room with a Heineken. I'm able to catch a quick glimpse into the kitchen, seeing a few boxes of Arm & Hammer baking soda and a big clear bag of plastic vials. One of the cabinets has been left open, revealing two scales.

It sounds like the tenants downstairs are having a party. Their music is so loud that it sounds like it's coming from somewhere in Kelly's apartment.

Trey asks, "Where's Kev and Mike?"

"They shouldn't be long. They went out for something to eat. I cook, but the shit I cook ain't exactly edible, if you know what I mean."

They laugh really hard. I must be dumb because I don't find Kelly's joke to be that funny. It finally hits me. I'm so slow. She cooks cocaine. I get it, but I still don't laugh.

Trey says, "I got you, what you been up to?"

"Working, holding down the fort."

"You coming to my party tomorrow?"

We hear somebody moving around outside the upstairs door. There's a loud round of knocking at the door. Then the knocks turn into loud pounding. I'm visibly shaken.

Kelly remains calm and makes her way to the door. "I can't make it, wish I could. I heard your boy's coming home. Hold on, let me get the door."

Kelly opens the door without looking through the peephole or without asking who is at the door.

I think, *Please, God, don't let this be the police because I'm too pretty to go to jail.*

She opens the door and says, "I knew it was y'all knocking like the damn police."

Two guys that look like rejects from the Wu-Tang Clan enter the apartment carrying grease-stained brown paper bags. Looks like they picked up a few ghetto chicken boxes from a carry-out restaurant. One of them is carrying a duffel bag similar to Trey's.

The short stocky guy devours a chicken wing and at the same time says, "What's up, y'all?"

I think, *Disgusting!*

The tall slim guy says, "I bet we scared the shit out of y'all knocking like Five-O. The downstairs door was unlocked, so we just came right up. What's up, Trey?"

They do that handshake, half-hug bullshit that guys do. Trey does the same with the other guy. They must be Kev and Mike. Mike is the little stocky guy and Kev is the slim, ugly, loudmouthed one.

Kev asks, "Who's this fine-ass girl right here, boy? She looks way better than your other ones."

Mike says, "You ain't lying."

Trey turns to me and says, "These are my partners from Brooklyn, Kev and Mike. This my girl from the west side, Jessie."

I look at Trey out of the corner of my eyes and think, *Your girl from the west side, what kind of shit is this? What does this nigga have, an east side, north side, and south side girl too?*

I say, "Hey, how y'all doing?"

Kev says. "No, how you doing?"

I say, "I'm fine."

Kev says, "You sure are, finer than a motherfucker."

I feel for my little cowboy gun because I swear I will shoot this ugly bastard if he gets an inch closer.

Trey says, "Stop trippin' and let's get down to business. Leave my girl alone 'cause she don't want your ugly ass."

Kev says, "I might be ugly, but I'm rich, and a woman will take a paid ugly nigga over a broke ugly nigga any day, know what I'm saying?"

"Alright, I hear you. Let's go in here and talk business and leave the ladies out here."

Kelly yells, "Hold up, where my chicken boxes at? I hope y'all had them put salt, pepper, and ketchup on my fries."

I think, *Oh my God, they got this white girl speakin' ebonics.*

Mike says, "We had them put salt, pepper, and ketchup on everything. They put hot sauce on your wings just like you like 'em, baby."

He hands Kelly her greasy paper bag filled with two boxes of chicken wings and fries. Mike smiles at me as he passes on his way to the bedroom with Trey and Kev. As Mike passes by he slaps Kelly on her big flat ass. The slap on the ass makes her feel sexy. She laughs and does a silly little dance like she is on cloud nine. This is so pathetic. I understand now. They treat her like a sex goddess and in return Kelly processes and packages their drugs.

Kelly says, "Thanks, baby." She kisses Mike on the lips.

Trey looks at me as if to say, *Act nice.* He says, "We'll just be a minute."

I say, "Alright."

He picks up the duffel bag. Mike puts his arm around Trey and they go into one of the back bedrooms.

Kelly is about to tear into her chicken boxes. She asks, "Jessie, you want some?"

"No, I'm okay."

"I don't usually share my food. So you must be special."

"Thanks, but no, thanks."

"Girl, you better stop acting so damn funny. You family now. This chicken is the bomb."

I laugh. "It smells good, but I don't eat a lot of fried foods."

"Don't tell me you're scared of getting fat. Trust me, brothas love a girl with a little meat on her bones."

I laugh. "Okay, I'll take a wing and a few fries."

"That's more like it. Here you go."

Like I always say, misery loves company. Kelly hands me a napkin and moves one of her boxes in my direction. I pick up a wing and about four fries. The food smells good, but I really don't want it. All of a sudden my mouth starts to water. I'm just a victim of peer pressure. I ask Kelly to direct me to the bathroom so I can wash my hands. She points me in the right direction because her mouth is too full to talk. I hate leaving my food with a stranger all unprotected. I arrange my napkin a certain way so that if it's tampered with I'll be able to tell right away. When I enter the bathroom the stench of urine almost knocks me the hell out. I refuse to look in the direction of the bathtub or toilet. Kelly never even entertained the thought of washing her hands.

Between bites she manages to yell out, "Girl, you gotta excuse that bathroom. While you're at it, excuse the whole house."

I reenter the living room air-drying my hands because I wanted to limit the things I touched in the bathroom.

I say, "Kelly, I ain't even paying your house any attention. Don't even trip." I think, *Your house is nasty, you're nasty. It's a damn shame.*

I can't believe I'm about to eat in this place. I say a quick prayer and bite into my chicken. It surprisingly tastes twice as good as it looks or smells.

I say, "Umm, this chicken is the bomb."

Kelly smiles. "Told you."

"Can I have another wing?"

Big Nasty Kelly's bad habits are already starting to rub off on me. I'm getting all comfortable living on the dangerous side and eating in this dirty house. I guess it's human nature to imitate the company we keep.

Kelly says, "Oh, at first you didn't want none of my chicken and now you wanna eat it all."

I laugh and say, "Well, you started it. It's like a good man, I can't just have one."

"Girrrrrrl, you scandalous. I guess you gotta be a little scandalous, right? 'Cause guys do it to us. Here you go." She hands me another wing with a napkin.

I ask, "Is Mike your man?"

"Yeah. He comes down every now and then to check on me. I know he got another girl in New York, but I don't care as long as he looks out for me. I'm his good thing and he's mine. I'm what he likes to call a pharmacological genius. I cook it, cut it, and package it. Plus, I give good head. He needs me." She laughs.

I don't know what to say, so I just smile and say, "Wow, I don't know what to say. I'm impressed." I'm lying. I'm wondering what's taking Trey so long, because I'm ready to head to our hotel suite.

Kelly goes, "It's nothing."

For some reason I can't take my eyes off Kelly. I'm trying to see what the hell Mike finds attractive about her, besides her brains and her ability to keep this underground operation going. Her hair looks like it hasn't been washed or combed in weeks. She needs her ends trimmed. Her eyebrows need to be arched. The thick dirty glasses definitely have to go. She does have pretty eyes, and some clear contacts would work. She has nice teeth and her lips kind of look like a sista's. She has big boobs, but her big jelly-belly draws all the attention away. She's in serious need of liposuction.

She asks, "Why you looking at me like that? You crazy, girl."

"Sorry, I was just imagining you with a haircut, contacts, and . . . and—"

"A tummy tuck, gastric bypass, liposuction, or after a year of Tae-Bo classes?"

"No, not that extreme, just a little makeover. I could do your nails and my girlfriend is a beautician."

"You're so shallow. I can't believe you're sitting here analyzing me like this. Who are you to judge me?"

"Oh, I'm sorry. I really didn't mean any harm."

"No harm. I know I'm a big girl, but I'm comfortable with it. My man doesn't complain. You're just like that rest of them. That's why I don't mess with females. I thought you was cool at first, but now I see how you really are and how you think."

"It's not like that."

"I shared my chicken with you too. Shit, I wish they'd hurry up, so you can get outta here."

This chick is bugging out over nothing. She's breathing all hard and fogging her glasses up. If she steps to me, I swear I'll shoot her right in her belly.

I say, "Kelly, please calm down. I really didn't mean any harm. You're beautiful, you just need a little help enhancing your features."

"I know you think you're God's gift with your pretty face, long silky hair, and petite build, but you're not. You're nothing special. I could've had Trey's fine ass if I wanted and I still can. He's got a lot of women and you're just one of many; like I said, you're nothing special."

"You fat bitch, I'll kill you!"

Thank God, the bedroom door opens. Trey is the first person out of the room. I think he's carrying that other duffel bag now.

He says, "Alright, shorty, we're all done here. We've got one quick stop to make and then we can head to the hotel."

Kelly yells, "Good, get this little conceited bitch outta here."

Trey asks, "What's going on?"

Mike asks, "What happened? Y'all were all buddy-buddy when we went in the room."

Kev just stands there smiling like he's enjoying watching the drama unfold.

Kelly says, "She started criticizing my appearance, after I fed her skinny ass."

I say, "Kelly, I swear I will kick your *ass* in your own house if you mouth off to me again. Don't make me call my girls." I'm a real bad ass now.

Trey says, "Damn, Jessie, calm down. Here, take the keys and wait in the car. I'll be right down."

I snatch the keys out of his hand. I head out the door, down the steps through the front door, and to the car. I don't believe this shit.

She made it seem as if I did something wrong. Now they're up there consoling her. I'm a sista, they should be lookin' out for me. They ain't shit.

Finally, Trey comes down. He has this you-shouldn't-have-done-that look on his face.

I say, "What? Don't even try it."

"No, you're wrong. How could you hurt her feelings like that?"

"She did that to herself. She's uncomfortable with her appearance and she's obsessed with you. That's what all that was about."

"What?"

"She hates herself 'cause she's overweight and hates me 'cause I'm with you. She said you had a lot of girlfriends, what's with that?"

"She'd tell you anything because she wants me and I hope you don't let this spoil our night."

"It doesn't have to spoil our night, I just think you should apologize for jumping on her side so fast."

"I wasn't taking sides. I was just trying to keep a valuable employee calm and happy, that's all. I'm sorry."

I say, "That's still not good enough." All of a sudden, Trey gives me this bitch-you-must-be-crazy look. I forgot I was dealing with a fool. I say, "I'm just playing, everything is okay."

"Good, 'cause I got too much on my mind with my party and all to put up with a bunch of bull."

"Alright." I give Trey a kiss.

Trey starts the car and we're off. We speed down the street with DMX blasting from Trey's eight-speaker sound system. My blood rushes, I smile, and my heart . . . my heart beats-beats-beats to DMX. The car accelerates, the music flows harder, and my rush intensifies.

I love the fact that Trey doesn't sweat petty issues. I look over at him as he drives. Trey's seat is slightly reclined. He has one hand on the wheel and the other on his crotch. His jaw is tightly clenched and his head bounces to the beat. He has this intense look in his eyes like he is in a zone. He looks so focused on doing his thing. He is a drug dealer and I know it. That should bother me, but for some reason it doesn't. I'm caught up in something with a dangerous and powerful allure. I can't explain it. I have a strange attraction to Trey and this whole lifestyle. He looks as if he is willing to take out anybody and anything that gets in his way.

We pull over on the corner of North and Greenmount Avenues.

The streets are alive. It's cold as hell outside, but there are junkies and little corner boys all over the place. All I can do is shake my head at such a pitiful sight.

This is the real shit. I hear a siren and see flashing lights, an ambulance speeds by us. There's not a policeman in sight. I'm not sure if that's a good or bad thing. This is the same corner I saw on *Fox 45 News* two nights ago where three people were shot and one later died at Shock Trauma.

Without hesitation Trey says, "I'm gonna leave the car running. I need you to wait here for a minute."

I think, *No, this fool ain't leaving me in the middle of a battle zone. Can't we just skip this and go to the hotel where it's warm and safe?* Instead I say, "Go 'head, I'm alright."

Trey gets out of his car with his duffel bag gripped tightly. The corner boys and junkies greet Trey as if he were some type of celebrity. He talks to some of the guys for a minute. I hear one of the guys say, "Alright, Trey, be safe." To me *be safe* really means *I hope you get shot, so I can move up the ranks and take your place.* Trey makes his way down the block and suddenly disappears. I lose track of him within a few seconds. Like I said before, this is the real shit and I like the way Trey moves. He's probably headed to one of his stash houses.

I sit here watching, but I have the strange feeling that I'm being watched. The weird thing about being out here is not knowing who to trust. Trey is a big dog, but I know one of these little nobodys would love to take him out.

I look over to the bus stop and I see a mother struggling with bags and her two small children. They look cold and tired. I would hate to be stuck on a bus stop this time of night in the cold, especially in this neighborhood. People walk in and out of the liquor store across from me. Two young boys and a silly-looking grown-ass man have just ridden by on bikes. Looks like they move their product around here any way they can. A white Ford pickup truck pulls up in front of me. The driver is a middle-aged white guy. He gets the attention of one of the corner boys and he rushes to the truck like a moth to a flame. For all these fools know, this white guy could be an undercover cop. Greed completely takes over and what little common sense these corner boys possess is out the window. Five-O probably has this entire intersection under surveillance, which includes this car. I bet the white guy in the truck is part of the whole thing.

One of the junkies makes his way toward Trey's car. He has an obvious limp. His face grimaces like he's suffering from a case of excruciating arthritic pain. Most people in his condition would be home in bed. I guess he's out here trying to get medicated. His eyes are fixed right on me as he moves closer with his crippled bop. My stomach is in knots. Although I'm scared I can't let it show. We make eye contact and I hit the switch to lock the door. It makes a funny sound because the door is already locked.

The junky looks at me and to my surprise he says, "Don't nobody want you, bitch." He turns around slowly and goes back in the opposite direction with his crippled bop.

I laugh and think, *Well, excuse the hell outta me.*

The longer I sit here I become more uneasy with this whole situation. Young hustlers and chemically dependent, disease-infected junkies surround me. The guy in the truck was either a cop or an addict from a different neighborhood. Everybody around me right now is black and in serious need of help. This is really a harsh dose of reality that sends me reeling back to my senses. Sitting here watching this vicious cycle play out instantly takes the appeal out of this world of money, power, and respect and puts it all into perspective. Without realizing it we're victims of a different type of terrorism. African-Americans are victims of biological and chemical warfare. AIDS and drugs are killing us and that's reality. There's nothing fake or phony about that. I'm ready to get out of here.

It's too quiet. All of a sudden someone pounds on my window and it scares me half to death. There's a tall thin girl with a big gold tooth and braids standing here signaling me to lower the window. I lower the window just enough to hear her voice.

I say, "Yeah?"

Instead of watching her I stare right at her big gold tooth as she prepares to speak to me.

She asks, "Isn't this Trey's car?"

"Yeah, it's his car."

"I thought so. You his girlfriend?"

"No, I'm just a good friend."

"What's your name?"

I hesitate and ask, "What's *your* name?"

"I'm Latonya."

"I'm Jessie."

"Thanks, that's all I need to know." She simply walks away like her mission is complete. I knew I was being watched. I don't know if she is Five-O or just some jealous little hood rat. Either way, I messed up and gave her my real name. I'm glad I got the chance to experience Trey's world, but this is just a little too much for me.

A faint pop-pop-pop-pop rings out in the night sky. I know it's gunfire being exchanged, but I refuse to acknowledge it.

Trey finally returns to the car breathing hard. He says, "You ready to go?" He looks at my disgusted face and asks, "What's wrong?"

"Nothing. Thanks for letting me experience your world. This is really interesting and all, but it's too real for me," I say in a very snobbish fashion.

"What happened?"

"Everybody around here seems to be numb to the affects that drugs have on our community."

"Oh, shit, here we go again. Let me get you to the hotel, to the more glamorous side of my lifestyle that you enjoy."

"You're right. Seeing all this upsets me. At least when we're shopping or lying up in an expensive hotel, I don't see all these young boys putting their lives on the line and all these pitiful drug addicts. I know those weren't gunshots I heard a few minutes ago."

"You need to get real. This is how it goes down around here. And I'm the same regardless of whether I'm here or there. Whether you see it or not, all this really exists. You need to ask yourself why you're with me."

"I love you, but being out here like this makes me feel like I'm playing an active part in destroying my community and I hate that."

"I understand. If this is too much, you're free to go at any time."

"I wish it was that simple. Can we just go to the hotel? I need to feel your tongue between my thighs, so I can relax and exhale."

"A'ight, but remember what I said."

"I'm free to go. I remember."

Trey cuts the conversation short and pulls off. We didn't solve anything. We just act as if that whole thing didn't happen. I double-check the door locks and he seems to zone out again, letting the music take him away.

Chapter 7

Jamal

I woke up this morning with Jillian Smith on my mind again. That happens every now and then. She and I went to Edmondson High School together. Jillian was an exceptional girl and I was attracted to her for years. I was just a little too immature to know how to approach her. She was one of those full-figured girls with a beautiful face, the warmest personality, and the prettiest smile you'd ever want to see. She was always appealing to me, but I was too worried about what my friends would think of me if I dated her. I always wanted to open up to her and shower her with compliments, but I didn't.

The day of our senior prom she asked me to give her a ride home. I was driving Coach's car and on the way to her house we talked a little about the prom. That's when I asked who she was taking to the prom. She paused for a few seconds and said, "No one, I'm going alone." I was taking this girl from our school named Chanel. The only reason I was taking her was that I knew she was an easy lay. Chanel was pretty, but she had no substance or character like Jillian. Even knowing all that, I took her anyway. Deep down inside I knew that Jillian should have been my date. To make matters worse, on our way to Jillian's house we stopped at a red light and three of the most popular girls from school pulled up beside us. They were all smiling. I felt like they were laughing at me for being with Jillian.

One of them said, "So, Jamal, is that your prom date for tonight?" Like a dummy I yelled, "Who, Jillian? Nah, I'm just giving her a ride home. I'm taking Chanel Tanner."

I said Chanel Tanner like they should have been impressed or something. The entire time Jillian didn't say a word. She just sat there smiling, but I could tell that she was hurt. Later that evening I saw her at the prom and she looked absolutely beautiful. I was too much of a punk to even speak to her or ask her to dance. She looked too beautiful to be alone. I could have given her a night that both of us would have cherished forever. Instead, I hurt her and that's what I'll always remember most. I often think about what I could've, would've, or should've done. I can't help wondering what happened to her. It would be nice to see Jillian again, but that's all in the past now and Jessie's my future.

I've been up since 6:00 A.M. thinking about that girl Jillian and painting. My art is an intricate part of my being. It defines me. Art is my great escape and I mean that literally. When I have a paintbrush in my hand something magical and romantic happens. I get caught up in a creative vibe. My mind, eyes, hands, and heart all make a virtual connection causing me to completely get lost in my work. My passion overtakes me and I make love to the canvas or whatever medium I'm using. Art is my passion, my release, and my great escape all in one.

So far this morning I've done a quick still life painting of a bowl of fruit with a floral background for Grandma. I'm in the middle of working on an oil painting of Coach. The sight of him in Grandma's recliner is forever etched in my memory. No matter how much I try, I just can't stop picturing him. My goal is to create a portrait of Coach that instantly draws attention. I want it to capture the same emotion I felt when I first clicked on that lamp and laid my eyes on him. I want to recreate that same sense of urgency and fear that I saw in his eyes. No one wants to remember a person's pain and suffering, but creating this portrait is somewhat therapeutic for me. Inspiration comes in the strangest forms. Throughout history people have been immortalized on canvas and this is my tribute to my uncle.

I think I'm suffering from a severe case of anxiety and that's why I'm trying to stay busy. There's so much on my mind right now. I can't help wondering what Jessie is doing at this exact moment. She will be back in town later today. Trey's party is on my mind too. I don't want to go. Usually I would never go to a party like this, but this is something for Jessie. I know if our relationship is going to work I'll have to compromise and that's exactly what this is all about.

There's a knock at my door. I put my paintbrush down and lift my easel, turning it in the opposite direction because I don't want anyone to see my painting until it's complete.

I make my way to the door. I look through the peephole and see Jessie on the other side.

I open the door and say, "Hey, I was just thinking about you. I wasn't expecting you back until later."

"We left New York early this morning."

"I missed you. How was your trip?"

We embrace and I give her a nice long, passionate kiss. I inhale, taking in Jessie's fragrance. God, I missed her. She smells good enough to eat. I think, *Sounds like a plan.*

She says, "I missed you too. What can I say about the trip? It was an overnight shopping trip, so you can imagine how much fun I had."

I smile and ask, "What did you get me?"

Instantly a puzzled look comes over Jessie's face. I can tell that she forgot all about me. She tries her best to gather her thoughts in order to form a major lie.

She says, "Hold up. Let me see."

"Nothing, right?" I shake my head in disgust. "That's messed up. You went all the way to New York on an overnight shopping trip and you forgot all about your fiancé." I think, *She's selfish as shit.*

This makes me think back to the time when Jessie bought a cinnamon bun from the mall. The next morning she heated that thing to perfection in the microwave. Her apartment was filled with the aroma of cinnamon. The scent of the bun and the sight of that sweet white frosty topping made my mouth water. Since there was just the two of us, I couldn't resist asking for half. I figured fifty-fifty is the way most couples do things. But being the little selfish good-for-nothing she is, Jessie only gave me a tiny morsel. I asked for a bigger piece and she acted as if I asked her to do something that was completely against her religion. She actually refused to share any more of her cinnamon bun. That ignited an argument. I was so angry and disgusted by her that I ended up leaving her apartment. We later made up and the next day I went back to her apartment. I entered the kitchen as if I had some sort of tracking device guiding me. I looked toward her trash can and what did I see? My eyes focused on a half-eaten cinnamon bun. The half that she could simply have shared with me and avoided an argument. I know it sounds petty, but the whole incident really hurt my heart. I haven't forgotten it and I never will. I'll probably take it to my grave. It sounds ridiculous, but it's the principle of the whole thing. She just didn't want to share with me and that's what really hurt. Love is about sharing and compromising.

I look at Jessie and say, "I didn't need anything anyway. Just like I didn't need that damn cinnamon bun."

"What? Oh my God, not the cinnamon bun thing again. It's been over a year. Please leave that alone. Now, back to shopping, you know how picky you are. You probably wouldn't have liked what I picked out anyway."

"You're probably right, so we might as well change the subject."

"I'll make it up to you by taking you out to lunch."

"Where are you getting all this extra money? I see that expensive-looking diamond pendant around your neck."

"This cheap thing? It just looks expensive."

"It makes you look rich and it goes real nice with your new engagement ring. C'mere."

I smile and Jessie smiles. We kiss and everything is okay again. I'm always so forgiving. There's just something so enticing about Jessie.

I say, "You feel so good in my arms. I missed you and I miss making love to you. My grandmother is gone to breakfast with Ms. Pearl, her girlfriend from church."

"Good. I want you, right now."

Jessie lays a wet kiss on me. She really tongues me down. She's more aggressive than usual. She begins to unbutton my shirt. I'm excited and I begin to take off my pants. I grab a Trojan from my dresser.

Jessie takes the condom from my hand and says, "I wanna feel you inside me. I mean, I really wanna feel *you*. Skip the condom."

I look at the condom in her hand like I'm having second thoughts. I ask, "Are you sure? Is this what you really want?"

"Yeah, I'm on birth control. Besides, we're engaged and I wanna share everything with you. We need to experience the real thing, not that synthetic sex."

I smile. "I agree. Sounds good to me."

I thought this day would never come. This is what I've been waiting for. Jessie has finally opened up to me. Usually there's some sense of hesitation on her part. Her body language or a strange look in her eyes often gives her away. But today is different, there's no apprehension. There's nothing better than uninhibited lovemaking. Finally Jessie wants to feel the real me.

I say, "If you don't mind, I wanna take my time and make love to you slowly, so we can enjoy every second."

"I'm ready."

I like foreplay, but I can't help thinking about *raw penetration* because this is a new experience for us and I'm excited. No matter what, I can't skip the foreplay because Jessie's a lot like an oven and it's definitely to my advantage when she's properly preheated. She honestly works even better when she's been warmed up for ten minutes or more. I hate comparing my woman to an oven, but it's true.

Jessie is completely nude and I go to work right away. I back her to the closest wall and begin to seduce her. Jessie's body is incredibly sensitive and very receptive to my touch, my kisses, and my tongue as it glides ever so gently. My love seems to activate every little nerve ending, especially when my tongue hits the right spot. Her nipples are erect and she's nice and wet. With every passing second Jessie's anticipation grows and that's what this is all about. She becomes hotter and hotter, damn near begging to feel me inside her.

Jessie stands against the wall with her knees slightly bent. I kneel down, exploring and creating intense pleasure between her thighs. Jessie places both of her hands behind my head, pulling me in deeper. As I stimulate and gently tease with my tongue, she looks as if she is about to explode.

Jessie moans, "Ooh . . . Ooh. Oh God, that feels so good! Please don't stop! I love it. I love you. Your tongue . . . inside me . . . good! I'm gonna come!"

As I continue to please her I mumble, "Not yet."

Jessie lies on her back and I position myself between her legs. I slowly penetrate her wetness and it feels ten times better than I expected. As we make beautiful love her inner walls tighten and seem to pulsate as I slide in and out. Jessie holds me tight and her breathing intensifies as I thrust deeper. I raise her legs, bending her knees while riding high, putting just the right pressure against her clitoris. It feels so good that she touches herself down there.

Jessie screams, "That's it! Ooh, that's my spot! Oh God, I'm coming!"

I can't hold back, because this feels too good. I reach my climax too and for the first time I actually ejaculate inside Jessie. The feeling is incredible.

I yell, "Ah, Jessie, I'm coming!"

This is the greatest release I've ever felt. Jessie's body goes through spasms. Her facial expression makes me want to laugh, but I don't because I'm caught up in the same orgasmic vibe. After a minute or so, Jessie begins to shiver like she is cold. I lower myself, putting my hot sweaty body against her cold moist skin. We slowly begin to make love again.

After making love for about an hour we just lie here holding each other, breathing at the same steady pace.

I ask, "What are you thinking?"

She says, "I'm feelin' too good to talk. I love you."

"I love you."

We kiss.

"I think that was the most intense experience we've ever shared. What do you think?"

"Uh-huh. I feel so mellow. I wanna stay close to you. Let's lie here forever."

"We've worked up a real appetite. I'm ready for that lunch you promised me."

"How can you think about food after all that?"

"'Cause I'm hungry."

She mumbles, "Okay, me too, I guess. So, where do you wanna go?"

"Somewhere that's nice and quiet. Somewhere different."

"I have somewhere nice in mind. It'll be a surprise. Have you seen my panties?"

"They're in my drawer. I want 'em."

"What? You got some type of panty collection going on?"

"Just yours. It's a new fetish."

She laughs and asks, "What's that all about?"

"The color, the cut, the texture, and the smell of 'em."

"You're nasty."

"I know and you love it."

"Let's swap underwear."

"You must be crazy. There's no way in hell I'm wearing panties."

"No, stupid, not like that. Give me a pair of your boxers, so I won't have to be ass-out."

Jessie and I take a hot shower together, dress, and head out on our lunch date. The idea of Jessie wearing my boxers is a major turn-on to me. It's special when a woman loves a man enough to wear his clothing. In general, I think it's sexy seeing women in boxers.

We make it out of the house just before my grandmother and Ms. Pearl return. Grandma has a keen sense of smell and can smell sex in the air quicker than a bloodhound. Grandma heard me and Jessie having sex in the house a few months ago. She didn't interrupt, but when Jessie left I had to hear this long lecture about how it was disrespectful for us to have sex under her roof without being married. Good thing I didn't have to listen to all that noise again. That rule shouldn't apply to me, considering I'm renting space. If I were a stranger it wouldn't apply, but that's just a minor sacrifice.

Jessie and I end up going to a nice little restaurant in the village of Cross Keys called Crossroads. This is one of our favorite spots. Jessie orders stuffed flounder in lobster sauce. I order the Marylander, which is an award-winning jumbo lump crab cake on a potato roll.

I say, "This is delicious. Now I forgive you for forgetting about me when you went to New York."

"You know I didn't really forget about you."

I look into Jessie's eyes and get an overwhelming feeling of love. I think, *She is so beautiful and she's all mine.*

Crossroads has a very relaxed atmosphere. There are just a few African-Americans here, but Jessie and I feel very welcome. I can't help noticing this mural on the wall. There's a painting of a countryside with a patchworks-looking landscape. It's really bad.

I say, "They could have paid me to do that mural. It reminds me of the crap I used to paint when I was about twelve years old."

"It's not that bad. I don't believe you. You're never this hard on other people's work. You're mean."

She's right. I might be a little jealous because my paintings aren't showcased like this anywhere. I hate critiquing someone else's work. Art is subjective. But this painting is still really bad.

I say, "No, look again. I mean really look at it. The perspective is all wrong."

"Oh, now I see. You're right. The perspective is all wrong."

I pause for a minute. Jessie is bullshitting me. I laugh. "You have no idea what I mean, do you?"

She laughs. "No, not a clue." All of a sudden she says, "Oh my God,

I hate to change the subject, but I almost forgot to tell you. I know who Tank killed!"

"Shhh! Who? And how'd you find out?"

"Trey told me."

That overwhelming feeling of love I felt now feels more like anger. Jessie and Trey are a little too close. I'm tired of hearing Trey's name. It's bad enough I have to be around him tonight for his party.

Jessie's face has this weird look of excitement. She says, "He killed the boy named Bernard. Do you remember him?"

"Yeah, how could I forget? He was a real nice guy. I heard he was murdered execution style."

"He was, but the whole thing was an accident."

"I don't think so."

"It was. Trey made me promise not to tell anybody about this and I swore I wouldn't."

With an angry look on my face I ask, "Why is he trusting you with information like this?"

"I'm not sure, I guess he trusts me."

A burning sensation radiates throughout my gut. I hope it's not the start of an ulcer. I stare at her in anger because I can't understand why Trey is sharing secrets like this with my girl. Something's up with that and I'm going to find out what.

Jessie continues, "Trey said that when he, Tank, and Bernard were in the ninth grade they cut out of school early and went to Bernard's house to watch college basketball during March madness. They were getting high and playing around. Tank was being his usual badass self and wrestled Bernard to the floor. Trey held Bernard down while Tank wrapped duct tape around Bernard's hands and feet. I guess they were in training to become little gangsters. They dragged Bernard up to his bedroom closet."

"So how did Tank kill him?"

"I'm getting to that. Trey said that Tank taped a plastic shopping bag around Bernard's head."

"What? Why the hell did he do that?"

"He was playing around and didn't expect to kill the boy. They were best friends. You know how stupid young boys are. I guess he was just trying to scare him and left the bag over Bernard's head too long. They were all smoking weed and it impaired their judgment. Tank left Bernard upstairs for a couple of minutes and by the time he made it back to Bernard's closet it was too late. He had already suffocated. Tank and Trey were scared shitless and ran home leaving Bernard's body in the closet for his mother to find."

"I just lost my appetite."

"I'm sorry."

"It's just that I knew Bernard and I hate to think of how he died. He didn't deserve that shit. I still can't understand why Trey felt the need to share all that with you."

"I asked who Tank killed and he just opened up like that. I didn't ask for that much detail. He said Tank really did shoot four people in high school, but none of them died."

"With you telling me all this I really don't want to go to Trey's party now."

"Okay, what if we just go for an hour or so? Everybody who's anybody is gonna be there. I really wanna be there."

"I don't know." I look at Jessie and think about compromising. "I guess so."

"Thanks. I love you. You love me?"

"Yeah, I love you." For the first time I sound kind of unenthused while telling Jessie that I love her.

"You look like something's wrong. Please, please keep what I told you to yourself, okay?"

"Don't worry, I won't tell anybody. I just feel bad for Bernard's mother finding her son in the closet like that. To this day she doesn't know who killed him."

"I know. Everybody thought that it was drug related."

"He never had anything to do with selling drugs. Everybody just drew their own conclusions."

A bad feeling has just come over me. Bernard's mother lost her only child and his image is forever tarnished, not to mention the fact that he lost his life because two assholes wanted to play around. I wish Jessie had kept Trey's little dirty secret to herself and more than that, I wish Trey had kept his mouth shut.

Chapter 8

Jamal

Trey's house is located in a very exclusive community in P. G. County. His house sits about a quarter mile up a long driveway. As we approach his front gate a guy with a flashlight signals us to stop. He's dressed in a tight-fitting red jacket with a white shirt and black bow tie.

He says, "Good evening, your invitation please."

I look over at Jessie and she reaches in her purse and whips out the invitation and hands it to me. I never imagined that things would be this formal. Trey is really putting on a front. He isn't this big-time kingpin type that he wants everybody to believe. At least I don't think he is.

I hand the invitation to the guy and say, "Here you go." I notice something very familiar about him. "Hey, is your name Greg?"

He smiles and says, "Yeah, but tonight I'm Gregory, one of Mr. Bryant's helpers."

I smile and say, "That's cool."

He says, "I guess. Anyway, you two enjoy your evening."

"Alright, Benson, have a good night."

I drive away laughing. Jessie didn't find that funny at all. She stares at me as if she thinks I'm an idiot. Guess she doesn't like me disrespecting the help. She must be mad about something else. I'm just trying to stay loose because I don't want to be here anyway.

Jessie asks, "Why are you messing with him?"

"Don't tell me you didn't recognize Greg. Come on, that was Greg the crack head from around our way."

"What? You sure that was him? It didn't look like him."

"Yeah, it's him alright. I would know Greg anywhere. Whoo, he's in serious need of a laxative."

"Why would you say that?"

"'Cause he must be backed up. His breath smelled like he had shit coming out his mouth."

Jessie bursts out laughing and says, "Shut up! At least he's trying. It's good to see him working."

"Yeah, working for Trey. Trey is probably paying him with crack and Greg's dumb ass will be right back on the streets tomorrow looking dirty again."

"Can you just be quiet and drive? But seriously, baby, was his breath rotten?"

"His shit was *rotten!*"

"Why didn't you give him some gum?"

"Yeah, right, then his breath would just smell like minty-fresh shit."

As we make our way up the long driveway I notice almost every kind of fancy car and SUV on the market: Jaguar, Lexus, Mercedes Benz, Lincoln, Cadillac, Range Rover, Acura, and even a stretch Hummer. This looks like a damn car show or police auction and I'm representing for the economy-class cars. I have the cheapest ride within a ten-mile radius. I can tell by the expression on Jessie's face that she is impressed and ashamed at the same time and doesn't want to be seen getting out of a Chevy Cavalier.

I ask, "Am I embarrassing you?"

"How?"

"With this car."

"Not really, but can we park right here?"

"You're right. I don't wanna get too close to the house 'cause somebody might see us getting out of this piece of junk. I wish I had known things were gonna be so fancy because I would have rented a car or borrowed Shadow's Benz."

"That's not like you. You don't need to front for these people. I love you for who and what you are."

"Well, in that case, I'll try to get us as close to the house as possible."

Jessie shouts, "No! Please just park right here."

I laugh. "I knew it."

"Okay, I am a little embarrassed."

"Now that's what I was looking for. Just be honest. To be completely honest with you, I'm a little embarrassed too, rollin' up here like this."

"The hell with these people, park anywhere. This car doesn't define who we are. We look good and we have nothing to be ashamed of."

"You're right. I'm gonna get out now and you can park this piece of shit right next to that brand-new Escalade."

Jessie hits me on the arm. She yells, "Boy, stop playing!"

Trey's house is probably the most immense and well-designed home I've ever seen in the state of Maryland. For some strange reason I have a new respect for him. I'm filled with both envy and intrigue. This house is outstanding. Jessie and I enter the house through these huge double-mahogany and stained-glass doors accented with fancy gold fixtures. The foyer is a vast wide-open space with trees, cathedral ceilings, and skylights. If I'm not mistaken this is Italian marble flooring. Above us on the left-hand side is a loft with two turntables and a DJ from Old School Productions. He has a classic club mix playing. Directly in front of us is a reception area with hors d'oeuvres and four giant ice sculptures in the shape of diamonds topped with dollar signs. People are lined up signing guest books as an attractive young girl serves them champagne. She serves them Cristal and I stand back thinking that stuff costs over four hundred dollars a bottle.

To the right of the reception area is Trey, standing there looking like he's worth a million bucks. By the looks of this house he just might be. To the right of him is the shiniest black baby grand piano. That thing is beautiful. It looks like a jazz quartet is setting up to provide some smooth sounds. Trey has a DJ and live entertainment.

Right above the piano, glaring at me, is a masterpiece that I would recognize anywhere in the world. Perfectly centered on the wall in plain sight for everyone to take note of is a very impressive portrait of Malcolm X, my portrait of Malcolm X. This is the same portrait that sold at the auction last year for three thousand dollars. It should have sold for at least ten times that amount. I never knew who purchased this painting because I wasn't present when it was auctioned.

My painting looks like a priceless masterpiece mounted on this wall. The lighting accentuates every minute detail the painting conveys. I never realized how spectacular this painting was. It's weird seeing it here. At this point I'm not really sure what to think of Trey. I tap Jessie on the shoulder and point to the painting.

I say, "Does that painting look familiar?"

"Yeah, it's Malcolm X."

"No, I'm not talking about the person. I'm talking about the painting."

"Oh my God, baby, that's your painting. It looks so good up there."

"I know."

"Did you give it to Trey?"

"No, he must have got it from that auction last year."

"C'mon, let's go talk to him."

Jessie is so excited that she grabs me by the hand and pulls me along like a stubborn puppy. We root twenty-five or thirty people waiting to greet Trey.

Jessie says, "Hi, Trey. Did you know that was Jamal's painting up there?"

Trey smiles and says, "What's up, baby? Of course I did, that's why I bought it. I'm glad y'all could make it. I see you got my dawg, Jamal, with you. What's up, cuz? Welcome."

I can't believe he's still stuck on that fake cousin stuff after all these years. We shake hands and I say, "What's up, Trey? Good to see you. Thanks for buying my portrait and for inviting us. This is nice."

"Well, I'm just trying to do a little something. I knew you'd like seeing your painting up there. Give me a minute and I'll show y'all around. You know, give you two a little personal tour." Trey steps away. He says, "May I have everyone's attention for a second, please?" The crowd calms and Trey continues. "This portrait of Malcolm X was painted by my cousin over here, Jamal King." With a big smile on his face, Trey points me out and everyone gives me a quick round of applause.

This is totally unexpected. At first I didn't want to be here and now I feel at home. I can't lie, I love the attention, and Trey kind of blows me away with that. I owe him big time.

I smile and say, "Thank you. Thank you so much."

After a quick moment in the spotlight, Jessie and I move off to the side and I feel a tap on my right shoulder. I turn around and it's Shadow and John. Shadow and I embrace. We all exchange greetings. For some reason Shadow has always been short with Jessie. It's obvious that they're not the best of friends. John seems to have plenty to say to Jessie. He takes her away from me and starts a conversation with her, leaving me and my sister alone to talk.

I say, "What are you doing here?"

"Same thing you're doing here, bighead, getting exposure."

I laugh. "I can't believe I'm here and I'm shocked as hell to see you."

"These days you might run into me anywhere."

"So, this is your type of crowd, huh?"

"Hell yeah. There are people here from local government, the Washington Wizards, the Baltimore Ravens, and the music industry. As a matter of fact, the white guy over there is my program director from the station. That guy right there is my gynecologist."

"Really?"

"Yes, really."

"Damn, I guess just about everybody knows Trey. He's the man! Anyway, I haven't seen or talked to you in over a week."

"I've been incredibly busy. If you need to see me you can catch me every weekday at noon and at six o'clock."

"That's the only time I get to see you is on television."

"And now you get to see this beautiful face in person, don't you love it?"

"I love it so much that I wish you were on television right now so I could change the channel. Nah, I'm just playing. You know I love you. I'm so damn proud of you."

"I'm proud of you too. Your painting is getting some major attention tonight." She looks at my painting, then back at me. "You're all different now, but I see you're still a little silly."

"I can't change. You need to stop by the house ASAP to check on Coach. He's not doing well at all."

"I have to stop by the station tomorrow, but I promise I'll go by to see him and Grandma tomorrow. Tell them I said hi and I love them."

"I will. We've got a whole lot of catching up to do."

"Okay, I promise I'll stop by. Oh my goodness, look at my stupid husband and your hot-ass girlfriend over there flirting with each other. Let me go break them up before I have to hurt somebody."

"Wait! Jessie is more than my hot-ass girlfriend, check the ring. She's my hot-ass fiancée."

Shadow's eyes look like they're about to pop out of her head. "What? You big dummy, don't make the same mistake I made. I mean, you're making a mistake, but I guess I'm happy for you."

"Oh, you've got a real nice way of making me feel good about myself."

"I'm sorry. We're about to get outta here. See you tomorrow."

"Alright."

John walks over to me and says, "This is a good woman you got here. She showed me the ring. Congratulations. We all have to get together and celebrate."

Shadow rolls her eyes. "Call us. We're outta here. Congratulations, you two."

Jessie whispers, "I can't stand your sister."

"Shhh! Thanks again. See you tomorrow."

Jessie says, "Bye, John."

John smiles and waves good-bye while Shadow walks away very nonchalantly.

A few minutes later Trey comes back over to take me and Jessie on the tour. We start on the first level. This guided tour reminds me of an episode of MTV's *Cribs*, a really nice house and a really big showoff. I guess I should feel privileged having Trey take us on a guided tour, but I don't. This is so unnecessary. Throughout the entire tour all I can do is smile, nod, and say, "That's nice" over and over. The kitchen with its center island, the family room with the huge fireplace, the sunroom with exotic trees, the living room done up in cream leather furniture with mahogany tables, the Jacuzzi, the game room, the three flat-screen televisions, the five bedrooms, and the four bathrooms are just some minor details that kind of stand out a little. It's obvious that Trey is doing this to impress Jessie and at the same time make me feel inferior. Jessie is hard to read, but I'm sure she is very impressed by all this. She's oblivious to Trey's egotistical game. I thought Jessie and Trey would be a lot more cordial to each other. They're not their usual extra-friendly selves and I'm glad because that kind of makes me uncomfortable.

Chapter 9

Jessie

I'm so mad that I could explode. I was pissed from the moment we arrived at the front gate. This whole thing is like a big slap in my face. I've been to Trey's house in the city countless times, but this one in P. G. County is all new to me. The house in the city is nothing compared to this one. He probably reserves this house for his other girls. All my life I have considered myself beautiful and above average in all categories. Trey probably has girls that look twice as pretty as me and they're the ones that get to enjoy this house. That isn't fair to me considering how much I've put on the line sneaking around with him. He gives me money and all, but so what? I'm supposed to be treated special.

I have this angry feeling inside that just won't subside. Maybe his punk ass didn't think I was good enough for this house, and that hurts. He should have shared this with me a long time ago. He could have brought me here even during the construction phase.

In some ways I've underestimated Trey. He appears to be a lot wealthier than I imagined. He appears to possess so much more style and class than I initially gave him credit for. I'm starting to feel like I don't know him anymore. My opinion of Trey has definitely changed. I'm not sure if that is a good thing or a bad thing.

As we toured the house I looked around for evidence of a woman living here, but there wasn't a trace. Trey wants to give the impression that this is the ultimate bachelor pad. This house is much more than an ultimate bachelor pad. This is my ultimate dream house. Name it and this place has it. Trey is a man that has everything and nothing at the same time. He isn't truly happy, and happiness is everything. He needs someone like me in his life full-time. He should have me right by his side greeting our guests. When Trey spoke of networking with people on the golf course, I laughed. I'm not laughing now. I didn't think he had what it takes, but of course he has proven me wrong. It seems as though he has charmed everyone at the party. Trey was blessed with some sort of wonderful insight. He is one of the most charismatic men I've witnessed in a long time. I'm sure that most people here know that he is a drug dealer, but they're more concerned about what he can do for them. I hate to say it, but Jamal probably fits in that same category. He's been having the time of his life ever since he saw his painting on the wall.

Being here tonight has me reevaluating my position in Trey's life. What do I mean to him? What does he mean to me? I'm in need of some serious soul-searching. I know that money can't buy true happiness, but it sure can ease the pain of poverty. Just thinking about money makes me smile. My dream is to live a comfortable lifestyle, which allows me to do whatever I want, whenever I want, or to do absolutely nothing if I please. Having money means never having to worry about living beyond my means or worrying about making ends meet. I dream of possessing the ability to shop without ever looking at another price tag again. Everyone dreams of having a little fun, and the thought of bringing my girlfriends here and showing them around would be nice. I'd love to call this place home, but I know that's a far-fetched idea. I'd give almost anything to live here.

This will never be my home because I've kind of committed myself to Jamal. I look over at him and he looks so happy just standing around eating shrimp and sipping champagne. It looks as if everyone here is having a good time, except me. Guess I've brought myself down by thinking too much.

Trey is the only person who can bring so many different people together to party like this. There are people here from corporate positions and street-level positions. This is definitely a new age. In some cases it's hard to distinguish who's who. So many of these guys have Afros, bald heads, cornrows, twists, locks, and braids. These days brothas have no idea what they want to do with their hair. At least Jay keeps a close, conservative haircut.

He turns to me and says, "You alright? Want some Cristal, a Heineken, or a Smirnoff Ice?"

"No, thanks. You seem to be having a good time." I think, *You big phony-ass sellout.*

"Yeah, this is nice, much better than I expected. Wanna dance?"

"Not really."

"What's up with you? At first you were all excited about coming here and now you're acting like somebody died."

"I wanna live in a house like this one day and I don't see how we could ever afford something like this."

"So, that what's bothering you? Girl, I've got this all worked out. Just give me a few years and we can move into our little starter home in the city. Then five to ten years later we can think about working our way up to something like this. I told you I've got that potential wealth thing going. If my art career really takes off, we can be in a house like this in no time."

Now I really want to explode because I want this house right now, not years down the line. I can't even respond to Jamal. He's such a fucking joke and this is the man I'm supposed to marry. I can't do this. I wish Trey would take me away because I'm not cut out for a life in a starter home. This is all the starter home I need right here.

I don't respond to Jamal, I simply grab him by the hand and say, "C'mon, let's dance."

Oh my God, what the hell was I thinking? Out of frustration I forgot Jamal can't dance. Now we're in the middle of the dance floor and he is all kicking and shuffling around like a big retard wearing two left shoes. Can my night get any worse? I feel like people are laughing at us. I want to scream or run off the dance floor, but instead I just take it like a woman. I keep dancing because this is the man and the life I've chosen. I'll just have to learn to suffer with Jamal. He looks goofy, but in a strange way he's so cute. All I can do is smile.

After Jamal and I finish dancing, Trey comes over and takes him away. I guess they're going off to do some male bonding. I'm all alone, but not for long. Some local singer named Khalil steps to the microphone and it's almost as if he is singing to me. He's fine as hell.

Khalil has the looks, the moves, and a smooth voice to match. His song is like a sweet lullaby. He reminds me of a low-budget version of Maxwell, but still I don't think there's a dry pair of panties in the house. As I look around the room every woman in the house has that same euphoric expression. Well, almost every woman, except these two girls staring directly at me. I mean, they're really staring. I give them this what-the-hell-y'all-looking-at-me-for kind of stare. Lesbians? This tall WNBA-Amazon-lookin' girl gives me a dirty look. The other girl just keeps staring. She gives me a friendly little smile and now she is making her way in my direction. I'm not really in the mood to mingle with females. I'm too busy enjoying Khalil.

The girl says, "Hi, how you doing? I'm Alicia. Was that your man who was with you earlier?"

"Which one?"

"Which one? I'm sure not talkin' 'bout Trey, 'cause he's my man."

I think, *Oh, shit, this is Alicia, Trey's baby's mother.* She's a lot prettier than I imagined. Trey never said she would be here. He's wrong. I'm nervous, but not intimidated.

I say, "I'm sorry, you mean Jamal. Yeah, he's my fiancé."

"That's nice. I was wondering how you knew Trey. Don't you love this house?"

"Yeah, it's so pretty. Who decorated this place?"

Alicia smiles and says, "Me and an interior decorator. Trey bought this house for me and the baby. He treats me like a queen and Anitra is his little princess. I wanna have like two more kids by him. Do you have any kids?"

Why is she talking to me? I wish she would go away with all this bullshit. I feel like being completely rude. I want to shove her by the side of her head and yell, *Get the fuck out of my face!*

Instead I say, "No, I'm not ready to wreck my body all up. I have a thing about my weight and keeping my shape. I'm not trying to take anything away from motherhood. I just think most guys go out on their pregnant wives and girlfriends, especially when they have to make it through those six weeks without sex. That shit messes a lot of guys up. There aren't a lot of men that can go six weeks without sex, you know?"

"See, that's the kind of shit I hate. Women are always calling men dogs, but then there's those little greedy bitches that don't have a man or don't have a good man and try to mess things up for sistas like me."

"All I can say is, life's a bitch."

Alicia signals for her big Amazon-lookin' girlfriend. This tall, slim, ugly girl with a big gold tooth steps to me. There's something familiar about this girl. Her hair is different, but the big gold tooth is the same. She is the girl from North and Greenmount. She is the hood rat that asked my name when I was in Trey's car that night.

The big girl asks, "You 'member me? Yeah, you the girl Jessie I told Alicia about. The one who thinks she's Trey's new sidekick and shit. We gonna have to show you different."

This can't be happening like this, not here in front of all these people. I say, "I know y'all aren't gonna start any trouble in here, especially in front of all these people."

Alicia says, "Why not? This is my damn house. Now what you gonna do?"

All I can do is stand here, biting my bottom lip, clutching my purse, and trying not to look too scared.

Chapter 10

Jamal

Trey takes me away for a minute for some guy talk. It's the same shallow bullshit conversation that guys always have. I just put myself on automatic pilot because I'm already preprogrammed to talk about sports, cars, money, and sex. I greet about four guys I already know from my neighborhood. It's funny because Trey has the same views on sports as Jessie. I swear she gave the same sports commentary a few days ago. After Trey and I finish our small talk he introduces me to his friends from Brooklyn, Kev and Mike. These two idiots are standing around talking openly about how they used to transport cocaine on Amtrak trains a few years ago until the feds started busting people. Now they transport keys up and down I-95 in the back of $19.95-a-day U-haul trucks. They figure it's less likely a state trooper would stop a brotha riding in something that inconspicuous.

Kev and Mike have no idea who I am. For all they know I could be an undercover agent. Guys like this get real cocky over time, and in most situations their bragging leads to their arrests.

Trey says, "Jamal, remember Tank?"

I turn around to see this little short chubby guy step from behind Kev and Mike. He says, "How you been doing, my brother?"

I think about Bernard and how Tank murdered him. At first I'm kind of reluctant to shake hands, but he is very different from the Tank I remember. He looks pitiful. He is only twenty-nine or thirty years old, but he looks and sounds about fifty. To be honest, he looks sick.

I say, "How you been, Tank? It's good to see you."

"It's good to be seen, my brother. I've been away for a long time and God has blessed me with my freedom and I plan to make the best of the rest of my time I have left here."

I say, "I thought this was a welcome-home party for you, but I haven't seen you all night."

Tank says, "I've been all around the house talking to people, spreading God's word."

I feel so sorry for this man. All those years in prison have really humbled him.

He says, "You look good, Jamal."

I think, *Oh no, he looks so bad. What can I say?* All I can do is lie. "You look good too, Tank."

"That's what I keep hearing. You're about the twentieth person who's said that tonight. Thanks."

Damn, I'm the twentieth person to lie to him. He looks like he died last week and Trey brought him back to life just for one last party. He looks like death warmed over, like Trey warmed his ass up in a big microwave on high for five to ten minutes.

Trey pulls me away from Tank and we talk between ourselves again.

He says, "Tank is my dawg and all, but he looks bad, right?"

"He looks different, that's all."

"You're lying, but I respect that. You're my dawg too, and you're welcome here any time you wanna come out. You really like this place, don't you?"

"You know I do."

"Did you see my new Escalade out front?"

"I did, and what's your point?"

Trey looks kind of insulted that I'm so blunt with him. It's just that I hate a person that constantly brags about material possessions.

Trey says, "What's my point? My point is I saw you pull up in that tired-ass car of yours. I wanna help you. You know, help you make some loot. Push a phat-ass whip like mine."

I ask, "So, what you gonna do, commission me to do some paintings for you?"

Trey laughs. "Nah, cuz, I'm pushing some major weight and I wanna put you down, know what I'm saying?"

"I hear you, but I ain't trying to go to jail. That ain't my style."

"It ain't my style either. You think I'm trying to go jail? I don't believe you. I invited your generic ass to my house, offered you a business proposition, and this is how you react? I can't believe you."

"Believe it. How you gonna call me generic?"

"I'm sorry. That was wrong. I'm not trying to corrupt you or disrespect you. Do your thing, son. If art is your thing, then God bless. Here you go, have a Heineken."

I reach for the bottle and my mind takes me back to that night in my car when I found that Heineken bottle under my seat. I smile because it's like mathematics, it's all starting to add up. I think back to Jessie getting kind of emotional for no reason earlier, the sports commentary, and now the Heineken. I feel bold and crazy at the same time.

I say, "Trey, you got a condom? I'm trying to do a little something with Jessie tonight, but I'm out of rubbers."

He laughs and says, "I got you, dawg."

Trey reaches for his wallet and pulls out a Lifestyles condom, the exact kind that I found in my car.

Before Trey returns his wallet to his back pocket, he flashes his license at me and asks, "Do you look hard-core like this on your license or are you smiling, looking like a soft-ass nigga?"

Suddenly everything is so clear. Now I know why Jessie wanted to see my license the other morning. I swear it seems as if the room becomes brighter. It's the light I've been looking for. I feel strange like something's taking over me. My body temperature rises and my muscles are pulsating. I'm mad as hell. I feel like hurting somebody. My mind snaps and I look right into Trey's eyes.

I ask loud and clear, "Why are you fucking Jessie? Why?"

Without even thinking Trey says, "I'm sorry, dawg, it just happened. I was wrong, but I wasn't trying to hurt you."

My world has come to an end. I feel like a fool. I'm defeated. All that time and energy is gone to waste. I loved that girl. I proposed to her. All this time I've been walking around wearing my heart on my sleeve and it just took a mighty blow. Jessie said she loved me, but it was all a lie. I look over my shoulder and she's talking to two girls. I look back at Trey.

He says, "I know you're mad and you wanna hit me, but trust me, that would be a big mistake."

Trey's boys overheard what he said. They all laugh at me, except Tank. He just shakes his head in disgust.

Trey says, "Anyway, I hate fighting. If you hit me I'd have to kill you. I'd make you famous though, just like all the other dead artists. Your paintings would be worth a lot more money then."

He laughs, but I never respond because I hear a major commotion going down on the other side of the room. People are scrabbling everywhere. Ten or twenty people are on cell phones. I can't believe my eyes. Jessie is standing on the other side of the room with her purse dangling in one hand and a little silver gun in the other aimed directly at those two girls she was talking to a minute ago. I ignore Trey and without thinking I rush over to help Jessie.

I yell, "Jessie, what's going on? Please put the gun down."

She says, "No, they started this shit and I'm gonna end it right here, right now."

"Listen to me. It's okay. Put the gun down. Relax, relate, and release. Give me the gun."

"I can't!"

"You can!"

Trey yells, "Don't give him shit! Everybody get off the cell phones. This is not happening."

One of the girls that Jessie has the gun aimed at asks, "What are you doing, Trey?"

Trey pulls out his gun and says, "Go 'head, Jessie, now give Jamal the gun."

It's as if Trey has some strange power over Jessie. She instantly hands me the gun. This feels weird, as if it's all a bad dream. I look around for Tank, but he's nowhere to be found. I guess he's really had enough of prison and wants no part of this.

Trey looks at me and says, "Now, give it to me."

I look at the gun, then at him, and say, "Trust me, motherfucker, I wanna give it to you for real." I ignore Trey and say, "Jessie, I know all about you and Trey. I know everything so there is no need to lie to me anymore. His dumb ass told me everything."

She cries, "I'm sorry. I'm so sorry for what we've done to you. I've ruined your life. I ruined us. Please give Trey the gun. Jamal, don't shoot him. You're too good for that."

I shout, "Do you really think so? Am I too good for you? I should shoot you, but I love you too much. Here you go, Trey, take the gun and take her too, I don't have any use for either one of them."

I hand Trey the gun and he laughs as if this is all a big joke to him. He says, "I'm sorry, everybody. This was a big, big misunderstanding, but everything's under control."

I hear sirens in the background. Trey hands the guns to one of his boys and he takes off like a runaway slave out of the room. The guests all scramble around trying to get the hell out of the house before the police arrive. Looks like nobody wants to be a witness.

I turn to Jessie and say, "All I wanted to do was to make you happy and make you love me, but I couldn't. I couldn't do it. You never loved me." She looks at her ring like she's questioning whether she should give it back or not and I say, "Whatever, you can keep the ring."

She says, "I do love you. I do."

The tall girl yells at Jessie, "Shut up, bitch!"

She punches Jessie right in the mouth and other girl jumps on Jessie. I simply walk away. I think, *I've saved her for the last time. I can't be her fool anymore. That's an ass whipping she deserves.* Trey and his boys slowly break it up.

Chapter 11

Jamal

That was unreal. I still have a little buzz going on from all that alcohol. I keep reminding myself that it actually happened. Jessie is gone and I'm drunk as hell.

I was lonely with or without Jessica, so what's the big deal? She really can keep that ring. Maybe I'm a little crazy or a little mixed up right now. It's even hard for me to understand. All I can say is the same thing I used to say as a child when my building blocks would come tumbling down, "All fall down." That's exactly how I feel right now because nothing lasts forever. Although I lie here crying, my heart is happy. No more worries, no more wondering, I know the truth. I'm alone, but I'm not lonely and there's a big difference. I'm happy with me. Most of all I'm happy to be me because I'm free from Jessica. She was only out for herself. She never really loved me. No matter how hard I tried, I couldn't make Jessie feel something that wasn't there. She was only out for what I could do for her.

Trey made a fool of me. I felt like the whole world was laughing at me, and now the whole world is smiling with me. This is a happy heartache or a happy heartbreak. I'm smiling and my heart is smiling too. There are a couple of sayings that go, *Too blessed to be stressed* and *One monkey don't stop the show.* Those sayings perfectly express how I feel.

I pick up Jessie's picture and say to myself, "No more you and me. You're gonna be lonely without me."

Jessie and I could have been a wonderful work of art. I'm talking about a beautiful family and all. God knows that was a fine woman with the ability to produce some beautiful offspring. That was all physical beauty though. My goal is to prepare myself for my next girl-friend, that special lady who's worthy of my love. I need someone I can trust, someone I can call my own. I promise to go out of my way to make her happy.

I say, "God, I'm ready for my Ms. Right."

All of a sudden, I hear a bloodcurdling scream echo throughout the house that sobers me right up. "He's gone! Lord, Lord, Lord, he's gone! Jamal!"

My heart drops to the floor. For the moment I'm paralyzed because I know that the angel of death has just paid this house a visit. Coach is gone and now I have to drag myself upstairs and try my best to comfort my grandmother because her baby brother is gone.

I say a little prayer, "God, give me strength. I hope you've prepared a home for my uncle and he finds peace."

When I get upstairs to Coach's room Grandma is right by his side with his hand in hers and her head on his chest, next to his silent heart.

She says softly, "Coach, wake up."

He's unresponsive. Dead. I feel so bad because I feel like there was something I could have done. I didn't even get to say a last good-bye. I was too wrapped up in nonsense. This is it. Death is so final. So many thoughts and memories zoom through my head. I can't take my eyes off my grandmother.

I say, "Grandma, he's gone. It's all over. He's gone."

"I know. I know, baby." She stands up and places her arms around me tightly. Tears flow from her eyes and she moans in agony. I feel my own tears run down my face. I'm overwhelmed with emotions. As I hold my grandmother I peek over to Coach's body. He looks as if he died a horrible death. His skin is as dark as ever. The chemo has left him completely bald. His lips are parted and his eyes are wide open with a blank frigid stare. This is the look of death and it's frightening. I reach over and attempt to close his eyes, but they won't close. I hate seeing him like this and I don't want Grandma to look at him.

I say, "Call the undertaker and call Shadow. I'll stay here."

I feel like my breath has been taken away and I wish I could breathe life back into my uncle's body. This really hits hard because this is my friend, my family, and the man who was like a father to me. I hold his hand.

I look over to his nightstand and see Coach's old-fashioned cassette recorder. I don't know why, but I press PLAY. Instantly Coach's voice comes blaring out of the tiny single speaker. He's singing his favorite song, "Lean On Me," by Bill Withers. Usually hearing a dead man's voice would be disturbing, but this makes me smile. I smile because my uncle has the worst singing voice I've ever heard, but today it's the sweetest sound I could ever imagine.

Chapter 12

Jessie

The funny thing about life is how unpredictable it is. Here I am exactly where I dreamed of being. It was a hard and bumpy road though. God knows I took some bumps last night, but I'm still beautiful. Those maniacs were driven by jealousy and look who ended up with Trey. I'm in his bed looking around this beautiful master suite.

Alicia never lived here. She was just trying to provoke me. She won the fight, but I won the battle for Trey's heart. As he sleeps I kiss him because I love him.

Trey awakens and says, "Good morning, baby. How you feelin'?"

"I feel wonderful thanks to you."

"Welcome home."

"Ooh, say it again please."

If this is a dream I don't want to wake up. Hearing Trey refer to this place as my home is like music to my ears.

"Welcome home, baby. This is your house too. Alicia only dreamed of living here. I never wanna see her again. I love my daughter, but as far as I'm concerned, her mother doesn't exist anymore. I can't believe she caused a scene like that in front of all my guests. I had a beef with Jamal, but at least I didn't cause a major scene like that."

"Don't blame all that on Alicia. I accept some of the blame for that. I was the one who pulled a gun."

"I know. I was like, look at my little thug chick. I loved it. I was laughing my ass off. I thought you was gonna shoot her and her tall-ass bodyguard-lookin' girlfriend."

"Yeah, they thought I was gonna shoot them too."

"Seriously though, they beat your ass, but you still look pretty. You kinda held your own."

"At least I kept my face covered."

"Except when Big Foot hit you in the mouth. Damn!"

I have a flashback of Latonya's big gold tooth and hideous face and her lunging at me with her giant paws. The impact of her fist meeting my face damn near sent me into another world. Without any lateral head movement I was done.

With a silly look on my face I say, "So what? That's not funny."

"You're right. Jamal was funny though. That nigga was all fired up and didn't do shit."

"Leave him alone. I feel bad for him."

"Who's this? 'I love you, but you never loved me,' all crying and shit. I thought I was watching Denzel or somebody."

"You're wrong. We're both wrong."

"Yeah, but at least everything is all out in the open now. No more lies or sneaking around."

"True. I still can't believe how fast everything happened."

"That's life, shorty. I'm just sorry all that went down in front of all those people. I'm glad I know a lot of influential people, 'cause that's what cooled the cops down."

"Forget the influential people. I'm glad people fear you and do what you say."

"That's not fear, it's respect."

"I'm just glad everybody including Alicia stuck to the story you made up."

"Believe me, those cops wanted to keep everything simple. They weren't trying to fill out long reports. Everything was cool when they got here and that was good enough for them."

"Thanks for having my back. It's a dream come true waking up in this bed with you."

"That's not a big deal. You're my little wifey." He kisses me and my heart flutters. "Whatever I have is yours, you know that?"

"Thank you. I love you."

"Love you too. No doubt. Just hold me down, baby. That's all I ask."

"Look, Trey, I don't mean to sound greedy or selfish or anything, but can you put my name on a few things? You know the house, a car, or something."

He laughs. "You're a trip, but I got you. Hey, you gotta look out for yourself. Don't worry about going to work tomorrow, you work for me now."

"Doing what?"

"Keeping me happy."

Again, this is a dream come true. I'm so excited that I feel butterflies in my stomach. My eyes start to tear. All I can do is hug Trey and hold him as tight as I can. I'm never going back to the bank again. The first chance I get I'm going to call my supervisor and tell her to go straight to hell because she never really respected me.

Trey says, "I know you're not crying."

"I can't help it. I'm always real emotional. These are tears of joy, but last night I was hurt because you never even brought me to this house. And now I can't believe you're telling me that it's mine. You hardly ever talked to me about this place. I imagined you having all types of model-lookin' chicks here all hangin' around the pool and Jacuzzi."

He laughs and says, "What are you talking about? I spend most of my time in Baltimore. It's not like I was trying to hide anything." He looks me up and down, then gives me a quick, sexy smile. "You're the only model-lookin' chick I have in my life. Anyway, you never seemed pressed about coming out here."

"You always seemed to downplay whatever you had out here. I was just waiting patiently for you to bring me here."

"Trust me, I didn't mean anything by not bringing you out here. I just recently got this place together. Let me show you something that no one else knows about."

Trey gets out of bed butt-naked and slips on a pair of his Timberland boots. He looks rugged. I guess this is supposed to be the roughneck version of bedroom slippers. I've never seen anyone butt-naked in boots, but I like it. I follow Trey to the walk-in closet.

He says, "This house has a lot of safety features. Behind this wall is a hidden safety room." He opens a door to a small room with security monitors like the ones out in the master suite. Trey says, "Once this door is closed and this lock is activated, it can only be opened by the person on the inside. You're completely safe in here."

"Oh my God! This is slick. I've never seen anything like this."

"I saw this on TV and I contacted the manufacturer. Along with my builder they made this happen. There's enough nonperishable food and water to live in here for an entire year. It's fireproof, bulletproof, and storm proof. A lot of people are getting these installed. If something ever goes down and I'm not home, this is where you better head, okay?"

"You don't have to tell me twice. I'll probably end up in there whether you're home or not."

We laugh.

"Yo, if Scarface would've had one of these he'd be alive today," he says.

I smile and think, *You big dummy. He can't be serious. No, he is serious.* I say, "Excuse me, but Scarface was a fictional character in a movie."

"I know that was a movie, but it was real to me."

"I guarantee you that Tony Montana was a fictional character."

"You might be right, but at least I learned from him. Scarface was like a documentary on how to come up in the game."

End of conversation. I have nothing else to say about the whole Scarface situation. The black Tony Montana/Nino Brown over here doesn't know fiction from reality. All these young thugged-out wannabe gangstas sit back and watch gangster movies and get all kinds of wild ideas. In reality not many young black guys reach the level Trey has reached, regardless of how well they pattern their lives after fictional characters.

Trey says, "You're looking at me like I'm crazy, but I'm serious."

"I didn't say anything. We just have different views on *Scarface.* Basically the movie was just about guns and drugs."

"It was much more than that. It's my all-time favorite movie. My father was my biggest influence and then I learned from Tony Montana. After watching that movie I spoke with a Cuban accent for two weeks. Scarface was a good flick." Trey laughs. "That movie helped bring out another side of me, for real. I know I'll never be as large as Scarface and that's cool. It's rare to find a lot of blacks getting paid like that, but when the shit goes down we're always the first ones on the news looking like assholes being labeled as kingpins and everybody knows that's bullshit. I've never dealt directly with any Columbians or Bolivians. I don't own a boat or a plane. All I know about is how to hold it down on the streets and I'm slowly working on expanding this shit. I've got connections all up and down the East

Coast." He squints his eyes and gives me a funny look. "I can tell you don't wanna hear this."

"I'm listening. If it's important to you, then it's important to me."

"That's what I wanted to hear. I'm about to roll out for a little bit. Gotta get that paper. The keys to the house and the Infiniti are on the dresser."

Hold up, I guess now that Trey has the new Escalade that means no brand-new Benz for me. The Q45 is fine, but I still want my dream car.

I say, "Thanks."

"What you got planned for today?"

"I was thinking about inviting my girls over."

"That's cool. They can help get rid of some of those leftovers."

"That's what I was thinking too. I'm gonna hook that shit up so good they won't even know they're eating leftovers."

We laugh.

Trey says, "C'mere. I love you, and thanks for making me happy."

"I can't even begin to describe how much I love you or how happy you make me. You've given me everything I could ever dream of." I think, *Except a new Benz.*

"This is just the beginning. It's important to me to have a good woman in my corner. I owe you an apology."

"For what?"

"As long as I live I'll never call you a bitch again. No matter how I try to rationalize the use of the word, I was wrong."

"You are so sweet and full of surprises."

"I don't know about all that, but thanks."

Trey leaves the house on his way to do whatever he does best. He has given me a new life and I can't see myself sweatin' him over where he's going or who he's going to be with. I understand that a man needs breathing room. Regardless, a man is going to be a man.

Chapter 13

Jamal

Mornings are usually refreshing, especially after a cold, dark, rainy night. Sunlight shines through the window on the far side of my studio. It's a welcome sight. The rain really came down last night. Lightning lit the night sky, giving a brief illusion of daylight. Thunder sent shattering echoes across the sky as if it were God taking out His frustration on the world. I know He isn't happy. There is so much evil going on in the world that it makes my problems seem miniscule.

As my enemies move against me, God moves with me. I've survived a raging storm, but today is just the beginning of another storm. The undertaker came by around 5:00 A.M. to pick up Coach's body. I can't let my uncle's death or my breakup with Jessie get me down too much.

I'm tired as hell, but sleep is the last thing on my mind. I lie here alone wishing I had someone to hold, wanting someone to cuddle and keep me warm in this cold world. No matter how I try to deny it, I love Jessie and I always will. I thought this would be easy, but I was wrong.

I hear footsteps and voices coming from upstairs. The news of Coach's death is out and spreading like wildfire. I asked Grandma to make two phone calls and I'm sure she phoned everyone she knows. The news of a death travels faster than the speed of light, especially in the black community. For some reason, we love to spread bad news.

Black people have a habit of calling each other before the crack of dawn to spread the news that someone has died. I have to get myself together to greet visitors alongside my grandmother.

When I get upstairs I can't believe my eyes. We've never had this many people in this house before. It's too early for this, but I'm sure these people mean well. Grandma is nowhere in sight. There is a mixture of neighbors, distant cousins, and a bunch of my grandmother's church members here. It looks like the Edmondson Village Community Baptist Church's Sunday morning service were being held right here in our living room. All I can do is smile and greet people. I'm not even sure if they know who I am. It's almost as if the funeral were already in progress. Everyone is busy singing, praying, or crying. I should have had the undertaker leave Coach's body here and we could have gotten the funeral service out of the way.

I hate funerals. I know that we're born to die, but funerals just make things worse. The whole funeral process is so drawn out. Today is Sunday and Coach's funeral actually isn't until Thursday morning at 11:00. We're expecting family from out of town. Now for almost an entire week we'll have to host daily grieving sessions here. I'm not sure how much fried chicken I can stand. It appears that almost every person who has walked through this front door has brought fried chicken from KFC, Popeye's, or home. This reminds me of being at an old-fashioned revival or a small storefront church. Thanks to all these old church people our house smells like mothballs, cheap hand lotion, and fried chicken. I'm gonna be sick.

I haven't seen this much fried chicken or this many church hats under the same roof in God only knows how many years. Don't get me wrong, I love and respect a woman in a nice church hat. Church hats are truly expressive. These churchwomen around here are a lot like cowboys: No matter how much kicking, dancing, shouting, and jumping up and down they do they never lose their hats. One Sunday in church I saw a woman fall out and hit her head on one of the pews, and when the paramedics wheeled the sister out her church hat was still in place.

Finally, I see Grandma. She's in a prayer circle with Ms. Pearl and her other church members. I join the circle, taking Ms. Pearl and my grandmother by their hands. After the prayer Grandma and I embrace and talk for a minute.

I ask, "Did you call Shadow?"

"Yeah, her and John will be over later this afternoon."

"Have you heard from my mother?"

"No, and I don't expect to hear from her. She'll probably pop up early Thursday morning."

The doorbell rings and I make my way to the door. It's Church. He says, "Hey, Jamal, sorry to hear about Coach."

"Thanks. I'm glad you're here."

"I know you got a lot going on right now, but can we go somewhere and talk?"

"Sure!"

I'm sorry all this is going on, but at least it's keeping me busy. I really haven't had much time to think about Jessie or time to really process everything I experienced last night. Despite how everything went down, I'm really starting to miss Jessie. I have an urge to call her, but I won't. I just need someone to talk to and I'm glad Church is here. We head down to my apartment to talk.

Church says, "I heard about what happened last night at Trey's house."

"Damn, how'd you find out already?"

"You know it doesn't take long for gossip to spread around here. I can't believe Jessie was messing around with Trey."

"I can't either. It's crazy, but I can't stop wondering what she's doing or where she is right now. I wonder how she looks and feels. These girls beat her up pretty bad."

"I heard."

"I guess I'm in denial or something, but this time around I swear there's no making up. I'm a changed man. Let's just say I saw the light last night. I'll never let another female take advantage of me like that. I'm tried of being the softhearted pushover type. I'm a man and that's how I expect to be treated."

"I hear you."

"I could have killed Trey last night, but he wasn't worth it. I'm glad I didn't do anything crazy, because my grandmother really needs me by her side. Trey's hard to understand. He bought a painting of mine at an auction about a year ago. It was hanging on the wall above his baby grand piano and I got some major attention last night from that. He acknowledged me in front of all those people. And then a few minutes later he had the nerve to pull me up and offer me a position selling drugs. To top everything off I found out that he had been messing around with my girl. All that happened in one night. I hate thinking about him and Jessie having sex. I know they had sex in my car and that makes me wanna go kill them. That shows a complete lack of respect for me and I can't have that anymore. Trey will never respect Jessie the way I did. He'll just continue to buy her expensive gifts. I'm sure he bought her that fancy diamond pendant that I thought was a fake. I don't wish bad luck on anyone, but Jessie will never find true happiness with anyone because she's a miserable person. She doesn't know who she is or what she really wants out of life. She's so superficial and I don't need a woman like that. She thinks that life is all about her and looking good. All she knows is money and having a good time. She doesn't love Trey, she loves the lifestyle he gives her. The last thing she probably wants is a drug dealer. Jessie only wants what she can get out of him right now. Trey respects her so much that he took his time breaking up the fight because him and his boys were getting cheap thrills from seeing Jessie and those girls fight."

"Aw, man, I wish I was there. You gotta admit, female fights are a rare sight. To most guys it's a sexy thing to witness. All that wrestling, screaming, scratching, and pulling of hair. Guys just wanna see a breast pop out before stopping the fight."

I laugh. "That's true, but I was too mad to stick around for that. I'm bitter as hell now just talking about all this."

"You have every right to be. I'm mad at my girl, too. We broke up a couple of days ago."

"You and Keisha broke up?"

"Yeah. She had the nerve to walk up to me and say, 'Here, you need to start taking these.' She handed me a bottle of antibiotics."

"Oh no. That's messed up."

"Tell me about it. She's been sleeping around with some other dude."

"So, what kind of disease did she give you?"

"I don't have nothing. I think she's got chlamydia. I don't have any symptoms."

"I heard you can have it and not have any symptoms. You better take those pills anyway, every last one. I can't believe this. We're nice guys and our women dogged us."

"That's what we get for being nice guys. Most of these women aren't used to that. I used to talk to some other girls when me and

Keisha were together, but I never slept with any of them. I never really thought about cheating on her."

"You know I never cheated on Jessie."

"I know. You never had time to cheat."

"You're stupid. It's not that I never had the time, I never had the desire. I thought about other girls before."

"Like who?"

"I can't believe I'm telling you this. Do you remember that girl from high school named Jillian Smith?"

"Yeah, that fat, pretty girl. Man, she was fine, but nobody wanted to step to her because of her size."

"We were so immature then and couldn't appreciate her for who she really was. I'm a man now and things are different."

"I know what you mean." He gives me five. "I'm about to roll out, but before I go you think I could get at some of that chicken upstairs?"

"Yeah, we got enough food to feed an army."

"That's one thing I won't miss about Keisha, she never cooked. Her idea of preparing breakfast was pouring milk into a bowl of Cap 'n Crunch. I eat at McDonald's like four times a week, but I'm just gonna start cooking for myself. I'm a man and I'm gonna survive, regardless."

"Me too."

About 1:00 in the afternoon, Shadow finally decides to show her face.

I ask, "Hey, where's John?"

"I don't know and I don't really care. We were in separate vehicles. I had some personal business to take care of at the station," Shadow says angrily.

"Damn, I thought I was in a bad mood."

"I'm sorry, Jamal. I know the last thing you need is to have something else bring you down. I heard about you and Jessie. I guess John and I left too soon. What time did all that go down?"

"I don't know. You act like you're sorry you didn't witness it."

"Well, you know I never liked Jessie anyway. She's pretty and all, but she always carried herself like she was God's gift to the world. She's definitely not God's gift to the world." Shadow smiles. "Because I am."

"You think you are. Who told you about what happened?"

"John told me. A friend of his was there last night and he called John this morning."

"That's embarrassing."

"Don't even worry about it. Jessie was the one who did wrong. We need to go somewhere and talk."

"We can go down to my apartment."

Shadow laughs and says, "You live in a fantasy world. You mean, we can go down to the basement."

"No, I mean exactly what I said, my apartment."

When we get downstairs I try to pay her back for her wisecrack. "Now, don't you feel bad for not getting here sooner?"

"Why should I? I loved Coach like a father, but don't get me wrong, he lived his life and I have to live mine. If people have a problem with what I do and how I do it, that's too damn bad."

"Nobody has a problem with that. Everybody knows how busy and important you are."

"I'm not that important. Everybody just has a way of putting me up on a pedestal."

"They see you as little Ms. Perfect. You are a little conceited, snob-bish, vain, arrogant, and self-centered."

"No, you didn't go there. Is that how people see me?"

"Maybe not in your world, but in this neighborhood, yeah."

"Are you just saying this because that's how you really see me?"

"Don't be crazy. Other people might see you like that, but I don't."

"Well, I'm not like that at all. It's not my fault that people don't under-stand me. I'm not any of the stuff you called me. I'm just proud."

"That's true. They just don't understand you, right?"

"Or they're just jealous and I don't know why. I'm just like every-body else. I'm nowhere near perfect. Trust me, I have problems too, but I just don't go around broadcasting them to everyone."

"You shouldn't."

"Back to your problem. I can't believe Trey and Jessie would mess around behind your back. Don't be surprised if one of them shows up around here or at Coach's funeral."

"They better not show up around here or at the funeral."

"Check you out, talking like you've got balls all of a sudden."

"Forget you. I always had balls, I was just blinded by love. Just think about all the things love can make you do and say, not to mention how crazy it makes you act."

"I can definitely relate to that."

"How can you relate to that?"

"I just can, that's all. I was wrong about Jessie flirting with John. They were just discussing investments and how to manage her money."

My blood begins to boil. "Damn, Trey must be giving her a lot of cash. I can't stand that little prostitute."

"Calm down. I know you're mad at her, but nobody's perfect. We've all done things we're not proud of."

"Including you?"

"Including me. I told you, I'm not perfect. People just think I am."

"Is there something you wanna get off your chest?"

"You can't handle it. My problems are a little too deep for you."

"Try me."

"Okay." Shadow pauses and looks down at the floor. She continues, "For the past three years I've been having an affair with Kyle Williams."

"Oh, shit!"

"Why else do you think we have such great on-air chemistry?"

"Listen to me when I tell you this. Don't ever mention that to anyone else as long as you live. I can't believe you've been cheating on John."

"Believe it. Told you I wasn't perfect."

"Everything seemed so perfect with the two of you."

"That's your perception. I'm happy with John, but I'm not in love with him. He can't please me sexually."

I think, *Yuck! Nobody wants to hear about your sex life.* I say, "I've heard enough."

"No, you opened this can of worms and now I'm gonna force-feed it to you."

"I can't believe he doesn't satisfy you sexually. All he ever talks about is how good he is in bed and how he used to have girls running after him."

"Yeah, he had *girls* running after him, but he can't satisfy a woman. John is a lot of talk. Let's just say his tongue is a lot bigger than his dick."

"Alright, I've really heard enough."

She bounces up and down on my bed and says, "No, it feels good to get this out."

"Okay, but I thought size didn't matter."

"That's a lie. It does matter. Women just made that up, so guys with little dicks wouldn't commit suicide. Come on, how you gonna knock it and rock it with a little thing?"

We laugh.

"I have no idea because that's never been a problem of mine. I can't believe we're sitting here having this conversation."

"Me either, but we're adults. Isn't it good to have a cool-ass sister like me?"

"Uh-huh. You're crazy and you know it. Thanks for making me laugh. You took my mind off my problems for a minute."

"This might be bad advice, but if you really love Jessie, get her back. She's just a young dumb girl that got caught up."

"I'm not trying to hear that. I don't want her back."

"I was just testing you. I guess you do have some balls after all. Don't be her little sucker again, okay?"

"I won't. Enough talk about Jessie. I miss Coach. One of his last requests was that the two of us stay close."

"We will. I'll always make time for my big brother."

We embrace. It's funny hearing Shadow refer to me as her big brother. I think I look up to her more than she looks up to me. I'm sure Coach is in heaven smiling down on us.

I love my sister. She is so unpredictable. Shadow and Kyle Williams. I should have known something was up with them. Shadow almost got me with her little test. I was almost ready to forgive Jessie until something in my subconscious jolted me back to reality. I guess I still need some type of closure.

A male voice says, "Can I come down?"

It's John. Shadow and I make surprised faces at each other like little mischievous kids wondering if they just got busted doing something wrong. We don't say a word, but I'm sure we're thinking the same thing: *How long was John standing there? Hope he didn't hear our conversation.*

I say, "Yeah, come on down, John."

John says, "Hey, baby." He gives Shadow a quick kiss. "What's up, Jay?"

"Nothing at all. What's up with you?"

"I'm just here to mourn with the rest of the family, that's all. I'm gonna miss my man, Coach."

I say, "Me too." I look over at Shadow. She doesn't say a word. I know my sister, she's trying to size John up, trying to see if he overheard anything.

A few seconds later Shadow says, "Is everything okay with you?"

John says, "I'm sad about your uncle. Besides that everything's fine."

"Good."

John asks, "Jamal, you wanna go downtown to the In-Zone later?"

Shadow answers before I can even open my mouth. "No. Y'all are supposed to be mourning, not to mention the fact that it's Sunday. How are you gonna be around half-naked women at a time like this? John, you're a married man and you shouldn't even wanna be around all that temptation."

I look at Shadow with this I-know-you're-not-talking kind of look.

Before I can open my mouth she says, "Okay, go ahead. I hope y'all have fun looking at those half-naked women at the In-Zone."

I say, "We will."

John smiles. "Jamal's going through a lot. The In-Zone will be a good experience for him. It's not like it's a strip club."

Shadow says, "I know what it is."

My sister is crazy as shit. I can't believe she has the nerve to sweat John like she does. Her insecurity is a dead giveaway. She is doing wrong and acting like the victim at the same time. Women are a trip. Shadow was right about herself, she's no better than Jessie. As a matter of fact, they're both scandalous as hell and pretending to be so innocent.

Chapter 14

Jessie

*B**ryant residence, home of Jessica and Treyveon,* I love the sound of that. I'm not quite a Bryant yet, but if I play my cards right that won't be too far off.

Kim, Toya, and Rachael should be here any minute. The four of us grew up together. We're girlfriends and sisters for life, regardless of what we may go through in life. We try not to get caught up in trivial issues, like who called who last. My friends and I are so tuned in to each other that we can pick up wherever we left off, even if we don't talk for weeks. The three of them couldn't make it to the party last night and I didn't make a fuss. Toya and Rachael are biological sisters. Actually I think Toya is closer to me than Rachael. Kim has a lot in common with me and Toya. We all have a little ghetto in us, but Rachael is the most refined sista in the group.

When we were younger, Rachael was the leader of our little clique and I guess she's still the one we look up to the most. Rachael is a registered nurse, married with three kids. Kim is a single mother of one and she's an arrogant sales associate at Macy's. Toya is a stay-at-home mother of two and she occasionally does hair out of her apartment. I probably consider Toya my best friend out of the three because she's so down-to-earth.

Food is warming in the oven and Cristal is chilling by the bar. I can't wait to see how they react to all this. The house looks immaculate. You can hardly even tell we had a party here last night. More than that, I look incredible. That tiny lip swelling of mine is almost gone.

The doorbell chimes. This is it. I open the door to the screams and cheers of my girls.

Kim says, "Hey, Mrs. Bryant!"

Rachael yells, "Girl, you did it!"

Toya is crying and all I can make out is, "I love you!"

The three of them attack me with hugs. They're so happy for me and that makes me feel good. These are my girls and that is how it's supposed to be, all love.

I say, "Thanks, I'm so glad to see y'all. Come on in."

Toya says, "This house is bad. You got a maid yet?"

I say, "Not yet, but I will."

Kim says, "The house looks unbelievable and you look beautiful. We heard about what happened last night."

I say, "Just a little baby-mama drama. Alicia won't be showing her face around here anymore."

Toya says, "If we had been here none of that would have happened. You wanna go around Alicia's way and get some payback?"

I say, "Don't worry, I handled that shit last night. I had to whip out my little gun on 'em."

Rachael says, "I can't believe you. You're too old and you have too much class to deal with people like that."

Toya says, "Shut up, Rachael. You're crazy. Those little jealous hookers had it coming. They're just mad Jessie got Trey and this badass house. I'm glad one of us made it big. When I tell Derrick about this place we might be moving around here, too."

Rachael laughs and says, "I doubt that. These houses are very exclusive."

Toya asks, "So what you saying, we can't afford to live around here?"

Rachael says, "You know that saying, *You can take a nigga out of the ghetto, but you can't take the ghetto out of a nigga.* Okay, I can picture you and Derrick out here with your house all dirty, you going door to door borrowing shit, grass tall enough to hide a body, and Christmas lights up all year long."

We all laugh.

Toya says, "Alright, you got me, maybe we won't move around here."

Kim says, "Forget all that, Jessie, I'm so happy for you. Show us around."

As I show the girls around the house Rachael asks, "Did you hear about Jamal's uncle dying last night?"

The news hits me so hard that I stop dead in my tracks. "Oh my God!" Instantly I begin to cry. "I'm gonna miss him. Coach was a nice man."

Toya says, "He was a real weirdo if you ask me. I can't believe you're crying. I think it's funny how people always have nice things to say about dead people."

"He was a nice man. I feel sorry for Jamal. He loved his uncle and I feel bad because I know he's going through a lot. I bet he's dying inside and it's my fault. I need to call him."

Kim says, "Leave it alone. You're probably the last person he wants to talk to right now."

I say, "I know, but I still need to call him."

We stop walking through the house because I need to take a seat and get myself together. They all join me in the living room.

Toya says, "Don't worry about Jamal. Shit happens. I'm just glad you did your thing before you let him do something bad to you. He was probably messing around with some freak on the side, anyway. I don't know what makes you think he was so special or so different. All men are dogs."

Rachael says, "You're wrong about Jamal. You just don't know, that man loves Jessie with all his heart."

I smile a little because Jamal would be happy to hear Rachael stick up for him. Out of all my friends he always liked her the most.

I say, "Trust me, Jamal wasn't cheating on me. He really loved me and that's what hurts the most. I shouldn't have played with his emotions like that. If Jamal had somebody, he would never have put up with all my little games. I know he loved me."

Rachael says, "Jamal is a good man. Give him credit. He put a ring on Jessie's finger before Trey."

Toya says, "So what! You act like putting her up in this house was nothing." Toya turns to me and says, "Stop crying. Girl, you should be happy. Trey is gonna take good care of you. I know you're not going back to the bank. Are you?"

Still crying, I say, "No, my new job is keeping Trey happy."

Kim says, "Are you serious? I don't mean any harm, but that sounds boring. Not to mention chauvinistic."

Toya says, "Keeping a man happy is a good job. I wouldn't mind having a job like that."

Kim says, "This house is beautiful and all, but after a few months, Jessie is gonna go crazy hanging around here all day." Kim turns to me. "You're talking about hiring a maid, you won't have shit to do around here. You need a life. What do you wanna be when you grow up?"

I think, *Look who's talking. You just started working two years ago and you still don't have a career.* I don't say a word because I'm not in the mood for an argument. Kim has a lot of nerve to open her mouth. Her boyfriend, Kareem, was a hustler and took care of her and her daughter from the time Kim was in the eleventh grade right up until the time he was arrested and sentenced to twenty years. It's funny how fast people forget.

Rachael says, "Kim's right. You definitely need your own. You don't want a man doing everything for you. He can snatch all this away when he's good and ready. I know you don't wanna be left like that. This is Trey's way of controlling you, and a lot of men do that. Meanwhile, they're never home."

I've had about enough of them analyzing my life.

Toya says, "Y'all don't know what you're talking about. Stop hating on a sista. Take it from me, Jessie, you've got it made. You're a home-maker now. Black people always act like homemaking is a bad thing. I'm a homemaker and I'm proud. Lots of white women are home-makers too. They're always on game shows talking about 'Hi, I'm Amy and I'm a homemaker.' I'm not saying you should be the next Martha Stewart around here or nothing, just know that you're not unem-ployed. Being a homemaker is a job. You need to give Trey a few ba-bies and that will definitely keep you busy."

I say, "I don't know if I'm ready for kids."

I don't know if I'm ready for all this. My life was so simple at first and now I'm facing issues I never even considered. I guess the grass isn't greener on the other side after all. The money isn't greener ei-ther, there's just more.

I feel so bad for Jamal. I can't wait for my girlfriends to go home so I can call him. I'm sorry I invited them here. I thought they would be happy for me, but now I'm not so sure.

Instead of putting them out I pick myself up and assume the pas-sive role of a pleasant hostess. I decide to continue showing them the rest of the house.

Chapter 15

Jamal

The In-Zone is like a local version of Hooters for the brothas. They have just what a man needs when he is having relationship problems: *new women*. Plus, the food here is on point for real. This is the best spot for Buffalo wings, beautiful women, and cold beer. These are some of the finest waitresses in the business. The thing I love most about the waitresses is the variety. The In-Zone definitely doesn't discriminate. I mean, they've got lots of slender, medium, and full-figured beauties. Along with the waitresses I love the relaxed atmosphere. Dim lighting in the right spots definitely adds to its appeal. This place is finished in oak and brass and there's sports memorabilia everywhere. They have a pretty effective air-filtration system, so smoking isn't a problem. This place is far from your average sports bar or old smoky pool hall. They even have an attendant in the men's room. There are several wide-screen televisions showing different sporting events and comfortable leather recliners appropriately situated throughout the restaurant.

I'm not too good at shooting pool, so I mostly mess around with the arcade games. Every now and then groups of women come here just to check out the brothas. Sunday is probably the best day of the week to be here.

Church spots a woman and says, "Ooh, look at that chick over there. She gives my penis a tingling sensation."

I laugh and say, "You sure it's not your chlamydia flaring up?"

"Shut up, somebody might hear you. I shouldn't have told you about that."

"John is on the phone. Nobody heard that except you."

Church and I carry on some small talk as we continue to check out the ladies. Meanwhile, John is on the phone with a client on a Sunday evening. Either he is talking to a nervous client who is worried about losing money or he has a girlfriend and they're speaking in code.

As I look around the room at the ladies it makes me wonder what's on their minds. So many single women here hanging out, looking for love, companionship, and God knows what else.

Church must have been reading my mind because he asks, "What the hell are women really looking for in a man?"

I smile and say, "I was just sitting here wondering the same thing. Look at them over there. I guess they wanna be loved and respected. Not all women are looking for money. Every now and then you might find one who's willing to work with a brotha."

Church says, "Yeah, right. Where is she? I need a woman like that. Every woman I know is looking for a brotha with a job, car, house, and benefits."

John speaks into his cell phone. "Look, I gotta go. I'll talk to you tomorrow." He hangs up his phone, then looks at me and Church and says, "Sorry about that. Just one of my clients. Well, here's my answer to the million-dollar question. Women want communication. A good listener is important. Sometimes a woman just wants to be held. A nice massage and some really good cunnilingus."

I laugh and say, "As long as she can perform some really good fellatio, that's cool."

Church asks, "Can y'all speak English? I can't enjoy myself when I can't understand the conversation."

John and I laugh because we can't believe that Church is serious. He has no idea that we were simply talking about oral sex.

Church says, "There are three good-lookin' women over there, let's holla at them."

John says, "Man, only one is nice lookin'. The other one is okay and the last one is kinda ugly."

Church says, "You're trippin'. She's far from ugly."

I say, "Nah, I think ugly is right on her heels."

Church goes, "She's fine to me."

I say, "Forget about them. Look over there. That redbone is banging and her friend is finer than a mutha."

John laughs and says, "That's not a redbone, that's a white girl."

"My bad, but she's still fine."

John says, "She sure is. I'd take five hundred years of slavery out on
that ass."

We all laugh and give each other high fives. I'm not really laughing
because I agree. I'm really laughing because I think back to Shadow
and how she said that John's tongue is a lot bigger than his penis. He
has no idea what I'm laughing about. He just keeps right on talking
all loud about what he'd do with his little penis.

As the two girls pass by our table the three of us watch them like
they were supermodels going down a runway. They're dressed in hip-
hugger pants and jeans with tight shirts that show lots of cleavage and
their tight bellies. I hope they wore some warm coats because it's a little too cold outside to be dressed like that. Some women will do anything for attention and it's working, because a bunch of guys are
looking at them.

All of a sudden Church blurts out, "Excuse me, miss, what are you
looking for in a man?" He directs that question at the fine sista.

She asks, "What? What kind of pickup line is that?" She wrinkles
her pretty face in disbelief. She appears slightly offended that Church
even spoke to her. She rolls her eyes.

In an attempt to clean things up I say, "He means, what qualities
are women looking for in men? It's just a general question."

I'm not sure if she likes me better, but she smiles and says, "Okay,
that's a little better. I can tell you what we're not looking for in a man
like, ashy-ass elbows, crusty feet, breath so bad that it falls under the
category of mouth odor. I can't deal with a brotha with breath that
smells like infection."

We all laugh. Her little joke breaks the ice.

The wanna-be redbone says, "We're looking for respect, honesty,
romance, and good sex. There's one other important thing. I love a
man who understands that a woman can achieve an orgasm with
something as simple as a finger. Sometimes we can reach our climax
faster with a finger than with a penis."

Everyone has this where-the-hell-did-that-come-from kind of expression on our faces. However inappropriate that was I understand

exactly what she means. Sometimes a woman just wants to be touched. Sounds good to me. She's a nasty girl and I like that. Instead of speaking I just smile and nod, signifying that I completely understand. I look at Church and think, *Don't say a word, especially anything stupid. Just let it go.*

Church says, "That's easy. I can provide all that."

The sista says, "Oh, I forgot to mention that we like guys with good bodies. A few muscles here and there are nice."

This is going kind of good because the girls ask if they can sit at our table. Everybody does a quick introduction. The fine sista's name is Renee and the wanna-be redbone's name is Carla.

Carla continues where we left off. She looks at Church and says, "You gotta have a six-pack, sweetheart."

Church says, "Muscles are overrated. Forget a six-pack, I got a keg. Y'all need a big, strong, cuddly, *teddy bear* like me. Now how you like that, sweetheart?"

It's weird seeing my brother-in-law interact with women. It's not that he is saying so much right now, but he has the tendency to get a little too comfortable with the ladies. He never announces the fact that he's a married man. I never say a word, even though he has a very carefree demeanor around certain women in my presence. That shouldn't bother me, considering my sister has been cheating on him, but it does. I admired their relationship for so long and now I see that they're just as messed up as everybody else.

Renee and I end up exchanging phone numbers, but I have the feeling that we'll never use them. Church ends up with Carla's number, so I guess his big, strong, cuddly-teddy-bear line worked after all. John ends up with a shit-eating grin on his face. The look on his face tells me that he was kind of expecting a lot more. Stuff like that makes me wonder how he operates when he's out by himself. Maybe Shadow isn't completely wrong for doing what she did.

I had a good time hanging out with the fellas. I think back to Renee and consider calling her. Just as I think of her, my phone rings. Something inside tells me that this is probably her calling. I think, *Bingo.*

In a deep, sexy tone I say, "Hello."

"Hi, Jamal."

Instantly I think, *Mental note: In addition to a cell phone get caller ID.* I say, "Jessie!" If I sound surprised to hear her voice, it's not an act.

"I'm just calling to tell you how sorry I am to hear about Coach and to apologize for hurting you. I'm so sorry."

"I'm not wishing bad luck on you, but what goes around comes back around and when it comes back around you better watch out. You're gonna find yourself lonely." Jessie is awkwardly silent and probably hurting just as much as I am. I don't feel like acting like a jerk, so I say, "Let me stop. I'm a little bitter, but I'm not the type of person to hold a grudge. We can be friends, nothing more and nothing less."

Immediately she brightens up a little and says, "You're so sweet. God broke the mold when he made you."

Now I hear light sobbing on her end and I ask, "Are you crying?"

"Yeah."

"Why?"

"Because I'm so sorry for what I did to you. Why are you so nice to me?"

I think, *It's called killing you with kindness.* I say, "Being angry and hateful isn't healthy. I wanna live a long, happy life."

"You will 'cause you deserve it. How do you really feel about me? And be honest. Don't worry about hurting my feelings."

I pause for a few seconds trying to come up with something sensible that kind of sums up my feelings for her. "You can't be trusted." I think, *That wasn't real clever.* I decide to tell her something she doesn't know. "This is how I see things. As beautiful and peaceful as a dove is, you'd find a way to crush its little heart and make it cry."

That line is sure to have a mighty impact on her. Jessie does that awkward pause again. This time it's a little longer.

She asks, "Am I that vicious?"

Despite all the bad things she has done to me I still find it hard to be mean to her. "No, baby, I'm just teasing you. I'm hurting. I was just thinking that we could have been so beautiful together, husband and wife, so happy in love. It's not right how you betrayed my trust. I keep asking myself, why? I was true to you, ready to settle down. Why Trey of all people?"

"I don't know."

"You don't know? You can do better than that."

"I guess we just started to spend a little too much time together. He was such a slick talker and I liked his style. More than anything I found myself in financial trouble. I lost my car and I couldn't stand to lose anything else. You couldn't help me and I had nowhere else to turn."

I want to say, *Poor you, so that's why you gave him my loving, for money? What kind of prostitute are you?* Instead I say, "That's still no excuse, you should have claimed bankruptcy."

"And it takes money to do that too."

She's right, but that's still a poor excuse to have done what she did. Usually when I speak to Jessie I have some type of vision of her and her surroundings in mind. Right now everything is cloudy. That's a sign that our connection is fading. She is slowly turning into a memory.

Not being able to picture her bothers me, so I ask, "Where are you right now?"

"I'm at Trey's house in P. G. County."

That isn't at all the vision I wanted to create in my mind. She is probably laid out across Trey's bed in some fancy Victoria's Secret lingerie.

I ask, "So he's your man now?"

"I guess."

The thought of Jessie being Trey's live-in lover makes me jealous because already she is giving him more than she gave me. That hurts me to my heart, so right away I go to work on her insecurities.

I say, "Trey is probably out on the streets doing God knows what with God knows who. I bet he left you all alone and you're probably lying up in his bed talking to me right now. Am I right?"

In a sad tone she says, "Yeah, he's been gone all day. I hate being alone like this."

"What a shame. Guess you better get used to it. This is so funny because when you were mine I was always there for you. I miss you, but I'm different now. I'm undergoing some type of metamorphosis. Our entire relationship was like one big learning experience. You just helped make me a better person. You made me realize that your beauty is only skin-deep."

"I'm glad you learned from me. But my beauty is more than skin-deep. Sometimes you just have to look a little closer."

"Okay, I'll keep that in mind. Remember this, all that glitters ain't gold."

That must have really hit home because that awkward silence has just made its way between us again. This makes me realize that Jessie is truly sorry for what she did to me, but it's too late for apologies because I'm moving on. What's done is done and there's no changing that.

I purposely add a little insult to injury by saying, "I went to the In-Zone today with John and Church."

"You're trying to replace me already, huh?"

"Not quite. I'm just testing the waters a little. I got my big toe wet and I realized that the world is just one big cold ocean."

"I made it like that for you, right?"

"You said it, I didn't. I'm not sure what I'm gonna do. I've been told countless times that artists are loners, but not me. My love is meant to be shared."

"Share it then. Share it with as many people as you want. Good luck, Jamal. I hope you find what you're looking for." She pauses and I hear sniffles. "I don't know what else to say. I'm not gonna make it to Coach's funeral, I'll keep you and your family in my prayers."

"And I'll keep you in mine. Jessie, I don't think badly of you and I don't have any ill feelings toward you. No matter what, I'll always love you. Take care of that ring, okay?"

With more sniffles she says, "I will and I love you too. Good night."

I hang up the phone and let out a long sigh. Oh, that girl still has my heart. Trey'd better treat her right. If anything ever happens to her I'll come running and nothing could stop me. I should have told her that if she needs me I'll be there for her. She probably already knows that. It's hard to hate what I love. It's just not in me to hate. Guess that was the closure I was so desperately seeking; then again, maybe not.

I'm the type of guy that lives for love. There was a flame in my heart for Jessie, but she slowly extinguished the fire with her subtle changes and infidelity. Now my heart is just a smoldering heap of burnt-out emotions looking to be reignited.

Chapter 16

Jamal

The scent of fresh flowers, the sounds of my mourning family, the sight of my uncle's handcrafted redwood casket, and the feeling of deep sorrow all envelop my senses. Externally, I appear numb. I've been able to hold back any visible signs of pain. Tears want to pour from my eyes, but for some reason I can't cry. Internally, I'm an emotional wreck. At some point I might explode, but then again I'm a man, so my emotions are used to remaining bottled up. Eventually they'll just be reabsorbed by some natural internal mechanism.

My thoughts echo within my mind so loudly that it seems as if the entire world can hear. At the same time I feel like I'm narrating one of the most painful days of my life to a captive audience that couldn't possibly comprehend this surreal experience or my agony. For countless hours this day has played over and over in my head. Regardless, nothing could have prepared me for this moment, the closing of my uncle's casket.

The funeral is about to begin and the undertaker calls the family forward for a final viewing before he closes Coach's casket for the last time. Most funerals don't play out like this, but Grandma chose the order of the service. My eyes are fixed on the magnificent craftsmanship of the casket. My mind tries to venture off somewhere else, but I'm quickly reminded that the man lying in that casket is the only father figure I've ever known. He is the only man who truly dedicated time to making me the man I am today.

None of this seems real.

Grandma takes my hand and we proceed to the casket for our final viewing. John holds Shadow as she lets out a screeching moan and she becomes almost limp in his arms. In the background I hear someone mutter, "Pray, child, you gotta pray."

Someone else cries, "Hallelujah! Hallelujah!"

Reverend Thomas reminds us that this is a celebration of a life, not the mourning of a death, and in unison all of the Christians in the chapel begin to sing God's praises. This is somewhat comforting to me. Grandma arrives at the head of the casket first. She touches Coach and gently kisses him on the cheek. As I look down at my uncle I realize that he is no longer here. Never will I see him on earth again. As much as I love my uncle, something inside me won't allow me to kiss him. I can't help thinking about all the things his corpse has been through in preparation for this day, so I simply touch his hand. This is just a shell and hopefully his spirit is with God.

The undertaker has done a wonderful job of restoring some of Coach's natural appearance, but regardless of how well he looks today, nothing would please me more than knowing that Coach is truly at peace. I can't erase the thoughts of how much he suffered. He had so much on his mind and he took some deep secrets to his grave. Sometimes it's better that way. He really wanted to share what was on his mind, but he wasn't able to express his thoughts.

I feel a tap on my shoulder and to my surprise it's Church. I never even realized that he was here. He's right alongside the family where he belongs. I can tell by the expression on his face that he is hurting. We embrace like brothers.

John and Shadow stand before the casket. They should have remained seated, because Shadow is too hysterical to view the body. An usher comes over to assist John with Shadow. She needs to be escorted out of the chapel, but instead they simply return Shadow to her seat. I hate to say it, but that is nothing except a bad case of guilt that Shadow is dealing with. She appears very lethargic and just sits there moaning.

I step away from the casket and whisper to John, "I think you should take her outside for a minute."

He says, "She's fine."

John is so stupid. Shadow is nowhere near being fine. It's almost as if he is enjoying seeing his wife like this. He acts as if he wants her to get a full dose of this traumatic experience. I simply leave this situation up to John. He's Shadow's husband and I have to respect his wishes.

As long as this community exists, Coach will never die. The Edmondson Village community loved and respected him so much. They will surely keep his memory alive. The people from the department of recreation and parks sent flowers in the shapes of a basketball, a football, and a baseball. A few of Coach's team jerseys lie in the casket beside him. There's even a flower here from Trey, a giant bleeding heart made of roses. I hate him, but I like the fact that he didn't forget my uncle.

As I make my way back to my seat I glance around the chapel, seeing the faces of so many people from the neighborhood. There is standing room only because about a hundred kids took off from school to pay their final respects to their coach, Richard Bailey.

There are two people noticeably missing from this crowd, my mother and Aunt Hunk. Before I sit down I notice two correctional officers leading what appears to be a very neatly dressed man into the chapel. I gently nudge Grandma and she seems to perk up a bit. I'm kind of embarrassed, but I'm happy to see my aunt. Everything seems to stop and almost every head turns to watch as Aunt Hunk is led down the aisle in cuffs and chains. People watch in amazement as if she were some sort of fierce circus animal. Nevertheless, she still looks good in her dark shades and her black double-breasted men's suit. Her hair is cut close and tapered on the sides. Her shape-up is neater than mine. The closer she gets the stronger the scent of her Polo Sport cologne gets. Her nose is pierced, but I guess they didn't allow her to wear her nose ring. I can still see part of her neck tattoo even though her shirt is buttoned up tightly. She made it here just in time to view Coach's body before the undertaker closed the casket.

Aunt Hunk stops in front of the casket and smiles down at Coach. She gently kisses him on the cheek in the same manner in which Grandma did. Grandma tries to hug my aunt, but one of the correctional officers quickly informs her that Aunt Hunk isn't allowed to have contact with anyone, not even her mother.

One of my cousins from Virginia yells, "That's her mother and this is a funeral."

All I think is, *Please, God, don't let my crazy family start a riot in this chapel over something so petty.*

Aunt Hunk smiles and assures everyone that she's fine. I'm not fine because the thought of my mother not being here upsets me.

My grandmother's friend, Mrs. Pearl, starts the funeral with a reading from the Old Testament. Soon after that my cousin Donna sings "Going Up Yonder." She sings that song with everything she's got and almost everyone in the chapel is on their feet singing along. Now this seems like a real home-going service.

I can't really concentrate on anything because I keep thinking that Karen King is the sorriest woman in the world to ever carry the title *mother*. There is no excuse for her not being here today. Only God knows where she is right now. I'm sure she knows that Coach has passed because she has a way of keeping up with everything that happens here. It's not so much that she isn't here for Coach, it's more like she isn't here for me and Shadow. My mother knows how much we loved him. This would be a good time for me to let out all of my pain and frustration, but instead I just sit here and ask myself, *What's the point?*

Chapter 17

Jessie

I'm sure Jamal has no idea that I'm here today. I figured it was the least I could do considering I'm the blame for at least half of his grief. That was probably the saddest service I've ever attended. One of the saddest parts was seeing Jamal's aunt escorted in wearing cuffs and chains. Shadow is one of my least favorite people in the world, but seeing her in such a sad condition was enough to make me cry. It's hard dealing with the death of someone so close. Jamal looked as if he somehow found the strength to bear the pain. I'm sure he is hurting. It's not like him to hold his tears back. If he had seen me inside I wonder how he would have responded.

I didn't feel right greeting the family because the thought of them knowing about what I did to Jamal last week kept me away. It's hard for Trey to face the family and that's why he isn't here. At least his flowers arrived on time. Trey thought the world of Coach and he still loves Ms. Connie. There's no telling what she thinks of me. I pray to God that no one here today knows anything about how I hurt Jamal. Usually I'm the one who's there to pick Jamal up when he's down, the one who breathes life back into him, but now I'm the one who knocked him down and took his breath away all at the same time. If I had another chance, none of this would have happened. If I could do it over again I would be the best thing to ever happen to him. God, I'm so sorry for what I've done. I feel my eyes start to water again. I wish we could go back to the days in the park. Nobody else ever took me on picnics by the lake. Even in the face of all this pain, my mind takes me back to the days we used to share under the same shady tree, talking and laughing on a blanket.

Jamal tried teaching me how to enjoy the simple things in life, but I wanted the complex or what seemed like the unobtainable. Now I'm caught up and disillusioned by the fast life. All that time never realizing what a wonderful life I already had with Jamal. Trey gives all the things that he thinks I need, but all I really want now is for him to spend time with me. To most people that's a simple request, but to Trey it's almost impossible. In reality all I ever wanted was to feel needed and receive extra-special attention from someone. Trey has given me so many material possessions and very little of his time. He surprised me earlier this week by taking me to R&H Mercedes-Benz and buying me a brand-new CLK Coupe.

This has been one of the strangest weeks in my life. It's gone from ups and downs to tears and fears. My grandmother used to say, "Be careful what you pray for." That's so true. I prayed for the opportunity to be with Trey and now that it's come true, I'm still not truly happy. I'm attracted to him. He loves me, but he can't buy my love. Maybe he can earn it with a little sincerity. I thought it was possible to buy love and happiness, but I was so wrong.

Trey is extremely weird at times. He's hardly ever home and it's obvious where his heart is, in the streets. He has no real reason to stay away from me like he does. Trey swears up and down that I'm his one and only. He's out all hours of the night overseeing his operation because he can't trust his workers and that's why he's having Kev and Mike move to Baltimore. Hopefully that will help free him up a little.

The other night I dreamed of being near a beautiful, cool, crystal sea with white sand. In my dream I wasn't alone. The man in my dream wasn't Trey; instead it was Jamal. It's so funny how we don't miss what we had until it's gone. I swear Jamal is my destiny. As I slept I accidentally called out Jamal's name. Of all times, why did Trey have to be lying in bed next to me? I woke myself and slowly became conscious of where I was and what was going on. When I opened my eyes and gained some sort of focus in the hazy darkness, Trey was staring directly at me like he wanted to kill me.

In a vicious tone he said, "You need to get that nigga out your system."

As a chill ran through my body I said, "Excuse me, I was asleep and I don't know what you're talking about. You're scaring me staring at me like that."

"You just called out Jamal's name in my bed!"

"I'm sorry! I told you I was asleep!"

"Don't matter. He's still on your mind."

"I don't complain when you wake up kicking and screaming from your nightmares."

"That's different and you need to leave that alone. You know that shit is about my mother. You don't act like you love me. I still gotta use condoms with you and shit. What's up with that? Did you used to let Jamal go up in you raw?"

"I'm not even going to answer that."

"'Cause it's true."

"It's late, good night."

Too bad a simple good night wasn't enough for Trey's crazy ass. That fool went on all night rambling about how I treated Jamal compared to him. There is no way I'm having unprotected sex with a man I don't trust. This is my body and nobody is going to dictate to me how to use it. The last thing I remember hearing Trey say is, "Nobody will ever love you like I do."

That line was so tired that it put me to sleep.

Women holding flowers line the walkway leading to the hearse. Coach's casket leads the procession out the front door of the funeral home followed by the family. Jamal and Ms. Connie are the first two family members out the door. Shadow looks a little better, but she is still leaning heavily on John. I've only seen pictures of Jamal's mother, but I think I could pick her out of a crowd. As I scan the crowd, no one resembles her.

Jamal holds Ms. Connie close as they walk right by me. In a way, I'm glad they don't notice me. Shadow is too weary to notice me, but John shoots me a friendly smile. Even with all this grief around us, John still finds a way to remain cordial. Simply put, he's a big flirt, or should I say a wanna-be player? He needs to stop because Shadow is a good woman and she deserves better.

I make my way over to the family car just before Jamal and Ms. Connie get inside.

I softly say, "Ms. Connie, Jamal, I'm so sorry for your loss. God bless y'all."

Jamal gives me a strange look. It's not a surprised look or any familiar expression. He has a very flat effect. This is a strange demeanor for him.

Ms. Connie steps away from the family car and gives me the most heartfelt embrace.

She says, "Hi, Jessie, baby, I'm so glad you're here." She turns to Jamal and says, "I told you she wouldn't let us down."

She has no idea that less than a week ago I completely broke her grandson's heart. I think, *Praise the Lord.*

Ms. Connie turns back to me and says, "Jamal didn't think you were gonna make it. As a matter of fact he said you weren't coming at all. Do you wanna ride in the family car with us, honey?"

I look at Jamal and he still remains silent. Now I think this is his uncomfortable look he's displaying. I've known him long enough to know that he's disgusted with me.

Without hesitation I say, "No, thank you, ma'am. I have my car here."

Jamal gives me a little cheap smile and extends his hand. I give him my hand and he says, "Thanks for coming. We've gotta be at the cemetery by one o'clock."

"I understand, but can we talk for a minute? Can I give you a ride to the cemetery?"

Jamal goes, "I . . . I . . . my grandmother—"

Ms. Connie says, "Go 'head, I'm fine. I'll meet you two at the burial site."

Jamal gives his grandmother a quick hug and agrees to come with me. I can't believe my eyes. My heart almost skips a beat. I'm nervous and excited at the same time. In a strange way this is like meeting Jamal again for the first time. I pray for a positive outcome.

Chapter 18

Jamal

A gloomy autumn sky and blustery winds almost seem appropriate for a day like this. Not even sunshine could brighten this day. The thought of being in this brand-new Mercedes-Benz CLK 430 purchased with Trey's drug money brings me nothing but more anguish. I wish I could spoil a woman like this.

Why did I even agree to ride with Jessie? I don't know what to make of her. Sometimes my impression of her is that she is incapable of truly loving anyone. I define her as innocence tainted by pure evil and greed. Let me stop, she isn't that bad. Exaggeration is a sickness. Jessie is still a little sweetheart. Again, exaggeration is a sickness. No matter what, I'm still a captive of her seductive influence. She doesn't have to say much, because just being in her presence has a way of neutralizing my anger. After all this time I can't even put a label on this mind-boggling gift that she possesses. No matter what, she deserves a little credit just for being here today. She has done something that my mother didn't have the decency to do.

I say, "I really appreciate you coming out to show your respect."

"It's the least I could do. I really appreciate you not telling Ms. Connie about what happened between us."

"Trust me, that wasn't exactly for your benefit. What happened between us isn't one of my favorite topics for discussion."

"I understand and again I'm sorry. Did your mother make it to the funeral?"

"No, she didn't make it and I'm pissed at her." Jessie mentioning my mother angers me a little. I pause for a few seconds to think about what else Jessie said to me. "Please stop apologizing. It's okay. Because I can look at you and see that you're not happy, even with the nice ride. Let me give you a quick rundown on what I think is going on in your life. I bet Trey isn't giving you the attention you deserve and you feel really neglected. Except for the obvious material things he provides like this Benz, you don't get much from him. You don't trust him because he's probably never home and you think he's like all the other hustlers with a bunch of hoochies running behind him. That unavoidable feeling of 'am I being played?' lingers with you. Should I continue?"

As the funeral procession slowly creeps along to the cemetery, Jessie is silent. I must have really struck a nerve with all that rambling.

She slowly turns to me with tears in her eyes and says, "You know me so well, don't you?"

"And you know me just as well and I'm sure you can understand what I'm feeling."

"I understand. Do you think we can ever get back to where we used to be? I feel like you're my destiny. I still have my apartment. Do you wanna go by there so we can spend some time together?"

My eyes widen and now my face begins to frown because my mind can't seem to process the crazy message my ears just received. "What kind of game are you playing? You want me to cheat with you on the man you cheated on me with." I laugh. "Damn, you're confused. All I can say is if we end this day as friends, then that's a good thing."

There's something Jessie just doesn't understand or refuses to understand. Our relationship is seriously flawed. She violated the golden rule of any relationship. We've been through too much to ever get back to the way we used to be.

She says, "Is this your way of getting payback? Because if it is, it's working."

"It's not about payback. It's about me being a man and getting the respect I deserve. Can you understand that?"

"So, it's over between us?"

"You ended it when you messed up. Hello, remember that? Remember when you cheated on me? I love you, but sometimes I feel like you're totally oblivious to what you've done."

"I know exactly what I did. I'll just have to learn to deal with the situation I've created."

"See, that's what you asked for, so live with it and love it."

"I'm sorry I came out today."

"You're so spoiled. This time you can't get what you want. You had me, but I wasn't good enough. Now Trey is showing his true colors. I can't believe you thought Trey would actually be willing or able to spend quality time with you." I look at Jessie's hand and notice that she is still wearing my ring. Wow! I quickly remind myself that she is a master of the Jedi mind trick and this is just a low-down trick. "Please stop crying."

"This is a funeral and I'm supposed to cry. Nobody has to know the truth behind my tears."

We arrive at the Maryland Veterans Cemetery. The entrance is covered with trees and a tall cobblestone wall topped with hollow steel blocks. I was too deep in conversation with Jessie to even notice the enormous size of Coach's funeral procession. The line of vehicles come to a complete standstill as we enter the cemetery. This is without a doubt the largest funeral I've ever witnessed. For almost a mile down the road, all I can see are headlights and neon orange funeral stickers.

The cemetery appears to be a very well-maintained perpetual garden. We begin to move again. Cars have to double-park along the cemetery's narrow road. In the distance I see a bulldozer preparing a new grave. It seems as if this is just an endless landscape with so much undeveloped land.

Countless rows of flat white headstones line the cemetery. Jessie and I get out of the Benz and make our way to Coach's final resting place. I tighten my black wool dress coat as the blustery wind blows through the various types of trees and gives movement to the rows of miniature American flags standing at attention like well-disciplined soldiers. This is a perfect representation for these men of honor.

A large American flag drapes my uncle's casket. A few feet from the grave a soldier plays "Taps" on his bugle. There is a group of soldiers standing in formation waiting patiently for the next segment of the service to begin.

My heart is heavy and my head hangs low. To Jessie's surprise I take her by the hand as we join my family. In reality I find comfort in having her by my side right now. Nothing makes this easy, but this does help alter the perception of my pain. Although there are hundreds of people here, I feel that Jessie and I can still have somewhat of a candid conversation.

In a whisper just a few inches from Jessie's ear I say, "I noticed you're still wearing my ring. I like that, makes me think you still really want me."

In a whisper she answers, "I do. Glad you noticed. I never plan to take it off."

"What does Trey have to say about that?"

"He bitches all the time."

Softly I say, "Shhh! Watch your mouth. This is a funeral."

"Sorry, but there's nothing Trey can do except complain. I'm not taking it off. Destiny, remember?"

"I hear you. Anyway, if he was a real man he'd replace it. What's he afraid of?"

I guess Jessie doesn't want to discuss this topic any further, because she simply shakes her head and shrugs.

The soldiers fire a twenty-one-gun salute. The blast from the rifles resounds like thunder and seems to startle the crowd of mourners. To me it's the most outstanding salute to a hero. And Coach was truly a hero to many.

Two other soldiers fold the American flag that draped the casket with pride and distinction. They hand the flag to Grandma. I'm really proud because this all has played out better than Coach probably expected. We all place flowers on top of Coach's casket and Reverend Thomas says a final prayer.

As my family and friends disperse to their vehicles Jessie turns to me and says, "So, are you coming with me?"

Jessie has this look in her eyes that I usually find very irresistible. She resembles a sad little puppy. How can I say no to those puppy eyes?

"I can't. This is it, closure. I need to do something for myself. I need to see what else is out there for me. We'll always be friends. My number hasn't changed."

Jessie looks like she's having a problem processing the word *friends*.

For some strange reason I guess she thought I was going to give in to her again. I think, *I'm so sorry, baby.*

Jessie says, "Friends, I'm okay with that for now, but don't forget what I said."

"Destiny, I remember. Thanks again for coming out."

With tears in her eyes, Jessie simply says, "Uh-huh."

As I look into Jessie's eyes, my eyes get this stinging sensation that makes them water. Our familiar eye contact is slowly broken and Jessie begins to walk to her car. Not once does she look back. This seems so final. It's so hard to let her go. I take a deep breath. Something inside me wants to call her back and wipe away her tears, but I can't. A real man has to do certain things to survive, and to be honest, Jessie was killing me by being so selfish. She gave her body to another man, but I'll always love her.

My eyes focus on Jessie as she gets into her car and starts the engine. I dare a single tear to fall from my eyes. That tiny piece of bitterness in the bottom of my heart just dried up the smallest trace of a tear. That stinging sensation in my eyes is gone. I want to run over, grab her, hold her in my arms, let her go for a second, then shake some sense into her head all at the same time. Instead of doing something regretful, I just allow her to walk out of my life.

Chapter 19

Jessie

The bedroom door opens and it's Trey. I smell him. He's wearing CK One cologne. I'm wide awake. I've been lying here thinking about Jamal. He's so different now. He can be a cold bastard when he wants to. I'm powerless when it comes to persuading him like I used to. I even wore my engagement ring, hoping that it would spark something inside him. I honestly miss him, but I lied about never taking the engagement ring off. There's no way in hell I'd wear that ring around Trey, he would get so pissed off. It's bad enough that I still mention Jamal's name. That ring is safely tucked away in my jewelry box.

I was really touched at the funeral today. The service was carried out perfectly. Jamal was hurt that his mother didn't show up, but at least his aunt made it. Oh my God, that was a sight that I'll never forget. I thought I would die laughing when they escorted her crazy ass into the funeral home. At first it wasn't funny, but now that I look back, it's funny. Out of respect for Jamal's family and my life, I didn't laugh out loud.

Trey slowly creeps around the bedroom doing his routine stuff, like taking off his jewelry, taking out his wallet, unclipping his two-way, dropping his change on the dresser, and putting stacks of cash in his safe. I guess his tiptoeing around the room is supposed to be out of respect for me. Now, I hear voices from downstairs. The alarm clock reads 1:30 A.M. and this fool has the nerve to have company. He left this morning at 9:30. That's one hell of a workday. There is no way in hell he's just been working all day. I'm sure he was able to fit some pleasure in there somewhere. At first I was on cloud nine, but lately things around here haven't exactly been like seventh heaven.

Trey exits the bedroom.

Now it's time for me to do my routine thing. I know I'm wrong for doing this. Every night around this time I get out of bed and happen to find things like business cards and matchbooks from clubs. Of course I find money around the room, sometimes in and around Trey's wallet. If I knew the combination to his safe, I would open that bad boy right now. Trey gives me everything I ask for, but starting a rainy-day fund isn't a bad idea. I never know when he might decide to kick my ass to the curb without any cash. He has so much money he won't even miss it. For all I know his secretive ass is probably a millionaire.

In this house, there's no rest for the weary. Every night this week it's been the same thing, pleasant dreams about Jamal and nightmare after nightmare about Trey being tortured or murdered. That's what I get for watching the news every night before drifting off to sleep.

I'm really worried something bad is going to happen to Trey. Sometimes you can press your luck too far or go to the well one time too many. I'm sure that fool is downstairs tired as hell trying to entertain his friends. He's too busy being a bad boy to come up here and get some rest like a sensible man. Forget the nightmares because the sandman is calling me.

It's 2:15 A.M. and I'm awakened by the sounds of laughter and loud voices. I can't begin to imagine what's going on downstairs. I have to go see for myself.

The doors to the family room are wide open. Trey and four of his buddies are inside drinking Cristal, totally engrossed in a Play Station 2 game. I can't explain the fascination or fixation grown-ass men have with this overglorified toy. No one even notices me standing here.

Some bigheaded guy finally notices me. He looks at me all simple, as if his mouth is watering. He taps Trey on the arm and says, "Yo, your girl's at the door."

Trey says, "What's up, baby? We making too much noise?"

In a very seductive tone I say, "No, I was just upstairs missing you, wondering when you were coming to bed."

The bigheaded guy says, "Yo, if that was my girl, I'd put all y'all niggas outta here and I'd be upstairs gettin' busy for real."

Trey has this expression on his face like he wants his boy to shut up. His other boy says, "No doubt, I'd be gettin' real busy."

Now Trey looks me up and down. He nods. Trey looks as if he took those disrespectful remarks more as compliments. Usually he would get upset.

Trey twists his mouth, licks his lips, and says, "Yo, I swear y'all lucky y'all my boys, 'cause if not I'd slam both these bottles of Cris on ya' fuckin' heads for disrespecting my wife like that. Now apologize!" The two guys become very humble and apologize to me. Trey gives me a smile and says, "Jessie, don't pay these fools no attention. We got a Madden tournament going on, let me beat this fathead nigga and I'll be right up, a'ight?"

"Okay." I think, *Take your time. You wanna play with a toy, well, so do I. My toy gives me much more pleasure anyway, the kind I can really feel. What man doesn't enjoy sex?*

That's the last time I'm gonna be put on hold like that. I got more sex when I wasn't living here. If Trey can't give me what I need I'll just have to turn up the heat on Jamal a little more.

Trey says, "Oh yeah, they gonna spend the night. Think you can hook us up with some breakfast later this morning?"

Is that part of my job description? I guess that falls under keeping him happy, but what about him keeping me happy?

I put on the prettiest smile and say, "Sure, I'd be glad to put something nice together for you and your boys."

This is more or less a game to Trey. He's testing me to see how much more of his bullshit I'm willing to put up with. At some point we'll have to establish some boundaries.

I'm surprised Trey even considered bringing his boys here to spend the night. He can trust me, but he shouldn't trust them around his beautiful little wifey. Even though Trey threatened two of them, the other two haven't taken their eyes off me yet. I sound so conceited and I guess that's exactly why most women hate me.

Trey asks, "Why you still standing there? This is strictly for the fellas."

I must be some kind of freak because I'm enjoying the attention.

And I like the fact that Trey is jealous and becoming slightly irritated. He never even took the time to introduce me. I guess he doesn't want any of these clowns to get too familiar with me.

Trey says, "Okay, baby. You can go back to bed now. Get some rest for breakfast. We gonna be hungry again in a little bit."

I put on a pretty smile again and in a sexy tone I say, "Good night, guys."

They all sing out good night to me at the same time. I step away from the door. On my way back upstairs I stop long enough to hear their comments.

Trey says, "So what y'all really think of her?"

The bigheaded boy says with caution, "Definitely a dime."

I can tell his voice from the others.

One guy says, "She's fine as shit. I thought I was looking at Ashanti, Chilli, or one of those other fine-ass singers."

Another one goes, "I know you're killing that, son. She's like the finest thing I've ever seen you with."

Someone else says, "Yo, I swear you a lucky nigga. And she cooks, too."

Trey says, "Man, y'all need to stop trippin' and get back into this game."

I think, *Nah, you better stop trippin' and get back into this.*

I hate to be taken for granted. Even Trey's boys recognize that he's got a winner.

It's 4:00 A.M. and Trey decides to come upstairs. He has the nerve to just hop in the bed without a shower. I smell as fresh as a sweet summer breeze and he wants to put his nasty self in bed next to me after he's been out all day.

I say, "What are you doing?"

"Getting comfortable."

"Not smelling like old stale cologne. Please take a shower or something."

"Girl, I'm a grown man. If I wanna get in my bed stinking, I can. I'm tired."

"Well, I'm going down to one of the guest rooms then."

He quickly says, "A'ight, I'll take a shower."

Any other time Trey wouldn't have agreed so quickly. His boys are in the house and he doesn't want me wandering around the house unless everyone is in plain sight. Trey just proved two things to me without actually saying it. One, he's a very protective type of guy. Two, he hasn't been sleeping around, because I'm sure he would have hopped right in the shower without me saying a word. On second thought, he could have showered before coming home, so that second notion is dead.

Any female rolling with a hustler has to be two steps ahead at all times. I must be tired as hell because I'm thinking all kinds of stupid stuff.

Trey comes out of the bathroom wearing a towel.

He asks, "You still awake?"

"Yeah, got too much on my mind."

He looks concerned and asks, "Like what?"

"Like you and where you're at all day."

He takes a deep breath and has this here-we-go-again expression on his face. He says, "I'm out there making money trying to maintain all this, trying to keep you happy. Your little Benz wasn't free, you know?"

"I know, but that's not what I mean. I want us to spend more time together. I see less of you now that we live together. What's up with that?"

"Yo, I'm confused. I hope you don't think I'm out there trickin' with somebody else."

"No, it's not that."

"I'm just trying to make all the money I can while I'm still young. I ain't trying to do this shit five to ten years from now."

"This is all new to me. It's harder than I thought. It's just that every time you walk out that door I worry myself to death wondering if you're going to come back to me. I watch the news, I see and hear what's going on out there."

Trey smiles and says, "This is wild. Stop worrying. I never had anyone in my corner like this." He pauses. "When me and Alicia was together she hardly ever worried about me. As long as I kept her pockets stuffed, she didn't give a damn. Most women only seem to care about what a guy can give them in the form of cash and gifts. And you care about my time. That's wild."

"Spending time with you is what makes me happy. I can't even remember the last movie we saw together or when we've gone to a nice restaurant."

His smile quickly dissipates and is replaced with a serious expression. He says, "Look, you knew what you was getting yourself into."

"I thought things would change. I feel like I'm eating my favorite meal, but I can't taste a damn thing. When you're not around my life lacks a certain flavor."

Trey stands in front of me butt-naked, drying himself and talking. Whatever he's doing, it appears that he's making time to work out. His body is tight! He starts to rub his body down with a cocoa-butter-scented lotion. I kind of want to help, but I'm enjoying this. He looks funny being so expressive and naked at the same time.

He says, "I have to be out there like that sometimes. I'll try to do a little better. Let me be honest with you. I've never been in a real relationship before. My time has always been split between multiple women and working. This is new to me too."

He has a way of being sensitive and brutally honest. Those are two unique qualities that set him apart from the rest. I used to be one of those multiple women he mentioned. I still can't trust him and that's why I insist on him using a condom, just my way of looking out for myself.

He continues, "I'm committed to making this work. I'm sorry if the novelty is wearing off this relationship already. Sometimes for guys, it's like we're on the outside looking in. I'll try to see things from your perspective, a'ight?"

Trey gets into bed. We kiss and everything seems to be fine. That one kiss turns into multiple kisses all over my body. A certain wetness begins to emerge. Clitoral stimulation soon turns to penetration. Our body temperatures as well as the room temperature start to rise and our passion races, taking us to places we haven't been for far too long.

Screams of pleasure fill the room. Nothing's better than good make-up sex. We take out our frustration on each other.

Trey and I seem to have forgotten that we have houseguests. At this point we don't seem to care.

Chapter 20

Jamal

This is one of those dreaded sleepless nights. It's 4:45 A.M. and I keep finding myself drifting in and out of sleep, mostly out. Because of my drowsy state and the sheer darkness of my bedroom, everything is in a haze. Silence echoes all around me. Confusion clouds my perception of reality. My eyes begin to play tricks on me. Lines become shapes and soon shapes become vivid images.

At the foot of my bed appears a man sitting in a very relaxed manner as if he doesn't have a care in the world. I'm not at all startled. I'm more amazed than anything. I just keep reminding myself that this must be a dream. I laugh to myself because there is something familiar about this man.

He focuses on me, but remains silent. His face displays a silly grin and his clothes are clearly outdated. He's neatly dressed, but in 1970s fashion. That's when it hits me.

I ask, "Coach, is that you?"

He smiles and says, "Yeah, it's me. Who'd you think I was?"

"I wasn't sure."

At first I thought I was looking at Antonio Fargus, who played Huggy Bear on *Starsky and Hutch.* Coach always resembled him anyway.

He says, "When you go where I've been, you can come back looking like any version of your former self."

"And you choose the seventies version, huh?"

"That was my favorite time. I got the Fleetwood parked right outside. Wanna go for a ride?"

The thought of getting into a car with Coach gives me the creeps. "I don't think so."

He looks like I may have offended him a little. He says, "There's no need to fear me, Little Man."

No one has called me Little Man in years. That's what Coach used to call me when I was a kid. He used to call out, "Little Man and Shadow, stop running and making all that damn noise in here."

I feel that stinging feeling in my eyes and they start to tear. I think, *It's funny how we forget things.*

Coach says, "Ugh, aw, don't you go crying for me now. It's too late to get all sentimental and shit. If I was still alive I'd love to reminisce like we used to. How come you didn't cry for me at my funeral?"

"I couldn't cry then and I'm not gonna cry now. Actually, I'm happy for you. No more suffering, right?"

"I don't know about all that, but I'm here to let you know that I'm all right, Little Man."

He smiles and starts singing his favorite song, "Lean On Me." This is too weird and I want him to stop. Suddenly he stops singing. I'm not sure if he stops singing because he's tired of hearing himself or because this is my dream and I still have some type of control.

He says, "There's one thing that bothers me." Coach's happy face slowly turns pale and ghostlike. I continue to stare at him and witness the most frightening and hideous face anyone could ever imagine. In a very demonic and spine-chilling tone he says, "Your bitch of a mother didn't come to my funeral."

All of a sudden I hear a loud thump and glass shatter. I awaken out of breath and in a state of disarray, not knowing what's what. It's freezing in here. I click on my lamp and I can see my breath coming out of my mouth. I lie still trying to distinguish reality from my nightmare. That was a pretty disturbing dream, but it was just a dream. Somehow I think the loud noise was real.

I walk to the staircase in a sluggish manner. On my way up the stairs I notice a trace of light under the doorsill coming from the kitchen. When I open the door, Grandma is standing there wearing a robe and her fuzzy slippers sweeping up a broken punch bowl. Besides the broken punch bowl everything else appears okay.

I ask, "Grandma, you okay?"

"Yeah, I just dropped the punch bowl."

"Don't tell me you did a Florida Evans."

"What are you talking about?"

"You know. Damn! Damn! Damn! Then slam the punch bowl to the floor."

She laughs. "Stop being silly. You watch too much television. I was washing dishes and the bowl fell off the dish rack, that's all." She pauses for a second and smiles at me. "I got a big surprise in store for you in the morning."

"I'm already surprised. I can't believe you're up this time of morning."

"Something woke me up a few hours ago."

I hear footsteps coming down the steps. If it's Coach I'm about to run the hell up outta here.

A soft female voice says, "What's going on down here?"

Either I'm dreaming again or my eyes are playing a cruel trick on me, because Karen King has just stepped into this kitchen.

In a very casual way she says, "Hi, Jamal."

"Hi, Momma." It sounds so weird saying "momma." "It's been almost a year since we've seen each other and all you have to say is 'Hi, Jamal'?"

She laughs and says, "Boy, what did I tell you about calling me momma?" She points at my grandmother and says, "That's your mother right there. I keep telling you my name is Karen. Stop being so hardheaded and give me a hug."

Karen hasn't changed at all. She's still as pretty and crazy as ever. I swear my mother could double for Angela Bassett any day.

I say, "You look good. Where have you been? And why didn't you make it to Coach's funeral?"

"I'm staying with a friend up in Rhode Island. I'm still in school. I had class today and couldn't miss out even if it was my own funeral."

"Class? You should be a professor by now."

Grandma says, "Jamal, leave her alone. She just got here a few hours ago."

Grandma is protective because she's knows Momma ain't exactly in her right state of mind. She's been seeing a psychiatrist for the past couple of years.

"I don't know about y'all, but I'm dog tired. Time for me to head back upstairs. Jamal, we can talk about school in the morning over breakfast. I'm gonna get up early and make one fit for a king. Good night, y'all."

It's just after 11 A.M. and Grandma and I haven't seen a trace of my mother. Since my mother failed to fulfill her promise, Grandma is preparing that breakfast fit for a king. No big deal. Karen just happens to be one of those people who have a way of talking just to hear themselves spit out a bunch of nothing. My mother knew damn well she wasn't getting up this morning to make breakfast. As late as it is, McDonald's is even done serving breakfast.

My mother loves me, but just not the way nature intended a mother to love a son. That's just one of her idiosyncrasies. For years, regardless of whether my mother was present or not, Grandma always did the cooking around here, except the few times my mother tried to prepare meals. How can I forget her greasy deformed pancakes, her lopsided cake made from scratch that tasted like a giant biscuit, or her famous turkey that didn't need to be stuffed because it was already stuffed with something when she bought it? She meant well. Maybe it's a good thing Grandma is making breakfast.

Karen tried to be a good mother, but I think raising twins was just a little too overwhelming for her. Again, she meant well, but I thank God for my grandmother.

Back when I was about five years old I sat in Coach's Cadillac pretending that I was driving. Nobody knew I was even in the car. Back in those days you could leave your car doors unlocked and the windows down. Being the little badass I was, I did a *Dukes of Hazard* move and climbed in Coach's car through the window. I sat there pretending to drive, hopelessly trying to move a locked steering wheel and turn an ignition without a key. I turned knobs and pushed every little button in sight.

The ashtray caught my attention. I pulled out an old cigarette butt and pretended to smoke. Pretending wasn't good enough because inside that ashtray was a lighter. I had seen Coach light cigarettes thousands of times. I decided to do something I'd never seen Coach do before. Something about that little bright red heat coil of the lighter intrigued me and made me want to touch it.

The next thing I remember I was screaming like a little maniac, dropping the lighter inside the car, and running inside the house for my mother to do something to stop that excruciating pain. When my mother realized what had happened she panicked and ran to get my grandmother's help. Instantly Grandma went to the refrigerator and slapped some butter on it. The butter did nothing but add a buttery aroma to my burning flesh. In those days people thought that butter soothed burns. Wrong! That hurt so bad. It was soothing to me just to get some first aid and some TLC. My mother was a nervous wreck. She just stood there and watched.

There was the time when my mother poured alcohol on my knee abrasion. I wanted to kill her. The next time I skinned my knee Grandma tried to put peroxide on it and I almost fought her because I thought it would burn like the alcohol did. Grandma always knew how to make me feel better. When I ran into the wall and hit my head she smoothed my big Fred Flintstone knot down with a butter knife. That reminded me of how corner men put cold steel on boxers' lumpy faces. After getting the knife placed on the knot she would put ice on it.

In a short period of time my grandmother's parenting skills overshadowed my mother's. Shadow and I developed a special bond with Grandma that my mother resented. She really resented Coach trying to be a father figure to us. My grandfather had died before Shadow and I were born, so of course we never got the chance to meet him. All I know about him is that he loved his family, he had a bad heart, he loved the blues and Otis Redding, who he considered the greatest soul singer who ever lived.

Whenever Shadow and I would hear a bump in the night my mother would say, "That ain't nothing but Daddy." Hearing that from my mother was disturbing. Shadow and I didn't understand the concept of death, but we had enough sense to know that a person we couldn't see shouldn't be making strange sounds in the night. Grandma quickly explained to us that those sounds were just the house settling in the night.

My mother used to say, "I don't understand why this house always decides to settle at night. That's the craziest thing I've ever heard. It's a ghost in here."

From that point on we slept in Grandma's bedroom.

During terrible thunderstorms and blackouts we would rush to my grandmother's side to calm our fears. Shadow and I would sit quietly beside our grandmother while she read us stories by the light of a kerosene lamp. Any time a storm came we thought we had to turn off every electrical appliance in the house and sit quietly so the thunder and lightning couldn't find us.

Shadow and I saw my Grandma as our mother and looked at Karen as more of a big sister. Karen used to eat breakfast with us. We all ate cereal and watched cartoons. When we would run out of milk Karen would pour evaporated milk and water in our cereal, Shadow and I loved that. We were on the WIC program so there was no excuse for us to run out of milk, but we did because some days my mother would feed us cereal all day long. Those were mostly Sundays when Grandma was in church all day.

My mother was an adult, but still a teenage mother. Grandma bathed me and Shadow together until we started to notice some anatomical differences, and then she separated us. I usually had to use Shadow's leftover bathwater. Grandma called herself saving money that way. That's how poor people did things in those days. If I was lucky enough, sometimes Shadow would get my leftover bathwater. Most times it was the other way around because I was the dirtier of the two.

By no surprise I received most of the whippings. According to Grandma, she only beat me because she loved me. She always showed us unconditional love though. I'll never forget the birthday party Grandma gave me and Shadow at McDonald's. I felt like a rich kid for a day, but at the same time I felt guilty for having such a nice party. That was my first time seeing Ronald McDonald in person. I remember thinking, *He looks better on television. He needs to be in the hospital lookin' all sick and skinny at my party. He don't even sound like himself.*

Grandma used to try to get my mother involved in our care, but she was always reluctant. She used to say, "Wait a minute, I'm coming." I thought that was so cool not having to do something right away when your mother had just given you a direct order. I couldn't wait to say, "Wait a minute" to someone with authority. Regardless of the day or the time, my mother was too engrossed watching soap operas, *Soul Train, Good Times,* or whatever else was on television to take care of us. Soon all that got old. I remember some very heated arguments between my mother and Grandma. So much bad language was used, foul name after foul name was exchanged. One night it got so bad Coach had to come down and break them up. Things really got heated when Coach put his hands on my mother. He was simply trying to separate them before things got physical. Soon my mother's foul words were directed at Coach. As the days, weeks, and months went by my mother became more and more withdrawn from the family. One day she was gone and postcards started coming from all over the country and soon from overseas. In one postcard she mentioned that she had enrolled in college. That was the beginning of her strange cycle. I often think of that time as the beginning of the end. Although Shadow and I had our grandmother, we still needed our mother. We loved her, but we were too young to really know how to express that.

The most outstanding thing my mother did for me and Shadow when we were growing up was giving my grandmother tips on how to dress us. At first all of our tennis shoes came from the supermarket. Shadow and I were the last of the supermarket-tennis-shoe generation. We used to ride in the grocery cart and try on our shoes at the same time. We were so appreciative because all we knew was that we were getting new tennis shoes. I was five years old and to me there was no difference between those tennis shoes and brand-name shoes. I just thought getting any new pair of tennis shoes meant I was gonna be able to run faster.

We used to shop at Montgomery Ward, Kmart, and Sears, until my mother had some guy from down the street sell Grandma some stolen clothes at half price. This was our introduction to designer clothes and shoes. Shadow and I never knew those were stolen clothes. We thought that man just offered some type of door-to-door service selling nice clothes.

After breakfast I decide to go up to my mother's room to see what's up with her. She's staying in her old bedroom, which is the smallest of the four bedrooms upstairs. I knock on the door and she answers.

In a hoarse morning voice she asks, "Who is it?"

"It's Jamal."

"Come in."

I enter the room and the curtains are completely shut as if she fears sunlight. She's lying in bed in a fetal position with the covers over her head like a hood.

She slowly pulls the blanket from over her head, revealing a satin nightcap. She smiles and says, "Good morning, baby. I'm about to get up and get breakfast going."

By now I'm a little mad, but she's such a joke I have to laugh. My mother still looks young. God has blessed her with a youthful appearance. She definitely has my grandmother's genes.

I say, "You mean, good afternoon."

Her sleepy eyes widen and she says, "Don't tell me that! With these curtains closed I can't tell what time it is. I'm sorry for missing breakfast. Where's Mama?"

"She's downstairs cleaning up the kitchen."

"I guess she beat me to the kitchen. Is there any breakfast left?"

"Yep. We saved you some bacon and eggs. There might be a few cold pancakes left." I give her this strange look as if I'm trying to read her. Physically, she's the picture of good health, but mentally, the picture needs some obvious fine-tuning. "Momma, what's wrong with you?"

She says, "What did I tell you about that? Momma is downstairs. And what do you mean what's wrong with me?"

"Something's wrong. Like, why are you still in school after all these years?"

"Education is an endless journey and you should never forget that."

"I understand that and all, but it seems like you're scared of something. What are you hiding from? Are you afraid of the real world?"

I notice a package of birth control pills and a bottle of Prozac on the nightstand. No surprises there. I just think, *What a weird combination.* Momma is definitely a little disturbed and she's still in her child-bearing years.

She sits up in bed and says, "You really wanna know what's wrong with me? I'm gonna tell you what's been bothering me all these years." She pauses and repositions herself of the side of the bed, exposing her legs and feet. I'm almost scared to look at her feet. Her feet are nice. No corns, bunions, or hammer toes. Looks like she's had a recent pedicure.

My attention goes back to her face. I ask, "What? Tell me."

"I really wanna tell you what's been on my mind and troubling my heart all these years."

"If it's something to do with Grandma and how Shadow and I clung to her, I'm sorry."

"That just a tiny part of it. I'm glad you realized that hurt me."

There's a strange look in her eyes like she really wants to open up, but there's no way for her to express her problems or deep dark secrets without becoming an emotional wreck.

I say, "Whenever you're ready to talk I'm here for you. I love you and Shadow loves you too. She should be over later. We've both taken vacation time because there's a lot going on in our lives."

"Mine too. My life is really busy." She looks at her hands resting on her lap, then back at me. "I've seen and done so much in such a short time. My mind is full of knowledge that I'll probably never use, but just in case, it's there to be used. I'm proud of all of my accomplishments. I never even intended on going to college. When I left home I felt so inadequate. I needed a decent education to survive in a very elite sector of the world that most people only dream of, like on the soaps. My intellect and my appearance are what helped sustain me all these years. I have never once had a job, maybe an internship here and there, that's all. It's never been a money thing, but more about experience. I'm surrounded by rich people who love my company and I love them."

She should have said rich men who love her company. There she goes again saying a bunch of nothing. I've heard this same bull countless times.

"You know what, I'm glad you've enjoyed your life. Seems like you were always there for those other people who love you, but what about us? We love you too. What about us? You just left us."

She doesn't say a word. She just sits there with a blank expression. She's so brilliant, but she can't answer my simple question.

I say, "I'll see you later."

"Wait, don't leave me. I'm so sorry for leaving you and Shadow. I was young and didn't know any better. I hadn't seen anything. Now I can say that over the years, I've been to Africa, Asia, Europe, and South America many times. How many people can say that? My travels have truly made me a better person. I needed to get away. This wasn't a good environment for me to grow as a person."

"No excuse. What about us? We could have seen the world together, as a family. It was bad enough growing up without a father. You will never understand how hard it was growing up as a black man without a father. I really needed a father and more than that I needed a mother. If it weren't for Grandma and Coach I'm not sure where me and Shadow would be. All Coach ever tried to do was be a father figure to us and you even interfered with that."

"Don't even mention his sorry name to me."

"Why not?"

"I hate him. He's gone and I still hate him." She really begins to break down in tears. She shouts, "He got away with murder!"

"What?"

My mind goes back to Coach and that guilt he was dealing with. He must have confided in my mother at some point. He must have murdered someone close to her. Whoever it was must have been very special to her.

She looks over in the corner at this old La-Z-Boy recliner as if someone were sitting there. She says, "He committed a vicious crime."

"What did he do? Better yet, who did he kill?"

"He killed me!" Tears fall from her eyes. She puts her hands up to her mouth and begins to shake uncontrollably. My mother has really lost it. I'm afraid for her.

I pick up her Prozac and ask, "Did you take your medicine today?"

Grandma must have heard all the sobbing from downstairs. She steps into the bedroom and sees my mother all hysterical. She turns to me and asks, "What's going on up here? What did you say to upset her like that?"

I simply say, "I dunno."

Grandma knows a lot more about my mother's weakened mental state than I do. She asks, "Karen, what is it, baby?"

Momma says, "He stole my life . . . he stole my life." She looks as if she is completely gone. She begins to kick her feet a little. Her eyes look like she has seen a ghost.

Grandma asks, "Who? Who stole your life?"

Before she can answer I say, "I think she's talking about Coach."

Momma says, "I tried blocking all this out, but I can't anymore. I'm so tired of running and running, trying to find myself. No need to run anymore, he's gone now. I prayed that I'd see the day he died and now he's gone."

Grandma asks, "What you talking 'bout, girl? Tell me. You're having a panic attack. Calm down and tell me."

I say, "Take a deep breath and take your time."

Momma points at the old brown La-Z-Boy recliner and says, "That's the chair from the basement right there, isn't it?"

Grandma says, "Yeah. It was in the basement. I moved it up here 'cause Jamal needed space for his artwork."

My mother closes her eyes like she's trying to escape from this place, a place that has caused her some horrible and unforgettable pain. She takes a deep breath and says, "That's where it used to happen. He raped me. Coach raped me in that chair when it was in the basement."

Instantly my breath is taken away. My heart fills with empathy and is completely crushed at the same time. For now the earth stands still. I want to reverse time and take back my mother's last words because they're too hard and painful to believe. In all honesty, her words explain so much. A few sentences have just explained volumes.

Grandma screams, "Stop! Stop! Why are you making that up? Why would you say that about your uncle? He was a good man. He wouldn't hurt a fly."

Momma says, "Well, he hurt me! He hurt me, Momma!" She pauses and recollects her thoughts. "He always touched me and he finally took what he wanted when I was seventeen. I was still a virgin. What did you think my suicide attempts were all about? He raped me, Momma!"

I've never felt so empty in my life. I feel like I don't even know my family anymore. Every family has secrets, but this is too much.

Grandma cries out, "Oh, baby, I'm so sorry! I'm so sorry, I didn't know. I'm here for you."

Grandma drops to my mother's side and wraps her arms around her. I'm numb from head to toe, except for that stinging feeling in my eyes. It's probably the worst it's ever been. Finally, I just let it all go. All of my pent-up pain and frustration comes pouring out. I find an opening next to my grandmother and I hold my mother tight.

I say, "Nobody's gonna hurt you again. I'll never let anyone hurt you, I promise."

All I can think of is how selfish I was, pressuring my mother. I never knew her pain, but now I understand. I truly understand. That's the secret that Coach took to his grave. He tried to clear his conscience before he died. I hope that bastard burns in hell for what he did to my mother, for what he did to us. He's the reason she left.

One question remains. If my mother was seventeen when this rape occurred, who's my father? Nothing in my life can or will ever be the same. I ask, *God, who and what am I? I hope that story about my mother meeting my father at Fort Meade is true.*

Part II

A Taste of Honey

Chapter 21

Jamal

This has been one of the longest days of my life. Earlier I was full of evil thoughts and a vengeful type of hate. In my mind I formed a hit list with a dead man topping it. That makes no sense whatsoever, but it made me feel better. Now I understand why my mother was always lying in bed watching television trying to escape that awful situation that Coach created, his incestuous rage. I commend her on finding the strength and courage to actually escape from her tormentor and start a new life elsewhere. This almost puts an end to my abandonment issues.

Trey ended up being second on the list because he took my best friend and lover away, possibly changing the course of my entire life. But for all I know that could have been a blessing in disguise.

Jessie is third on my list. I'm on some type of emotional roller coaster when it comes to her. One minute I want to call her and say, "Let's forget the past and work on making a future together." But that can't happen because I can't ever look at her the same way. There will always be a serious trust issue there. As this emotional roller coaster moves from one extreme to the next, I want to love her and then again I wish there was a way that I could make her feel the same pain and embarrassment that she caused me.

My apartment isn't a place of peace and relaxation for me anymore because this is the place where my mother's innocence was stolen and that will forever stay on my mind. Knowing what happened down here gives me a weird feeling that I'm not sure I can ever adjust to. I think I actually hate being down here.

I ask God to give me the strength to accept the things I can't change. I'm tired of being angry and hurt. That's not my style at all.

I look down at Coach's old-fashioned cassette recorder sitting on my lap. Something tells me to pick this thing up again. I press the play button and silence fills the air. This is the point of the tape where Coach stopped singing "Lean On Me."

All of a sudden there's the sound of Coach clearing his voice. In a faint raspy tone he says, "Jamal, goddammit, boy, I messed up. I messed up real bad. If you're listening to this message right now that's means I'm long gone away from here. I'm gonna miss you, boy." There's a pause. "Lord have mercy on me for what I'm about to say. Regardless of how I say this, it will never sound sincere enough. I wanted to tell you certain things face-to-face, but it's just easier this way." He pauses. "I . . . I need you to understand that I didn't survive the war over there in Vietnam, I just came home, that's all. They sent me back home to be a dead man amongst the living. I thought I was invincible, but the war showed me different. I saw and experienced some weird shit over there. Everybody knew I wasn't right when I came back home. I went from the jungles of Vietnam straight to the streets of Baltimore without a cooldown period. They shouldn't have expected me to go back to a normal lifestyle so soon. Guess I needed some type of counseling or something. Back then it wasn't easy for me to admit that I had a problem. To be honest a major part of who I was died over there along with so many of my friends. I'm not trying to make excuses for what I've done. It's just that every man has another side to the image that the rest of the world sees, an evil side. The devil lives in every one of us. Years ago God told me not to worry, because I'm only responsible for half of the bad things I've done." He pauses, sounding like somehow his conscience has been cleansed. "How can I say this? I never meant to hurt your mother. God knows I loved that girl with all my heart." He begins to cry. "I loved her so much. She was my little cherry blossom, just as pure and innocent as she wanted to be. Karen was always a smart and quiet type of girl. I didn't want anybody to put their filthy hands on her. She needed to be protected, so I kept all those bad boys away, but I couldn't keep myself away." He cries with more intensity. "I hurt my little niece and I'm so sorry. God knows I am. The more time I spent with her the more I loved her. She was so beautiful and I ruined that. I hurt the person I loved the most and when I did that I couldn't stop until it was too late. I had gone all the way and there was no turning back from there. After I lost Freda I turned to your mother again to heal my pain, but by that time she was old enough to fight me off. I'm a sick man and I know it, sick in so many ways. And I deserve whatever God has planned for me. Kiss your mother for me and tell her how sorry I am. I wish I could have told her before it was too late. I want you to know that I never messed with none of those other kids in the neighborhood." There's a long pause. "I hope you found my will in my underwear drawer near my insurance papers. I'm leaving everything to you because there's a chance that you might be my son. You and Shadow might be mine and I know that hurts. Tell Shadow that I love her, but I didn't leave her anything because she's got John to take care of her. They've got so much and I just wanted to give you a helping hand. You were always like a son to me. Even if I'm not your father I always tried to love you and Shadow like I was. I hope you do something nice with my house and car. There's not much in my bank account, but enjoy. Tell Connie that I love her and I'm sorry for hurting her child like I did. Tell Hunk to get herself together and all y'all please pray for me. I just . . . just want redemption for my soul. I love you, son, and please don't hate me." The tape ends.

All I can do is sit here trying to accept, interpret, and digest Coach's message. This whole thing is too bizarre. I don't believe that Coach is my father or maybe I just refuse to accept it. I'm trying to find out if there is some type of hidden message behind the song "Lean On Me." I think Coach saw himself as a person everyone could lean on. The strange thing is that he saw himself as my mother's protector and he ended up being the one who violated her. He developed some type of weird obsession with her.

I don't know anything about a will. Once Grandma and I found Coach's insurance papers we left everything else intact. No one has been to his house since. My first notion was to turn down any of Coach's possessions, but I plan to sell whatever he left me right away. I don't want to live in his house or drive his car. I plan to give Shadow and Grandma part of whatever money I make from selling his junk. There's no way my mother would ever accept anything from Coach.

I feel like I'm going insane because I have no one to talk to. This isn't the type of problem you can discuss with just anybody.

Chapter 22

Jessie

Trey and I are on our way downtown to an upscale African-American restaurant called Britton's. Occasionally you might find a few hustlers there, especially on a night like this. This is one of their busiest nights and to my knowledge we don't have reservations, but Trey promised that he could get us a table right away.

Believe it or not, this is only my second time being out in public with Trey in the Escalade. A big, shiny, black chromed-out machine like this attracts lots of attention. I'm sitting up in the Escalade looking pretty and laid-back like I don't have a care in the world.

We pull up to the front door of Britton's to wait for a valet to park the truck. As we exit the truck all eyes seem to be on us and I love it. The butterflies in my stomach instantly take flight because I'm not used to all this attention. Although I try my best to act nonchalant, I can't hide my beautiful smile. It feels so good to be out with Trey like this. There's a small red carpet outside the entrance. The only thing missing now are the paparazzi taking pictures.

I notice a few girls giving me jealous stares and whispering to each other. I continue to smile and think, *Don't hate me 'cause I'm beautiful.*

Trey turns the Escalade over to the valet. He says, "Be real careful with this, my man."

The valet says, "No problem. I'll be real gentle with her."

"Don't think about going for a joyride, 'cause I memorized the mileage."

The valet laughs at Trey as if he's joking. Trey's facial expression tells me that he isn't joking and doesn't trust this guy with his truck.

I say, "Trey, stop worrying. He said he'd be gentle with her. I should be jealous. Would you act like that if you had to hand me over to another man for a few minutes?"

He laughs. "That would never happen and if it did, I'd have to hurt somebody for real."

As we walk toward the entrance I whisper, "Look at how these people are lookin' at us."

"You know you like this shit."

My smile widens.

Trey says, "Here, let's really give 'em something to look at."

Trey quickly pulls me toward him with one hand and lays a kiss on me. In my mind a flash goes off because this would make such a nice picture.

When we get inside I overhear the maitre d' tell a couple that there is a one-and-a-half-hour wait for a table and their smiles instantly turn to frowns.

The food here must be worth the wait, because they quickly change their expressions back to smiles and take a seat. The maitre d' spots Trey and signals for a waiter. He whispers something in the waiter's ear.

The maitre d' smiles and says, "Good evening, Mr. Bryant. Willie will show you two to your table. Enjoy!"

All of the people waiting for tables have this who-the-hell-are-they-supposed-to-be expressions on their faces.

I whisper to Trey, "So, I guess you've been here before, considering that guy knows your name."

He smiles and says. "Nah, see, what had happened was . . . I'm just kiddin'. Me and my boys eat here all the time."

"Yeah, right."

Trey thinks I'm stupid or something. He did have a matchbook from this place on the dresser the other night. This place is far too classy for him and his boys. I'm sure he's been here with a female or two.

There's only one empty table in the entire place, located in the rear dining room. Willie seats us and Trey orders a bottle of wine. This is how I've always dreamed of being treated.

I whisper, "Thank you."

"For what?"

"For giving me tonight. This is all I really wanted."

"Well, then you're easy to please."

"I'm not sure about all that. I think I let my girlfriends' little spiteful remarks get to me. They had the nerve to try and give me advice about us. They're not happy in their own relationships so I'd have to be a fool to listen to them."

"They don't know nothing about us. Don't let nobody try to tear us apart. People are gonna try to fill your head with all types of shit, but you don't have to listen."

"Nobody can turn me against you. Trust me, I know I have something special in you."

Trey smiles and says, "You better believe that and don't forget it." He laughs. "So, what you think of this place?"

"It's nice. Did you come here with Kev and Mike?"

"Yeah, by them being from New York and all, I knew they'd appreciate this good food."

"You haven't mentioned their names in a while. What's up with that?"

"Nothing. They're fine. You know I don't like to tell all my business."

"You can tell me. What's up?"

"Kev and Mike are helping me keep an eye on this clown in our crew named Derek. I don't trust that nigga no more. He was missing for about four days and didn't return none of my calls. I was trying to hit him on his cell and two-way like ten times a day, no responses. Then he finally decided to call me, talking about he was out of the country, down in the Caribbean with his girl. Right away I knew something wasn't right 'cause he's the type of nigga that likes to brag about wherever he's vacationing before and after the trip. When Derek got back he didn't have a lot to say. How's he just gonna go on vacation without telling me?"

"So what do you think that's about?"

"I think he got knocked by the feds and got lost in the shuffle. The feds found out who he worked for and now they're trying to set me up."

"It's time for you to make a change. We've got enough money to live comfortably for the rest of our lives."

Trey smiles and says, "Check you out, planning our future. Don't worry about us, no matter what, we gonna be all right. I'm definitely gonna make some moves in a minute. I just need a little more time."

"A little more time? That's why I keep having nightmares about you. I hope I'm wrong, but I think things are getting too risky."

"Everything's cool. We're here to have fun, not to talk business, so let's check out the menu before our waiter gets back."

The chef comes over to our table to personally introduce himself and he briefly goes over their specials. Our waiter patiently stands alongside the chef to take our orders. I've been to plenty of restaurants, but this is a new experience for me. This is absolutely VIP treatment.

After dinner Trey and I aren't up to going anywhere else, so we head straight home to burn off some calories.

A slow-jam CD of various artists echoes in the background as glowing candles softly light the master bath revealing the passion-filled image of two lovers exchanging pleasures. The wall behind us is mirrored and I can't keep from sneaking a peek at such a lovely sight. We're truly united. Physically and mentally connected. His shiny, wet, muscular brown skin combines with my all sensitive, shiny, wet, tight brown skin, just slipping and sliding, getting lost in each other. A kiss here and a kiss there. Intimate touches and caresses. Moans and screams. Pure intensity mixing with raw intensity, that's our love. It's breathtaking and spine-tingling. I'm really starting to enjoy this, starting to love it. I'm into this mind, body, and soul. If only every night could be like tonight.

All my stress and tension is slowly being released. With every motion my breathing intensifies and I get closer to ecstasy. Every muscle in my body seems to contract, then release. My head is so clear. My eyes are closed tightly and now I shiver with uncontrollable waves of pleasure. I begin to see vibrant colors blending at the speed of light and a quick image of Jamal that fades just as fast as it appears. I can't even think about him right now because I'm too busy thinking, *Heaven, oh, heaven must be like this!*

Chapter 23

Jamal

Somehow I had to get a grip because my thoughts had begun to slip deeper and deeper into the abyss of the dead man's evil deeds. On Saturday evening Grandma, Momma, and I sat down with Shadow and told her every detail of our family dilemma. Although Shadow took the news pretty hard, this entire ordeal has definitely brought us all closer together and has given us a deeper understanding of my mother's trials and tribulations. I finally found out the significance of the song "Lean On Me." Coach had it playing in the background when he did what he did to my mother. That sick bastard.

My mother surprised us by being so open and honest and sharing her horrific experience. No one asked her to relive her nightmare, but I guess she just felt like sharing. She spoke so openly that it made me uncomfortable at certain points. The women in my family have a way of forgetting that I'm around when their discussions get a little explicit. That's just one drawback of being the minority around here. We all agreed to keep this secret among ourselves. Shadow said that this was something too personal to share even with John.

The next morning I woke up scrutinizing my very existence. The thought of Coach being my father is enough to make me lose vital sleep for the rest of my life. As I shaved I really took a close look at myself in the mirror. I couldn't find a trace of a physical resemblance to Coach. Over a week ago I told Jessie that I was undergoing some type of metamorphosis and it's true. God is preparing me for something important, but I just can't figure out what.

As I looked in the mirror I closed my eyes to my living nightmare and I never want to speak on what Coach did to my mother again. Life is too short to dwell on something I have no power over, especially something that I can't change. Grandma's prayer worked.

I'm sure that there are people with problems ten times worse than mine, like a handicapped child, a heartbroken mother who just lost her only child, or a person newly diagnosed with an incurable disease. I don't have any problems.

Today is my first day back to work and this sounds strange coming out of my mouth, but it feels good to be back. Things are different around here and that includes the people. Mrs. Harvey looked incredibly busy when I entered the store. She didn't greet me with her usual hug, but Dennis did. It's not that I'm homophobic or anything, it's just that I tried to give him a handshake, half-hug thing and he turned it into a full hug. He told me how sorry he was about my uncle's death and how sorry he was about not making it to the funeral. Then he asked if we could talk privately. Of course that caused a little suspicion on my part because we've never talked in private unless there was a problem.

We head back to my office.

Dennis closes my office door behind him and says, "I wanted to talk to you about what you saw the other night."

"You don't have anything to worry about. You're an adult and who am I to question or judge your lifestyle? I promise not to mention it to anyone."

"Thanks, Jamal. I really don't want my mother to find out."

"Why not?"

"This is something you can't understand unless you've walked in my shoes. All my life I feared rejection. Every day is an ongoing battle to keep my life a secret."

"There are so many gay people coming out of the closet now. I think you'd be fine."

"Society isn't that accepting yet. There are homophobes everywhere."

"And there always will be. No matter what, you have to face your fears and be yourself. If people can't accept you for who you are, then you don't need them in your life."

"I just don't want to be labeled as a fag. I hate that word." He smiles and says, "Call me a bitch, sissy, punk, homo, or anything except fag."

I laugh and say, "I can't really relate, but you'll never have to worry about me calling you anything except Dennis, okay?"

"Thanks, Jamal. I didn't know you were so down-to-earth. I'm sorry for being such a jerk in the past."

"It's not a big deal. Anyway, I'm probably not as down-to-earth as you think I am." I feel the need to slip that in because the last thing I want to do is send mixed signals.

"Don't worry. I know you're not gay, if that's what you're implying." He pauses. "I think I wanna tell my mother about my lifestyle. I think it's time to come out of the closet and she'd be a good person to start with."

"That sounds like a plan."

"Can I bring her in here? Because I'd like for you to be around for moral support."

"Okay."

He knows I'm not gay, but I think he sees me as some type of liaison between gays and straights. Everybody has issues. I guess it can't hurt to help a brotha in need. Maybe God is working through me to help him.

Within a few minutes Dennis returns to my office with Mrs. Harvey. She enters my office with a puzzled expression on her face because she rarely sees me and Dennis talking.

She asks, "What are you two up to?"

I shrug as if I don't have a clue.

Dennis says, "Momma, I have something I need to tell you. And if you love me as much as I think you do, then you'll definitely understand."

She asks, "What is it?"

Dennis closes his eyes and puts his hands in a tight praying position. He takes a deep breath and quickly says, "Momma, I'm gay."

Mrs. Harvey gives Dennis a strange look and says, "Oh, baby. I thought you were going to tell me something I didn't already know."

I battle to hold my laughter inside because I'm supposed to be here for moral support. Dennis has this stupid surprised expression on his face because he thought he had been keeping a secret from his mother for years.

Mrs. Harvey says, "Baby, your father and I knew you were gay before you knew what gay was. Your homosexuality isn't so obvious. It's not like you're the most feminine guy in the world, but you're almost thirty-seven years old and the only time you ever brought a girl home was when you were four or five years old. That little girl used to bring her tea sets and dolls down to play with you. To be honest with you, Dennis, you enjoyed the dolls more than the little girl."

I burst out laughing. Dennis and Mrs. Harvey ignore me and keep talking.

Dennis says, "That's not the only time I brought a girl home. Let me see. There was . . . there was the time . . . the time when . . . You're right. I never brought a girl home."

"Regardless, you're still my son and I love you. Your father was a little disappointed, but it's been so long now that he's accepted it and probably doesn't give it much thought anymore. I'm sure other people know you're gay. You're always talking about these fierce females that no one has ever seen. You live alone with your cat and house-plants. Your favorite movie is *Mommy Dearest.* I think your favorite color is fuchsia. Your apartment is always neat and clean. You've got stacks of men's muscle magazines and you don't work out. Should I continue?"

Dennis smiles and says, "Okay, you're right. I guess I was already out of the closet and didn't realize it. Jamal, thanks for being a friend and sorry for being such a drama queen earlier."

"It's okay."

Dennis reaches over my desk and we shake hands. He turns around and hugs Mrs. Harvey, then exits my office.

Mrs. Harvey says, "Now that that's settled, let me update you on a major change around here. Your Thursday night art class has been taken over by another artist named James. I hope that's not a problem."

I think, *So that's what happens around here when you don't give people what they want. You get replaced. James must be giving you the attention I refused to provide.*

I say, "No, that's not a problem at all."

I'm not sure if she bought that last line. My facial expression said the exact opposite of my mouth. As soon as I stepped through the door this morning I could tell that something was different. Mrs. Harvey usually greets me with some type of physical contact or with her famous sex-starved stare. It's funny, but all of a sudden I miss her little flirting. Mrs. Harvey is just a regular boss now, strictly business. Oh well, there goes my dominatrix fantasy with the boss. She'd make the perfect mistress. What a weird image. I smile. I'm trippin'. I just realized something. I haven't had sex in a while and I'm horny.

Mrs. Harvey asks, "Jamal, are you okay?"

"Oh yeah. I'm fine."

"Sometimes you act like you have epilepsy or something."

"Nah, I just get lost in crazy thoughts."

Dennis knocks on my partially closed office door and sticks his head inside. He seems to be in a playful mood.

He says, "Ma, Regina Bishop is here to see you."

My stomach knots up at the mention of Ms. Bishop's name.

Mrs. Harvey says, "Where is she?"

Dennis pushes my door wide open, revealing the very beautiful Ms. Bishop. I feel as if an explosion just went off, because that's the kind of attention she draws. She exemplifies style, class, and sophistication.

Ms. Bishop says, "I'm right here, girl."

Damn, her presence makes me feel kind of insecure and intimidated. I'm completely caught off guard. Ms. Bishop slowly struts into my office. Her uniquely crafted antique diamond and pearl jewelry catches my attention. She has on some type of expensive-looking black designer pantsuit and her coat is draped over her right arm.

Regina Bishop is an art dealer and probably the most influential African American in the art world. Ms. Bishop is also the owner of a world-renowned art exhibit called the Umoja Collection, which features artists from the African diaspora. She's responsible for shaping the careers of countless numbers of prominent artists worldwide.

Mrs. Harvey and Ms. Bishop embrace like long-lost sisters meeting for the first time. Actually they've been best friends since childhood. They both grew up in the original Northwood community in northeast Baltimore.

Dennis walks away and these two stand in front of me conversing in my office as if I were invisible. I wish I were invisible because I'd be out of here in a second. Ms. Bishop suddenly stops talking because something steals her attention. She seems awestruck by my painting called the *Montage*. It's a very sensual painting that depicts an African-American orgy with nude models of varying shapes, sizes, and skin tones.

Ms. Bishop says, "Excuse me, but this is a unique piece. It's really an attention grabber." She walks up to the painting for a closer look, smiles, and adds, "Kind of mind-blowing even. Who's the artist?"

Mrs. Harvey turns to me and says, "I'm so sorry. Jamal, we were acting like you weren't even here."

Ms. Bishop looks at me and says, "I saw him and then again I didn't." I think, *What a snob.*

Mrs. Harvey says, "Regina, allow me to introduce the two of you. This is my fantasy lover, slash future store manager, slash artist extra- ordinaire, Jamal King."

Ms. Bishop cuts in and says, "Girl, you haven't changed a bit. Hello, Jamal, it's a pleasure meeting you. I like your style. And you . . . you're a very handsome young man."

I look her up and down and think, *I like your style too. You and your sexy little self.* Instead I say, "The pleasure's all mine. This is really an honor having you here like this, Ms. Bishop."

"Please call me Regina."

Regina looks around my office at some of my other paintings. She thumbs through a few on the floor. Besides a few paintings on the wall, my office is very impersonal. I never wanted to get too comfort- able here. That's all part of my potential wealth scheme: if I get too comfortable in my current position that's where I'll remain.

Regina says, "You have such raw talent and I absolutely mean that in a complimentary way."

I think, *We aims to please, missy.* I simply say, "Thank you. I'm glad you like what you see." I feel like a bum standing here in my Old Navy jeans and a Nautica T-shirt. This big silly *Jamal* name tag isn't helping either. Regina is so beautiful and extravagant that she makes me feel as if I'm ugly or something. I laugh to myself because I've never met anyone who has had this type of affect on me.

Regina says, "I do like what I see. I really do."

Ms. Harvey says, "I'm gonna leave the two of you alone to get better acquainted."

Neither of us says a word, we just maintain eye contact. As Mrs. Harvey leaves, Regina moves back and forth around my office observ- ing my paintings.

"Jamal, did you attend an art college?"

"No, I haven't quite gotten around to that yet."

"No need. It'd just be a waste of time. You're already exactly where you need to be. Why are you wasting your time working here?"

"I have to eat, you know."

"We need to talk. How does dinner tonight at the Bayou Blues Café sound?"

I smile and say, "That sounds real nice."

"Can you pick me up at the Hyatt at six-thirty?"

All of a sudden the embarrassing image of this sophisticated lady riding in my hoopty pops into my head.

I quickly say, "I can meet you at your hotel, but I don't think you'd like to ride in my car. It's a piece of junk."

"Don't be silly. I'm just a regular girl looking for a good time." She smiles and says, "I can't believe I said that out loud. A little business mixed with pleasure never hurt anyone, am I right?"

I can't believe she's flirting with me and just a minute ago I was invisible. "You're right."

"Oh, and please dress casual."

"Okay. By the way, I love your coat. Is that cashmere?"

"Yeah. Just like the song, 'Pink Cashmere.' A good friend of mine from New York designed it."

"I've never seen anything like it before."

That's a really nice touch and a bold artistic expression. I bet the coat cost a lot of money.

She says, "Stick with me and I'll show you lots of things you've never seen before. See you later, Jamal."

She gives me her suite number and continues to flirt with me. "I'll see you at six-thirty."

All I can do is smile and wave as Regina leaves my office. I'm so impressed I'm speechless. This is a dream come true. At first Regina seemed like such a snobbish diva type, but she's, as Dennis puts it, down-to-earth.

This morning my spirits and confidence were pretty low and tonight I'm having dinner with a woman who has won both an Essence Award and an NAACP Image Award.

I don't know why, but for some strange reason I expected my mother to become a regular part of my life. When I get home from work Grandma tells me that she begged my mother to stick around a little longer, especially with Thanksgiving being just a few days away. My mother is famous for making abrupt exits.

It's hard to understand what goes on in the mind of someone who has been through such a traumatic experience. All I know is that life goes on. I love my mother with all my heart, but I can't stop living my life because she chooses not to be a part of it.

Chapter 24

Jessie

Gunshots ring out from downstairs and my adrenaline completely takes over. Without hesitation or regard for my own safety I jump out of bed and race downstairs. The last thing I remember was being in bed watching *Fox 45 News*. They were broadcasting a report about two substantial drug busts executed throughout the city over the last few days. With these busts the Baltimore City Police Department recovered a combination of over twenty-five handguns, shotguns, and semiautomatic assault rifles. The police had the weapons proudly displayed on a long evidence table. On the same table alongside the weapons were twenty keys of cocaine with an average street value of over one million dollars.

When I get to the bottom of the steps the first thing I see is Trey lying facedown in a pool of blood. I scream for help and then I rush to his side. I put my head on his chest to listen for a heartbeat, but there's nothing. Luckily Trey's brother, Carlos, and another guy are here.

Carlos yells, "Jessie, hurry up, they went that way!"

For some reason I jump up like a fool and run toward the open front door as if there's something I can do to whoever did this to Trey. Hysteria has a way of making people react without thinking.

As I rush to the front door I hear a loud boom and then something zips past my right ear. When I turn to see what's going on Carlos has a gun aimed at me with the facial expression of a possessed killer.

He yells, "Yo, get her ass!"

Somehow I'm able to get out the front door and now I wish I had just stayed upstairs and headed to the safety room like Trey told me to do in situations like this. Carlos and his friend take off after me.

As I run down the driveway at full speed, bullets sail past my head. I know they want me dead, but my legs just won't cooperate. Each leg feels as if it weighs a ton and with each passing second they gradually become heavier and heavier. My feet begin stick to the ground as if they've been magnetized. Carlos and his friend jump on my back and tackle me to the ground. I feel their hands on my neck and shoulders and they call out my name. I close my eyes tight and start to fight for my life.

I hear Trey's voice say, "I'm here, baby, it's okay. Wake up. Jessie, wake up."

I open my eyes and tears stream down my face. Trey is a sight for sore eyes. He holds me in his arms and tells me that everything is okay. I hold him so tight it hurts.

My breathing calms a little and I say, "I'm so glad to see you. I just had the worst nightmare ever."

"What happened? Look at you, all crying and everything."

"I don't want to talk about it, because it was too real."

"It was that bad, huh?"

"Worse than bad, it was horrifying."

"Don't worry. I'm here, baby. Calm down. You're breathing like you were running."

"I was running and fighting too. What time is it?"

"Six forty-five."

"Is it morning?"

"It's still evening."

"Oh, you're home early. I must have fallen asleep watching the evening news."

"What you been doing all day?"

I laugh and say, "Nothing, just chillin'. I'm bored out of my mind doing nothing all day."

"Come on, let's go out tonight."

During the entire ride to the ESPN Zone I hold Trey's hand and lay my head on his shoulder. That dream really made me take a minute to think about what Trey really means to me. Now I know that I started to take him for granted. I was acting as if he were guaranteed to be by my side every day. If he was ever killed like in my dream I couldn't go on. I can't even tell him about my nightmare, because I fear talking about it just might make it come true.

I ask, "What's going on with your brother?"

"What makes you ask about him?"

"Haven't heard you mention anything about him in a while."

"He's good. He's still at Morgan and he stopped talking crazy. He doesn't have any desire to follow in my father's footsteps or mine."

"What changed all that?"

"One of his little partners was shot eight times on Baltimore and Hilton last week."

"Why didn't you tell me?"

"I hate talking about things like that."

"I didn't see it on the news."

"They don't show everything on the news. Just 'cause it's not on the news doesn't mean it didn't happen."

"When's the funeral?"

"Shorty survived. I guess God just wasn't ready for him."

"That's a miracle."

"I don't know about all that. He ended up losing a lot of blood and he lost a kidney. The boy had liver and intestinal damage and now he's gotta use a colostomy bag."

"Who'd he piss off?"

"I don't know, somebody who wasn't down for no Mickey Mouse bullshit. These young boys be out here wildin' out and these older thug-type niggas don't play."

"That's a hell of a wake-up call. I hate to ask this, but what will it take to wake you up?"

"Man, why you gonna say something like that? You always have a way of spoiling shit, trying to be all critical."

"I'm being critical because I love you. That's why I'm like this. Look around, Trey. Brothas out here are going down left and right. I had a dream your little brother and his friend took you out. How much money do you need and is it really worth it?"

"For real, I ain't gonna lie. I came home early because Five-O is shutting shit down. We had to move our stash house on North Avenue twice this week. I'm definitely feeling some pressure. Plus, I told you something is up with Derek. I don't want him around me at all 'cause I can't trust him."

"Who the hell can you trust?"

"Besides you, the only other people I can trust are my father, Kev, and Mike, and that's it. People have to earn my trust and that's not easy."

"Why do you trust Kev and Mike so much?"

"Because they're just like me. They're about business and they have a vision for the future. That's why I asked them to move down here. As a matter of fact I want us to go on this cruise with them and their girlfriends. If you wanna go, the cruise leaves from Miami on Friday."

"This week?"

"Yeah, the day after Thanksgiving."

"That's awful short notice, but that should be okay."

"Good 'cause I already booked us."

"Why'd you even bother to ask?"

Trey makes this stupid face. "I don't know, I was gonna surprise you at first."

"Uh-huh, you're trying to be slick. You weren't planning to take me at first. You were probably going to take one of your other girls. That's exactly what this trip is about."

"There you go with that again. I can't get over on you like that. This is what really happened."

I cut him off and say, "Yeah, slick, tell me what really happened."

He starts sweating. "I paid for the trip awhile back and it was originally supposed to be a getaway for me and my boys, but now we decided to invite our girls along." Trey wipes his forehead. "You're always two steps ahead and that's good."

"Yep, I learned that from you." I pause for a few seconds because there's something else on my mind. "I don't like the idea of you teaming up with Kev and Mike, because those two were already partners and they could easily double-cross you."

"See, you are learning from me. I already thought about that. When I take on new business partners I take things like that into consideration. Trust me, the way things are set up, they would never double-cross me. The only person I'm worried about right now is Derek."

"Well, the only thing I'm worried about is Thanksgiving because we don't have any plans."

"Do you want me to invite my father and Sharon over for dinner?"

"That'd be nice. I haven't seen your parents in over a month."

"That'll give you something to do tomorrow."

"I'll go out and get some new cookware and dinnerware."

Trey laughs and says, "While you're at it why don't you go get a new wardrobe for the cruise?"

He's joking, but I'm serious. "I already thought about that."

The thought of going on a cruise makes me smile even with Kev and Mike going along. I need a vacation to help put my mind at ease.

Chapter 25

Jamal

I arrive at Regina's suite at the Hyatt at 6:30. Being the diva she is, of course she isn't ready. Regina answers the door wearing a white monogrammed terry cloth robe and slippers. She has Mozart playing in the background and it's beautiful. I have to smile because for the first time in my life I actually consider Mozart beautiful. I'm sure it has a lot to do with the classy woman who chose the selection. Regina is already having an effect on my life. A little style and class never hurt anyone.

She offers me a drink to help me mellow out for this major production she's about to have me sit through. Regina starts telling me about a few of her successes and her life story in great detail as if we weren't going to be spending the rest of the evening together. She goes on telling me things that I already read about in magazines or on the bio page of her Web site. Regina briefly mentions her ex-husband, Stanley, and her twenty-three-year-old daughter, Kia. Soon her lengthy monologue turns into a much more interesting fashion show.

Regina changes in and out of several appealing outfits, none of which really suits the casual but sophisticated look she's trying to capture until her beige leather pantsuit and chocolate-colored blouse puts a huge smile on my face. The suit really complements her shape. Regina is a very sensual woman. I like the sexy way she moves and her body language. I can tell by the definition in her arms and legs that she's involved in some type of physical training program. She is the type of woman who seems to get better with age.

Regina and I are on I-83 North, headed toward I-695 en route to White Marsh Boulevard. We're about fifteen minutes from the Bayou Blues Café.

Throughout all the interviews and publicity Regina has received she has never revealed her age and I'd never ask. Mrs. Harvey is fifty-five, so my guess is that Regina is between fifty and fifty-five years of age.

Regina begins to drill me with tons of personal questions. I'm momentarily dazed because I can't take my eyes off her sexy beige leather pants and the contour of her thighs. Regina asks me the most dreaded question imaginable.

She says, "So, tell me about your parents. What do they do?"

I want to tell her that my mother is an award-winning criminal psychologist who has been married for over twenty-five years to my father, who heads a major corporation. Being the person I am, I can't lie. I'm who I am and that can't be changed.

I say, "My grandmother raised me and my twin sister. I've never met my father, and my mother . . . she lives in Rhode Island. She actually has degrees in law and psychology, but she isn't currently practicing either. She's kinda taking a hiatus from her hectic schedule."

Regina smiles and says, "There's nothing wrong with that. So, you're a twin, huh?"

"Yep."

"Your mother sounds impressive. Sorry you never met your father. My grandmother raised me too. My parents were together and all, but my grandmother happened to stay with us one summer and that summer turned into a lifetime. She stayed with us for years, right up until the time she died."

Regina and I go back and forth sharing our pasts until we arrive at the restaurant.

From our table we enjoy the sounds of a live blues band. The restaurant is kind of busy for a weeknight, especially the bar area. I guess the live band has attracted the majority of the crowd. Most of the patrons here are Caucasian and so is the band. This band is obviously a crowd favorite because the crowd is able to interact and sing right along.

I look around and say, "I remember when black people were more into blues."

"White audiences are the ones who keep blues artists' pockets filled. What do you know about blues, anyway?"

"I know enough about blues to know that those rookies up there can't touch John Lee Hooker, B.B. King, Muddy Waters, or Robert Johnson."

"Alright, you've proven your point. You know a little something. You seem like you'd be more into hip-hop and R & B."

"Actually I am, but let's just say I'm the type of person who can appreciate just about any category of music. As time moves on it's only natural for people's musical tastes to change. I guess music is becoming more universal. The color lines don't really exist anymore. Look at rap. Who would have thought one of the top-selling rappers would be a blond white kid?"

Regina laughs and says, "I happen to be a fan of pop music. You gotta respect N' Sync. I love Justin. The boy's got soul."

"Oh, no, not you too. I hear a lot of sistas say they love that guy. Actually, I think those boy bands pretend to be interested in sistas just to help boost their record sales."

Regina says, "Stop, you're hurting my heart talking like that. Let's talk about something else. What's your personal philosophy on art?"

"No one has ever asked me anything like that before. I'm just gonna give you the first answer that popped into my head. If I can see it, feel it, live it, then I can create it."

Regina looks as if that wasn't exactly the kind of answer she was looking for, but it'll do. She simply says, "Sounds good. What's your inspiration?"

"Life, love, interesting people, and my surroundings."

"You know a little something about the Umoja Collection, right?"

"Of course I know a little something about your world-renowned collection. I know that it's currently in South Africa. Your collection features over one hundred paintings and sculptures from twenty-five artists. Your collection has gotten all kinds of recognition for being in museums and galleries that had never featured black artists until you came along."

Regina smiles and cuts me off. "Blah, blah, blah . . . I've heard enough. You've got something brown on the tip of your nose." She laughs and says, "Just kiddin'."

That's a good sign. Regina is comfortable enough to joke around with me. She is starting to relax and let her hair down. There's a glowing look of happiness in her eyes. It's a major compliment to me that she can be so comfortable in my presence, and at the same time she helps to ease my inhibitions. Still I'm not ready to totally relax around her. The last thing I want to do is turn her off by being too comfortable or too familiar too soon, because we just met.

I smile, slowly nod, and say, "Alright, you got me with that, but honestly I wasn't brownnosing, just giving you your props."

"I know and I appreciate you recognizing my hard work. I was just being silly. How would you like to be one of my featured artists?"

Bells, whistles, lights, and sirens all go off in my head from hearing Regina's last statement. I don't think there's anything else she could have said that would make me happier.

I try to remain composed and say, "That'd be a dream come true."

"The collection will be back in the States next year and that's when I'd like to add some of your paintings to it."

"I don't know what to say. I can't find the words to explain how happy I am right now. Thank you so much for even considering me for your collection. You're unbelievable. And not only that, you're beautiful, intelligent, and very considerate. I'm sorry. Was I brownnosing again?"

Regina sips her wine, but it appears that she wants to laugh at the same time. She gives me a strange look and signals me with her hand to give her a second. She's fine, but at first I thought she was about to choke. I smile because she's so cute.

Regina swallows her wine, takes a breath, and quickly says, "I wasn't ready for that. You weren't brownnosing. I like hearing compliments like that. There's nothing better than a man who's willing to express himself. It's not every day that a young handsome guy like yourself showers me with such flattering remarks."

"That's hard for me to believe."

"You've got me feeling so good that I wanna dance."

I'm not much of a dancer. Occasionally I do a little something. The last time I danced I think my dance moves embarrassed Jessie half to death.

I look around and say, "Nobody's even dancing."

"They probably don't know how. Let's show these white folks how to dance to the blues."

"You might have to teach me a little something. I'll do my best, but don't hate me if I end up busting a few dance moves that have me looking like Carlton from the *Fresh Prince of Bel Air.*"

We laugh.

Regina leads me to the dance floor and soon our excitement and infectious energy spreads around the restaurant. Other couples follow our lead and begin to dance. The band loves the added energy and excitement that all the dancing brings.

Regina and I dance for a few songs. The best moment comes when the band plays an instrumental piece and Regina and I hold each other close. The lead guitarist plays a sweet melody that totally puts everyone within listening distance at ease.

After dinner Regina invites me back to her room, so we can share a few more personal thoughts and our views on art. She wants to toast our new partnership. Regina has had one drink too many, because we've already toasted to our partnership twice at the restaurant. Maybe it's just that she really enjoys my company or either she's just in the mood for some romance or a passionate sexual encounter. Whatever the case may be, I'm having a really good time. Almost nothing compares to the spontaneity of a first date.

To us it seems that age is nothing more than a number, because not once this evening has our age difference presented a problem. Actually we never even mentioned anything about age.

All that wine is starting to take effect on Regina. I have no plans of taking advantage of an inebriated sista, that's not my style at all. Regina tries to act as if the alcohol isn't having an affect on her by carrying on a regular conversation.

Regina and I stand together at the window, taking in this beautiful panoramic view of downtown Baltimore's skyline and the Inner Harbor.

She asks, "How do you promote your art?"

It looks as if she struggled to put that thought together and it damn near killed her to get it out of her mouth.

I act natural and try not to laugh. "I'm my own promoter. I sell my paintings at beauty salons, festivals, flea markets, over the Internet, local art shows, and just about anywhere else people allow me to."

"You need a corporate or an individual sponsor to get your work into art shows across the country. The fees for art shows are expensive and at the level you're at right now, you'd be lucky just to break even."

"That's true."

"I wanna help you in any way I can. I can make you a household name in the art world. After a little hype and one major exhibit you can pull in thousands of dollars in one night. I just want to inspire you. Can I do that?"

"Sure."

Regina silently sips her wine and continues looking down at the different shops and restaurants. I step away from the window and kick back on the sofa, casually sipping my wine while listening to Coltrane blow. In her silence, Regina makes her way closer to me. We make eye contact and our eyes become fixed in a seductive stare-down. To my surprise Regina slowly runs her soft hand and manicured nails down my face and around to my mouth. She runs her finger across my lips as if she loves the texture. I kiss her fingertip and slowly begin to mimic her actions. I run my index and middle fingertips across her lips and she kisses my fingertips. She slowly licks my index finger and then she gently inserts it into her mouth. She sucks it. Her mouth is warm and I love the fact that she takes her time as if we have an eternity to seduce each other.

We kiss and surprisingly her kiss makes me feel unfulfilled as I pull away. I felt nothing. Our first kiss is empty and meaningless. For some reason I wanted my heart to feel something. I have to keep in mind that this is probably nothing more than a one-night stand.

In an attempt to get a little more intimate and comfortable, Regina removes her leather jacket and unbuttons her blouse, revealing a chocolate-colored embroidered Victoria's Secret bra.

I refocus and say, "You're so sexy."

Regina says, "Ummmm," as she returns to sucking my index finger. "I don't usually do this type of thing on the first date, but you make me hot. I hope you don't feel like you're taking advantage of me, because I'm not drunk."

That makes me feel better about this whole situation. My eyes instantly focus on Regina's pants, my mind shifts to the thought of getting them off. Seconds later my free hand puts that thought into action. I unbutton Regina's pants and work the zipper downward. She lifts her bottom and with her right hand she helps guide her sexy leather pants down, revealing the matching chocolate-colored panties to her Victoria's Secret set.

Regina takes my middle finger inside her mouth and begins to suck it along with my index finder. She pulls them both out of her mouth and slowly licks them up and down. She damn near takes my breath away. Regina guides my hand down into her panties, stimulating her clitoris. I slide my fingers down a little lower and feel how wet she is. My middle finger penetrates her tight vagina while I continue to give her clitoral stimulation with my other hand.

I decide to penetrate her with both fingers. She squints her eyes and opens her mouth. "I can't take two fingers. Ooooooh!"

My fingers are kind of thick, but I say, "Yes, you can!"

I continue to give it to her and she says, "It feels good! Deeper!"

In a slow and deliberate motion, I gently give Regina a very pleasing and rhythmic internal massage. My fingers are like magic wands controlling and satisfying her soul. If only my eyes could see exactly where my fingers are submerged. Better yet, if only my penis could be where my fingers are right now.

At first Regina seemed to be levels above me and now I've dropped her down a few notches to my world and she's not complaining. She loves this. I remove her panties with my free hand. Regina lifts up slightly to unfasten her bra. Her eyes guide me to where she wants my mouth. I continue to please her with one hand and with the other I grab a handful of her right breast. I slowly glide my moist tongue around her erect nipple.

At this moment Regina doesn't seem to be able to verbalize anything. She moans. Her eyes have rolled back in her head and her body language lets me know that I'm doing her right. She crosses her legs and holds my hand in one spot and with her inner thighs she applies a viselike grip, adding incredible pressure to my hand and almost crushing it. As she reaches her climax, she quickly withdraws my fingers from inside her as if she doesn't want to be touched anymore.

I stare at her wishing I could share in her blissful state, but that seems far from happening tonight because Regina looks completely done. She slowly positions herself in a fetal position while caressing herself. I climb on top, kissing her right shoulder and cheek. Regina acts as if I'm no longer in the room.

I think, *What's up with that?*

All of her previous sexual energy has quickly turned to a blatant form of insensitivity. Somehow her satisfaction took precedence over everything.

Regina looks at me and says, "Thank you. I needed that. I really did."

I ask, "Are we done for the night?"

"It's late and I think we should call it a night."

I think, *What about me?* Instead of saying what I think I start to undress myself in hopes of reversing this unpleasant outcome that has played out. Regina gives me a funny stare.

I say, "I have a condom." I reach for my wallet and pull it out. I flash it in front of her like I'm doing a condom ad. "Trojan, the best on the market."

"I'm sorry, Jamal. Not tonight. I usually don't go this far on a first date, I swear."

"Let me show you something."

I take Regina's hand and guide it to my erection. This proves to be a very awkward moment for her because when her hand gets close to me she acts as if she's afraid to touch me. Her hand begins to tighten and cripple up as if she's instantly struck with a severe case of rheumatoid arthritis. I can't quite understand what happened here.

Regina says, "I can't."

"Try. What happened here? At first you were all pumped and once you got your release everything came to a screeching halt. That's not fair to me."

This is a different type of experience for me and I'm not sure where this is headed. Now I'm afraid of offending the woman who possibly holds the key to my future.

Regina's tensed facial expression quickly turns to a smile. She says, "Poor baby, I'm sorry. I have a tendency to be a little selfish sometimes."

Regina pulls me in close to her and gives me a quick peck on the lips and then holds me in her arms as if she is trying to console me.

She says, "I don't mean to leave you hanging like this. I'll have to satisfy you another night. If you'd like, you can take a cold shower here and if you're tired you're more than welcome to stay. This sofa is a bed, you know?"

She still doesn't get the point.

"Yeah, I figured this was a sleeper." I pause for a second. "You're a trip. If you can't join me for that shower or if we can't sleep in the same bed, I honestly don't see the point of me staying the night."

"You're right. There I go ruining things between us already. I have a bad habit of mixing business with pleasure. Don't hate me."

I laugh and say, "No. I can't hate you. I'm looking forward to working with you."

"So am I. I have an early flight, so can we call it a night? I promise to stay in touch. Look, we'll have plenty of opportunities to make up for tonight."

Regina's sincerity calms me down. We exchange contact information, kiss, and say good night.

On my way home all I keep thinking about is Regina and how sexy she was, all that sweetness gone to waste. My mind goes back to the moment of our first kiss and that empty feeling I felt. I'm not sure what that was about. Usually a fine woman like Regina would have given me sensations throughout my body. She looks nice and all, but she was definitely lacking something.

Regina said she always had a problem mixing business with pleasure and that almost proved to be a dangerous mixture. I briefly think of all the other male artists that came before me. I'm sure I'm not the first to get a little intimate with her. I thought about how I could possibly have ruined my art career in its infancy. A woman with Regina's influence could easily turn my name into mud.

My little encounter with Regina proved to be an enlightening experience. In a lot of ways I overestimated her and in other ways I totally underestimated her. She's a wealthy woman who felt comfortable in my hoopty and that's a rare find. Regina is a good woman and all, but I hate a selfish lover. Regardless of what happened I still look forward to working with her. A chance like this doesn't come along too often and I plan to take full advantage of it. Most times making it big is all about who you know, being in the right place at the right time, and the right hype. I'm sure there are other artists out there with twice the talent of mine and they might be twice as deserving of this opportunity, but this is all mine. That's just the way things work out and I thank God.

Chapter 26

Jamal

When I arrived at work this morning Mrs. Harvey rushed to my office and bombarded me with all types of questions about my date with Regina. She asked questions that I was sure she could already answer on her own because Regina had called her from her plane just before I arrived. I think Mrs. Harvey wanted to hear me answer the same questions, hoping I would add in a few new details. Nosey people have all kinds of little tricks when it comes to getting the inside scoop. In reality there wasn't much of a scoop. Mrs. Harvey congratulated me for landing a spot in the Umoja Collection. I thanked her for the connection and for putting everything in motion.

A few minutes later Regina called me apologizing again for last night. She had just arrived in Atlanta. She told me that she was in the process of getting a domain name for my new Web site. Regina asked me to take about twenty photographs of my best paintings and sculptures to send to her so she could post them on my Web site.

Meeting Regina was truly a blessing and the thought of having a booming art career makes me want to do something impulsive, like quit my job and paint for the rest of my life. I haven't even made a cent and I'm ready to start planning major moves. More than anything it's good to have someone who believes in me and who's willing to back me. Regina must see some serious potential in me, because she's about to invest a lot of money in my future.

Regina is such an animated person. She and I talked about art and became excited from it as if we were having phone sex. She asked me to close my eyes and imagine my first big art show at a gallery. Regina kept emphasizing that this is the start of something big. She said there would be hundreds of wealthy people at the gallery willing to pay outrageous amounts of money just to say that they were among the first to own one of my original pieces. She described the gallery so perfectly that I could see a room full of rich people decked out in formal attire. I could hear the tapping of champagne glasses toasting my achievement and see photographers taking my picture for the arts-and-entertainment section of the newspaper.

Regina said she was having a contract, cell phone, and laptop computer sent out to me within the next couple of days.

In all actuality, my new partner isn't doing all this just because she likes me, she is getting a major commission from all my sales. Regina definitely deserves to be properly compensated since she's the one financing and directing all the business my way. Without Regina my art career would probably remain right where it is, the local art scene.

Regina was an artist herself until her love of collecting art quickly outweighed her desire to create art. Collecting art was in her blood. The Umoja Collection was originally her grandfather's. After his death in the late 1980s, she inherited the rare collection and began to add new artists as it gained recognition.

It's late evening and I just had a relaxing hot shower. I'm hungry as hell, but I'm not in the mood for a plate of Grandma's hog maws and chitterlings with black-eyed peas and corn bread. Her cooking has hit a serious rut. Somehow she lost track of her usually appetizing meal plan. I don't know what's up with the new menu. I haven't eaten hog maws and chitterlings in years. Last night she made liver and onions, the night before pig feet, and now hog maws and chitterlings. Grandma might make a big ole pot of pinto beans and ham hocks for dinner tomorrow. I have to go to the supermarket, McDonald's, or somewhere.

On my way to the supermarket I speed through the intersection, barely avoiding getting my picture taken by one of those stupid red-light cameras. I hate the fact that we have those cameras at almost every major intersection in my neighborhood. Nevertheless, I still love my neighborhood. Just like every other ghetto it's nothing more that a huge mosaic, blending shapes and colors. The people and backgrounds all come together perfectly, forming a beautiful abstract image.

As I approach the next intersection I notice a panhandler. This is an entirely different breed of panhandler. He has abandoned his typical WILL WORK FOR FOOD sign and has resorted to standing on a median strip holding a huge paragraph written on cardboard with far too many words for the average passerby to read. I keep my eyes focused straight ahead hoping this guy keeps moving to the next car. I'd rather donate money to a homeless shelter than contribute to his alcohol or drug habit. I laugh at myself because I sound like a snobbish young urban professional with that condescending attitude and I'm far from that. I beep my horn and signal for the panhandler to come over to my car.

I hand him a dollar and say, "Here you go, brother. Put that to some good use."

As he looks down at the dollar I wait to hear a sarcastic remark, but instead he says, "Thank you. Thank you so much. Something good is gonna happen to you for helping me. Have a blessed day."

I smile, roll up my window, and proceed through the intersection. At other intersections around the city there are Mexicans selling roses, recovering addicts selling M&Ms and handing out treatment literature, and Muslims selling bean pies and *The Final Call* newspaper. Baltimore is changing, but pretty much remains a segregated city.

I end up going to Metro Food Market on Baltimore National Pike. I'm glad I stopped here, because the place is full of gorgeous women. I notice attractive women of all ages.

That old song "Holding Back the Years" by Simply Red is playing over the intercom system. Hearing good music over the intercom makes shopping here a pleasant experience.

This is the first time I have thought of the supermarket as a pickup spot. As I make my way down the aisles I pay more attention to the music and the women than to filling my shopping cart. It's hard to keep my mind on what I'm actually here for. I start to pick up a few things. I don't have a clue about what to make for dinner. Soon my cart is loaded with a big bag of Skittles, Breyer's yogurt, raisin granola bars, bananas, apples, turkey burgers, chicken strips, and boneless, skinless chicken breasts. Now I'm headed down the cereal aisle. The Frosted Flakes boxes catch my attention.

I love this market. Now they're playing "Groove With You" by the

Isley Brothers over the intercom system. Everybody in the market is straight-up grooving to the Isleys.

All of a sudden I feel a shopping cart crash directly into my right Achilles' tendon and the pain radiates up the back of my leg. I close my eyes in agony and take a deep breath trying to calm myself down enough to avoid slapping the mess out of the person who hit me with their cart.

Before I even turn around the sweetest voice says, "Excuse me. I'm so sorry. Are you okay?"

As soon as I turn around and lay eyes on the beauty in front of me, my anger is instantly neutralized. This woman has a very powerful and familiar aura about her that seems to summon my soul. Every inch of me is drawn toward her. Her eyes are hypnotic and her lips look as if they're made for kissing. They're full, perfectly shaped, and moist. It's almost as if I've known her from a past life. She has such a glow that her beauty gradually blinds my eyes and somewhat numbs my mind. As my eyes scan her face and body, my mind searches through millions of mental photographs and mental notes trying to match a name to go along with this beautiful face. Within seconds I come up with Jillian Smith. She's still as beautiful as ever, but she's made some very noticeable changes to her appearance. Jillian has shed her baby fat. She has a look of maturity with curves and a certain thickness that any man could appreciate.

I say, "Jillian!" I give her my best smile and say, "Hey, girl."

She returns this cover-girl smile. "Oh my God, Jamal King!"

Jillian and I are taking up precious space in the aisle, but neither of us cares. We embrace and she feels so good in my arms that I don't want to let go. I don't want to come off like some type of weirdo or pervert, so I gradually let go after a few seconds of feeling her body pressed against mine and taking in her lovely scent.

I say, "I can't believe this."

"Neither can I. I'm so embarrassed for running into you with my cart like that. I know that hurt."

"Nah, I'm fine. How have you been? You're looking extra good."

"So are you. Looking like Tyrese. It's so good to see you. I can't believe we haven't seen each other since high school."

"You won't believe it, but I've thought about you a lot since then."

"Really?"

"Really."

Jillian says, "It took me a minute to realize who you were. I was so busy listening to the music that I lost track of how close my cart was to you."

"It's okay. These classic slow jams are nice and they have the tendency to mess you up. I think everybody in here was in a trance listening to this baby-making music."

"The Isleys have that type of effect."

We pause, staring each other up and down, and then we go back to this hypnotic eye contact. Jillian has the whitest and straightest teeth, a real Hollywood type of smile.

Finally I ask, "What do you do for a living? Are you single, married, or what?"

"I'm single and I work for Pfizer Pharmaceuticals as a pharmaceutical rep. So, what do you do? I bet you're married."

"I'm single and I'm an artist and an assistant manager at Peaches' Arts and Crafts downtown. My art career is about to blow up for real. I'm going to be working with this woman who's gonna be like my agent, publicist, and sponsor all in one. I'm gonna be a featured artist in her art collection next year."

"Congratulations! I'm happy for you. It's nice to hear that one of my former classmates is doing well. Lord knows, too many of them made bad choices after high school. I can't tell you how happy I am for you. I remember some of your artwork from back in the day."

"It's a lot better now. You seem to be doing alright for yourself. A pharmaceutical rep, that's a good career."

"It's pretty good. I've been with the company for three and a half years and I love my job. Not to say that it doesn't get a little monotonous at times, because it does. If I'm not in some sort of training, my job consists of the same routine day in and day out. My schedule is like a never-ending cycle of visiting the same physicians and promoting the same drugs." She laughs. "On the other hand the salary is very competitive. I have a company car, a Ford Taurus, which isn't exactly the fanciest ride on the streets, but at least it saves me from a car payment and insurance. Also, the position came with stock options, a 401k, and a nice expense account to wine and dine my physicians."

"Damn, I told you that was a good career. I'm proud of you." I pause for a second. "I'm not gonna take up too much more of your time, but I'd love to get your number, so we can hook up and continue this conversation."

"Sure."

"What are you doing for dinner tonight?"

"I was about to ask you to come over to my place, so I could cook something special for you."

"I hope you're serious, because I'd love that."

"I'm serious."

"We have a lot of catching up to do."

After we finish shopping I follow Jillian to her house. Meeting up with her again has me more excited than I've been in a long time and she seems to be equally excited.

Chapter 27

Jamal

It's hard to believe that I'm on my way to Jillian's house. She lives in a quiet town-home community called Fox Ridge. I know a lot about this community because they used to have an infomercial that aired locally every Sunday morning. A Japanese builder designed these homes and they've won numerous awards for their design.

When I enter Jillian's house the first thing I notice is her little fuzzy brown dog barking at me. Jillian introduces me to Munchie as if the dog were a person. It works, because Munchie calms down and seems to welcome me. I can't believe how new everything in her house looks and smells. There's absolutely no pet odor. Her place is nicely decorated in earth-tone colors and has sort of an Afrocentric theme. Looks like she needs a couple of my paintings around here to add to the décor.

"I love your house. Everything looks brand-spanking-new."

"Thanks. Most of this stuff is new. Make yourself at home. There's plenty of room in the freezer for your food."

Jillian and I unpack our groceries. She has a spacious kitchen with a huge side-by-side refrigerator-freezer. Grandma would love this kitchen. When I make it big I'm gonna move her into a community like this. Knowing how set in her ways she is, she wouldn't want to leave that old house.

I look at Jillian and say, "Alright, now tell me some things I don't already know about you."

"Don't get me started, 'cause I can talk, even though I have a pretty typical story to tell."

"Go 'head, I'm a good listener. I wanna know about everything you've been doing with yourself."

"You don't wanna know everything, do you?"

I laugh and say, "Maybe not everything. Just tell me as much as possible. I've always thought you were interesting."

"I don't know why, my life is so boring."

"I wanna know your story, what makes you tick, your likes and dislikes."

I'm not really trying to be nosey, it's just that this might be the start of something good for the both of us and communication is important.

"Alright, since you think I'm so interesting, I'll share some of my personal experiences with you if you help me prepare dinner. How's that sound?"

"That'll work."

Jillian doesn't start off by talking about herself; instead she tells me about this recipe for baked Dijon chicken that she claims has a zesty fried-chicken taste straight from the oven in fifteen minutes. She washes her hands in the kitchen sink and that stops me dead in my tracks because my grandmother raised me to never wash my hands in the kitchen sink. She said that we carry certain germs on our hands that don't belong near the dishes. Since Grandma isn't here and there aren't any dishes in Jillian's sink, I go ahead and wash my hands.

We decide to use my chicken breasts. Jillian preheats the oven at 375 degrees. She pours some evaporated milk into a bowl and I mix in some Dijon mustard.

As Jillian turns the chicken breasts from side to side in the mixture, she says, "Here we go. Once upon a time I was a fool."

"Oh, you're gonna tell it to me just like a real story."

"Shhh, I thought you said you were a good listener."

"Sorry."

Jillian is finished flipping the chicken breasts around in the mixture and now it's my turn to sprinkle bread crumbs over the chicken. She prepares two baked potatoes in the microwave and I clean some fresh spinach for steaming.

Jillian punches the proper cooking time into the microwave and says,

"Here we go again. Once upon a time, I was the type of woman with high expectations and low self-esteem. You know I used to be a lot heavier."

"I remember."

"I'm constantly battling a weight problem or something more like an eating problem. I've always loved food, always found comfort in it. Now that I've lost weight men refer to me as beautiful. That's funny to me because not too long ago people referred to me as the fat girl with the pretty face. At one point, terms people used to describe me hurt, but now they give me strength. I love comedians like Mo'Nique, with her big-girl jokes. It's good to see full-figured women in the spotlight being sexy and loving their appearances. Being sexy is more about attitude than appearance, anyway."

"That's true and you're definitely sexy."

Jillian smiles and says, "Thanks and so are you."

The chicken is in the oven, the spinach is steaming, and the potatoes are in the microwave. Jillian leans against the counter and continues talking. I kind of tone her out for a minute because I'm caught up looking around her house as I stand here. I can tell a lot about people judging by the condition of their home and what's in it. Jillian likes to have things her way and there's nothing wrong with that. She doesn't settle for second best. Her West African paintings are authentic, unlike the cheap prints I've seen in other people's houses that come from roadside art wholesalers. More than anything her place is clean and well organized and that speaks about her health and lifestyle. The fact that she instantly invited me here says that she's proud of what she has and doesn't have anything to hide.

"Why are you so quiet all of a sudden?"

"I'm looking around here and listening to all the things that your house says about you."

"This kitchen is probably telling you that I eat too much and I'm overweight. Don't listen, it's lying."

"Don't put yourself down like that. You really look good."

"I'm not putting myself down. I am overweight and I've always been. I was born thick. I came out weighing ten pounds six ounces, looking like a flesh-toned cannonball."

We laugh.

She asks, "Do you remember people calling me by my nickname, Honey?"

"Yeah, I thought you had a nickname."

"My grandmother nicknamed me Honey Sugar Dumpling when I was a baby. She had the nerve to name me after food."

Our laughter echoes throughout the house again.

Jillian continues, "My mother's thick, her momma's thick, and I think her momma was thick too. Big bones run in our family, except for my little sister, Natalie. Do you remember her?"

I peek at the chicken and say, "Vaguely. Do you remember my sister, Shadow?"

"She went to Edmondson too. Isn't that her on the news?"

"Yeah, that's my little sister."

"I thought so. Well, my sister, Natalie, is a year younger than me and I used to resent her body shape and size. In high school she always got all the guys' attention and stole the spotlight from me. High school was rough for me, being a big girl and all. I went to my senior prom alone, but that was by choice."

That last remark leaves me standing in the middle of the kitchen floor with a cheap look on my face because Jillian and our senior prom have always been touchy subjects for me. I'm embarrassed that she even brought it up. For years I've been beating myself to death for not asking her to the prom.

She says, "The guy that was supposed to take me to the prom was only doing it because he felt sorry for me, or at least that was what I thought. He wanted to appear like the sensitive type by taking a fat girl to the prom in hopes of gaining the attention of some more attractive girls. I wasn't aware of this guy's true intentions until he confessed to one of my girlfriends. That hurt because I actually thought the guy liked me. Naive doesn't even begin to describe what I used to be." She smiles and says, "Another guy that I won't mention by name wanted to take me to the prom, a guy that I had a major crush on, but he took the easy way and punked out of asking me. I guess he didn't want to go to the prom with a fat girl."

I think, *Oh, damn!* I'm overwhelmed with guilt and my conscience makes me say, "I'm so sorry for that. You just don't know how I've been kicking myself for years for not asking you to the prom. If I could go back and change anything from high school, I would have taken you to the prom. I was just so immature back then."

She smiles again and says, "I understand, really I do. Thanks to two years of Tae-Bo under Billy Blanks's intense guidance, I've shed pounds of fat and gained discipline, determination, and muscle tone." She acts silly and starts flexing. "Now if only I could just do something about my love life."

"Mine could use a little help too."

"Mine could use a lot of help. I have a habit of letting things like infatuation, male domination, and perpetration disguise themselves as love. Recently they sent my life into a whirlwind. I thought I knew love, but let's just say that love don't live here anymore because I kicked his ass out three months ago and replaced him with something new called celibacy."

"What? You're wild."

"With a little soul searching I was able to reclaim my body for myself and learn how to please me. That's such a powerful thing. Along that journey I met a new friend called me. I love me and I'm glad I found myself. Thought I needed a man to define me, but that was just a myth. It's so hard to give love to someone else when you don't even know how to love yourself and it's especially hard when you don't even know yourself."

"I like that and I like the way you express yourself. You're intelligent and you keep it real. So, what happened between you and your man?"

"His name's Khalil. I gave him the best three years of his life and in return he gave me the worse heartache ever. I'm just gonna be honest. There wasn't anything I wouldn't have done for him. Nothing was too good for him. I worshiped the ground he walked on. Needless to say, he ripped my heart out of my body with his bare hands and crushed it right before my eyes. Then he went around town showing it off to all his girlfriends, laughing and toying with my emotions. Khalil was the sexiest and yet the most manipulative man I've ever known. He's a musician and I fell into the trap of taking care of a brotha with a dream. Big mistake. Told you I was a fool. As soon as that dream gained a little momentum, that brotha started trippin' for real. There I was trying to work with a brotha and instead I got worked. He walked around like his shit didn't stink, but it did. I know it did because we shared a bathroom for almost three years. I didn't want his shit to get too funky that he couldn't smell mine, if you know what I mean."

I laugh and say, "I know what you mean."

"One day he had the nerve to tell me, 'Jillian, we need to talk. Things are changing for me. Some big things are happening for me.'

His music career was starting to take off and he gained a few local fans, female fans. When he said big things are happening for *me* and not *us*, I knew something was wrong."

"Damn."

"I remember what he said to me word for word. He was like, 'I don't know exactly how to say this, so I'm just gonna say it. The caliber of women I've been dealing with lately are on a completely different level. And you just happen to fall short of my new definition of attractive. I think we should just be roommates.' I completely snapped."

"That's crazy. What did you say?"

"Excuse my language, but I yelled, 'What the hell did you just say to me? You got a lot of nerve. I'm not attractive? I'm alright with me, so you should be alright with me too. You can't even spell, much less define attractive, you ignorant bastard. How the hell do you think we're gonna be roommates and you've never given me a cent toward my mortgage? It's time for you to get to packing and get to steppin'.'"

Jillian is so dramatic with her eye contact and tone while describing what she said to Khalil that I feel as if she were fussing at me. I'd hate to bring out her bad side.

After a delicious dinner we sit on her sofa near the fireplace talking, eating Jillian's homemade deep, dark, rich chocolate cake, and drinking coffee. There's nothing better than a beautiful woman who can cook a good meal and back it up with homemade chocolate cake. Jillian has a good job and she's intelligent. If she can get busy in the bedroom like she does in the kitchen, this could possibly be the future Mrs. Jamal King.

I say, "This was starting to look like another one of my typical boring evenings until I ran into you. Thanks for inviting me over and sharing your story. You make me laugh."

"I like to laugh."

I tap my coffee mug against hers and say, "Here's to our friendship and to new and exciting possibilities."

Jillian smiles and looks unsure of what to do or say next. She gives me a simple "Okay."

I've kind of thrown her off by toasting with coffee mugs. "I really appreciate you showing me such a good time. This is nice and cozy. It's almost winter and usually I consider it a depressing season because I like warm weather and hate the fact that daylight turns to night too soon this time of year."

"I feel the same way about winter. I'm glad you decided to come over and brighten my evening. It's nice having you around. Thanks for being here to listen, 'cause I've got issues."

We laugh.

"So does everybody else. I recently broke up with my girlfriend, Jessie."

"Really?"

"Yeah."

"Do you still have feelings for her?"

I smile and say, "Don't ask me stuff like that. You still have feelings for Khalil?"

She laughs and says, "Alright, I've been real all night and I'm not about to hold back now. As much as I thought I loved him, he had to go. That bloodsucking, good-for-nothing, son of a you-know-what had to go before his words and actions hurt my heart too bad. Give a brotha a hand and he'll take your whole arm. Let's just say I gave Khalil the finger."

I laugh, but Jillian's facial expression is serious. "I'm sorry."

"It's okay, I get mad just thinking about how dirty he did me. I kept a roof over his head and dressed him in the finest clothes. Please excuse me for saying this, but during sex I had that brotha's toes curling."

"Damn, you put it on him like that?"

"Yeah, I had him calling my name, God's name, and speaking in tongues. I did all that because I wanted to keep him happy and he totally took advantage. He couldn't appreciate my feminine strength or generosity, so he went astray like a dog in search of what he thought he was missing at home. Khalil was so dumb or got so careless that he used to come home smelling like his other woman. Just about every day he'd come home in the evening smelling like Dove, Camay, or some type of fruit-scented soap. He smelled like soaps we never even had in the house. A few times he came home wearing that distinct rubbery smell of a condom. This asshole even came home with lotion or baby oil left on his back. His breath always had that kissable fresh scent, his sex drive abruptly fell off, he started wearing designer underwear when all he ever used to wear were old raggedy Fruit of the Loom drawers, he started wearing cologne and working out like there was no tomorrow and coming home late telling blatant lies about where he'd been. Simply put, he was cheating. Heck no, I don't still have feelings for him."

"I'm sorry you had to experience all that. In case he never told you, let me apologize for him. I'm sorry for all the times he lied to you, disrespected you, cheated on you, and broke your heart. I sincerely mean that."

Jillian eyes begin to well up with tears and I hold her in my arms. It's hard to find the right words to describe how good she feels in my arms. She's in somewhat of a vulnerable state and the last thing I want to do is take advantage. On the other hand, her irresistible lips are extremely close to mine. I slowly bring my lips closer. They touch. Her lips are so soft and supple. Our kiss is electric and sends sensations throughout my body. It gives my heart the feeling I was looking for. When our tongues meet, I'm not even myself anymore. It's as if I become my tongue and my goal is to give her the most intense and passionate first kiss she has ever received. Our kiss is so precise and consuming that we just go on for a few minutes. As our kiss winds down I sneak a peek at Jillian. Her eyes are closed. She is completely zoned out. Our lips separate, but I keep her close.

Jillian opens her eyes and says, "You're so sweet. It's hard to describe, but you were giving me unbelievable sensations with your tongue."

"That's a good thing, right?"

"It is. You've got me all messed up. I don't even know what I'm saying, but I wanna kiss you again. I think I felt something special in that kiss."

I smile and say, "I felt it too."

A few minutes pass and somehow we get on the topic of love verses sex.

Jillian has regained her composure. She says, "Most men can't distinguish the difference between love and sex because they love with their penises, and women, we love with our hearts and minds. I know I sound like some type of feminist, but I like dropping a little knowledge every now and then for my sistas, so they won't end up making the same mistakes I made in the past. I'm all about uplifting sistas physically, mentally, and spiritually. Black women are making major strides in the business world. That's an obvious fact because every day I look around in rush-hour traffic and see us dressed in business attire, driving to and from work in nice cars. *Essence* magazine always has feature articles about us in business. We still don't get the respect we deserve, but that's an entirely different topic."

"I understand what you mean. Go 'head and represent for the sistas, but I have to defend my brothas. Not all men love with their penises. I'm not bragging or anything, I happen to know a lot about sex. You could call me a sexpert."

She laughs and says, "Oh, really?"

"Go 'head and laugh. Hopefully one day I'll get to show you some of my skills."

"I'm not saying a word. Go right ahead, Mr. Sexpert."

"Thank you. Let me use myself for an example. I love with my heart and mind. During sex I love with my entire body and I like when the woman I'm with does the same. You can easily tell a man that loves with his penis, because he's the one who suffers from premature ejaculation or the brotha goes straight to sleep after sex. It's important to balance out your pleasure to other regions, especially the mind, and not just concentrate on the erogenous zone between your legs. It's important to remember that the mind is the greatest sex organ."

Jillian says, "I like that. You make a lot of sense."

"Now we understand each other and I value the opinions of a strong sista like yourself."

"I'm glad you understand because it's time that brothas recognize our true worth. I'm not hating on my brothas, 'cause I love, respect, and need y'all. Throughout my life I've only dated black men. A lot of sistas think that the only thing a white man can do for them is sign their paychecks. I never said all that, I'm just not looking for a white man. I believe that love is color-blind and if I happen to fall in love with a white man, then that's fine, but again I'm not looking for one, because nothing beats an intelligent, hardworking brotha. There are those raw instances where it seems as if brothas are a little intimidated by me. Once they get a taste of my strength and a whiff of my new nononsense, I'll-believe-it-when-I-see-it attitude they're ready to step off. I've said a lot tonight and I hope I haven't offended you or turned you off in any way."

"I don't think you could do or say anything to offend or turn me off."

"You said I was interesting, you're the interesting one. I'm so glad you're here. Sometimes it gets lonely in this big ole house without a man. I'm not the type of woman that doesn't need a man or anything. Trust me, I ain't too proud to beg or ask for what I need, want, or lust for. My walk-in closet is still empty on one side. There's space under my bed for a large pair of shoes, there's a spot for an additional toothbrush, a *his* towel, razors, and shaving cream in my bathroom. Despite all that I've experienced, there's always space in my heart and in my bed for someone special."

"Are you inviting me into your life or what?"

"I'd like to make you part of my life. Time has a funny way of healing old wounds. I need a friend more than anything right now."

"I can be whatever you need."

She smiles and says, "I like the sound of that."

The doorbell rings and Jillian looks as if she doesn't want to answer it.

She says, "Excuse me for a second, Jamal. This can't be anybody except my neighbor, Darien, at the door. He reminds me of one of those pesky neighbors from a sitcom, who always likes to hang out at his neighbor's house."

She gets up and opens the door to Darien's smiling face.

In a deep voice he says, "What's up, sexy?"

"Nothing. What's up with you, married man?"

Darien says, "Damn, Honey, what's up? You're lookin' all fine."

"Thanks, bro, but I'm not in the mood for playing around tonight. I've got company."

"My bad. I had no idea."

Darien didn't notice me at first and now his whole demeanor changes. Jillian introduces the two of us. Darien and I shake hands and he tries to get a little firm with his handshake, so naturally I tighten mine.

Darien turns to Jillian and says, "I was just trying to add a little life to this slow evening. Just wanted to see if you wanted to go out to dinner with me and Nedra, but since your friend is here, I guess not."

Jillian says, "Thanks for keeping me in mind. Maybe the four of us could do a double date sometime."

I say, "That sounds good."

Darien says, "Maybe. I'll keep you guys posted. I bet we'd all have a good time."

Jillian laughs and says, "You better go home to Nedra and have a good time."

Darien smiles and says, "Alright, Honey. Nice meeting you, Jermaine."

I say, "It's Jamal."

Jillian says, "A'ight, married man, get it right."

Darien finally leaves.

I say, "What the hell was his problem? I think I already know."

"Darien is a trip."

"He's annoying."

"He's cute."

"He likes you."

"I like him too, but not like that. I know he likes me and that's why I constantly refer to him as 'married man' so he won't forget the real deal. Darien's really intelligent, friendly, and comical as hell. He's good to have around. I allow him to hang out sometimes, but only for a few minutes at a time because I'm not trying to start something with a married man. I've lived in this neighborhood for three years and Darien and his wife, Nedra, are the only neighbors I know by name. The only thing my other neighbors get from me is a simple hello."

"I guess Darien is okay, but there's something about him I didn't like. That chump couldn't even get my name right."

"He didn't mean anything by that."

"He's jealous of me being here. He tried to break my hand when he shook it."

Jillian laughs and asks, "Are you serious?"

"I'm serious. He's kind of protective."

"He did act like he was kind of uncomfortable leaving us alone. I wasn't going to say anything, but did you see how he kept looking over his shoulder at you when he was leaving?"

"You know I saw that, I'm very observant."

"What did you observe about me?"

"You're flirtatious."

"Good observation. I do flirt with him a little, but I know how far to take it. I think that's why Darien comes around, so I can make him feel like he's still got it."

"Flirting with a married man can be dangerous. Are you close to his wife?"

"We're kind of close. She's a very attractive woman. Nedra is secure with Darien stopping by here every now and then."

"Good thing I'm here to keep you out of trouble. Can I give you an erotic massage?"

"Where'd that come from?"

"I have attention deficit disorder, especially when my date keeps talking about other men."

"I'm sorry. What's the difference between an erotic massage and a regular massage?"

"With the erotic massage I get to touch you anywhere."

"Ooh, that sounds good, but I'll take a regular massage for now."

"Are you sure?"

"No, but we'll start with a regular massage and see where it takes us."

Jillian goes to her bedroom and returns with a small bottle of baby oil. I drop the baby oil in a cup of hot water in order to bring the oil to the right temperature. I ask Jillian to take off her blouse and she removes it without hesitation.

I love the fact that Jillian is so comfortable with her body, and she should be because she's beautiful from head to toe. She's still slightly overweight, but more like plump than chubby. I like the added thickness, especially to her hips, thighs, butt, and breasts. She's fine as hell and I liked how she said that being sexy was more about attitude than appearance. Jillian personifies sexiness in so many ways. She looks good and she has lots of attitude.

Jillian unfastens her bra and lies on a towel on the floor in front of the fireplace. She appears to be very relaxed in my presence. Her modesty is out the window because she gave me a quick peek at her breasts. I act natural and drip oil into my left palm and then rub my hands together.

I say, "Take slow, deep breaths and imagine yourself in your favorite place."

"This is my favorite place. I can't think of any other place I'd rather be or any other person I'd rather be with."

"I like that and I feel the same way."

Alternating from my palms to my fingertips, from gentle to firm, I begin to massage Jillian's back in slow circular movements. She moans in a soft tone as I gradually loosen up her most tensed areas, her neck and shoulders.

The living room is dimly lit. Jillian's skin glistens from the oil as it reflects the flames of the fireplace.

I say, "Your shoulders are really tense."

"I know. That feels nice."

Her skin is incredibly soft and I love the feeling of running my hands up and down her back. She especially likes the feel of my thumbs isolating certain areas and giving a miniature rubdown. Holding her skin taut and massaging with my free hand gives the perception of penetrating right down to the muscle. I add more oil and move my hands with a slow in-and-out motion, almost soothing the entire back with one motion. I speed up the pace of the rubdown, and the friction adds the right amount of heat. In some areas my hands are firm and in others my touch is so light that it's almost as if I'm teasing her flesh. Jillian's muscles are almost completely relaxed and I'm sure her blood is circulating at an increased pace, sending sensations throughout her body.

Jillian lowers her pants, revealing her sexy round ass and thick, shapely legs. I try to act natural, but it's hard. I instantly smile because she has legs that remind me of Beyonce's from Destiny's Child.

Jillian takes my breath away. She's absolutely gorgeous, so precious and irresistible.

This massage quickly turns into a full-body massage, but stays within the guidelines of a regular massage. There isn't anything regular about the way I'm touching her. This is more like a sensual massage.

"I hate to sound like all those other guys, but you're so beautiful. My God, just look at your skin. I love your honey brown complexion. It's so even and just flows perfectly."

In a relaxed tone she says, "Stop lying. I know you see those stretch marks and little dimples in my butt."

"They're so minor I barely noticed them. They're okay. You don't have to be absolutely flawless to be appealing in my eyes. You don't see what I see."

"Well, if they don't bother you, then they don't bother me."

"Good. Like I said, you're beautiful."

By the time I finish with Jillian's massage she falls asleep. I take off my shirt and cuddle up next to her. When Jillian wakes up she offers to give me a massage. At first I give her a hard time because I wanted her to relax and get around to me another time. I finally give in to her.

As I take off my pants, Jillian watches my every move. She looks as if she's studying every little aspect of my body.

She asks, "Has anybody ever told you that you are beautiful?"

"Never."

"Well, you are. I love your physique and your chocolate skin tone. Can I touch you?"

Before I even answer Jillian starts to run her hands all over my arms, shoulders, and back. I'm still standing and she doesn't use any oil. I laugh because this isn't a massage; it's more like a groping session. I don't mind because Jillian has a nice touch.

"Your hands feel nice."

"So does your body."

"Do you want me to lie down?"

"Not yet."

Jillian stands behind me and slowly works her hands around to my chest and abdomen. Her touch has me aroused. I turn around and we kiss. I put my hands around her waist and slowly lower them, grabbing a handful of her ass.

She says, "I want to do something different. Have you ever had a facial?"

"No."

"You'll love it. It's very relaxing."

Jillian goes to her bedroom and comes out with a basin of warm water and an entire line of skin-care products. I lie on the same towel in front of the fireplace and Jillian takes her time cleansing my face. Next she exfoliates my skin with a facial scrub. Jillian gently massages my face with a moisturizer, paying special attention to my jaw muscles, forehead, and temples. I relax and waves of pleasure radiate throughout my face and body. This is nothing but tender love and care at its best.

After my facial Jillian completely blows me away with a very invigorating massage. Although we dread the inevitable, this night has to come to an end. Jillian helps me get dressed and we kiss good night about twenty times and keep discovering new topics to talk about before I actually leave her house.

Chapter 28

Jamal

Over the past two days I've gone out with two very interesting women, with Jillian being my top pick of the two. She's affectionate and has a warm personality that draws me to her. In addition to that, she possesses a lot of appealing physical characteristics that drive me crazy, like her complexion, round facial structure, high cheekbones, constant smile, dark slanted eyes, her physical build, and overall sex appeal. She's a definite eight on a scale from one to ten. More than anything she made my heart feel something special. I'm excited again.

I like the fact that Jillian is so down-to-earth and she likes to speak her mind. She talks a lot, but she's very straightforward. Khalil didn't know what he had in her. She talked about him a little too long, but I understand that she needed to vent.

Last night was nice, from the conversation down to the massages. I wanted to give Jillian an introduction to the exquisite pleasures that I knew my touch could bring. I enjoyed taking my time exploring her body like that. She has a tender touch too. That facial was a nice show of affection and it left my skin feeling refreshed. Our evening was sexy, but at the same time subtle.

Jillian told me about how her family moved out of my neighborhood a few years after we graduated from high school. They live in a big single-family home in the Ashburton community, a community Jillian refers to as a haven for uppity black folks. Her father was a member of the Maryland House of Delegates and now he's a state senator for the Forty-first Legislative District. Jillian's mother is a social worker who works with pediatric AIDS patients and their families. I could tell that Jillian loves her family by the look on her face when she talked about them. She told me about how she and her mother helped her father campaign during the last election. They went off meeting and greeting people for months and going to campaign fundraisers. I've known about Senator Smith for years, but I never knew he was Jillian's dad. I voted for him purely on name recognition.

My phone rings, I pick up, and a female voice says, "Last night was incredible. I mean, you're such a gentleman."

It's Jillian. She just skips the usual hello or hi, Jamal. I just play right along. "Thank you."

"You scare me, man."

"Why?"

"Because I don't know what to do with you. All I can say is, you better be careful. I might have to put it on you real good and then you're guaranteed to fall in love with me."

"I'm a man, I can handle it. I might have to put it on you real good and have you acting like a little schoolgirl. I can see you now lying around the house writing my name on everything and drawing hearts around it."

"Is that right?"

"Yeah, that's right. Test me if you think I'm playing."

"I might kill you, man. You know I've been celibate for three months." She laughs. "Then again you might kill me. I'm feeling like a virgin again."

"I like the sound of that, you got that recycled virgin thing going on."

"You ever been with a virgin before?"

"No."

"I might scream like one."

"Stop playing. Can we hook up this evening?"

"You got it bad too, huh?"

"Yeah, I can't stop thinking about you."

Jillian laughs and says, "Neither can I. I thought about you all night. I can't wait to see you."

"Can't wait to see you."

"I have to go now, got work to do. Have a good day and I'll talk to you later."

"Alright. Can we meet at that restaurant called Hops?"

"Yeah. Seven o'clock?"

"I'll meet you at the bar."

"See you then."

I head upstairs for breakfast and hear Grandma's radio blasting her favorite gospel station, Heaven 600. She's listening to a song called "When I See Jesus." This isn't just any old gospel song, because it has her dancing and shouting. I haven't seen her catch the Holy Ghost like this in a while. She doesn't notice me, so I ease back downstairs and give her a few minutes alone.

When I enter the kitchen a little later, she looks at me and says, "Good morning, William, I mean, Henry, Jamal, boy, whatever your name is."

William and Henry are two of my grandmother's brothers who have been dead for years and years. When something's worrying Grandma she gets a mental block and starts calling me by the names of her dead siblings.

I laugh and say, "After all these years you still don't know my name."

"Stop laughing at me. You know what I was saying. Keep putting your shoes on and see how many names you forget."

I guess the saying *keep putting your shoes on* is Grandma's way of saying, Keep doing the simple, everyday tasks and as you get older the simple things become complex.

I say, "You're right, I was just teasing. What's been going on with you lately? You've been cooking all this down-home soul food."

"I don't know. My heart is so heavy right now. I miss your grandfather. I miss my momma and daddy. Cooking like that reminds me of home, that's all."

I don't know exactly what to say, because Grandma looks sad, like she's lost her best friend. Outliving everyone is really starting to bother her, because it's not too often that she talks about Granddad, her parents, or Virginia.

"Are you depressed?"

Her eyes begin to tear. "Maybe I am. Everybody's gone away from here and soon it'll be my turn to go. All I hear about is sickness and death. When I see Jesus, oh, it's gonna be such a glorious day. I'll be reunited with everybody I've lost."

"Stop talking like that. You're starting to sound like Coach right before he died. You're healthy as I don't know what, so stop worrying. God's not ready for you yet. He needs you here to continue doing His work. Where's your faith? You always taught me that if I lose my way let faith be my guide. If you lose your faith this family is in trouble."

"You're right, baby. I should be thanking God instead of worrying and complaining. I don't know what I'd do without you, Jamal. Thanks for sticking by my side all these years."

I put my arms around Grandma and say, "I love you and I plan to be here for you as long as you need me."

"I can't ask you to stay here forever. You gonna meet another nice girl soon and probably get married and have a family."

"I ran into a girl I went to high school with, last night at the supermarket. Her name's Jillian and she's really pretty. She lives alone in a town house not too far from Shadow and John. She's intelligent and has a good job too."

"She sounds like a nice girl. Did you tell her you were still living here with me?"

"Yeah, and she was fine with that."

"She probably thinks you're retarded or something living here." We laugh.

"I see you're alright now. I'll be sure to ask her if she thinks I'm retarded. She knows I'm here helping you out."

"I wouldn't want a man who lives in his grandmother's basement. These young girls these days want a man with his own house and car."

"You're killing me. It's more than a basement. It's my studio and I'm comfortable here."

"Don't get too comfortable here or you'll never wanna leave. I just don't want you feeling like you missed out on something because you decided to stay here looking after me. Have you thought about moving into Coach's house? Have you even been down there since you and I went down there together?"

"No. I don't even wanna step foot in there."

"You have to. It's your responsibility to keep the place up. If you want, I can help you clean it up."

"I'll get around to it sooner or later."

"No matter what Coach did he was my brother and I loved him. I miss him right now. He had problems and he needed help. I don't think he meant to hurt Karen."

I give Grandma a strange look and say, "I don't wanna talk about him."

The doorbell rings and I make my way to the front door. There's a FedEx guy at the door with a box for me. I see that it's from Regina.

I open it to find a box with my new laptop computer, a cell phone, a contract with a note attached telling me to sign and return. She even threw in a check for five thousand dollars, which is supposed to be an advance for art supplies. Regina expects me to do a lot of paintings. I can work with this.

Grandma has no idea what all this is about. I forgot to tell her about my good news. When I tell her, she's elated.

The next thing I have to do is call in sick from work and then cash this check. I need to head to Mr. Tire for new tires, a tune-up, and an oil change. I need some new clothes, shoes, and maybe a few art supplies.

I'm sitting at Hops drinking a beer when I notice a few of the guys at the bar turn their heads toward the door. Jillian has just stepped inside. Right away she spots me and gives me the most beautiful smile.

She steps up and greets me. We embrace and her double-Ds feel nice pressed against me. I give her a nice little kiss on the lips.

She asks, "How was your day?"

"I called in sick because I had a lot of important things to take care of. My car needed some attention. How was your day?"

"It was fine until this physician decided to harass me by asking a bunch of personal questions and then asking me out on a date."

"I don't blame him. He was just doing what comes natural. You don't understand the power you have over men."

She smiles and says, "No, it's not that at all. When I conduct myself in a professional manner I expect the same in return. I was going through my usual sales pitch and product updates when I noticed he wasn't paying me a bit of attention. His eyes were fixed right on my breasts. He had no respect for me or for his wife. Men flirt with me a lot, but married men are the worst. When I'm in the field I'm all about business. I'm not there to be harassed by horny doctors."

"I understand what you mean, but don't worry, everything's cool here. Try to relax. You want a beer or something?"

"I'll take a lemonade. I need something to eat and maybe then I'll be okay. Here comes our waitress."

I pick up my beer as the waitress directs us to our table. She seats us at a booth. We sit facing each other at the booth unlike the couple across from us; they're sitting side by side. I prefer to face my date so I can enjoy a nice frontal view.

I look Jillian directly in the eyes, smile, and say, "I think we're good for each other. I've been through a lot lately, feels as if I've survived a raging storm and you're my rainbow."

"That was so sweet and I can relate to where you're coming from because you're like my pot of gold at the end of the rainbow." She acts surprised and says, "You're smiling."

"You do that. All I have to do is just look at you and I smile. I can't begin to tell you how good you make me feel."

"You better stop. I told you, you're gonna fall in love with me. I keep warning you."

"And what's wrong with that?"

"Love is a serious thing."

"Love is serious. What else does it mean to you? Define love."

My question causes Jillian to make a cute dumbfounded facial expression. Now it appears that she's quickly formulating a response.

She says, "Love is a powerful whirlwind of beautiful emotions. We can see and feel it. Love is unconditional. Love is blind and indiscriminate. It accepts all of our imperfections and shortcomings. Love is endless."

"I like that."

"Since you put me on the spot, you define love."

Our waitress comes back with Jillian's lemonade. She orders a crispy chicken salad with honey mustard and extra chicken minus egg whites and bacon bits. I don't want to appear as if I can't think for myself, but her salad sounds so good that I order the same.

"Okay, you need to answer my question even though it's unfair because you had an extended period to think."

"The extra time doesn't make a difference. This is simple for me because I live for love and it's always on my mind. First of all, God is love. Love is what inspires me to create. Love is a need. It's our greatest and deepest desire. Love is the king of all emotions. Love is faith, passion, and tenderness. Love is both selfish and unselfish. Love is what drives us and it's the reason we do all the things we do."

"I'm impressed. Sounds as if you know a lot about love. I bet you could write a book about it."

"I just might do that. It'll be a love story called *You and Me*. Would you like that?"

"You're good. I usually don't like smooth talkers, but I give you credit, you're one of the best."

"Come on, this is the real me. I'm not putting on some sort of act to impress you."

"We'll see."

"I'm just making small talk, trying to get to know you a little better. Here's another question. What's sex to you?"

"What's up with you?" She pauses for a second. "I'm going to impress you with this. Sex is a yearning to connect with another soul. Sex is having your innermost desires met. Sex is beautiful, fulfilling, and spiritual." She smiles and says, "Your turn."

"That was good. Okay, check this out. Sex is powerful and priceless. Sex is the ultimate and the most intimate exchange of physical, mental, and emotional pleasure shared by two people."

"Wow, you make it sound so good. Can I have my breath back now? I have to admit, most guys wouldn't have answered these questions like you did. You're different and I think that's what scares me most about you. You might be the first guy I've ever met who actually loves with his heart and not his penis."

"Not that again."

She laughs and says, "I was just giving you a compliment because you're different."

"I am different from other guys in a lot of ways, but at the same time I'm very similar."

"You sound complicated, but I understand. I love your personality."

"I love yours too. You make me feel good about myself."

"You don't need me for that. You're very confident."

I stop smiling and say, "Don't be fooled, that hasn't always been the case. I've learned from experiences. Why are you blushing?"

"It's nothing."

"Come on, this is me you're talking to, you can tell me. It's not like you to hold back."

"You're right. There's just something about you. You were able to penetrate my defenses with such ease. I was bitter and not really looking forward to talking to a guy so soon in terms of starting a relationship."

"I never even noticed that you were bitter or had any kind of defense. You instantly welcomed me into your life. How did you even end up at that market last night? You live miles away from there."

"I don't know. I was on my way home from work and something told me to stop there. What made you pick that market out of all the markets in your area?"

"I passed two other markets on the way there. I'm not sure why I picked that one."

"Do you think it was fate that brought us together?"

"It was either fate or the fact that the first market I passed smelled like rotten meat and old musty fish and the second market I passed was too expensive. I'm just kiddin'. I'm sure it was fate."

"We've probably been soul mates since high school and never realized it. Do you even believe in soul mates? If so, do you think God only intended for us to have one soul mate and once we find that person we're meant to settle down for the rest of our lives?"

The waitress brings out our crispy chicken salads in two giant glass bowls.

Jillian says, "You have to answer my question before you touch your salad."

I look at Jillian and think of how beautiful she is to me. It's just ridiculous how perfect her face is. It's rare to see a person with such attractive features. To top all that off I really enjoy her company and our crazy but interesting conversations.

I smile at her and say exactly what's on my mind. I ask, "Who are you and where did you come from?"

She simply says, "Answer my questions."

"Okay. I got lost staring at you for a minute."

"You're stalling."

"First, you have to ask yourself, what exactly is a soul mate? Who can really define what it is? To me a soul mate is a person you're deeply in love with and a person who equally returns that same love. A soul mate taps into your being and is someone who understands your physical, emotional, and spiritual needs. I'm talking about that special someone. It's like when you hurt, I hurt, when you cry, I cry. I feel your pleasure, you feel mine, and together we can stand the pain kinda thing. You feel me?"

"Oh yeah, I feel you."

We begin to eat, but that doesn't stop our conversation.

I say, "Most people believe that we can only love or be involved with one person at a time, but in reality we're constantly looking, comparing, and fantasizing. And there are those of us who act out our fantasies. Love is an abundant emotion that's meant to be shared, but society limits us. All I can say is, love is a wonderful thing and nothing compares to new love. I don't know how you feel, but I believe in monogamy."

"So do I."

"I believe that we can have more than one soul mate in a lifetime. There's probably one for each and every phase of life that we experience. It's possible to outgrow the person you thought was your soul mate."

"Have you ever experienced that before?"

"Maybe once, but I'm not sure. You?"

"I'm not sure either."

"Thanks for stimulating and opening my mind. I haven't had an interesting conversation like this in years."

If the sun forgot to shine Jillian could still brighten my day. That's how special she is. She seems to give me sanity in this crazy world.

After dinner we head back to Jillian's house. Munchie is locked in the basement barking like crazy. Jillian and I take him for a walk.

Out of nowhere she says, "I'm not sure how long I can keep this celibacy stuff going."

"Take as long as you need, I'm not going anywhere."

"You say that like you mean it."

"I do."

"I don't think I can last much longer. You gonna think something's wrong with me for saying this, but last night at the market I got wet when I was trying to pick out the right cucumber for my salad. They were all big and long."

I burst out laughing. "And green. I shouldn't even laugh, because I got a hard-on the other night while I was at the gas station."

"How and why?"

"I had the nozzle in my hand inserting it into that little hole and that was it. Wham! My thing was erect."

"We're two weirdos together."

When we return to Jillian's house she sends Munchie to the basement and shows me around her house. She purposefully makes her bedroom our final stop.

Chapter 29

Jessie

Directions:

1. Collect urine specimen in clean cup.
2. Remove test strip from plastic foil package.
3. Dip test strip into urine for six seconds.
4. Remove strip from urine and let sit for one minute.
5. Read result. (Single use strip only. Discard after five minutes.)
*Single blue line indicates negative result.
**Double blue line indicates positive result.

My monthly visitor is late and that's not a good sign. If this test comes out positive, that means two things, Jamal is going to be a father and Trey is going to kick my ass out of this house for sure.

I could do something underhanded like have unprotected sex with Trey and pretend that he got me pregnant, but I couldn't live with a lie like that.

It seems as if this is the longest and most critical minute of my life. I'm nervous as hell and my eyes begin to tear because I know my body and I've already figured out what the result is going to be.

My stomach gets this bottomless, sinking feeling. Two lines appear on the test strip and all I can do is stand here with my hands in a prayer position pressed against my trembling lips. I keep telling myself that this can't be happening. *I'm pregnant!* An error must have occurred somewhere and I automatically think back to that day I decided to have unprotected sex with Jamal. What the hell was I thinking? That was nothing more than me and my guilt overcompensating for what I had done the previous night with Trey.

Tears flow from my eyes because I'm afraid to think about what's going to happen to me. I've never felt more alone in my life. Things have just begun to come together for me and Trey and now this. We were on the road to a perfect life and I had to ruin it. This is my first pregnancy and the worse scenario possible. I always dreamed of having a planned pregnancy where my husband and I would sit down together to choose a name, a pattern for the nursery, and make a guest list for my baby shower. At some point I'll have to tell Jamal, but how? He wouldn't believe in a million years that this is his baby. I don't even want to think about telling Trey because I wouldn't even know how to explain to him that I'm carrying Jamal's baby, especially after I lied, telling him that I always made Jamal use condoms when we had sex.

I wish I had a mother, sister, or someone to turn to. I can't trust telling any of my girlfriends about my pregnancy. I can't even trust Toya because she has a sneaky way of letting at least 25 percent of our confidential conversations leak out to our other girlfriends. The only reason she keeps the other 75 percent on the hush is that it's boring information. I could trust my mother because she doesn't have any friends and she would be too ashamed to tell other family members. I'd love to share certain things with her, but too bad I can't get over the way she mistreated me all my life. I should call it abuse.

As much as I fear being in the delivery room alone, I'd much rather be alone than have her miserable ass there. I finally got up the nerve to confront her about abusing me and I'll never forget the last thing she said to me. I called myself doing something therapeutic and it wasn't my intention at all to offend or belittle her. When I opened up and let out all those years of pain, frustration, and hate, my mother had the nerve to get offended. She's such an evil woman that she actually said, "You know what? If I never see you again in life that would be too soon for me. You're dead to me." She really meant that.

I was so hurt that I could barely keep myself together. I said, "If ignorance was an illness you'd be on your deathbed." I walked out of her house and never looked back.

*   *   *

I sit in the Jacuzzi trying to forget my problems, but nothing seems to work. Not even the forceful flow of the water jets can make me feel better. This is something that I'll have to deal with on my own. I believe in abortions, but I would never even consider having one.

I just lie here bathing in self-pity, rubbing my abdomen, and thinking about how it will eventually expand to a big round belly to accommodate my baby's growth. I can't stop crying because I'm afraid for my body to undergo the stages of pregnancy, no matter how beautiful other women say it is. To me becoming a mother is nothing more than a precursor to becoming a grandmother. Call me the queen of vanity, but I love my youthful appearance and I don't want it to change. I'll probably gain forty to fifty pounds and get stretch marks. Forget that.

All of a sudden a warrior mentality overtakes me. I plan to stay fit and be one of those beautiful glowing pregnant women. I heard that applying different types of oils to the abdomen prevents stretch marks.

All I know is that once the news of my pregnancy gets out, lives are going to change forever. I know what Trey is up to and where he is. I wonder what Jamal is doing and where he is.

Chapter 30

Jamal

Jillian and I are in her shower stall very noticeably admiring each other's nakedness. We're dripping wet, excited, and somewhat anxious. We both wanted this so badly and now our inhibitions have been set free.

Her body is much more beautiful than I had envisioned. Last night I was only able to explore certain aspects of her body, but tonight she's fully exposed for my pleasure.

I stand aside watching the water run down her voluptuous body. Jillian's shoulder-length hair is dripping wet. My eyes move from her face, to her succulent breasts with the prettiest erect nipples, to her abdomen, to her neatly trimmed V-shaped pubic region, to her hips, thighs, legs, and manicured toes. She's a breathtaking vision of loveliness.

Jillian must be equally impressed with my body because she gives me a look of adoration that says that she really wants me. Her eyes move from my chest to my abs, and now they're focused on my penis. She takes a deep breath and touches it as if she's astonished by the size and firmness.

In a low seductive tone Jillian says, "I like. I like it a lot. Is all that for me?"

"Every inch."

Jillian asks me to hold my hands above my head and keep them there no matter what happens. I'm somewhat reluctant, but I do it anyway. She lathers up her hands and begins to massage my chest, arms, and back. Then she quickly makes her way back down there. Her hands feel so good that I just close my eyes and completely relax. She strokes it up and down with both hands, then moves one hand down to cradle my scrotum.

Jillian reaches for the faucet, gradually increasing the water temperature. She rinses my body. The water is a lot hotter than I usually like it, but I'm not about to complain. The steam thickens slightly, obscuring our nakedness and making all this appear hazy and dreamlike.

Out of nowhere she drops to her knees and begins to kiss me down there.

I say, "I like. I like that a lot."

Jillian returns to her feet and we move in closer, making our bodies appear as one. Passion guides our lips together and our tongues meet, gently caressing each other.

I hold Jillian close to me with my chest pressed against her breasts. We continue kissing as our hands move up and down exploring each other. I grab the handheld showerhead and focus the water on Jillian's neck and back. She hands me a bottle of botanical shampoo and I begin to wash her hair. This isn't what I really want to be doing right now, but it helps to build the anticipation. I take my time running my hands through her hair and gently massaging her scalp. It seems as if we've been here before and we've done all this at some point, but that was a dream of mine. This is real.

"I love for a man to wash my hair. To me it's part of foreplay."

Jillian is so different. I have to ask, "Who are you and where did you come from?"

Jillian doesn't answer, she simply gives me a cute little smile. I rinse her hair and she stops me from doing anything else. She takes me by the hand and guides me to her bed. I know where this is headed so I grab a condom.

She lies on the bed and I'm instantly struck with the urge to kiss her all over and I really mean all over. I slowly trace her body with my tongue and it makes a surprise visit between Jillian's thighs. She tries to say something, but she simply shudders and whimpers as I explore her inner lips, uncovering her ultimate pleasure zone quietly hidden under a veil of skin. She's so beautiful.

This is our sanctuary from the rest of the world. Everything around us could come crumbling down and we would never notice. That's how intense our lovemaking is. Jillian makes the most beautiful and most awesome sex sounds I've ever heard as I thrust my love deep inside her.

We reverse our position with Jillian on top riding me to her own rhythm. As she moves up and down I return pelvic thrusts from underneath, immersing every inch of myself inside. All of a sudden, Jillian holds steady and lets out a loud orgasmic moan. My toes curl and my eyes roll back in my head.

I think, *Oh God, who is she and where did she come from?*

A few minutes later we're lying still wrapped in a sheet kissing and caressing each other. I watch as tears stream down Jillian's face.

I ask, "What's wrong?"

"Nothing. I'm happy, but I just can't stop crying. I never felt like this before."

I hold her closer and wipe her tears. "What is it?"

"It's just that this is moving so fast and it's a lot more serious than I imagined. I kept joking with you about falling in love with me and now I feel myself falling for you. I'm scared because I don't want to be hurt again. I've been celibate for three months and I want this to mean something."

"It does mean something. I need you. I'm not going anywhere, if that's what you're afraid of. I would never do anything to hurt you. I'm scared too, but I really want this. I'm willing to put my heart on the line because I know you're worth it."

She smiles and says, "I'm gonna put my heart on the line as well, but please be gentle with it."

"I will."

I feel myself falling for Jillian as well. The energy between us is incredible. She's right, we've only been together for two days, but this feels so right to me. The feeling is so right that I decide to spend the night. I take a minute to call my grandmother to let her know not to listen out for me because I won't be coming home.

The next morning when I get home Grandma tells me that Jessie called me several times leaving urgent messages. She left her number and I decide to return her call.

After a brief greeting she says, "Can we meet somewhere? Because I have something really important to tell you. Let's meet at the park."

"I can't meet with you. Whatever it is you can tell me over the phone."

"That's not how I imagined telling you."

"Just tell me!"

"I'm pregnant."

"Whoa! I can't believe you called to tell me something like that. Congratulations!"

"Congratulations?"

"What else can I say? I guess you have everything you've ever dreamed of now. You and Trey need to make it official and get married."

"You don't understand."

"No, you don't understand. I really couldn't care less, 'cause I've moved on. I have a new girlfriend, so have a good life and I'd appreciate it if you didn't call me anymore."

Jessie goes, "It's—"

I hang up before she can even finish her sentence. I'm trying my best to move on, but hearing Jessie's voice kind of messed me up. I should be hurt by her news and maybe I am. I don't know what I feel right now. How could she get up the nerve to call me with some bullshit like this?

My phone rings.

I say, "Hello."

"You're so damn stupid. Don't hang up on me again. I was trying to tell you that this is *your* baby."

"How do you figure it's mine?"

"Because I know."

"I wish you'd just leave me alone. I don't bother you. Can you please stop calling me? I've got something special going right now and you just want to ruin it."

"Shit, you're not that important to me. I was just trying to tell you that you have a baby on the way."

"That's Trey's baby and you know it. Let him take care of that baby just like he's taken care of everything else. Bye!"

"Jamal, don't hang up! I swear this baby is yours. Remember that day in your basement, no condom?"

"I'm not trying to hear this now. When the baby comes, we'll see who the father is. Until then leave me alone."

"Don't treat me like this. I deserve better."

"Maybe you do, but this is as good as it gets from me. I have to go. If that's my baby I'll do what I have to."

"You still love me, don't you?"

"I do, but I have to love you from a distance. Look, I gotta go."

I hang up the phone again because I'm not trying to let Jessie put a baby on me. To me we never even had this conversation and there's no way I'm going to mention this to Jillian.

Jillian and I arrive at a spot on Charles Street called Gallery 409. It's an African-American art gallery that features art as well as poetry and music. The art and the poetry are cool, but we're really here to see one of my favorite groups called Fertile Ground.

The place is packed with a mature crowd, mostly couples and a bunch of single women. Everyone's smiling, laughing, and exchanging greetings. The room is kind of dark, but still light enough to cast shadows. This kind of reminds me of a set for a neo-soul video. There are candles lit on each table, giving the room a dramatic appearance. A majority of the people here are dressed in black, which includes me and Jillian. It seems as if everyone is more interested in standing in the rear of the room than having a seat at one of the tables. Standing around must be the stylish thing to do.

I notice a few familiar faces, but none that I know well enough to introduce to Jillian until I notice Jessie's girlfriend Rachael. She's on her cell phone yapping away. She sees me and automatically heads in my direction. I'm surprised to see her here. I'd much rather run into her instead of Jessie or one of her other friends because I consider Rachael the lesser of the four evils.

Rachael gives me a hug and says, "Hey, Jamal. How are you doing?"

None of Jessie's friends are ever this kind to me. The hug makes me suspicious. With little emotion I say, "Hi, Rachael. I'm fine. How've you been?"

"Good. Guess who I'm talking to."

"I have a good idea who it is."

"Jessie sends her love."

I shake my head and say, "Whatever. This is my friend Jillian."

Jillian knows all about Jessie. She remains very pleasant and greets Rachael.

After their quick greeting Rachael's attention goes back to her conversation with Jessie. "Girl, you should come here real quick 'cause the show hasn't started yet. You don't wanna miss this."

Rachael's husband, Todd, comes over to us. I introduce him and Jillian. I don't really know him too well, but I still give him a few words. He says, "This is a nice place. Man, it's amazing what we can do when we put our heads together. I've never been here before, but I've heard lots of good things about it. Aren't you a painter?"

I am a painter, but I hate it when people refer to me as a painter, because I prefer to be called an artist. When I think of a painter I imagine a guy in oversized coveralls, a cap, with a ladder and pails of paint from Dutch Boy or Sherwin-Williams.

I say, "Yeah, I'm an artist."

Todd asks, "Any of your paintings here?"

"Not yet. Pretty soon my artwork will be recognized worldwide."

"Really?"

We continue our small talk for a minute or so and then I say goodbye to Rachael and Todd.

Rachael gives me another hug and whispers, "Jillian is really pretty, but I didn't know you were into big-boned chicks."

I don't say a word, but my facial expression says, *Fuck you!*

Jillian and I head over to a table and soon the other people follow our lead. I sit in my usual laid-back pose, acting as if I'm totally oblivious of these women at the table across from us checking me out. They know that I'm not alone and I think it's disrespectful for them to stare at me. I peek over my shoulder and they're all smiling at me. Women are always trying to tempt guys. I'm not trying to be a fool, because I have everything I need right here in Jillian.

I watch Jillian as she gazes around the room with her dreamy expressive eyes. I'm sure she's aware of the flirtatious women across from us.

Out of nowhere Jillian says, "It's okay to look at them."

"Thanks for your permission, but I wasn't looking at them. They're staring at me."

She smiles and says, "I know. I consider it a compliment. The fact that other women find you attractive makes you more appealing to me. You are nice to look at. They can stare at you all they want, but you're going home with me."

"And you're going home with me. Don't act like these guys haven't been giving you smiles and eye contact too."

"You noticed?"

I smile and say, "Yeah, I saw that guy trying to holla at you when I was talking to Rachael's husband."

"I wasn't trying to hear anything that Bama had to say. I've got the finest brotha here."

"And you know those chicks over there ain't got nothing coming. You're all I need."

We kiss.

Everyone's attention goes toward the stage. A tall, slim, dark-skinned guy comes out to warm up the crowd with some poetry. He states his credentials, which include an appearance on HBO's *Def Poetry Jam*. Everyone sits back and gets ready to experience a true genius at work; well, at least that's what he leads us to believe.

When the poet is done he announces that we're privileged to have a special guest in the house that's going to come up and perform. This is their way of stalling because Fertile Ground isn't quite ready to come out.

He says, "Ladies and gentlemen, please give it up for Baltimore's own, Khalil."

Jillian cringes in her seat. She looks disgusted and uncomfortable. Just hearing Khalil's name appears to make her blood run cold. I can't believe this is happening, but I don't expect this to spoil our evening.

This Eric Benet, Maxwell-looking brotha makes his way to the stage to do his solo thing. Right away I recognize him as the singer from Trey's party.

I ask, "So, is that him or what? Is that your Khalil?"

"I don't believe this shit. He's nothing to me, absolutely nothing. Are you ready to go?"

"No, we already paid to see Fertile Ground and I'm not about to leave because of his dusty ass. Anyway, I've seen him perform before and he's pretty good."

I'm curious to see how this plays out. This is such a small world.

Khalil adjusts the microphone and says, "Good evening, everybody. It's a real honor for me to be here with you guys tonight. I see someone who's very special to me in the audience and I don't need to mention her name because she already knows who she is." He looks directly at Jillian. "I put her through a lot of unnecessary changes and I'm so sorry. I'd like to dedicate this song to her. It's entitled 'Beautiful.' "

Khalil sits on a stool on a dark stage with a spotlight aimed directly at him. He dazzles the crowd with his acoustic guitar and then he begins to sing, pouring his heart out to my girl. His voice is smooth and hypnotic. The song actually has meaning and substance. The title is appropriate and so are the lyrics.

Khalil is very convincing and Jillian appears to be mesmerized. She looks as if she's caught up in a flashback. No matter how volatile things were in the past, these two have a long history together in comparison to the past few days she and I have been together. To Jillian, the past few days probably seem like a drop in the bucket. She begins to cry her eyes out. Khalil is killing her softly with his sweet little love song and this is all my fault because I refused to leave. His song seems to summon some emotions that Jillian denied existed. It's obvious that she still has feeling for this Eric Benet, Maxwell wanna-be.

Jillian looks at me. She shakes her head and says, "I can't sit through any more of this shit. Jamal, you can stay here if you want, but I have to go."

"I'm sorry. You're right, let's go."

Everyone watches as we exit the room. They all know that Khalil was singing to Jillian and this is embarrassing to her. I feel their eyes on me, hear snickering, and notice a few concerned faces. In any other situation I'd be embarrassed, but right now I'm too worried about Jillian.

When we get to my car she says, "I owe you an apology for that. If you want to take me home I'll understand. I can't believe I lost it like that."

"You don't owe me an apology. I should have listened to you and got you outta there."

"It's not your fault I'm such a bag lady, carrying all this old useless-ass baggage with me everywhere I go. I never thought he could get to me like that."

I'm not commenting, because I have just spotted Jessie going into Gallery 409.

I say, "Oh, shit."

"What?"

"You won't believe this, but that pretty little peanut-head girl right there is Jessie."

Jillian squints her eyes, looking in Jessie's direction. "I guess I'm not the only one with baggage. Welcome to the club." Jillian pauses for a few seconds. "She's pretty, but she's tiny. Oh my God, she looks like a little girl compared to me."

"Stop trippin'. She's not that small. How weird is this, seeing our exes on the same night?"

"Too weird. Jessie is small, compared to me. What attracted you to me? Jessie and I are complete opposites. Are you sure I'm your type?"

"I don't have a specific type. Why should I limit myself? You're a beautiful woman and that's what I like. Enough said."

"I don't have a self-esteem problem or anything, but . . ."

"But what?"

"She's really pretty and I'm sure you're not completely over her yet. Come on, you can't be. I feel bad because I tried to act like I didn't still have feelings for Khalil."

"Look, I'm just gonna be honest with you. If Jessie were on that stage tonight singing a sweet love song to me, I probably would have lost it too. You shouldn't feel bad."

"Since you put it like that I don't feel bad anymore. This just proves that we both still have feelings for our exes. So, where do we go from here?"

"Don't give it a second thought. We talked about it last night. I told you that it's possible to have feelings for more than one person at a time. Look, we can sit here all night talking about our exes or we can continue with our evening."

"Where to next?"

"I know of a nice private gallery you've never seen."

We head to my place.

When we get to my apartment I smell the aroma of food coming from upstairs. It's Grandma getting a head start on Thanksgiving dinner. I take Jillian upstairs to meet Grandma, but she's not in the kitchen, Aunt Hunk is. She's sitting at the kitchen table writing her name on a carton of orange juice and a box of Ritz crackers with a black Magic Marker. She hasn't changed at all.

"Hey, what are you doing here?"

"Hello to you too, little nigga, and for your information I live here now. I'm sitting here watching this food for Momma."

"I'm sorry, Aunt Hunk. How you doing?"

"Fine. Happy to be home."

"This is my friend, Jillian, and this is my aunt Marsha."

"Call me Hunk, baby."

Jillian has this what-the-hell kind of facial expression. She smiles and says, "It's nice to meet you."

Grandma is at the top of the steps. She hears us and comes down. I introduce her and Jillian and they seem to hit it off instantly.

Aunt Hunk stares at Jillian as if she's the most beautiful girl she has ever laid eyes on. Jillian doesn't pay her any attention and continues to talk to Grandma. Jillian seems comfortable even with Aunt Hunk staring and Grandma asking tons of questions.

Grandma excuses herself and goes to the bathroom, leaving me and Jillian alone with my crazy aunt.

After sizing Jillian up, Aunt Hunk decides to use her charm and get a little personal with my girl. My aunt is a smooth operator from way back. She tries to come off sweet and subtle, but at the same time she's like a hungry beast, carefully luring her prey into her powerful grasp. The sad thing is that Jillian has no idea that she's being set up for the kill.

Aunt Hunk goes, "Jillian, now that I've told you a little about myself, I'd love to hear more about you. What do you like to do in your spare time? You seem like a real spontaneous type with an adventurous side."

I laugh and say, "She's not that adventurous. Leave her alone. She already answered a hundred questions."

Jillian tries to downplay the whole thing. "It's okay."

I say, "No, it's not."

Aunt Hunk looks defeated. She waves her hand and says, "That's alright, baby, we can talk some other time. I didn't mean any harm. I was just trying to get to know you better. Shit, that's why he brought you here. Too bad my nephew is threatened by me."

"You're phony. You don't threaten me at all. I just know how you are and I know what you're up to."

I hear the toilet flush and a few seconds later Grandma reenters the kitchen looking clueless, drying her hands with a paper towel.

Aunt Hunk shouts, "I'm going upstairs!" No one really seems to care. She extends her hand to Jillian and says, "Good night, beautiful, it was a pleasure meeting you."

Jillian acts natural and says, "It was a pleasure meeting you too."

Aunt Hunk says good night to me and Grandma, then exits the kitchen. When no one else is looking I glance out in the hallway and Aunt Hunk smiles, then waves her middle finger at me. That's her little way of telling me that I was right, she did like Jillian.

Jillian and I end up spending another hour talking with Grandma. This is a good sign that they like each other. Jillian is almost an honorary member of the King family. Tonight was a major stepping-stone, but her official initiation will actually take place tomorrow during Thanksgiving dinner.

Chapter 31

Jamal

It's Thanksgiving and everything is going well now that I'm away from Jillian's stuck-up family. We agreed to stop by her parents' house for an abbreviated dinner engagement. We drove down this long narrow street and pulled up to this huge all-brick two-story single-family home with wooden accents neatly trimmed in a brilliant white finish. The spacious yard was neatly landscaped and the grass still held a healthy shade of green. By most standards it's a nice piece of real estate. I had no idea that houses in the city had that much land. There was a classic red diesel Mercedes-Benz, a brand-new gray Jaguar S-Type, and a white Dodge Caravan in the driveway. The entire setup told me that this was definitely an upper-middle-class family.

From the start I already had two strikes against me. The first strike had to do with the fact that I was poor and the second dealt with the fact that Jillian's parents felt cheated because I was taking their daughter away from them on such a special day. They wanted her to be with them all evening.

Jillian's mother seemed pleasant, but we spent very little time together because she was so preoccupied in the kitchen. Jillian's father was kind of a jerk, which was surprising to me. In a lot of ways he did have his good points. Jillian introduced us and right away her father asked that I address him as Senator Smith or simply Senator.

Let's just say that the senator lost my vote. I had planned to stay in the kitchen talking with Jillian and Mrs. Smith. The senator took me away from Jillian and her mother within minutes of me entering the kitchen. He acted as if I were strictly there to spend time with him. We made our way to their sunroom so we could get better acquainted, as he put it. I drank a Coke as the senator sat across from me sipping cognac and smoking a nasty cigar. He threw a variety of topics at me just to see where my head was. I wondered if he saw me as his equal or if he'd be proud to have me as a son-in-law. As he spoke I barely listened because my attention was more focused on the jazz he had playing in the background and the hissing and crackling sounds of his brand-new wood-burning stove.

We talked about international politics, the stock market, the global economy, reparations, and the current state of black America. Senator Smith had an array of ultraconservative views that I was totally unaware of. Listening to him speak made me realize that I had voted for him simply because of name recognition and the fact that he was a Democrat and not because of his personal views.

Senator Smith said, "First off, let me say that I don't believe in reparations. We don't need anymore handouts. We're privileged to be in America. Face it, this is the greatest country in the world. Slavery was somewhat of a blessing in disguise. Look at it like this, even the poorest African-American is wealthy in comparison to the poorest African."

The senator's remarks had me boiling inside. He's nothing but a Republican in disguise. He probably became a Democrat because he knew that was the quickest way to get voted into office in this district. I wanted to curse him out for being in such a powerful position and being a sellout at the same time.

Out of respect for Jillian I bit my tongue and simply said, "I disagree with that because we're still feeling the impact of slavery today and will probably feel it for many more generations. We can't forget. This government promised us forty acres and a mule and failed to fulfill that promise. For a long time we were denied our civil rights. They owe us for the lack of respect, the beatings, and the lynchings. No matter what anyone says, the government owes us."

The senator gave me this spiteful, I-knew-you-felt-that-way kind of look and said, "The government doesn't owe us anything."

We talked a little more about reparations and then he switched the conversation to personal matters. I was glad he switched the subject, because I began to feel like I were beating a dead horse. Senator Smith asked what college I had attended. He asked about my family, what church I attended, if I was a registered voter, my short-term and long-term goals. Right away I could sense that he wasn't impressed by any of my responses, except the fact that I was a registered voter that helped put his sorry ass in office.

Senator Smith did me a favor by laying out my family issues and concentrating on the issues that I had direct control over, like my education. He stressed the importance of a decent college education and the importance of having letters behind my name. He said that a college degree added validity to a person's character. He talked about his fraternity brothers and how he wouldn't trade his experiences at Howard University for anything in the world.

I explained to him that I was blessed with a natural talent that couldn't really be taught and that my niche in the world was preplanned. I told him that as an artist my potential was limitless. He wasn't trying to hear what I was saying at all.

We talked for an hour and still couldn't see eye to eye. Somehow we got on the topic of athletes leaving college early to pursue careers in professional sports.

I said, "I agree with athletes leaving school early to pursue million-dollar contracts because it's a once-in-a-lifetime opportunity. They can always find time to go back to college."

Senator Smith said, "I can't stress the point enough that a college education should always come first. As African-Americans, the time has come for us to have dignity over dollars. That's why our people are going to hell in a handbasket. Look at what rap music has done to this generation."

I got defensive and said, "I'm part of this generation. Actually hip-hop, sports, and entertainment in general are making more young African-American millionaires than ever before."

"But at what cost? They're hurting us, son. How many of them truly have good educations? They're easily controlled and the white man wants to keep those idiots in the forefront in order to control our future. Look around, who are our role models?"

Finally Senator Smith made a valid point. He started dropping some serious knowledge. The senator regained my respect, but I was glad when Jillian came to my rescue. She could see that I was worn out listening to what her father had to say. Jillian could tell by the look on my face that things weren't exactly going well and that I had spent way too much time with the senator.

Jillian pulled me aside and promised that we'd be out of there in no time, but first she wanted me to meet her sister, Natalie, and her boyfriend. When I saw Natalie we both smiled because we were already kind of familiar with each other from high school. She's a tall, slim, beanpole-looking girl with a smile similar to Jillian's and that's where the similarities ended.

Natalie's boyfriend, Earl, looked a lot like a big black version of that cartoon character Shrek. In addition to meeting Earl I had the opportunity to meet the Smiths' other stuck-up guests. Jillian and I said our good-byes and headed straight to Grandma's house.

I'm home, right where I belong on a day like this. Aunt Hunk, John, and I are watching football in the living room while Grandma, Shadow, and Jillian set the table. My family likes Jillian and she seems to like them as well. For the first time Shadow actually gets along with one of my girlfriends. She knows Jillian from high school, but the rest of the family act as if they've known her for years and John is his typical overfriendly self. I think he and Shadow are still having some serious marital problems because they arrived in separate cars. Their problems have been going on a little too long.

The six of us gather around the table and prepare for Grandma to bless the food. She looks at me and asks me to bless the food. I know God and all, but I'm not really prepared to do an official Thanksgiving blessing.

I say, "I can't. I feel like you're putting me on the spot. I haven't blessed Thanksgiving dinner since I was like five years old."

I think back to that day, twenty years ago, and how disappointed I was. That was our first Thanksgiving without Momma. I remember seeing Coach and Aunt Freda sitting in front of me, encouraging me to bless the food. They were so proud of me and all I could think about was how much I missed my mother.

Grandma tells me that I should say a prayer and the rest of the family agrees. I'm getting the same encouragement I received twenty years ago. Seems as if little has changed around here.

Jillian nudges me and says, "You can do it."

Grandma says, "Don't be ashamed to pray. If you're ashamed to pray, that means you're ashamed of God. I know you don't want Him to be ashamed of you on judgment day."

Shadow says, "That's right, don't be ashamed of God." She taunts me like we were still kids.

I seem to turn into a kid again. I say, "Shut up, dummy. I'll do it." I pause for a minute to prepare myself. I say the first prayer that comes to mind. "God is great. God is good. Let us thank Him for our food. Amen."

Shadow bursts out laughing and says, "You're the biggest fool I've ever seen."

Aunt Hunk looks at me out of the corner of her eye and says, "He sure is."

Grandma says, "You're a grown man sittin' up here talkin' 'bout 'God is great. God is good.' He is, but don't you know a better prayer than that? You should be ashamed of yourself."

John jokes and says, "I'm ashamed for him."

Jillian doesn't say a word. She just sits next to me laughing her butt off because she's not used to having this much fun at the dinner table with her stuck-up family.

John is about to carve the turkey when the doorbell rings. Shadow jumps up from her seat to answer the door. She returns with a surprise guest.

Kyle Williams enters the dining room. I have a bad habit of referring to Kyle by his full name.

He greets us with his famous overexaggerated anchorman voice. "Good evening, everyone." That's the same way he opens the evening news. He kills me being so expressive, moving his eyebrow up and down as he speaks.

John yells, "Ain't this a bitch!" He turns to Grandma and says, "Excuse me, Ms. Connie. Everybody, please forgive me, but this ain't right."

I think, *Oh no! The shit is about to hit the fan.*

Jillian looks shocked.

I whisper to her, "I'll explain later."

Shadow says, "Calm down, John."

Kyle Williams says, "Yes, can't we all just get along?"

I look at John and he looks as if he's about to snap. He grips the knife tightly, raising it from the turkey. At this point, that knife is more of a lethal weapon than a simple carving tool.

I look at John and say, "Man, won't you just let me carve the turkey?"

John says, "Don't worry, Jamal, I got this."

Shadow says, "John, you acted as if you weren't coming today, so I invited Kyle. I didn't feel right canceling his invitation just because you decided to show up at the last minute."

John says, "That's unfair and also untrue. I'm still a member of this family no matter what's going on between us." John points the knife at Kyle Williams and says, "He's the unwelcome guest. Today is Thanksgiving and you're with him every day. Can I have a day with you for a change?"

Kyle Williams puts his hands up and says, "I can go. Really, it's okay. I'll leave."

Shadow says, "No, I want you here."

Kyle Williams says, "I must go. Good evening, everyone. I'm sorry for the inconvenience."

Shadow gives John a wicked stare, then quickly follows Kyle Williams to the front door.

Grandma says, "What the hell just happened?"

Aunt Hunk laughs and says, "Lord have mercy. I'm glad I came home in time to witness all this drama unfold."

John has tears in his eyes. He lays down the knife and says, "I can explain. Kali and I have been experiencing marital problems for years. Last week she decided to leave me and the life we've worked so hard to achieve. She left all that behind for Kyle."

Shadow bursts back into the room like a crazy woman. She yells, "I can't believe you're telling them all our business! If I wanted my business broadcasted I could do it myself. Since we're airing our dirty laundry, I've loved Kyle since the moment I laid eyes on him."

With a sarcastic grin John says, "Oh my God, tell us something we don't know. Everybody could see that you two had something going on for years, except me. I never had any real proof so all I could ever do was sit back and wonder."

Aunt Hunk says, "Shadow, I don't mean to be all in your business, but John's right. Even the people in my cell block could see that you and Kyle had something going on."

Shadow says, "Kyle and I were just good friends for a long time. We never did anything to disrespect my husband, until John starting making accusations that something was going on. Sometimes you can make a person do things just by mentioning it over and over. There was always something special between us and since John kept blaming me for something I wasn't doing, I felt that I might as well let something happen between us." She looks at John and says, "You never wanted me and that's why I asked for a divorce."

He yells, "Bullshit! That just goes to show what I said was true. Men and women can't be friends without being sexual."

Shadow says, "Kiss my ass, John."

"Grow one."

I can sense what Shadow's about to say next and the last thing John needs is for the rest of the family to know about his little penis. Before I can get a word out, Grandma cuts in.

She yells, "Please stop! Do not spoil my day. Y'all are sitting up here arguing after I damn near killed myself preparing this meal and it's just sitting here getting cold. We can discuss everybody's problems after dinner. Jamal already blessed the food, so everybody shut the hell up and let's eat."

Everything goes back to normal as if Kyle Williams never arrived. John finishes carving the turkey and we all make our plates. I'm only half as surprised as everyone else because I had an idea about what was going on, but I had no idea that John knew about Kyle Williams and Shadow. She never told me that she had planned to leave John. I guess she just couldn't take being with him any longer.

Jillian is the sweetest thing. She never says a word. She just acts natural and blends in right along with my dysfunctional family.

Chapter 32

Jamal

After dinner we're all in a pretty good mood sitting in the living room talking about old times. My family loves to reminisce because it makes us laugh and that's a good thing. Aunt Hunk keeps mentioning things about Coach and how crazy he was. She, John, and Jillian are the only ones who laugh because they have no idea what the rest of us know about Coach.

We hear somebody at the front door fumbling with keys. Everybody that has a key to the front door is already here, except for one person, my mother. It has to be her or else someone is trying to break into the house. Everybody stares at the door with anticipation.

Just as we suspected, it's Momma and she has a friend with her. Her friend is a tall, slim older guy about my complexion. He looks nervous as hell like he owes somebody some money and is hoping they won't mention it.

Since today's a holiday it makes us all extra-sentimental and friendly. Everybody jumps out of their seats to greet Momma and her friend. Again Jillian just blends right in and follows the rest of the group. She gives my mother a big hug as if she has known her for years. I quickly introduce them and then I introduce myself to my mother's friend and I find out that his name is Martin. I've never seen my mother in such a good mood.

With a big, bright smile she says, "I know we're late for dinner, but I had to meet up with Martin first. I have some good news that I can't wait to share. I want everybody to sit down for this. Then you can jump out of your seats, scream, dance, or do whatever you want." She moves closer to Martin and says. "Are y'all ready? Guess who this man is. This is my old, and I mean that in a nice way, and very dear friend Thomas Martin Butler. Martin, this is everybody."

The name Thomas Martin Butler seems to echo throughout the room a million times. Those of us who are familiar with that name are momentarily frozen. I get this stinging feeling in my eyes and I'm not quite sure what to do or say. I've never seen this man's face before, but I always thought I would be able to recognize it anywhere. I was wrong.

I look at Shadow and she looks at me. I look at my mother and ask, "Is this really our father?"

Martin answers, "I sure am. Y'all c'mere and give me a hug."

Within seconds I feel happy, sad, nervous, nauseated, cheated, and relieved at the same time. Shadow and I jump to our feet and embrace our father for the first time. Today is Thanksgiving and Father's Day all in one. We've never had a reason to celebrate Father's Day until now. I've dreamed of this day all my life. I thought this man was dead or just completely lost to the world. I can't believe I'm standing here with my mother, father, and sister. I look at Grandma and she's just overwhelmed with emotions. I try to laugh to keep from crying. I try to hold back my tears in front of Jillian because I'm not sure how she feels about seeing a grown man cry. When I look at her she's already crying for me. John even appears teary eyed. My hard-core aunt is even crying.

My prayers have been answered. Grandma told us to put all that hate to rest because she knew that God would work things out and He did.

My father is hurt because he never knew that Shadow and I existed until my mother found him on the Internet. He's been living in Virginia all these years. Out of nowhere Shadow and I begin to bombard him with all the questions that have been floating around in our heads for years.

Martin sits down with us all and begins to tell us about himself. Everyone pays close attention to him as he speaks.

"Let me just say that it's good to be here with my family. I can't believe I'm the father of twins. You guys have asked so many questions
that I'm not sure where to begin."

I say, "It's okay, Martin, take your time."

I wanted to call him Dad, but it doesn't feel natural referring to
him like that right now. Shadow is quiet and seems to stare at Martin
in amazement.

Martin says, "I've had a good, but pretty uneventful life. I married a
woman I met while overseas. Then we moved to Virginia after I finished serving in the army. I'm a retired government steelworker. My
wife died two years ago and we never had any kids." He pauses, looking for the right words to say next. "I want y'all to know that I'm so
thankful to finally meet my children and I'm sorry that we missed out
on so many years together." His voice cracks and he begins to cry. "I
didn't get to see y'all grow up and that hurts, but I'm here for you two
now. I really wanna be a part of your lives, if that's okay."

This is without a doubt the weirdest and happiest day for me and
Shadow. We both welcome our father into our lives with open arms.

Part III

The Flavor of Money

Chapter 33

Jessie

At this point I should be used to my pampered lifestyle and in addition to that I should be used to this undeniable feeling of guilt. Trey blankets me with love and at the same time there's a shroud of guilt that hovers over me. I'm grateful for all of the things that Trey provides. I really thought I deserved this special treatment after being so deprived all my life. Deep down inside I know that I don't deserve it, especially since I'm pregnant with another man's child. It's hard acting like everything's fine while Trey spoils and praises me. Trust me, I can do it, but it isn't easy.

We just returned from our seven-day eastern Caribbean cruise with Kev, Mike, and their surprisingly cool-ass girlfriends from New York, Trina and Daphne. Trey loves to play the role of the big spender. He treated his boys to a vacation. Even though I didn't like it I kept my mouth shut because it's not my place to complain or give suggestions on how he should spend his money.

Kev and Mike called themselves getting more familiar or trying to get a little friendly with me, but as always I refused to open up to them. Trey never said it, but I know he doesn't want me to get too personal with anyone in his little clique. I keep my distance from Trey and his friends because it helps to avoid conflict.

Around our third day at sea, I was relaxing by the pool, sitting in a chaise lounge minding my own business when Kev approached me. I instantly felt uneasy because Trey was still in our cabin and Kev's girl-friend, Trina, was still in their cabin. Something about this whole situ-ation didn't feel or look right.

Kev started off with some small talk and then had the nerve to ask, "How did a nice girl like you get mixed up with somebody like Trey?" He said it in a joking way, but I still didn't like him asking me some-thing so out of line because it was like the pot calling the kettle black. Kev can't talk bad about Trey because he's out there doing the same thing Trey does.

I said, "Go to hell, Kev. Leave me alone."

"Damn, girl, why you always acting like that? Me and Mike joke around with you and you treat us like shit. What's up with that?"

"I just don't like y'all. That's what's up with that."

"You don't even try to hide the fact that you don't like us and that's cool. You might need us one day, though."

I took off my shades and looked him right in his ugly face. "What the hell is that supposed to mean?" Something in his words made me feel threatened.

He threw his hands up and said, "Nothing more than what I said. You might need us one day and we'll be here for you. But you make a nigga not wanna look out for you. I didn't mean any harm."

I felt more at ease, but I still didn't want to talk to him and I defi-nitely didn't want Trey to see us alone by the pool talking.

I smiled and said, "I'm sorry. I just don't take to strangers too well. I guess I have a problem trusting certain individuals and that's way too deep for me to go into right now."

"I love you like a sister, shorty, and I'd do anything to help you. Me and Mike always say that Trey is lucky to have a woman like you. For real, Jessie, you don't take a lot of shit and that's good. I'm gonna back off and I'll ask Mike to do the same, because the last thing we wanna do is make you uncomfortable."

"I don't mean to be a bitch or nothing, but I'm just trying to re-spect Trey."

Kev said, "I understand where you're coming from. Trey's like a big brother to me and I'd never do anything to disrespect him."

Kev got up and gave me my personal space again. Afterward I felt kind of bad because I was limiting my contact with certain people. In all actuality, I knew it was a good thing.

While we were on vacation I tried my best to have a good time, and each moment I tried to relax the anxiety that comes along with my predicament/pregnancy brought my joy to a screeching halt. Our ship, the *Explorer of the Seas,* was incredible. I never realized the ocean would bounce our ship around like it did. I was nauseated for days. I couldn't tell whether it was seasickness or morning sickness that caused my nausea. Of course when Trey asked what was going on I blamed my nausea on seasickness.

Trey and I hardly spent any time in our cabin because there was so much to do and see like live shows, gambling, shopping, dancing, and food and drinks galore. We were on a floating city. When we were in our cabin I did enjoy the ocean view. A few times I was actually able to fabricate a smile. Trey could sense that something was wrong and the last thing I wanted was to let my discomfort spoil our vacation.

I kept saying, "I'm seasick."

Trey took me to the ship's doctor and he prescribed a medication for motion sickness, but I didn't take any.

Our nights were romantic and that was tough for me to deal with because I didn't want Trey to touch me, at all. Everything was so perfect and ordinarily I'd be in a sexy kind of mood, but I was far from feeling sexy. *Disgusted* is a better word to describe my mood. It was hard going along pretending that everything was okay. Every time we made love I had to refrain from screaming, "Stop, get off me!" Thank God I was able to keep myself composed. Acting is just one of the many talents that women are blessed with.

Our ship took us to ports like St. Maarten, St. Thomas, Nassau, and San Juan. My anxiety brought my joy to a screeching halt and in the back of my mind I kept hearing that unbelievable and terrifying phrase, *I'm pregnant!* I would relax and then I'd hear it again and again.

I repeatedly experienced the same annoying cycle and I can feel that same anxiety right now.

Trey and I are on our way home from BWI Airport. We're on the Baltimore/Washington Parkway stuck in traffic behind an endless sea of red glowing brake lights. A giant flashing arrow is forcing the traffic in the right lane to merge left because there's a road crew with heavy machinery hard at work laying new asphalt. I might be wrong, but it seems like they're always repairing this same stretch of highway.

As we slowly creep along at a snail's pace I notice the moon behind a row of trees. It's as if the moon is playing peekaboo with me because it hides behind the trees and only reveals itself every five to ten seconds. This reminds me so much of when I was a little girl and thought that the moon was following me. I thought the moon knew that I was hiding something or had done something wrong and followed me because I was bad. No matter how fast I ran or how many corners I had turned, it continued to follow me. I was so silly then, but to be honest I'm not much better now.

Trey says, "This doesn't make any damn sense. I can't believe they're doing roadwork on this highway again."

"I was thinking the same thing. Every time we come this way they're doing roadwork. We should've gotten on I-95 earlier instead of coming down this far."

Trey turns on the map light, I guess in order to get a better look at me. "Are you feeling any better?"

"I'm fine. The nausea is gone."

"You've been acting strange. I'm still worried about you even though I figured out what's going on with you."

My stomach instantly gets this weird, nervous, sinking feeling. I look away from Trey and wait to hear him say that he noticed that my period is late.

"You can't hide stuff from me. I figured it out on the cruise."

I give him this pitiful look and ask, "What?"

"You're upset with me for treating Kev and Mike to the cruise. Plus, I know you can't stand them."

I smile and can hardly hide the relieved look on my face. "Yeah, along with being seasick that stuff was kind of bothering me too." My mind goes into overdrive trying to manufacture quick details to go along with these petty issues Trey brought up. In my book being a good actor and a good liar definitely go hand in hand. "I'm worried that Kev and Mike might think you're getting a big head or getting ahead of yourself. Y'all are equal partners and you spending all that money on them and their girls makes you look kind of cocky. Of course that's just my opinion."

"I see what you saying, but the cruise was just my way of saying I appreciate our friendship and for them looking out for me."

"You sure they didn't see it as your way of showing them who has the real money in the partnership? It kind of looks like you were saying, 'I'm the boss and this is your reward for being good workers.' "

"Not at all. They ain't like that. If anything, they act like they want me to step up and be the boss, leader, or whatever you wanna call it."

"I just don't want any friction between you and them."

"You're lying, 'cause you'd love if I got into it with them; then you wouldn't have to see their ugly asses again."

"That does sound good."

"They're good guys. You're just judging them on their appearances. I know they're a little rough and could use some polishing."

"In a way you're right. I do judge them on how they speak, how they treat women, and how they carry themselves. Don't lie, you know they remind you of two rejects from the Wu-Tang Clan."

Trey laughs.

Traffic begins to pick up and we're able to exit the Baltimore/Washington Parkway and get onto I-95. Trey speeds up like a bat out of hell in an attempt to make up for the time we lost earlier in the traffic jam. I hate telling a grown man what he should or shouldn't be doing, but I do it anyway.

"Trey, please, stop speeding."

"I'm tired and I can't wait to get home."

Out of nowhere I see flashing blue and red lights. My stomach gets that nervous sinking feeling again.

As Trey pulls over he says, "Aw, shit. As tired as I am, why they gotta be doing this racial profiling bullshit tonight?"

"Honestly, as fast as you were going and as dark as it is that state trooper couldn't tell your race."

"They don't need to see my face because they can tell that I'm a young black male by what I'm driving."

Nobody told his dumb ass to go out and buy this Escalade and get it all chromed-out with twenty-two-inch rims to draw extra attention. Black people always have to stand out.

I play stupid and say, "I didn't even think about that. I told you to slow down, but no."

"I ain't trying to hear all that I-told-you-so stuff, okay?"

"Alright. I hope everything's clean in here. You know what I mean?"

"Everything's clean. My gun is under the seat, that's all."

"Oh my God. But it's registered, right?" Trey gives me this stupid look. I ask again. "Right? Please tell me that it's registered and I'm not in a truck with a gun with God only knows how many bodies on it."

"Shut up and stop acting so damn nervous. Think of this as a routine traffic stop, even though I know this is racial profiling. Remember this guy just wants to go home just like we do. This is nothing major. A'ight?"

I never thought we'd go down on a simple traffic stop, but that's usually how it happens. It's hard for me to hide how nervous I am. My hands are trembling and my heart is beating out of my chest. All I hear are the sounds of my pounding heart and my quick shallow breaths. I think, *I'm too pretty to go to jail and I'm pregnant too.*

Trey quickly pushes his gun farther under the seat. He places both hands on the steering wheel. He looks cool and very composed and all I can do is try my best to mimic his response to this unexpected situation. Trey has been in situations like this before and he pretty much knows what to expect, so I put my trust in him. I slow my breathing and think about trusting in someone else. I close my eyes and say a quick last-minute prayer.

Lord, if you get me out of this situation I promise that I'll be the first person in church Sunday morning. God, please let this be a nice cop and give Trey the proper guidance so that we all can make it home safely. You know my heart and that I'm a good person. I'm depending on your help, Father, please.

The state trooper is taking his time to approach us. He shines his searchlight directly on us and I'm instantly blinded because the side-view mirror just reflected the beam of light into my eyes. I feel as if I were having an out-of-body experience, because I'm seeing this whole experience from the perspective of the state trooper's dashboard-mounted video camera just like I've watched so many scenes like this play out on television.

As the state trooper gets out of his patrol car and approaches the driver's side Trey says, "Shhh. Stay calm and let me do all the talking."

Trey lowers the driver's-side window. I look over at the trooper and he has a very serious look on his face. Now he appears angry and Trey acts as if he wants to match that same anger.

"Good evening, sir. License and registration, please."

Trey doesn't say a word, he simply pulls out his wallet, then reaches for the glove compartment to retrieve his registration.

The trooper looks over at me and says, "Ma'am, I'll need to see some identification." Before Trey hands the trooper his license and registration the trooper asks, "Sir, is this your vehicle?"

Trey looks even more pissed now. He says a simple "Yeah."

I quickly hand Trey my license and he passes it to the trooper along with his license and registration.

The trooper takes our information. He looks down at Trey and says, "I'll be right back."

The trooper gets into his car to run a check on us.

I say, "I don't believe this."

"Stop worrying."

"You're right. We're fine as long as he doesn't check under your seat. You don't have any warrants or traffic violations against you, do you?"

"I don't know."

"What do you mean, you don't know?"

"Put it like this, none that I know of. Can you be quiet? I don't need any more stress right now."

"I need to know what's going on with you because I can't go to jail."

Trey laughs and says, "Look at you breaking down already. Damn, you're a trip. That's why I'm glad you don't know shit about me, 'cause I honestly believe you'd tell everything you know to save your own ass."

"Don't make fun of me, because I'm not like that."

Trey knows me well, because if this doesn't turn out right I'll tell about everything I know to keep from going to jail.

A few minutes later the trooper comes back to the truck and says, "Mr. Bryant, you were going eighty-five miles an hour and the posted speed limit is sixty-five miles an hour, which means you were a serious hazard to the safety of the other motorists."

Out of nowhere Trey says, "If you're gonna give me a ticket just give me a ticket. I don't need a lecture."

My heart starts beating out of control again because I can't believe Trey is getting an attitude with this trooper. He's going to piss this man off even more and make him search this truck.

I can tell that the trooper feels a little threatened and insulted, because he puts his hand on his gun. "Sir, you need to cool down. Luckily you don't have any warrants or violations against you. I was just trying to explain to you exactly why you were pulled over."

"Man, I already know why I was pulled over and so do you. I'm black and this is what y'all do to us. Can I just have my ticket so I can get home?"

Even though Trey asked me to be quiet I have to say something to break the tension in the air. "Officer, he doesn't mean any harm. We're just coming back from our vacation and our flight was delayed for a few hours. The airline treated us poorly and if he seems a little frustrated it's not about anything you've done. He's still frustrated about our flight."

The trooper looks back at Trey and says, "Sir, I want to keep this as simple as possible considering that we're both having a bad night. If it weren't for this young lady I'd ask you to step out of your vehicle and I'd search it, but I can see that you're just returning from your vacation. I won't put you through all that. I assure you that this stop had nothing to do with the color of your skin."

"I'm sorry, Officer. I appreciate that. She's right, I'm still frustrated about the delay at the airport. Again, I apologize."

The trooper hands Trey our information along with a ticket for a hundred and twenty-five dollars. Trey signs the ticket and the trooper lets as go and I'm so relieved.

As soon as we pull off I ask, "What were you thinking?"

"He made me mad talking down to me like that. I forgot all about what I had under the seat. I'm glad you spoke up, but next time you better listen to me."

"Please, I saved us. I couldn't believe you were talking to that state trooper like that. Sometimes you can be so ghetto."

"Look who's talking."

We laugh, but that situation could have ended much worse than a bruised ego and a ticket.

When we pull up to the front gate of our house there's a car waiting there. Within seconds I realize who it is. It's Trey's baby's mother, Alicia. Trey sees her and tries to ignore her. Alicia jumps out of her car and steps right in front of the truck as if Trey isn't crazy enough to run her ass over.

Right away I realize that something is wrong when I get a good look at her. Alicia really looks bad. She has dark rings under her eyes. Her hair looks like she got caught up in a windstorm and her lips look white and crusty like she's extra-hungry.

She steps around to the driver's side and yells, "Trey, I need to talk to you!"

Trey cracks the window and asks, "What do you want?"

"I been coming over here for the past three nights looking for you."

"Didn't I ask you not to come out here?"

"I need money and the baby misses you."

Alicia acts as if I were not even sitting here. I say, "Hi, Alicia."

She twists her crusty white lips and says, "Congratulations, you've got everything I wanted and now I have to beg for this nigga's help. Don't talk to me, bitch."

Trey hands Alicia a handful of money, mostly ones, fives, and tens. He asks, "Where's Anitra, anyway?"

She ignores him and looks down at the money and asks, "What's this shit? We need more money than this. You know how that girl can eat."

"Stop complaining. Crack is cheap and you can get all you need with that. That's all I have for you tonight." He gives her a disgusted look and lets out a sigh. "You look terrible. Where's my baby?"

"She's at Tonya's house. C'mon and see her." She laughs. "You need to stop with that crack stuff 'cause you know I don't mess with drugs. Me and the baby need some Christmas money."

"Christmas money, huh? Well, that's all I have right now."

"Stop lying to me. You giving Jessie all your money, that's what it is. Okay, I'll fix you. You better give me some more money or I'll squeal on you and you better believe I will."

Trey lowers the window all the way and says, "Alright, I was wrong. C'mere, I got something else for you."

Alicia smiles and eases her way up to the window. Out of nowhere Trey grabs her with both hands and jacks her up.

He yells, "Don't ever threaten me with that shit. Now take your junky-lookin' ass away from here. You're an unfit mother and I'm gonna take my daughter from you."

I yell, "Trey, stop! Please let her go!"

He releases Alicia. She begins to cry and says, "I'm gonna get you for that. Don't come around my way anymore, 'cause I'm gonna get somebody to kill you. I feel sorry for you, Jessie, 'cause he's not who you think he is. You'll find out though."

Trey ignores Alicia, but I heard what she said. As the front gate opens Trey puts his window up and takes off up the driveway, leaving Alicia standing there.

Chapter 34

Jamal

I'm no longer a stranger to myself. The day I met my father made all the difference in the world. For the first time in my life I have a clear understanding of who made me and who I am. No matter how much people try to alter the truth about having biological parents in your life, they're irreplaceable. No one could have been a better parent or could have had a stronger influence on me than Grandma. The fact that she was a good parent never stopped me from wondering about my parents or took away my abandonment issues. Trying to visualize my family together was always a challenge to me. In my mind there was always this distorted image of what we would look like together. It was virtually impossible to ever imagine us uniting. What happened on Thanksgiving Day was nothing short of a miracle. John took a Polaroid of me and Shadow with our parents and we all agreed that it was a family portrait that was long overdue. We can't ever get back the years we've lost, but in reality I'm extremely grateful that my mother had the strength and the courage to bring our family together.

Shadow was excited that we finally met our father, but unlike myself she never dwelled on the fact that he wasn't in our lives. To be honest she never really dwelled on the fact that our mother wasn't in our lives either. Shadow was more goal oriented and able to persevere and in a lot of ways I let my abandonment issues get the best of me.

My life is constantly changing and that's a good thing. I've never really been one to fear change, but at times I do stop and wonder. It's funny how one event makes everything else fall into its proper sequence. Jillian asked me to help turn her house into a home by moving in and I did. The day I moved out Grandma tried to be strong for me because she didn't want me to feel guilty for leaving. At first she stressed how ready she was and how important it was for me to get out and really be on my own until the time actually came for me to leave. As I loaded my last box on the U-Haul, Grandma looked at me as if it was going to be our last moment together in this lifetime. She cried worse than a preschooler with separation anxiety on the first day of school. Regardless of how much it hurt the two of us, I had to make a major move as soon as possible. I tried to move quick because I thought it would hurt less, sort of like when you remove a bandage from a really sensitive spot on your skin. I was wrong because it hurt so bad. I felt like I was turning my back on the one person who always gave me unconditional love and the one person who always gave a damn about me. My heart was flooded and I fought to hold back my tears. Grandma actually stood at the back door and watched as I hauled away all of my worldly possessions. What a sad sight.

Even Aunt Hunk has made a major move. As the new owner of Coach's house I made a deal with Aunt Hunk. I told her if she would clean up the place she could stay there for the first two months rent-free. The place is a complete mess so it's a pretty good deal. It will probably take her two months to clean it up anyway. I don't plan to charge her any rent until she gets on her feet, but I didn't tell her that because she's kind of typical and would take my kindness for weakness.

Mrs. Harvey bought Coach's Cadillac from me for her old playa-playa husband. I sold the small things like his jewelry, stamp, and coin collections to a guy at the flea market. I hated selling off all the possessions that my uncle left me, but those things were totally useless to me. I donated his clothes and tools to Goodwill. I gave all of the cash from Coach's bank account to Grandma so she wouldn't feel the financial impact of me leaving right away. Even though I'm gone I still plan to look out for her. I put the remaining insurance money into a mutual fund that John suggested. I offered Shadow half of the insurance money, but she flat-out refused to take a penny of that money.

Lately I've had several dreams about the baby that Jessie is carrying. Sometimes it appears in my dreams as a bigheaded boy that looks just like me and other times it's a beautiful little girl that's the spitting image of her mother. I have my doubts, but I know that there's a strong possibility that the baby is mine. I'm starting to realize that Jessie doesn't really have much of a reason to lie. I often wonder if she has more to lose or more to gain based on who's really the father of her baby. Sounds like a real win, lose, or draw situation. Honestly, the last thing I want is for a kid to come into this world with the same abandonment issues I dealt with. If I'm truly the father of this child, it's important to me to be more than a sperm donor. I don't plan to be an absentee parent simply sending a child-support check. I want to be an everyday presence with a definite impact on the kid's life, a real father.

I plan to do something about the whole situation, but when I'm ready. I refuse to let Jessie dictate my life, especially when she's such an insignificant factor. *Enough of that.*

Jillian is like a breath of fresh air to me. Living with her is unlike anything I've ever experienced. This is her house, but she refers to it and everything in it as ours. She welcomed me into her home and into her life with open arms and I mean that literally. Jillian never mentioned anything about me paying bills around here. Being the person I am, I've agreed to pay half of the mortgage and utilities. The last thing I want to do is be a burden on her like that freeloading Khalil. Jillian makes a lot more money than I do, but it's only right that we split things down the middle. We're slowly making plans for the future and I love contributing to something so special. This is about us. Every day we talk, laugh, and share. I've never been the romantic type, but I read to her and when I do it's incredibly sexy and romantic at the same time. Most men have no idea what passion and sexy secrets lie in contemporary African-American novels. I was introduced to a new world when I picked up a novel called *Love Don't Come Easy.*

I have the privilege of getting a behind-the-scenes look at Jillian's life and vice versa. I'm constantly learning more and more about her. She has shared some of her fears and innermost thoughts. She even sings and last night she surprised me by singing "Lovin' You" by Minnie Riperton to me. I don't know how she knew it, but that's my all-time favorite love song. As she sang, it really touched me because it seemed as if she meant every single heartfelt word.

Jillian is mature, funny, sexy, self-directed, and independent. She's strong, but she knows how to be a lady. I classify her in the passive-aggressive category because although she's mild mannered she knows how to get her point across without losing her cool.

During sex she's submissive, but she has the tendency to be dominate at certain times. I find no fault in her take-charge nature. She excites me and the mere thought of her turns me on.

Jillian loves to cook. She wakes up early every morning and makes breakfast. This morning we ate omelets, grits, and country-style biscuits. At first I thought she had a thing for breakfast in bed, but now I know that she likes to eat every meal in the bedroom instead of in the kitchen. It's crazy, but we have most of our meals in our bedroom in front of the television. This reminds me of being kids and doing whatever we like because our parents aren't home.

I've made the transition from being a single, semiresponsible adult to being a responsible man in a committed relationship without even realizing it. That's how fast all this happened. I no longer sleep in a single bed. I now sleep in a king-sized bed made for two. A few times Jillian has awakened me in the middle of the night and made love to me. I'm loving every minute of this. One of the best things about being here is that I get to wake up every morning and stare into Jillian's beautiful face.

I'm lying in bed flipping through the pages of Jillian's *Essence* magazine when she steps out of the bathroom wearing nothing but a plush dark purple towel. She instantly steals my attention. The magazine is now facedown on the bed because I've never been the type of guy that could just sit back and do nothing while an attractive woman dries her body. I'm especially captivated by Jillian. She has her back to me as she stands in front of the wide-angled mirror above her dresser. As she dries and studies herself in the mirror, I slowly approach her from behind like a stranger in the night. Jillian doesn't expect this and that's what makes it so hot. She quivers when my lips gently make contact with the back of her neck. My nude body unites with hers and our contours mesh perfectly as if we were made for each other. Jillian closes her eyes as I wrap my arms tightly around her waist, kissing her neck. She arches her back and raises her arms above her head. Her right hand grips the back of my neck as her left hand aimlessly moves back and forth from my head to my face. Her body is still warm and moist from her hot shower. She's kind of firm, but still soft in all the right places.

Jillian can feel me getting hard. She starts to give in to me, arching her back even more and pressing her ass against me, signaling that she wants to be penetrated from behind. This is her unique way of inviting me inside her love without saying a word. She lends forward and I gladly oblige.

I'm harder than hard. I mean, my thing is so rigid that it feels artificial. I watch as my forceful thrusts send shock waves through Jillian's body. She unleashes the most beautiful sexual screams and moans and it's like music to my ears. I lean forward, grabbing a handful of her hair. I continue to thrust as we stare at each other in the mirror. She clenches her teeth and squints her eyes, never losing eye contact with me. She loves this and I can tell that she wants it harder and faster. Usually I'm gentle with her, but not tonight. This position is wild and animalistic, allowing for deep penetration, and that really turns me on. Jillian is long overdue for a good workout and I'm feeling athletic tonight. I plan to do her until we're both dripping wet with sweat.

Both of our hands meet between Jillian's legs. She guides my hand to the right spot and then she brings her feet together. Her legs tighten and she lets out a deep soul-cleansing moan that gets all of my undivided attention.

Jillian hyperventilates and becomes weak in the knees. She's exhausted, but satisfied. I pick her up and gently lay her down on the bed, wrapping myself around her, becoming a natural heat source. I lie here kissing and stroking her.

Chapter 35

Jessie

The past couple of nights around here have been pretty unusual. Trey has been spending an excessive amount of time around the house. I can tell that something is bothering him, but I'm not sure exactly what. It might have something to do with the fact that the feds, along with the local police, have really been making their presence felt on the streets of Baltimore.

I'm sitting Indian style in the middle of our bed eating a big ole bowl of butter pecan ice cream. I'm wearing my favorite white silk pajamas and matching robe. For the second consecutive night Trey is home chillin' in bed curled up in a fetal position with his back to me watching *Comic View* on BET. He isn't laughing at the show at all. I'm not sure if it's because he's seen this particular episode too many times or if he just has something on his mind. He's not saying a word.

I ask, "Baby, why aren't you laughing?"

With his head still facing the television he mumbles, "I'm not in the mood for jokes."

"Is there something I can do to make you feel better?"

He slowly sits up in bed and says, "Yeah, you can answer one question."

"What's that?"

"Would you ever steal from me?"

I think, *Oh, shit, this penny-pinching bastard must know about my rainy-day fund.*

He gives me this angry look and says, "The look on your face says it all. Let me tell you something: Never bite the hand that feeds you, a'ight?"

All I can say is, "A'ight."

"Why steal from me? I give you everything. Anyway, you can't steal from a hustler. I keep count of everything. You should have known that sooner or later I'd find out."

"I was just trying to set up some emergency cash, that's all."

"What for? You plan on going somewhere?"

"No. That was just in case you decided put me out. I don't have anything to fall back on. I don't wanna end up on the streets penniless and hopeless."

Trey scares me. He snaps and jumps out of bed. He runs over to his safe and opens it. He pulls out stacks of wrapped cash and starts throwing them at me. Trey is angry and out of control. He throws the money really hard, hitting me all over my body, and I try to shield myself with pillows.

As he throws the money he yells, "Here you go! You want cash? Here's a load of cash! You need to get rid of that chicken-head mentality of yours! You're better than that! You wanna take my money and leave me! Here! Take it and go! I should've known you couldn't be trusted. I lied when I said my insurance policy was in your name. I'm glad I didn't put your name on it. I thought you were different, but I was wrong!"

I yell, "Stop, I am different. Please, stop!"

"I thought you loved me!"

"I do love you!"

"Then why are you stealing from me! Tell me the truth!"

Finally he stops throwing the money at me. I'm really upset and I begin to cry.

Again Trey says, "Tell me the truth."

"Oh my God, I can't tell you the truth."

"Why not? You better tell me!"

I put my hands up to my face, catching my tears. I know he might kill me for what I'm about to say. I take a deep breath and look Trey directly in the eyes and say, "My period was late and I did a home pregnancy test and it was positive."

"That doesn't make sense. How the hell are you pregnant?"

"I don't know."

"What do you mean you don't know? We use condoms! Did one of them break or what?"

"I don't know. I don't know." I want to lie, but something inside me won't let me because I am different from the other girls Trey is used to. I pause for a few seconds, looking down at the floor for a way to tell the truth. "I can't lie to you anymore. I lied when I said I used to make Jamal use condoms with me. There was one time he didn't."

"Why'd you lie to me like that? I believed you too. You're no better than the rest of those bitches."

"You said you'd never call me that again."

"Well, I lied. Just like you lied to me. Get out . . . get out of my house right now!"

"See, that's why I started taking the money. I knew you'd kick me out when you found out I was pregnant. I'm not like the rest of those girls. I could have played you, slept with you without a condom, and told you that this was your baby. You wouldn't have known any different."

Before Trey says another word he notices one of the security monitors. It picks up a black Navigator at the front gate of the house. The gate was left open and the truck makes its way up the driveway.

Trey sees the truck on the monitor and says, "That's Derek's truck. What the fuck does he want?"

Trey grabs a pair of sweatpants and a T-shirt off the chair and quickly slips them on. As he gets dressed another monitor clearly shows Derek and two other guys getting out of the truck and walking up to the front door. Trey is obviously shaken. He grabs his cell phone and orders somebody to come right over.

Trey turns to me and says, "I'm not sure what's up, so you might wanna go to the safety room real fast."

We head to the safety room. He opens the door and walks over to his gun cabinet. Trey puts on his bulletproof vest and a jacket, then pulls out an automatic handgun and a big assault rifle. I'm so nervous I can hardly move. Trey steps out of the safety room, then guides me inside. Before leaving me he makes sure that I know how to lock it correctly.

I look at him and say, "I really love you."

"I know you do, but save it. This isn't the time for that."

Trey gives me a quick kiss and then he looks away, closing the door. From the inside monitors I can see him walking out of the bedroom, downstairs, and then toward the front door.

Derek rings the doorbell. The intercom system at the front door picks up everything he says.

Derek says, "Yo, I know the nigga in there."

One of the other guys says, "He's definitely in there."

Trey puts his hand up to his nose, throws his head back, and shakes it like he's losing his mind. He opens the door as if he has no fear of facing his destiny. He has a real cocky whatever-whenever type of attitude.

Trey says, "What the hell you want, Derek? I can't believe you, bringing strangers to my house."

Derek looks at Trey's assault rifle and says, "All that's not necessary. We just wanna come in and talk business. These are my buddies from Philly, Dre and Lamont."

Trey says, "Yo, I ain't trying to hear that shit. Get these feds away from my house. My boys will be here in a couple of minutes, so y'all better get away from here with a quickness."

Derek says, "So it's like that now, Trey?"

"It's like that."

Derek says, "So, you don't wanna do business with us?"

Trey says, "Us? What you talking about, nigga? You work for me. I don't know what kind of business you talking about. All I know is that y'all better get away from here. I can't believe you turned on me like this, bringing feds to my house. These don't even look like niggas you would be around. Dre, Lamont, whatever the hell y'all names are, tell your people they need to try a lot harder 'cause y'all don't have shit on me, so stop harassing me."

A black Yukon and a black Expedition pull up to the house. Kev, Mike, and those guys that were here playing PlayStation with Trey get out carrying guns.

Derek says, "See, Trey, all we wanted to do was talk and now you're turning this into a war. You're gonna be sorry, 'cause we can't lose."

"Get the fuck off my property and don't come back."

Derek and the two guys get back into the truck and drive off. Trey stands outside talking to his friends for a few minutes and then he comes back upstairs to me. I open the door to the safety room and he steps inside and we embrace.

"We need to talk."

I look him in the face and notice something white on his nose. Usually when I see something in or around somebody's nose I ignore it because I don't have the heart to tell them, but this is different.

"You have something white on your right nostril. Please tell me that's not what I think it is."

Trey sniffs, snorts, and wipes his nose. "What do you think it is, huh?"

"I think it's coke, that's what I think."

He laughs, trying to downplay what he's done. "It was just a little something that helped me get revved up to deal with that bullshit."

"Now I'm starting to see what Alicia was talking about."

"She didn't know what she was talking about. So what you gonna do now, go running back to Jamal?" He wipes his nose and says, "This is nothing. That was my first and last time doing that, I swear. I need you more than ever because it feels like everything I worked so hard to get is crumbling around me. Now I see how Jamal feels about you. You could do just about anything and I'd forgive you. You have some type of power over men. You're not gonna leave me, are you?"

"No, I'm not going anywhere."

"Good, 'cause we can work this out. I figure you can get an abortion and then things will be back to normal."

"But everything else is crazy. I think the feds are actually closing in on you and this thing with Derek has me worried."

"I know. I'm gonna handle all that tonight. I'm gonna call my father and he can help me work some of this out. Kev and Mike are gonna stay out at the front gate while I'm gone. Stop worrying. I can fix all this. Everything is gonna be all right. I promise. If you need anything those two will look out for you."

Trey kisses me, then goes outside and hops into the truck with his boys, leaving Kev and Mike outside the front gate to watch the house. Trey is off to handle his business and to make things better. In my heart I know that things aren't going to get better and I'm definitely not getting an abortion. I don't want to be with Trey any longer because he frightens me. From this point on I know that things will never be the same between us. I love Trey, but he's not at all who or what I need in my life.

Chapter 36

Jamal

My bags are packed and my flight to New York leaves in less than four hours. I'm excited about experiencing life in the Hamptons, even if it's only for a few days. Jillian doesn't want me to leave and I guess she's trying to keep herself busy.

She says, "I can drop you off if you're ready to leave now." She sees that I'm busy checking my e-mail. "Come on, Jamal."

"I guess that makes sense, considering how much you have to go through at airports these days."

"You need to get off that computer and double-check your bags to see if you forgot anything. Can I check my e-mail real quick?"

Jillian is starting to sound like a nagging wife. I log on to my e-mail account to see if Regina sent anything and she did. It's probably one of her seductive messages. Jillian rushes me off the computer so she can check her e-mail. I quickly close the e-mail that I was reading and let her take over my computer.

A few minutes later I say, "You were all rushing me and now you're the one holding us up."

"Okay, whatever you say. I just need a few more minutes."

"What's taking you so long anyway?"

Jillian yells, "Don't worry about it, you lying bastard!"

All of a sudden I sense that there's trouble in paradise. Jillian called me a lying bastard and now I have a shocked look on my face because nobody told me that there would be moments like this, especially around here.

I walk over to her and ask, "What you talking about?"

Jillian looks up from the computer with this disgusted expression on her face. "I thought you said that nothing ever happened between you and Regina."

I look down at the computer screen and see that Jillian has my mailbox open, reading my e-mails. That's when it hits me. Oh my God, all those seductive and sexually explicit messages from Regina. I lied to Jillian, telling her that Regina mainly e-mailed me about business. I messed up. Before I can move or say a word, my mind goes into instant replay and I can't remember logging out of my e-mail account. All I did was close my e-mail and hand her my computer. My first impulse is to play it cool.

I play dumb and ask, "What are you talking about?"

"I'm talking about this e-mail that Regina sent your lying ass last night talking about how she can't wait to pick up where you two left off in her hotel suite. And how badly she wants to make love to you. Looks like she sent you a bunch of little freaky messages. Listen to the titles. *missing you, sexy surprise, I want you, dreaming of you,* and *I'm so wet.* All that really sounds like business, right? She's nothing but an old freak that's after your body and you're all caught up thinking that it's about your art."

"You shouldn't even be reading that. Damn, the least you could do is respect my privacy. Plus, you're jumping to conclusions. I don't plan to do anything with Regina."

"Sounds like you already did. Why did you lie and say that you never kissed her?"

"I knew you'd jump to conclusions like you're doing right now. Trust me, this is more about my art than anything else."

"Regina doesn't see it that way. If she does I can't tell by these e-mails. She only mentions you artwork twice."

"My art is my focus and I can't help it if Regina is focused on something else."

"She's taking advantage of you and you're too stupid to see it. You act like you need her validation. You're an artist with or without her."

"I know that and don't call me stupid."

"I'm sorry. You're too blind to see what's going on. She's taking advantage of you to get what she wants. If she comes on to you, will you stop her?"

"Of course. I'm a man and I know how to handle myself."

"That's what I'm afraid of."

"You need to stop trippin'. If I was a woman you'd say, 'Go ahead, girl, and use what you got to get what you want.'"

"So, is that what you're doing?"

"No, I was just using that for an example, that's all. Look, my life is at a standstill and I need to expand my horizons. This is an opportunity for me to mingle with important people in an important place. I'll be featured at an art show in the Hamptons. Come on, this is big and I'm not going to pass it up because you don't trust me."

"It's not you that I don't trust. You know what I've been through."

"I'm not him! How many times do I have to hear about what Khalil put you through? Get over it!"

"I don't believe you. I don't have the time or the energy to go through this shit again. I'm always trying to accommodate for black men's shortcomings and I'm tired. I love black men to death, but I think I need to stop limiting myself, because this isn't panning out."

"So what are you saying, you're gonna go hook up with a white guy or something?"

"No, I'm just saying that I'm tired of dealing with lame-ass brothas like you."

"You don't mean that about me and I know you don't. You're mad and maybe a little space will do us some good. Can you imagine how much we'll miss each other after three days apart?"

"If you walk out that door, don't ever come back. I mean it, you better take all your shit with you, because it won't be here when you come back. Give me my door key."

"Come on, Jillian. This is me you're talking to. I can handle myself, you gotta believe me. I know you're upset and you don't mean all this stuff you're saying. I know that we have something special here. I'm not like Khalil and you need to see that. You really need to see that."

"You're right and I'm sorry, but if you leave I don't want you back."

"Baby, come on, this is a once-in-a-lifetime opportunity and I can't pass it up. This is my chance."

"Don't leave me, not right now. I need you. Things were just starting to get good between us."

"I know, but I have to go. You just don't know what you mean to me."

"Tell me. What do I mean to you?"

I don't know why, but it's hard for me to express my feelings verbally to Jillian. "I gotta go. You know how it is at the airport. I'll drive myself."

"If you walk out that door, then this is good-bye and I mean it." She pauses, then looks directly in my eyes and says, "If only you knew how much I loved you, you wouldn't go."

"I have to. I really do."

"Do what you have to then. Good-bye."

"Okay, since this is good-bye, then tell me something I've been dying to know. Who are you and where did you come from? Can you answer that?"

"I'm nothing but a figment of your limited imagination. Just like you said, I'm too good to be true."

I simply shake my head in disbelief. "Here's your key. I gotta go. I'll just drive myself. Thanks for everything and I'll see you in a few days. I promise to be good, alright? I'll call you as soon as my flight lands in New York."

"Good-bye."

Chapter 37

Jessie

Trey didn't come home last night. I feel like there's a black cloud over me and I really can't deal with this anymore. It's time for me to make a move. Trey's a drug dealer, probably a coke addict and God only knows what else. I don't feel safe here so I have to go. My bags are packed and I have managed to stash some of that money Trey threw at me last night. Along with my rainy-day fund and the money he threw at me, I should be set for at least a year.

I'm in the bedroom all alone in this big house and out of nowhere I hear a loud pounding at the front door. I look at one of the monitors and see Trey's father banging on the front door. The other monitors show that Kev and Mike are still parked out front and everything appears safe. I head downstairs to let Mr. Bryant inside. I haven't seen or talked to him since Thanksgiving.

When I open the front door the first thing I notice is that Mr. Bryant looks scared to death. He looks like he's been up all night.

He says, "Hey, Jessie, something came up and I need to get you outta here fast."

"Where's Trey? He didn't come home last night and he's not answering his cell phone or his two-way."

"I'll explain in the car. We just need to get the hell outta here."

"What's going on? Is Trey okay? I need to know."

"He's fine. I had to help him get away from all this madness. The feds raided his house in the city early this morning and that's why I gotta get you outta here."

"Okay, I just need to grab my bags and then I'll be right back."

He steps inside and says, "Make it fast. Is there anything I should take with me?"

Before I can even say a word or take a step, about twenty police cars, trucks, and vans pull up to the house. My first impulse is to take off running upstairs to the safety room, but that won't do any good.

Seconds later about two-and-a-half-dozen local policemen and DEA agents flood the house.

I begin to cry and say, "I don't know what's going on. What should I do?"

Mr. Bryant says, "Just be quiet and do what they ask."

The agents begin to question me about Trey and his whereabouts. They cuff Mr. Bryant and question him too, but he doesn't say a word. He looks at me and shakes his head, signaling me not to answer them.

I say, "I don't know where he is, really I don't. I'm just a friend of his and I don't know what's going on."

The agent says, "Okay, that's fine."

I feel relieved. All of a sudden the agent grabs me and handcuffs me. This is like a nightmare come true. This is actually happening, but it's not real to me. I can't believe that this is happening to me right here, right now. It feels as if this were no longer my life. I must be living someone else's life because this isn't supposed to happen to me. I realize that this is actually happening and I'm the only one responsible for me being here. I can't place the blame on anyone else, because I knew the consequences.

The cuffs are on so tight that they're hurting my wrists and the officer refuses to loosen them.

Mr. Bryant says, "Leave her alone, she doesn't know anything."

The agent says, "Yeah, we know she's innocent just like you. That's why I've got her handcuffed."

I cry out, "I don't have anything to do with what's going on here. Please, you have to believe me."

The agent says, "Okay, I got you."

This man isn't listening to me at all. I feel like telling him that Mr. Bryant knows where Trey is so he can let me go, but that won't happen. I look up and see Kev and Mike walk in escorted by a bunch of cops. Damn, they got them too. I thought they would have been long gone away from here, especially when they saw all those police pull up.

I yell, "Ask those two right there. They might know where Trey is."

What I see next almost makes me lose it. Kev and Mike look at me with these save-the-bullshit kinds of expressions. I can't believe what I'm seeing because they're wearing badges around their necks. They were undercover agents all along.

Kev walks over to me and whispers, "I told you to be nice to us because you might need us one day."

This is the end for me and all I can say is, "I'm sorry. I'm so sorry."

Mike says, "Keep the father and let her go. She's just some young dumb girl that got mixed up. She hasn't done anything wrong."

Kev looks at me and says, "You don't have a clue what this is all about, do you?"

"I don't. I really don't."

Mike says, "Get outta here, girl."

I look out the open front door at my freedom, but something makes me think about what I left upstairs. "Can I grab my bags real quick?"

Kev escorts me upstairs to my bags.

He says, "Get your bags and go. I want you to leave here and never look back. Forget everything you know or thought you knew about Trey Bryant. Do you understand what I'm saying?"

"I understand, but it's hard to believe you're an agent. I don't even feel right talking to you."

"You don't have to say anything else. You didn't commit any crimes. We've been watching you. Remember that night on North Avenue?"

My mind goes racing back to that night in Trey's car. "Yeah."

"We were just waiting for the right moment to arrest Trey. That's why everything went so smoothly with cops the night of his party and the traffic stop on the parkway. I bet you thought all that was just plain old luck."

"I don't know what I was thinking. I just wanna get outta here."

"Good. One of the officers will take you home."

"Oh, my car is right out front."

"It's not yours anymore. That car was purchased with drug money."

"No, it wasn't. It's in my name."

"We know for a fact that the car was purchased with illegal funds." He laughs and then says, "Don't ever say that the police didn't help you. We've got a ride for you. Get outta here, and take care of yourself."

Kev gives me a quick hug, then escorts me out to a patrol car, and I get in. When I look around I see Mike standing near a group of officers. He waves good-bye to me. I give him a simple wave as we pull off down the driveway. Kev and Mike actually liked me and for the first time I can honestly say that I like and respect them.

Tears run down my face as I think about Trey for a few minutes, wondering where he might be, and then I let go and think about how I'm going to improve my life. I'm not going to take my freedom for granted.

I think about how policemen use their power to arrest or set free anyone they want. I thank God that this worked out in my favor.

Chapter 38

Jamal

It's 11:30 A.M. and I called earlier, leaving a brief message for Jillian, letting her know that I arrived safely. Regina picked me up from MacArthur Airport a few minutes ago and now we're on our way to her house in East Hampton. This is a cold, gloomy day . . . gray in every sense, forty-one degrees. The sky is expressionless, dull, and unimpressive. Back home the weatherman referred to our streak of unseasonably warm days as an Indian summer. I was hoping it would be just as warm up here, but I knew it was highly unlikely. Instead it's cold and dreary and a day like this does absolutely nothing to uplift my somber mood. Jillian got my day off to a terrible start and that's why I'm in such a bad mood. The whole art show thing has me feeling weird. I'm both nervous and excited.

Regina is her usual self with that type A personality in full effect. She seems to be all about business and fully focused on making the art show a success instead of carrying out the sexual fantasies that she mentioned in her e-mails. I'm grateful because right away she has proven that this trip is all about business. Nevertheless, she continues to intrigue the hell out of me because she's so unique, creative, sophisticated, beautiful, and energetic.

Regina's spirits are high and she has no idea that I'm in a bad mood. She's very talkative. As she drives along this stretch of highway she talks to me about the history of this area and about how it's a mixture of new and old money. She begins to give me a quick rundown of who's going to be at the art show and how it's supposed to flow. She brags about it being a black-tie affair and how most of the guests will arrive in limos. I should be paying attention to what she's saying, but for the moment I'm not interested. Instead of listening to her speak, my thoughts are on Jillian. How could I have just left my girl like that? I messed up bad and I'm starting to realize it. She should be here right by my side. I was so self-absorbed that the thought of inviting her here never crossed my mind. Jillian is such a shrewd individual that she was probably waiting for me to invite her. Inviting her would have meant a lot to her and would have made all the difference in the world. I'm sure she had too much pride to ask me if she could come along. If I had asked Jillian to join me it definitely would have made my relationship with Regina appear much more platonic and now that I didn't invite her it seems as if I have something to hide. If Jillian were here, that could possibly have cured her doubts.

On the other hand if Jillian trusted me she wouldn't have any doubts in the first place. I don't feel that it's important for her to tag along with me everywhere. Every now and then we need our personal space. But no matter how I look at this situation Jillian should be here sharing this experience with me. I can't lie to myself because subconsciously I think I want something to happen between me and Regina.

I'm wrong, but so was Jillian. She actually had the nerve to look over my shoulder at my laptop while I was online a few days before she read the e-mails that Regina sent. Jillian began to sense that something just wasn't right when she saw the size of the paragraphs in Regina's e-mails. I allowed her to take a quick look at the screen because I didn't want her to feel like I had anything to hide. The fact that Regina kept calling me around the clock on my cell phone didn't help matters much either.

With a concerned look on her face Jillian asked, "Why is Regina sending such long messages and calling you off the hook? Are you sure you two are just business associates?"

Talking to Jillian about my relationship with Regina bothered me, but I was able to keep a straight face. "What else would we be?"

"I bet the two of you have kissed or done something wild at least once. You ever think about being with her sexually?"

"Hell no! She's only e-mailing me like this to keep me updated on events and to check up on her investment. Stop being so paranoid and jealous." I tried to lighten the mood with a little joke. I smiled and said, "If I ever cheated on you it wouldn't be with Regina, trust me. It would definitely be with somebody like Halle Berry."

Luckily Jillian caught on to what I was trying to do. She smiled, let out a little laugh, and nodded. "Is that right?"

"Yeah, that's right."

"Well, if I ever cheated on you, I'd definitely have to cheat with Morris Chestnut. Oh, while I'm at it let me add Denzel Washington to my list too."

"List? See, why you gotta get greedy having two fantasy affairs? Since you have two, I wanna add Jada Pinkett to my list. How you like that?"

"That's fine just as long as Regina Bishop doesn't end up on your list."

Regina and I are still on our way to her house. She continues to talk as her Will Downing CD plays and I go on ignoring her, thinking about Jillian. I wonder if things are really over between us. I think Jillian was bluffing, but then again, she's hard to read when she's upset.

Regina asks, "How does that sound to you?"

"Huh?"

"Did you even hear what I said?"

"No. My mind is somewhere else right now."

"You need to get it together. This is your coming-out party, your introduction to the art world. This is a special occasion for both of us. I was saying that my daughter, Kia, is here and she's going to perform a ballet and a local pianist is going to perform as well. How does that sound?"

"Nice."

"I'm putting all this time and energy into this show and all you have to say is *nice?* What's wrong with you?"

I'm able to summarize it with one word. "Jillian."

"I know you miss her, but it's okay to get away from her once in a while."

"No, it's more than that. I think she broke up with me because of this trip."

"Was it the trip or was it something else?"

"Mostly you."

She looks surprised. "Me? What did I do besides try to help her man become a better person?"

"It's my fault. I messed up real bad. I forgot to log out of my mailbox and she hit the back arrow and it took her right to my mailbox. She read most of the e-mails you sent."

I just dropped what I thought was a bomb and Regina looks like she couldn't care less. "She'll get over it. Stop being so hard on yourself. If she trusts you, then there's nothing to worry about. I understand what she's feeling, but I can't make you do anything you don't want to, am I right?"

"You're right."

She gives me this devilish smile and asks, "Are you sure about that?"

I shoot her this confused look. I'm momentarily speechless.

She smiles and says, "I'm just kidding."

"I told her that my life was at a standstill and I needed to get away. I pretty much left without hesitation. I just wanted to see what life was like away from Baltimore. That's all I know and it's time for a change. I wanna meet new and interesting people. I wanna sip champagne, eat lobster and caviar." I have to laugh at myself for mentioning caviar. "Well, maybe not caviar, but definitely the champagne and lobster."

"You'll get used to caviar, it's an acquired taste. Don't worry, I'm gonna take good care of you. We're just a couple of minutes from my house and once you see what I've got in store, you won't wanna go back to Baltimore or anywhere else. You've never partied until you've partied in the Hamptons."

I begin to relax and take in the sights of East Hampton. As I look out the window of Regina's Range Rover I see rows of trees, the ocean in the distance, and a few historic buildings and houses with the same aged, brownish gray wooden siding. I see a huge white farmhouse and I think it's nice, but I'm hoping it's not Regina's house. There's a group of modern, expensive-looking houses and we're heading in that direction. These houses are mind-blowing. I'm excited, but I don't want to let it show too much because I don't want Regina to think that I'm not used to the finer things in life. She turns and we make our way down a long deserted road. We come upon this huge isolated compound.

My eyes widen and I say, "Don't tell me this is your house."

"This is it. What do you think?"

I kind of lose my composure because Regina's house looks like something from a movie or an *Architectural Digest* magazine. "I've never seen anything like it. I shouldn't have expected anything less from a woman like you."

Regina's house is beautiful. It's a secluded oceanfront home that sits on a lush elevated landscape along the Atlantic coast. This place is nothing less than a contemporary architectural masterpiece composed of glass and an attractive sandstone finish.

I get out of the truck and look down at this multilevel patio and a breathtaking view of the ocean as it slams against the beach. I'm completely taken away by the vacation atmosphere of Regina's home.

"Damn, this is the life. I feel privileged to be here."

"Don't be silly. You've earned the right to be here."

"Thank you."

"For what?"

"For being who you are and helping to bring out the best in me."

I feel strange like I want to give Regina a long, passionate kiss for making my dream come true. I'm frozen in one spot staring down at the ocean trying to think of a way to repay Regina for her generosity.

Regina says, "We can stay out here all day enjoying the view, but you haven't even seen the inside of my house."

I laugh and say, "I know, I'm all impressed with the exterior. How many acres is this?"

"Four and a half. You haven't seen anything yet. Come inside."

The interior of Regina's house is also finished in sandstone, giving it a unique and natural appearance. The foyer has a high vaulted ceiling with the grandeur nearly equal to a place of worship. The entire rear wall of the house is an extensive unit of glass that allows light to flow in naturally even on an overcast day like today.

I say, "This house is a work of art in itself."

"Thank you."

Regina leads me down a few steps to a spacious room, which is her personal gallery, filled with twentieth-century paintings and sculptures. This is Regina's sanctuary and I can tell that she loves it. We spend an hour or so looking at her private collection that's worth millions. It's hard to believe that someone could be so fascinated with art. I'm an artist, but I'm not nearly as passionate about art as Regina. This is what she lives for.

Without saying a word Regina smiles at me. I understand exactly what this smile is about. She's proud of what she has been able to accomplish in such a short amount of time and the amount of lives she has been able to influence. Regina has been able to affect the lives of urban artists as well as artists from Third World countries who could only dream of America, and now they're featured in some of the finest museums in this country.

"I think you're incredible."

"No, you're incredible. It's people like you that allow me to do what I do best and that's to inspire others." She slowly steps down to a painting of a cute little black ballerina dressed in a pink leotard and pink ballet slippers. "This is a painting of my daughter, Kia. I painted this years ago."

"Like I said, you're incredible. This is really nice."

"Stop it. Would you like to meet my daughter? She's probably in the main gallery rehearsing as we speak."

"Sure, I'd love to meet her."

"Are you hungry or thirsty? The caterer will be here shortly to bring by a sample of the food for the art show."

"I'm too nervous to eat or drink. Why is the caterer only bringing by a sample? Shouldn't he be setting up for the show?"

"Don't worry about that. Do I make you nervous?"

"No, I'm just thinking about the art show. What time are we getting started anyway?"

Regina squints her eyes, giving me this silly look.

I ask, "What? You said it was this evening, but you never gave me a time."

"Relax. Actually, the art show isn't today. It's tomorrow evening."

I explode. "Tomorrow? Tomorrow? Do you have any idea what I went through to get here today? I've possibly lost someone really special to me because you rushed me here. What's the purpose of me being here so soon?"

"I wanted you to get a feel for the place and make sure everything wasn't so rushed. People can tell when things are rushed. Do you understand what I mean?"

"Not really. Be honest, what's going on?"

"Okay, it wasn't really necessary for you to be here so soon, but I was hoping we could spend some time together before my mad rush of guests arrive." She pauses for a few seconds. "Are you upset with me?"

"Yeah, but it's not that serious. I went through hell this morning trying to leave Jillian. That girl loves me and she suspects that we've got something going on."

Regina looks me in the eye and says, "We do, don't we? At least that's what I've been led to believe, or did you forget that night at the Hyatt?"

"I'm sorry, but things have changed since then. Jillian and I are involved. I told you that."

"You did, but I don't see her here. Evidently you wanted to be alone with me. You read my e-mails, right?"

"I did. Look, if I had the chance to do it again she'd be here. I was wrong for not inviting her."

"No, you weren't. And back to the e-mails, if I'm not mistaken you responded to them, right?"

"I did respond, but I thought you could tell that I was mostly focused on the art show."

"Don't worry. It's not a big deal. I got the wrong message. Let just chalk it up to a big *misunderstanding*."

"I'm sorry."

"Don't worry about it. I said it's no big deal. C'mon, let's go see, Kia."

"Okay."

I follow Regina to the south wing of her house feeling like a complete idiot. Along the way she shows me the remaining rooms on the first level. Each room in her house has the right symmetry with its own individual appeal based on the furniture, color, and eclectic pieces.

I'm starting to feel uncomfortable. I'm kind of guilty of sending mixed signals, but I thought I made it clear that I was involved with Jillian. I feel bad because Regina is trying to act as if she's okay, but I know she's not.

I hear a piano playing in the background. We enter the main gallery and I instantly notice my paintings as they line the walls. Some of them are displayed on easels. My painting titled *Ground Zero* steals my attention. It's my tribute to 9/11. I actually saw it in a dream. It's sort of an opposite interpretation of the real Ground Zero. The picture depicts the Twin Towers standing proudly in the midst of ruins as if the rest of the world has been destroyed and they've been left behind to serve as timeless reminders of this nation's invincibility. I'm so proud to see my paintings on display that I could cry.

Regina has done something for me that no one else has. I feel guilty and then I quickly remind myself that she's getting something out of this as well. She didn't have to do this, but she did. I really appreciate her giving me this opportunity.

Some guy plays the piano as this attractive girl dances a ballet. This is obviously Kia. She's as beautiful and graceful as any ballerina, but she's added her own sista-girl kind of flava, which enhances her performance even more. Kia has strength and discipline unlike any other dancer I've ever seen. Her moves are very precise and she possesses the ability to make her audience fall in love with her just by watching her dance. That says a lot for her talent.

Regina says, "There she is. Look at my baby. She choreographed something special for tomorrow. That's Robert on the piano. Those two have been practicing for hours. See how important you are to us?"

"I see and I appreciate it."

When the routine is over Regina introduces me to Kia and Robert. I can tell that Robert isn't really interested in meeting me. He must see me as competition because he doesn't have much to say. Guys have a bad habit of doing that.

Regina says, "Robert and Kia were part of our first annual arts festival that we plan to hold every July out back on the lawn in a huge air-conditioned tent. People in this area are in love with the arts and are major supporters. You'll see tomorrow."

Kia smiles and says, "Jamal, you should come back next summer and be part of our festival. I know you'd be a welcomed addition."

I say, "Only if your mother still wants me around after tomorrow."

Robert doesn't say a word, he simply does the fake laugh. He makes me laugh because he's so phony.

Regina says, "Don't be silly, I love having you around. You could stay here forever if you'd like."

Kia says, "You better watch out because she means that."

I say, "I know. Thanks for the warning."

Regina says, "I'm not that bad. Am I?"

Robert says, "Of course not. You two leave Ms. Bishop alone. She's good people." Robert lets out this fake sigh as if he were really tired and says, "It was nice meeting you, Jamal, but Kia and I have to get back to work. We'll get to see you later, right?"

"Yeah, I'll be here."

Kia says, "He's right. We have a lot of work to do. It was nice meeting you, Jamal, and I look forward to talking to you later."

Robert says, "Ms. Bishop, I was wondering if my sister could stop by here tomorrow. She plays the harp and I think that would add a nice touch to the art show. What do you think?"

"I'll leave that up to Jamal."

Everyone looks directly at me. "That sounds good, but do you think you can get Jay-Z up in this spot?" I laugh. They all give me this you-can't-be-serious kind of expression. "I'm just kidding. I think your sister and her harp would be a nice touch."

Regina takes me back to the foyer to pick up my bags and then we head upstairs to the bedroom where I'll be sleeping. We enter this huge bedroom. I look surprised because this has to be the master suite.

"This is my bedroom and I'm giving it to you for the next couple of nights."

"No. I can sleep anywhere. I don't wanna put you out of your room."

"I insist and there's nothing you can say to make me change my mind."

I quickly scan the room and then walk over and feel the bed.

"Try it out. Go ahead and lie down. It's okay, I won't attack you."

I laugh, then lie down. "This is nice. I'm so tired that I don't wanna do anything else right now except get some sleep."

"I don't blame you. There's a relaxing whirlpool bath and sauna in the bathroom. Make yourself at home. I want you to be as comfortable here as possible."

"Thank you. I really, really appreciate this."

"I know." Regina turns to exit the room; then she slowly turns back around. "One quick question."

"Go ahead."

"Are you in love with Jillian?"

"That's a good question. Right before I left she told me that she loved me, but I didn't respond."

"Why?"

"I felt that things were dramatic enough and I didn't want to say something that I was unsure of in the heat of the moment."

"You still didn't answer my question. It's a simple yes or no. Are you in love with her?"

"No."

She smiles and says, "That was quick."

"Wanna hear something interesting?"

"Yeah, go ahead."

"I'm still in love with Jessie. Isn't that crazy?"

She gives me this funny look and says, "It sure is. The craziest thing I've heard all day."

"You're the only one who knows that."

"Well, I guess that makes me special then. I've got some things to take care of, so enjoy yourself for the next couple of hours. There's food and drinks in that little refrigerator over there. If you need anything you can reach me on my cell."

"Thanks, but I'm fine. All I'm thinking about is that whirlpool and getting some sleep."

"Enjoy and I'll see you later."

Regina gives me her little beauty queen wave, then exits the room. I remain lying comfortably on the bed and feel myself slowly drifting off to sleep.

Chapter 39

Jamal

It's about 5:30 in the evening and I've already called Jillian four or five times since I woke up. I've called her at home and on her cell phone and each time it's the same thing, no answer. This is what I feared. She doesn't want to talk to me even after having several hours to cool down.

I decide to call her one last time and her answering machine picks up.

I say, "Hey, Jillian, it's me again. I left a few other messages at home and on your cell. I just wanted to let you know that I'm thinking about you. Can you please give me a call when you get this message? I miss you and I'm bored to death." My tone changes a little. I am sorry and all, but I'm starting to get pissed. "I know you have caller ID and I hope you're not just sitting there ignoring me. I hope to hear from you soon, alright?" Now I shift to being more apologetic. "Sorry for leaving you like that, but I'll be home Monday evening and I promise to make it up to you. And again I miss you and I'm sorry."

Just as I'm about to hang up I hear someone pick up. Jillian yells, "Stop calling me! Don't call me at home or on my cell! It's over! It's overrrrr! Get it through your thick skull. Leave me the hell alone! You're where you wanna be. You proved to me who and what was more important to you. Good-bye!"

"That's not true," I say to a dial tone.

* * *

I'm in the whirlpool bath being silly singing "If Only For One Night" by Luther Vandross. This bathroom is finished in this expensive, coffee-colored, large-block tile, which really adds nice acoustics to the room. It's impossible for me to hit a sour note in here. My voice echoes off the walls real smooth, but in reality I can't sing a lick. There isn't a sound in here except my voice and the sound of the whirlpool's motor. The water feels so good that I close my eyes and sink down into the tub allowing the hot water to come up to my neck.

All of a sudden I sense someone standing behind me and before I can move I feel hands under the water touching my left shoulder and chest. It scares the living shit out of me because I thought I was alone. I quickly open my eyes and break away from the hands. When I look behind me Regina is standing there completely nude.

She laughs and says, "I didn't mean to scare you like that."

I'm mad and embarrassed. "What are you doing? What's wrong with you?"

"I thought you might like a little company."

"Not really."

"Come on. I thought you were singing to me."

"That's embarrassing. I thought I was alone. I was just singing like some people do when they're alone in the bathroom."

"I had no idea you had a voice like that."

"I don't. It's this room. It's called bathroom acoustics. If I was on the Apollo, Sandman would beat me half to death with his chair, then tap dance on my head."

She laughs. "You're silly. Can I join you? It's kind of cold standing here like this."

I look at her body and she looks sexy standing there all exposed. My attitude softens as something else begins to harden. "I'm sorry. Come on in. The water feels real nice."

Regina slowly submerges herself into the water and begins to touch my chest and shoulders again. This time I don't resist at all. I'm relaxed and the water is so deep that I can feel myself start to float a little. Regina's hands move slowly up and down my body. Finally she touches me down there. I open my eyes and see that she's completely focused on pleasing me and I like that.

"I knew you'd give in eventually. How does this feel?"

"It feels good. Relaxing. I'm light-headed."

"Just tell me what you want and I'll do it."

Regina reaches into a ceramic pot on the side of the tub and pulls something out.

I ask, "What's that in your hand?" She holds up a condom. "Do you treat all your guests like this or was that strategically placed there for me?"

"I'm offended by that."

"You don't look offended."

Regina smiles and says, "I'm not. I planned this for you. This is all for you."

This isn't what I had planned, but I'm mesmerized by her sex appeal. I say, "You're so beautiful."

We kiss.

She says, "I thought this would never happen. I'm crazy about you."

"Why?"

"You're young, strong, handsome, and you look so innocent. But I know you're not. You're just sexy and I want you."

"I want you too, but I don't know about this."

"What's the problem?"

"I can't cheat on my girl."

"News flash. Look at us, you're already cheating."

"It's not actually cheating unless I put my thing in you, right?"

"Whatever you say. We all have our own definition of cheating." She laughs. "Seems like you're ready to cheat, because your thing is harder than petrified wood. Give me your hand and feel what you're missing. Don't you wanna be inside?"

She opens the condom wrapper and starts to put the condom on me. I can't think straight or move a muscle. She's got me. The condom is in place and Regina is about to straddle me.

"I knew I could get you. You're all mine now."

All of a sudden she gives me the creeps and turns me off. She should have just kept her mouth shut.

I say, "Hold up." I put my hands up so she can back off. "Hold up. I swear I thought I wanted you, but this is wrong. I can't cheat on my girl. I shouldn't be here without her."

"Stop trying to act like you're so different. It's okay, baby. All men cheat. You know you want this, so cut the *bullshit*." She cops a quick attitude. "After all I've done for you the least you can do is fuck me."

"Like I said, I'm not gonna cheat on my girl."

"She broke up with you, remember?"

"Because of you."

"I was worth it, right?"

"To be honest, no."

"What? You need me, because without me you're just an arts-and-crafts-store employee with a dream."

That hurt coming from someone who I thought respected my work. "Is that how you really see me?"

"People with your talent come a dime a dozen. The only thing that really made you special was the fact that you had me backing you. Like I said, you're nothing without me."

"And you're nothing without me."

"What's that supposed to mean?"

"I'm not staying for this stupid-ass art show. I'm outta here!" I get out of the tub dripping water everywhere. I make my way into the bedroom.

Regina lifts herself out of the tub and yells, "You're still under contract. Try leaving and I'll have your ass in court so fast it'll make your head spin. Try me and I'll sue."

"You can't get anything from me because I'm a broke arts-and-crafts-store employee, remember? I'll show you how much I care about an art show. You can keep all those paintings and we'll call it even."

"Do me a favor and take them with you. You'll never have an art career. Consider yourself ruined. Your name will be mud in the art world courtesy of me."

That last line has me steaming mad. I'm so upset that I start getting dressed in the same clothes I wore earlier. I never unpacked, so all I have to do is pick up my bags and walk away.

Chapter 40

Jamal

R egina warned me not to leave her house because it was cold, dark, and damn near impossible to get a cab. She said I would get a ride in a police car quicker than a cab. She offered to take me to the airport, but I refused to accept any more help from her. I picked up my bags, put myself into automatic pilot, and left her house. At the same time I kind of felt like I was leaving my dream of being a world-renowned artist behind and that hurt.

I think I must have walked for about an hour before Robert picked me up and drove me to MacArthur Airport. He probably had a good idea about what had gone down at the house, because he didn't ask any questions or try to talk me into staying. I never asked if he came to pick me up on his own or if Regina sent him. I was just glad to see him because it was too cold and too dark for a brotha to be on the streets of East Hampton.

I almost swallowed my pride and went back to Regina's when I found out that the next departing flight to BWI wasn't until 7:45 the next morning. I held steady and made myself as comfortable as possible in an airport chair. I slept in the airport and woke up with the worst neck, back, and right shoulder pain ever.

After my flight landed at BWI I took a courtesy shuttle to my car and headed straight to Jillian's.

*   *   *

I'm outside Jillian's house banging on her front door like crazy and the entire time she just ignores me. I decide to pull out my cell phone and give her a call.

"Hey, baby, that's me banging on the door. Please stop playing and let me in. I know you're home. I'm not going anywhere, so you might as well let me in. How many times do I have to apologize?"

About a second later Jillian's neighbor Darien opens her front door slightly with the safety chain in place.

He sticks his face out and says, "I think you should leave, Jamal. I'm gonna call the police if you don't. I don't want any trouble and neither does Jillian."

"What the hell are you doing in there this time of morning?"

"I'm just being a friend."

"Where's your wife? I don't see her car out here anywhere."

"That's none of your fucking business."

"*Do not* curse at me. I know you're not trying to get loud with me, are you? I'm not in the mood for games. Man, you just don't know. I've gone through some crazy shit and right about now I will hurt you real bad. Take the chain off the door and let me in."

"I'm calling the police."

"No, you're not."

I'm having crazy thoughts about why Darien is in Jillian's house this early in the morning. I look around again for his wife's car. My adrenaline starts flowing so much that I forget all about my aches and pains. I take a couple of steps back and charge through the front door like a crazy man, breaking the safety chain along with the wooden molding, knocking Darien to the floor. I can't believe my eyes when I look down at Darien. He's curled up on the floor moaning like a pregnant woman giving birth for the first time. He's wearing a white T-shirt, boxer shorts with those little yellow smiling faces, and a pair of long black dress socks. I look down at this geek and shake my head.

Jillian screams and comes running downstairs wearing a light blue terry cloth robe.

She looks at me and asks, "What have you done? Darien, are you okay? Look at him, he's not breathing right."

I ask, "Is Darien okay? What about me? He's alright, he just had the wind knocked out of him. What's up with this? Are you sleeping with this clown?" I lose it even more and give Darien a swift kick to the midsection and he moans even louder.

Jillian screams, "Stop! You're gonna kill him, you fool. Get out of my house! Get out!"

"I just want my stuff. That's all I want. Later for you and him."

"Your stuff is gone. Darien and I got rid of it as soon as you left. I warned you."

"You're gonna pay for my stuff." I turn toward Darien, draw my foot back, and yell, "And he's gonna—"

Jillian cuts me off. "Don't kick him again. I'm not paying for anything. You better pay for the damage to my front door."

Jillian helps Darien up. She takes him upstairs and helps him get dressed. I follow right behind them. Darien doesn't look at me or say another word. After he gets dressed he collects himself and limps home looking like a wounded chump.

Jillian and I are in her living room trying to sort things out. I turn to her and ask, "Why was Darien here and where's his wife? Did y'all have sex while I was away?"

She makes a stupid childish expression and asks, "Did you have sex with Regina?"

"Hell no! I told you I was a man and I knew how to handle myself. Look at you." I point my finger at her. "You played yourself cheap and slept with a married man. How could you do that to me? How does that make you feel?"

"Get your hand out of my face. I don't know who you think I am. You must have mistaken me for somebody else, putting your hand in my face. I don't play that and I didn't sleep with Darien, so stop accusing me. No matter what you say I know you slept with Regina. You can't tell me any different."

"Nothing happened."

"Yep, just like nothing happened here."

"You're lying and you know I know the truth. Look at me." Jillian isn't able to look me in the face. In a soft tone I say, "You can't even look at me. Why did you do it? You tell me everything else, explain that."

All of a sudden everything changes. Jillian begins to cry. "His wife left him just like you left me. Don't call me cheap for sleeping with him. I'm cheap for sleeping with you. At least he loves me and had the courage to tell me."

That hurt worse than Regina criticizing my talent. All I can say is, "I knew it."

"Don't give me that. You didn't know. Didn't you sleep with Regina?"

For some reason I feel bad for Jillian and I do something totally out of character. "Yeah, you were right. I love her and I made love to her the entire time I was away. There was never any art show. I made it all up."

I guess this is my way of getting out of this whole thing. Besides, Jillian would never believe the truth.

She screams, "I hate you! Get out of my house and don't ever come back."

"So, you're breaking up with me?"

"Consider us broken up. There nothing here to fix."

For some strange reason, just as I'm about to walk out the door I feel the need to explain myself a little.

"You couldn't let me be me. I was just trying to be a man. I'm not perfect. At least I tried to get to know you. I asked you over and over who you were and where you came from, but you never really answered. I guess you thought it was a joke or something. You never took the time to get to know me. It's like you never even saw me. Just like you don't see me right now. You never saw the real me. You only seemed interested in seeing through me instead of focusing on who I really am."

Jillian looks down at the floor and then at me. "You're right. You're absolutely right. You told me that I was too good to be true and you were right about that too."

"Well, I'm sorry about how things turned out. I hate ending on bad terms with you. I still consider you a friend even though you threw all my shit away."

"I'm sorry. This isn't like me. I've been through a lot and I carried a lot of baggage into our relationship."

"I could see that you had a lot of baggage, but I thought you'd let go of it at some point."

"I know. It was harder than I thought."

"So what's up with you and Darien?"

"I don't know. He's been after me for a while. To be honest, what Darien and I did this weekend was mainly about getting back at you for leaving me."

"That's stupid. Just promise me one thing."

"What's that?"

"That I won't end up being one of your dating horror stories like Khalil."

"I can't promise anything because you're part of my never-ending story. I guess this is good-bye. Good luck with your art career."

"Yeah, right. The only career I have in art is as an arts-and-crafts store manager. I guess that's going to be my focus from now on. Thanks for helping me cure my curiosity thing about Jillian Smith."

"You're weird and I'm gonna miss that."

I smile and say, "You'll get over it."

Jillian and I embrace and say our good-byes. This whole weekend makes me wonder what love is all about. I tell myself that love don't love nobody, not even me. It's sad, but true.

I lied to Jillian about Regina and me having sex because it was easier for her to believe a lie than the truth. I could have stood there repeating the truth till I was blue in the face and it wouldn't have done any good. Women are like that too often with men and that's why we lie so much. Jillian would never have believed that I actually had a big art show scheduled in the Hamptons at a multimillion-dollar ocean-front estate and walked away from it all partially because of her. One of the biggest reasons I walked away was something her father said to me. That man was only in my life for a brief period, but he made a lasting impression on me. I can still hear his voice in my head like a mental sparing partner pounding his philosophical messages into my head. He said something about African-Americans having dignity over dollars. I swear that's what I heard in my head when Regina started going off on me about how much I needed her. I wasn't about to sell myself short and I proved to her that I couldn't be bought.

Chapter 41

Jamal

It's funny how we find ourselves back at our starting points when things in life don't quite turn out the way we originally planned. I guess I'm in search of comfort and reassurance. I'm not in the mood for games, and Grandma is the one person who's always honest with me. She has a way of telling it like it is, plain and simple. After giving me the third degree for not calling her for almost a week she and I sit down in the living room and have one of our typical conversations. I deserved to have her get on me for not calling. There's actually something of value that comes along with her verbal lashing. She's schooling me on life and I've always been the type of person to respect my elders and their wisdom.

Grandma surprises me when she says, "Jessie called you yesterday, but I told her that you moved out and I hadn't heard from you all week. She told me to tell you that she's back at her apartment. And that's not all. She told me to tell you that she was really back and you'd understand what that meant."

Automatically I take that to mean that she and Trey have broken up.

"I can't believe she called." Under my breath I say, "She's got good timing."

"What was that?"

"Nothing. I was just talking to myself."

"You better watch it. You know they say the mind is the first thing to go."

"Yeah, I've heard that."

"Does Jessie know about that girl Jillian?"

"She does, but Jillian and I are done."

"You're sure having some bad luck with women lately."

"It's them, not me."

"You sure about that?"

I laugh and say, "Not exactly."

"Well, one good thing is that you recognized that Jillian wasn't the right one for you instead of jumping up and marrying her, then realizing years down the line that you made a mistake like Shadow and John."

"I don't even wanna talk about them." I shake my head in disbelief. "Have you heard from them?"

"Yeah, they're still separated. Now, back to you. It took you almost two years to figure out that Jessie wasn't right for you." Grandma gives me this strange look and asks, "Are you sure she isn't the right one for you?"

"I don't know."

"You let her go and now I think she's trying to come back to you. That ain't nothing but love."

"What makes you think that?"

"I just know. I've been around long enough to know love when I see it. She had a sense of urgency in her voice. I can tell that she still loves you and you still love her."

"You're exaggerating."

"I'm not. I like Jessie. I like her better than Jillian. You and Jessie make such a nice couple. She's really a sweet girl. One thing I can say is that she always showed me respect except for that one time y'all had sex in my house. I blamed you for that though."

"I remember. I need to tell you something."

"I'm listening."

"Jessie's pregnant with my baby."

"That's a blessing. Does this mean y'all are gonna get back together?"

"No."

"It's not important that you two get back together. What's important is that you're there for your child. Wait till I tell Pearl I'm gonna be a great-grandmother. I was starting to think you couldn't make any babies."

I laugh and say, "I wasn't trying to make any babies. I'm gonna be there for my kid no matter what's going on with me and Jessie. You raised me to be a responsible man."

"That's the truth. I wish you'd be responsible and go 'head and marry that girl."

"Stop!"

"Are you gonna call that child back?"

"Who?"

"Jessie, that's who."

"Maybe I'll get around to calling her tomorrow. I need time to finish getting myself together."

"Well, don't wait too long. You know how women are when we don't get our way."

"Trust me, I know. I'm hurting right now and I need to get myself together."

"You'll get over it. Everyone gets their heart broken at one time or another."

"No, it's not my heart. I mean my neck, back, and right shoulder are hurting."

"Oh, I can help that. I thought you were talking about your heart. I'll run you a nice hot bath with Epsom salt and then I'll rub you down in Ben-Gay or Icy Hot."

"Thanks, but no thanks." The thought of Grandma rubbing me down is sickening, but she means well. "The last thing I want is to walk around smelling like liniment. I will take you up on that hot bath. You're always looking out for me."

"'Cause you're still my baby, that's why. You sound just like an old man, talking about some liniment. I'm an old woman and I don't even say liniment anymore."

"You made me old like this."

We laugh.

Chapter 42

Jamal

I took Grandma out to dinner, just my way of saying thank you. I don't know what I'd do without her even though she kept talking a bunch of nonsense. All of a sudden she was really stuck on Jessie, which happened to be the center of every one of our conversations from the time we left home till we returned. It made me think that Jessie paid Grandma off to make her seem appealing to me again. This was nothing more than one of Grandma's profound lessons on forgiveness. She made references to the Bible, Adam and Eve, the serpent, and original sin. As she spoke I thought about myself, Jessie, Trey, and money, the root of all evil. Grandma never knew the real reason Jessie and I broke up, but she was able to make me see that no one's perfect and that at some point we all are led astray.

When Grandma and I returned from dinner we sat down at the kitchen table like an old couple and talked over two hot cups of Celestial Seasonings Herbal Sleepytime tea. It was a funny sight, but I really enjoyed spending the evening with her. Sitting at the table with her was like a glimpse into the distant future when I become a senior citizen. My aches and pains kind of added realism to that affect. The whole thing made me laugh. On a serious note, I realized that I don't want to grow old alone. Talking to Grandma convinced me that I missed Jessie and it made me realize how much I truly love her.

*   *   *

I hardly ever drink tea and I only drank it because Grandma told me that the tea would help me relax and it did. It's 3:30 A.M. and I just woke up from the weirdest nightmare. Jessie's been on my mind since Grandma first mentioned her phone call, and now I wish that I had returned her call. I dreamed that she had an abortion and it hurt me to my heart that she did something like that. In my dream Jessie knew that I was against it, but I arrived at the clinic too late to stop the procedure. I was furious because when I finally met up with Jessie, she told me the only reason she decided to go through with the abortion was that she wanted to hurt me for not returning her call. There were probably too many herbs in my tea and I hope that's why I had such a crazy dream.

I feel like calling Jessie because I'm curious to see what's going on with her. I'm in the basement wide awake listening to the sound of rain on my environmental sound machine. I hold my pillow tight, pretending that it's Jessie. I need her and I hope she needs me just as much.

Chapter 43

Jamal

It's daylight and I watch as snow flurries fall from the sky. Christmas is right around the corner and soon autumn will be nothing more than a memory.

I go upstairs and meet Grandma in the kitchen for breakfast.

"Good morning."

"Good morning, baby. How'd you sleep?"

"I did okay if you don't count my nightmare."

"Are those body aches gone?"

"Yeah. You must have worked some voodoo on me or something."

"Why'd you say that?"

"I wanna be with Jessie so bad that I can hardly see straight."

"That don't have nothing to do with voodoo. That's love leading you back to where you belong. Did you call her yet?"

"Not yet. I was thinking about going to see her in a few minutes."

"I know she'd like that. It's freezing out there and it doesn't look like this snow is gonna let up none."

"This weather is crazy. Just a few days ago people were running around in shorts and T-shirts. The weatherman blames this quick change in temperature on El Niño."

"I ain't thinking about no El Niño, that's God trying to tell us something. The end may be closer than we think. That's why if you love Jessie you better go be with her."

"Okay, okay, I'm going to see her right now. You're wearing me out."

Grandma is so proud of me that she stops me on my way out the door and gives me a hug and a kiss on the cheek.

When I arrive at Jessie's apartment her little Benz is nowhere in sight. I get out of my car anyway and greet Ms. Jenkins, Jessie's landlady, outside her building.

She says, "Hi, sweetheart, Jessie isn't home. She left early this morning."

"Thank you."

I automatically think that I'm too late. She's gone and my baby's probably gone as well. I pray that my stupid nightmare doesn't come true. It's all my fault if it does, because I was too sorry to pick up the phone. As I walk back out into the falling snow I notice a red Mercedes Benz coupe coming up the street. It's not Jessie. Lately there are so many people driving those damn cars around. My cell phone rings.

"Hello."

"Hi, Jamal. It's me."

"Regina? What's going on?"

"I need to start off with an apology. I'm so sorry for the way I acted. I was unprofessional and I don't blame you for leaving. Can you please accept my apology for the way I acted, especially for the things I said? I had no right to do what I did. I was totally out of line and that's not how I usually conduct business."

"It's not a big deal. It happened and it's over. I accept your apology."

"Thank you. Now that that's out of the way, I've FedExed a check for thirty thousand dollars to you. We did it, baby! We did it! The art show was a major success."

"How? I wasn't even there."

"Lets just say that your artwork and I represented you very well. I told everyone that you weren't able to make it due to an acute illness and they believed it. They all loved your work. When can we do another show? I'm ready, just let me know when."

"I don't know about that. I'm scheduled to go back to work tomorrow. I'm going to accept this new management position and try to focus my attention on that."

"Maybe you didn't hear what I said. We made a killing and your check for *thirty thousand dollars* will be in your hands tomorrow. Baby, you're an artist, that's your career now. You don't belong in an arts-and-crafts store wasting precious time."

"I don't know what to say."

"Your *Ground Zero* painting was the showstopper. At first I didn't pay any attention to it, but when I did, I cried and so did a few others. You're really special and far too talented to give up. It's time for a change. I can set up ten more shows in this country alone and I can almost guarantee the same return as the first show. I want to take you places and show you things you've never seen. How does that sound?"

"I'll think about it. I realized that art really isn't my passion anymore."

"You're not the first to experience that. We'll work on getting your passion back, okay? All this money will help give you a boost."

"I don't think you fully understand me. For me it's not about money. Right now I'm in search of happiness. I need time to think. I hope you can give me a little time to get my priorities in order. If not I can't miss what I never had. Shit, I've been poor all my life."

"Alright. I'll give you time. I need a break myself. I promise to respect you from now on. You said that I don't understand you, but you don't understand me. All my life I've craved the attention of men and now I'm gonna get help for it. I was listening to this Kirk Franklin song this morning and it made me realize that I need to go back to church."

I notice a yellow cab pull up and Jessie gets out. Trey must have taken her little Benz away. Jessie has my attention and I want to get off the phone. "I'm happy for you and I hope you really find the help you need. I'm sorry, but I have to go. I have some important business to attend to right now. I'll be in touch. I promise."

"Thank you. Don't let me down."

I rush over to Jessie as she gets out of the cab and without saying a word I take her in my arms.

I say, "Please, tell me you didn't kill my baby."

"What? I would never do that. What's wrong with you?"

"I had a nightmare that you went off and got an abortion."

"No. I did see my doctor this morning. This was my first prenatal visit. I stopped by the mall on my way home. Here, help me with these bags and let's go inside and get out of this snow."

When we get inside I can't take my eyes off Jessie. "You're beautiful and you're glowing."

"Thank you. You look like you put on a little weight. You look a little more muscular or something."

"Maybe, but that's not important. I have so much that I need to say to you and I don't even know where to start."

"You can start off by saying hi. You just rushed up to me, grabbing me, talking about 'tell me you didn't kill my baby.' Man, I thought you had lost your mind."

I laugh and say, "You're right. Hi, how have you been?"

"That's more like it. I'm okay. The doctor said I'm doing fine and that's what's important."

"I'm sorry for not being there. I'm gonna be here for you from now on. Whatever you need you got it. You don't have to go through this by yourself."

She begins to cry. "Thank you. That means a lot to me because I've been very emotional lately."

I take her in my arms and ask, "Can we try to get things back together again? I need you in my life. I love you, I really do. You still love me, don't you?"

"I do. I love you so much."

We kiss and I almost forgot how nice Jessie's lips felt. I take her by the hands, drop to my knees, and kiss her stomach. She gently rubs my head as I rest it against her stomach.

"I can't wait to go to the doctor's office so I can hear the baby's heartbeat."

"You just don't know how happy I am to see you. It hurt so bad being at the doctor's office and seeing all those couples together. I was ashamed. When the doctor and nurse asked me questions about the baby's father I fought to hold my tears back." She pauses for a few seconds. "Who would have thought that I would be the one to mess things up between us?"

I stand up and say, "Don't even worry about that. I messed up too. I was so self-absorbed with my art career that I lost track of us. I put everything in front of you and your needs. I couldn't see it at first and I'm sorry."

"I wanted and needed too much too fast, but now I'm different. Too bad I had to learn the hard way. Let's forget about the past because now we can focus on building a future as a family. We're going to be parents."

I smile and say, "I know. We've gotta make this work because what we share is special. Our love should have died a long time ago, but look at us."

"It's destiny, that's all I can say."

"All is forgiven."

"All is forgiven."

Jessie was my Ms. Right all along, but it just took time for me to realize it. All the time she knew that she was my destiny. I'm taking a chance with this, but this time is different. Anyway, I've heard that love is better the second time around.

Jessie is my modern-day Eve and whether I want to admit it or not I'd probably follow her to hell and back. It's almost prophetic or maybe it's just the way things were meant to be. We're hopelessly in love. Once we were parted souls, but from this point we're inseparable.

Epilogue

*H*_oly matrimony._ It's hard to believe that Jessie and I made it this far. Today's our wedding day and here I stand before God, family, and friends. Our beautiful little baby girl, Destiny, is here resting in her Great-Grandma Connie's arms. We just had to name her Destiny because she was the catalyst that brought me and Jessie back together. Destiny is like me in a lot of ways, but she definitely has her mother's angelic features. I'm proud to be her father. When I laid eyes on her it was love at first sight. She's my heart, daddy's little girl.

I can't forget Grandma because she played a major part in getting me and Jessie back together as well. As I wait for Jessie to make her entrance, I look around the church at all these smiling faces. I'm even smiling, because this is the happiest day of my life.

I was talking crazy when I said that I lost my passion for art. That would never happen because creating a masterpiece like my *Ground Zero* painting is what I live for. I have been doing a lot of art shows and I have three lined up with Regina next month.

Jessie and I go to the settlement on our dream house the day after we return from our honeymoon in Hawaii. We've always dreamed of vacationing in an exotic paradise. Jessie planned most of the wedding and I planned the honeymoon.

Church is my best man and Rachael is Jessie's matron of honor.

Shadow and John are in the wedding party, but they refused to be matched up as a couple. Their divorce will be finalized soon. Toya, Kim, and their boyfriends make up the rest of our wedding party. The flower girls are Rachael's daughters and the ring bearer is Toya's son.

Jessie tried to hide it, but I could tell that she was hurt knowing that her mother wouldn't be here. I was able to talk her father into showing up. I went through hell trying to get him here today, but he's here and that's what counts. Mr. Weaver was reluctant to come because he thought he'd be the last person Jessie would want to see. He's in the back with her now and I know she was more surprised than anyone to see him. My parents are here as a couple, a real couple. They're so in love. Aunt Hunk is here with her girlfriend, Jackie.

I take a deep breath as the pianist begins to play the wedding march. Everyone stands as the double doors swing open. The flower girls are first and then Jessie's father escorts her down the aisle to give her away. They're both teary-eyed.

Jessie looks absolutely beautiful in her wedding gown. Truthfully, beautiful doesn't even begin to describe how she looks. She's wearing a strapless form-fitting off-white gown with an eight-foot train. She felt that it was improper for her to wear white. We discussed this weeks before the wedding. I told her that we're all imperfect people living in an imperfect world. I explained to her that this was her wedding day and she could wear whatever she wanted. I have to admit that I'm surprised that she didn't choose the white gown.

Mr. Weaver gives me Jessie's hand and the ceremony begins. Reverend Thomas says a prayer, Jessie and I exchange vows, and then we say our I dos.

Church hands me the ring and I put it on Jessie's finger. I wanted to upgrade her ring to the platinum set she was dreaming of, but she wouldn't let me. This is the original set that I purchased and the one she fell in love with.

Reverend Thomas says, "If there is anyone here today who doesn't see fit for this man and woman to be married, let him speak now or forever hold his peace."

Reverend Thomas pauses. Jessie and I act silly, looking around. When we hear the moment of silence we were expecting, we look at each other and smile.

"In the name of the Father, the Son, and the Holy Spirit, I now pronounce you husband and wife."

We embrace and get caught up in this passionate kiss.

Church's cousin Woody agreed to come here and sing "Ribbon in the Sky" by Stevie Wonder. As Woody sings, Jessie and I hold each other close, slowly swaying back and forth at the altar.

After the song Reverend Thomas proudly says, "Ladies and gentlemen, I present to you, Mr. and Mrs. Jamal King."

Hearing Reverend Thomas introduce us gives me a rush and a feeling of pride. Everyone begins to applaud.

I hear someone in the rear of the church yelling, "Hold up! Hold up!"

Everyone quiets down in order to see what the commotion is about. Out of nowhere Trey quickly makes his way down the aisle looking like he's hit rock bottom. Just when we thought everything was okay, this fool resurfaces. Why now?

A few months ago Shadow called me just before she was about to go on the air with some breaking news. She said that Tank confessed to the murder of Bernard Clayton. Tank had a nervous breakdown and confessed to killing that boy Bernard. I was just happy that Bernard's mother could finally find closure.

The police were looking for Trey for being an accessory to Bernard's murder. He was already wanted in connection to several other murders and in addition to that he's wanted on federal kingpin charges. He's been on the run for months and there were rumors out that this guy named Derek had Trey murdered. We all thought that he was dead.

Trey looks a dusty mess. He looks like he needs a bath, a haircut, and a shave. I'm sorry that things had to turn out like this for him, because he could have done a whole lot more with his life instead of wasting it like he has.

Everybody that knows Trey is shocked to see him here.

I ask, "What are you doing here? What do you want?"

Jessie says, "You shouldn't be here."

Trey laughs and says, "Y'all should have known I'd show up sooner or later. I couldn't let my favorite girl get married without giving her a special wedding gift."

Reverend Thomas shouts, "Get outta here, son, and take your troubles somewhere else!"

He looks at Reverend Thomas and says, "Shhh. I need everybody to remain seated because you won't wanna miss this." He pulls out a gun and says, "This is for you too, Jamal. This is a wedding gift y'all will never forget."

Trey aims his gun at me and Jessie. I hear screams and our guests duck down in the pews. Everyone's petrified. All Jessie and I can do is stand here frozen just waiting to see what happens next. I think Trey wants to shoot me, but suddenly he points his gun directly at Jessie. I jump in front of Jessie to protect her.

Trey looks at Jessie and says, "I told you that nobody would ever love you like I love you."

Tears begin to stream down Trey's face. He puts the gun to his own head and is about to pull the trigger. He gives us this insane expression. He smiles and cries at the same time. He's as unpredictable and as crazy as sunshine on a rainy day.

I hold Jessie and whisper, "It's okay. It's almost over."

Reverend Thomas says, "Please, son, don't do this. Think about what you're doing."

Church says, "Trey, don't do this in my father's church."

Trey yells, "Shut up!"

Grandma stands up with Destiny in her arms and says, "Trey, please don't hurt yourself or anyone else. I've known you all your life and I know you're a good boy."

I can't believe Grandma is putting herself and my baby in danger like this. Trey lowers the gun and turns toward them. As he turns I let go of Jessie and slowly move in his direction. Before I can make my move, Trey sees something coming toward him. He turns around quickly and instinctively raises his gun in my direction. I hear a single gunshot. In an instant, everything seems to come to a standstill. Slow motion doesn't even begin to describe how this is playing out. Each second seems more like an eternity. I become numb and my mind takes me to a dreamlike state. This entire experience has déjà vu written all over it.

The strangest thing happens. I see a vision of myself falling to the floor and landing in a contorted position. As much as I want to, I can't move. It feels as if I was hit in the head just like in my stupid dream the night before Trey's party. All I see is darkness and I begin to feel cold. I fight so hard not to become somebody's annual statistic.

This isn't supposed to happen to me and I can't let it. But who am I to question God's infinite plan?

There's silence all around me and I'm overtaken by the smells of being outside, a mixture of earth, grass, and leaves. All of a sudden I see a bright light and when my eyes focus I see autumn leaves falling all around me. Pale green, amber, auburn, and crimson leaves and a vast landscape with mountains as far as my eyes can see. My paintbrush is in one hand and my palate is in the other. A blank canvas stands in front of me on an easel. As much as I want to paint this irresistible scene I can't because something that's more important steals my attention.

In the distance I see Jessie and Destiny on a blanket under a tree waiting for me to join them. Jessie smiles and waves her hand, signaling for me.

Just as quickly as that vision appears, my mind brings me back to reality. I realize that I'm not wounded. I stand still thinking to myself that my vision was just a glimpse of what could have been. Luckily, that wasn't a fate meant for me. Today is too special for me to go out like that.

All of a sudden I see Trey's body come crashing to the floor. I soon realize that Trey never even fired his gun. I look over my right shoulder and see a small but effective tactical team from the Baltimore City Police at the front door of the church with their guns drawn. One of them fired a fatal shot, hitting Trey in his left temple. The police must have been trailing Trey all along. I'm relieved, but I feel no joy seeing Trey, a brotha with so much potential, slumped over like an animal.

Family members and guests are horrified as they look on in disbelief. Reverend Thomas takes off his robe and drapes it over Trey's body and begins to say a prayer. Church and the other groomsmen rush over to comfort the bridesmaids. Within minutes the guests begin to discuss what they saw. As the tactical team secures the scene, other officers escort the guests out of the church in an attempt to calm things down.

I try my best to comfort Jessie. I hold her tightly in my arms and whisper, "Are you alright?"

Jessie appears to be in a state of shock, as if she refuses to believe what just happened. I see and feel her pain as she tries her best to stay composed. She looks at me with tears in her eyes and says, "Not really.

I can't believe what just happened, I just can't. But I'm alright as long as you and Destiny are alright."

I kiss her on the lips. "We're alright. Don't worry. Thank God we're all safe. And all that negativity from the past, it's over. Finally, it's all over. Nothing will ever come between us again."

IF ONLY YOU KNEW

Alex Hairston

ABOUT THIS GUIDE

The suggested questions are intended to enhance your
group's reading of Alex Hairston's
If Only You Knew.

Please feel free to contact Alex at **alexhairston@yahoo.com**
or visit him at **www.alexhairston.com**

1. Do you think that it was personally beneficial to Jamal's mother when she left her family or was she just avoiding her problems? Did it help or hurt her family in the long run?
2. Who was your favorite character? Why?
3. Jamal seemed very forgiving and at times blind to the things Jessica was doing. Why was he so determined to make things work out with him and Jessica?
4. Jessica's mother set high demands for her. Do you think her actions were justified?
5. Do you think Jessica's lifestyle was a result of her childhood experiences?
6. Was Jessica a true gold digger or was she just a sista trying to get her basic needs met?
7. What lessons did Jamal learn? What lessons did Jessica learn?
8. What was the turning point in Jamal's life? What was the turning point in Jessica's life?
9. Do you think Jessica really loved Jamal? Did she really know what love was?
10. Was Jessica's attraction to Trey purely financial or was she truly growing bored with Jamal?
11. What was the most memorable part of the book?
12. Did the story end like you expected?
13. Where do the characters go from here?